Tales of Fanged Fish

ISBN 978-1911438526

This is a work of fiction. Any resemblance to any real persons living or dead is entirely coincidental.

Cover art by Mark Watts

I0545911

For Caz

"Well then, kiss me – since my mother left her blessing on my brow,
There has been a something wanting in my nature until now".

(Sarah Williams)

Ben Blake is on Facebook at https://www.facebook.com/benblakeauthor

Follow Ben's blog at http://benblake.blogspot.co.uk

Email him at benblakeauthor@gmail.com

Also by Ben Blake

The Risen King
Blood and Gold (Songs of Sorrow volume 1)
The Gate of Angels (songs of Sorrow volume 2)
A Brand of Fire (Troy volume 1)
Heirs of Immortality (Troy volume 2)
The Ancient Dead (Troy volume 3)
Black Lord of Eagles (Blessed Land volume 1)

2

Tales of Fanged Fish

Ruphachiy   the burning

1

Taruka slithered backwards down the slope until his feet hung over the cliff, and then wriggled his body over and dropped to the spur below. Fear choked his throat. The dark man was here, one finger of Tezcata's many-clawed hand close enough to seize them all. The band needed to leave. Right now.

He looked into the valley where they waited, a loose group of men and horses on the slope below. Most were staring up at him. Some were not, which was when Taruka remembered one of the prisoners was trying to escape.

He'd thought it wasn't a problem. Too many Deer were too fast, and several had set off to run the fugitive down. One glance told Taruka he had been wrong.

The runner was well ahead, a flash of red that came and went amid the rocks and bushes of the valley's lower slopes. None of the pursuers had come nearly as far. One outlaw – former outlaw, Taruka corrected himself – set his feet and raised a bow. But the range was long, and the arrow skipped off a stone and into the stream. The red coat appeared again, darting past a boulder left by some long-ago flood.

The man was making for the cliffs. Taruka measured the distance with his eyes. The Thrain had a chance, though he'd have to be fast. With the thought he saw the man leap onto a rock and from there spring like Makisapa the monkey, flinging out an arm to curl fingers around a handhold. He swung around it and up to a ledge. No Deer could have done it better.

Taruka wouldn't even have tried it.

The Thrain was going to stay out of range. Down on the valley floor his pursuers had lost him now, and were hunting back and forth through the boulder field. Whoever had been guarding him had better have a good explanation when Taruka got back down.

Taruka turned to look along the high ridge he stood on, working out a route that would bring him out ahead of the fleeing man. He could only see one, and it wasn't easy. Not easy at all, but dithering over it wouldn't make much difference.

"No Deer could make that either," he said aloud, and added in his mind, *except me.*

He'd better make it, with the sorcerer across the ridge.

He ran back up the spur, timing it so he picked up speed just as the ground ran out. Then he hurled himself through ten feet of empty air with eternity yawning beneath him. He didn't land so much as smash into a rock face, fingers clawing for holds and his feet skidding on a ledge just wide enough for two rats to dance. His body rebounded and began to lean out over the chasm, and then two fingers found a grip and pulled him back. Air whuffled out of him. A flap of skin hung from his right hand, streaked with blood. He ignored it and shuffle-stepped to the right, where the ledge was a fraction wider. Another shuffle, a third, and he stood on a shelf wide enough that he could unlimber his bow.

"Not graceful," he said to himself. But it would do. He chortled and then saw his bow.

The limbs were cracked, probably when he'd thumped into the rock. Taruka swore, but there was no time to waste on regret. He moved on instead, eyes darting from the ledges and slopes to the valley below. He couldn't see the escaping Thrain but knew where he must be, somewhere on a cliff face between two clefts in the stone. The chasers had seen him now, but they were far distant. Their shouts came to Taruka as the cries of distant birds.

He tossed the bow away. The ledge was wide enough for him to jog now. He followed it along the top of one cliff and the foot of another, losing a little height as he went. A curve of the rock brought him a glimpse of his quarry, a red splash against the grey, and then hid him again. That was all right. Taruka knew where he was now.

He reached the right place and stopped, squatting on his heels, and pulled an axe from his belt.

The pursuing Ashir were still a hundred yards away when he heard the strained gasps of a man climbing below him. Taruka glanced over the edge, very quickly, and saw the Thrain nearing the top of the cliff a few yards below. The soldier was purple with effort, but he wasn't slowing down. There were faint cries from below as he was spotted, but the chasing warriors were too far away to matter now. The Thrain pushed himself up on his toes, reached over the top of the cliff, and dug his fingers deep into a crack in the rock.

Taruka brought his axe down onto the top of the man's head. The blade bit deep and the soldier's eyes rolled up at once, before he could even draw breath to scream. One hand flailed spasmodically towards the cliff, the body still trying to obey the last instructions from a brain that was now spilling from a crack in the skull, and then the soldier went limp and dropped away. He fell like a rag, down to the loose rocks below where he hit and tumbled, leaving splashes of blood and tissue on the stones as he went. Finally the corpse slid to the valley floor, where the first pursuers were just panting up.

Taruka hesitated, and then said, "Quilla smile on you, warrior. May Supay welcome you home. Go in beauty."

He had been a Thrain, and an enemy. But he'd been a warrior too. He deserved a prayer.

Taruka climbed down. He chose an easier route than the one the Thrain had tried to climb: it was harder going down, when you had to twist around sometimes to look for a toehold before you moved. Besides, he'd taken enough of a risk today, leaping onto that sliver of a ledge with a lethal drop below him. He'd torn the flap of skin from his hand and the skin beneath was raw and tender. He'd banged his hip, too. He was limping a little as he joined the warriors waiting by the dead man.

6

"I saw you make that jump," Waki said as Taruka came up. "Do you think you're Makisapa the monkey, trying to be an eagle?"

He snorted. "That soldier was more Makisapa than me. Besides, I couldn't think of anything else to do. He was going to get away unless I stopped him."

"You'll have to show me how to do that," one of the bandits said. He was grinning. "That's laughing in the Blind God's face, that is."

"I'm not going to show you that," Taruka said. The outlaw's expression darkened as he sensed an insult, and Taruka smiled. "Because I'm never, ever going to be so stupid as to do it again."

The man laughed. "Can't say I blame you for that."

"But if you truly want to laugh in the Blind God's face," Taruka went on, "all you have to do is stay here. The tunnel is gone, and half the mountain with it. And there's only one man on the road."

"Quilla's-mercy-be-upon-us," Waki whispered, all in a single hoarse breath. "One man? *Him*?"

"I'm sure of it. And he's close." Taruka turned and set off towards Kai and the others, not running, but walking as quickly as he could. "We need to leave here, and right now."

There were mutters of agreement. More than one man threw a frightened glance over his shoulder as he went, warriors and outlaws alike. Taruka supposed he should stop thinking of Burru's old band as outlaws, but it was a difficult habit to break. He wondered how long Apusuyu had been this way. Warriors on one hand and bandits on the other, and hatred always between them. Well, there was another enemy to hate now. Maybe they could learn a new way.

Ahead, Evain stood ashen-faced, the rest of his deserters clustered in a tight knot around him as though afraid of reprisals. Taruka would prefer to kill all of them, if he was honest, but he could see why that wasn't wise. Another new thing. He grunted, remembering something.

"Before we reach the others," he said, "I'd like someone to explain how one of the soldiers got away, when you were meant to be guarding them."

Waki gave a start, and then he went almost as pale as Evain. It was hard for Taruka not to laugh. Whatever else changed, some things never would.

*

"Alone?" Kai asked in disbelief.

Taruka nodded. "I saw nobody else, and there was only one horse. He's alone all right."

Kai looked at Evain. The Thrain captain was still white-faced, partly with shock at the death of the man who'd tried to flee, and partly out of fear of how Kai would react to that treachery. Maybe he expected to die now, he and the remaining Thrain. "What do you think?"

7

"You killed his son," Evain said bluntly. Shocked or not, the soldier didn't mince his words. "Terzian would have felt that immediately, and rushed north. I think it's quite possible that he's down there alone."

"But Chakanay is a good two days travel from here," Burru protested. "How could he reach the tunnel so fast?"

Evain shrugged. "Magic, probably."

"I could pick him off before he even knows I'm there," Catori said. He spun his bow around deft fingers as though to prove his point. "Any Deer can shoot, but I'm better than any I ever met. I move as softly as moonlight over mist, and when I aim, I don't miss."

"That's true," Taruka agreed.

Kai frowned at the two warriors, trying to think. If it really was Terzian down by the road, alone and vulnerable, there might never be a better chance to kill him. Certainly not before hundreds more men and women died, on both sides of the struggle. "What if he sees you?"

Catori grinned. "He won't."

"Senses you, then. With his magic." Just speaking the word made Kai's stomach clench. Terzian possessed powers unknown except among the gods, and the truth was the Ashir had no idea where they ended. He had managed to come here from Chakanay in a quarter of the time it should have taken, even at a mad run. The sorcerer might be able to pull the moon from the sky for all Kai knew. "He could make you tell him where the rest of us are."

Catori lost his smile. "Then if he sees me, I'll take my belt knife and cut my own wrists. I swear it."

"No!" Suchi snapped.

"It won't work," Evain added. "Terzian can heal almost any wound. Besides, he always keeps a –"

"This is not your choice," Catori said to Suchi. His large brown eyes were like obsidian, smooth and cold. "Care for our souls, priestess, and leave the fighting to those who understand it."

Suchi actually fell back a step, mouth open in surprise. Kai was hardly less astonished. She and Catori were old friends, and something more than friendship had been growing between them as well, but it seemed that was over. The chill in Catori's tone was proof of it. Whatever the reason for it, Kai couldn't spend time wondering about it now.

"Get ready to move," he said to the crowd. "We have most of the day ahead of us, and I want to use it to get as far away from that sorcerer as possible. Be quick, and be quiet."

The band scattered to gather their gear, and Evain spoke swiftly in his own language. Some of the Thrain darted to fetch the horses before he finished. Kai glanced at them, making sure no one else made a run for the rocks, and saw three Ashir with half-drawn bows standing not far off. All of them were women. They watched the Thrain with narrowed eyes, as though hoping one would try to slip away just so they could put an arrow in him.

8

"Are you really as good as you claim?" he asked Catori. "Truly, I mean, without any of the tall stories you warriors tell each other. There isn't time for boasting and I don't want to hear any lies. Could you guarantee that you'd kill the sorcerer with a single shot?"

Catori shook his head at once. "No one can guarantee something like that. I shot at a puma once, and I swear I would have hit him right in the eye, but a bird swooped through the trees and I hit that instead. You don't believe me," he added when he saw Kai's expression. "It's true, though. Sometimes the Blind God's gaze falls on you just at the wrong time."

"But when Catori shoots," Taruka put in quietly, "he hits what he aims at. Don't let him tell you different."

Kai hesitated. Part of him wanted to let Catori try, or even to go hunting the cursed magician himself, but the other half wanted to tuck in its tail and run for the hills. *The sorcerer is alone.* That thought floated in his mind, relentless. How often would he be so exposed?

"It won't work," Evain said beside him. "Terzian always keeps a screen of magic around himself, in case an assassin slips up without him noticing. It's a habit he learned long ago, when he thought his brother might try to kill him."

Kai's forehead creased. What kind of people were these Thrain, that they had to live their lives so afraid of murder, and by their own blood? He shook the question away. "So arrows bounce off this screen?"

"Yes. Knives too, or any blade. And besides that, Terzian can heal almost anything. Your arrow would have to kill him before he felt the barb."

"*Almost* anything?" Catori repeated, sharp-eyed. "There's a wound that could kill him, then?"

"Apparently magic can't heal the heart," Evain said. "His wife died giving birth to Ramian. Something was ruptured in her heart, or so the story goes. I don't know if it's true."

"You're saying there's nothing we can do," Taruka muttered. "No way to kill him at all."

"This is getting us nowhere," Kai said. How could you stab a man through the heart, or shoot him, when he kept a screen of magic around himself? "Catori, I can't let you try this. There doesn't seem much chance, and you might give the rest of us away. We'll wait for another day."

"It might be a long wait, *kamachi,*" Catori said. "How long will it be until he's alone again?"

Kai shook his head, dismayed by the echo of his own thought. "Come on. Let's get moving."

They rested two hours later, at the top of a steep trail with the sun sinking behind them, so the peaks were lit and the valleys lost in shadow. Both Burru and Taruka said they had three hours before the moon came up, and gave enough light for them to move again. Kai knew he should move among the men but he was deathly tired. He leaned back against his pack and closed his eyes, just for a moment.

9

He woke to a hand shaking his shoulder, and looked up at Achachi and said, "Dreams."

"Dreams?" the old man repeated.

""How do you stop a cobra from striking?"

"I don't understand."

Kai hesitated, then rubbed his face with both hands. "Me neither. Just sleep fears, I suppose."

The old man shook him again. "Tell me."

"It's nothing. Oh, all right. You stop a cobra from striking by staring into its eyes. Blink and you're dead."

"So?"

"I told you it was nothing," he said.

But he wasn't sure that was true. His dreams had been full of cobras rearing to bite, all black eyes and sibilant hiss, but there had been something else too. A flash of bronze blade, again and again. Like a light in darkness.

Cobras hypnotized their prey, waited until its eyes glazed over and then struck the killing blow. A man could never be fast enough to reach his knife before fangs went into his wrist, but you could still survive. If you met the cobra's stare with your own and never dropped your gaze, even for an instant, the cobra might just blink first – and then it was time for the knife.

"Best get going, lad," Achachi said. "There are clouds coming in, and they'll hide the moon. We need to move while we can."

Kai nodded and accepted a hand to haul him upright.

Taruka had wondered whether it was possible to kill the sorcerer. Maybe it was. Maybe Terzian would blink first. All Kai needed to do was find something to make him drop his eyes, and he thought he already had.

The *cizin* was a solid weight inside his coat. Kai reach in to touch the handle. *The knife.*

Magic against magic. He had never heard the voice of the Bearded God as so many of the *kamachi* were said to have done, but perhaps Viraca came to him in dreams.

2

They left the path the next afternoon. All day they'd walked through a forest that rose and fell with the hills. To their right a river came and went and returned again, glimpsed as pouring foam or a green pool. Rock outcrops jutted through the foliage, half hidden by hanging branches and jostling scrub, covered with lichen, and crawling with red-and-yellow backed *alqo* insects. A soldier picked one up out of curiosity, then dropped it with a shout when it stung his finger. An hour later his whole hand was mottled with green pustules, and sweat left streaks in the dirt on his face.

"It isn't fatal," Burru told Evain. Kai was walking behind them, close enough to hear. "He'll run a fever for a couple of days and then he'll be fine. His hand will sting like fury, though."

"How common are those things?"

"Alqo? There are more of them than stalks of wheat in the fields. Especially here, in the forest. But you don't need to worry about them."

"Good, because –"

"It's the *tanqa* beetle that should concern you," Burru said.

"The *tanqa?"*

"It lays eggs under your skin," Burru told the outlander. "Odds are you won't even know it until the eggs hatch. Then you have a thousand tiny beetles trying to eat their way out, and they don't know which way to go. Some dig deeper into the flesh."

"Redeemer's Mercy," another soldier said. "How many creatures in this forest want to kill us?"

"All the Ashir, for a start," Achachi said from behind them.

That put an end to the conversation. The Thrain avoided *alqo* afterwards, and stayed to the middle of the path. As though that would keep them safe from *tanqa* beetles.

The path had been winding between thrusting arms of the hills, twisting back and forth through the trees. Sometimes the rush of water would be behind them, only for a turn of the trail to bring it into view ahead a moment later. Once the track ran along the side of a vertiginous drop to the green pools and foam of another river, then veered away into a suddenly open bowl packed with trees and undergrowth, crowding in on both sides. Matlal would have loved this place. Sala would have wanted to know where the nearest village was, and the chance of a cup of *chicha* beer.

A clan of howler monkeys screeched their annoyance as they bounded away through the high branches in a shower of disturbed leaves, making most of the Thrain jump in surprise. Suchi flinched as well, almost as unaccustomed to the wilds of Apusuyu as the outlanders were.

One rock outcrop was clear of lichen, obviously kept so by someone. It was a *lanti*, a graven image, carved into the likeness of a man's face, but in caricature.

11

The eyes were too large and protuberant, the forehead back-sloped, and the cheekbones swept out to make the face nearly as broad as it was high. A triple line of ragged scars scored one cheek. Time and rain had softened the features but the scars remained clear, pale marks etched into the stone. The bulging eyes above them might convey pain, or perhaps anger. It was a marker stone and warning, both: go back, stranger, for if you would come this way you will dare our rage, and die screaming.

"It's unpleasant," Evain said when it was explained to him. "But it's also foolish. Why mark the trail for your enemies?"

Kai smiled. "This isn't the trail. See those three scars on the cheek? That's a code, for those who know how to read it. It's on the left cheek, so the trail is on that side of the *lanti*. But an enemy wouldn't know what the 'three' meant. Three outcrops along? Three sequoia trees? Or it might be dialect based, something the intruders had no chance to decipher."

"So which is it?"

"Three outcrops," Kai answered. "This is an ancient stone. The people who carved it understood code, but they weren't very imaginative."

"You might do them an injustice," Evain said after a moment. "Trees die. Even language changes, though too slowly to notice, most of the time. But the rocks would always be in the same place."

Kai hadn't thought of that. For a moment he felt irritation that this invader thought he knew more of Apusuyu's past than Kai did himself, but then he shrugged inwardly. Maybe Evain was right. Nobody understood very much about the ancient people who had carved this stone. They were gone, one of countless peoples lost deep in the barbarous past before Viraca had come across the ocean with his learning and wisdom. Even their name was gone, their language forgotten.

"Our fate," he said, "if we lose this war. To be known only by monuments nobody understands."

"Every people's fate, in the end," Evain said.

"No time for cosy chats." Achachi limped up, leaning on his snake-headed stick. "It will be four hours at least before we can climb out of the forest, and we really don't want to be caught in the trees at night."

"Pumas?" Evain asked. "Or more of those coloured beetles?"

Kai shook his head. "Trapdoor spiders. They're as big as your hand, and open their holes at night. If you lie down you'll be bitten in nine different places before you can yell for help. If you keep walking you'll put a leg into a hole sooner or later, and it will bite you out of fear. And one bite is fatal."

"My God," Evain said. "How do you go through alive?"

"Walk by day and don't leave the path," Achachi said.

Kai turned to him with a frown. "You know the trail, don't you? You've been this way before."

"Once, long ago." The old man snorted. "I was younger then, and didn't mind the climb. Not sure my knees will like it now."

12

"Nobody is meant to know about it."

"Bandits know the wild lands," Achachi answered. "We've known them for thousands of years. I doubt there are secrets we don't know."

Kai smiled. "You might be surprised. But you know this trail. Did you go as far as Pujyu?"

"The town on the hill? Never knew it was called that."

"Maybe the people who built it used another name," Kai said. "It's we Ashir who call it Pujyu. I want to reach it before dark."

"Come on, then," Achachi said.

The third outcrop was a jagged fist of stone splinters, some half-fallen so they leaned on each other like sleeping monkeys. It was only when you stepped close that you could see a gap between two of them, barely wide enough to admit the horses. Several of the animals whickered unhappily, rolling their eyes, before they were coaxed through. Kai watched with interest. Nobody ever tried to persuade a pig or a goat. If it didn't want to go somewhere you simply hit it until it did. Obviously horses were clever. He wondered what else they could do.

Off the path, daylight was reduced to dappled flickers, peeking into the gloom through the canopy of leaves. It was just enough to show the line of men and horses ahead, many of them muttering under their breath. One of the Thrain walked with his eyes squeezed shut and a hand on an Ashir's shoulder, tiptoeing along as though afraid to touch the ground.

"Spiders," Evain explained when Kai asked. "Young Lain is terrified of them. The moment you mentioned trapdoor spiders he started shaking."

It wasn't just the Thrain who looked uneasy, though. Every village in Apusuyu had its stories of dark things that lurked under the trees, malevolent spirits of mulch and gloom, drinking rancid water and eating live flesh. Several Ashir shuffled forward with their eyes darting from side to side, waiting for the bogeymen to leap out and seize them. One young warrior ahead glanced constantly around in ill-concealed fear, until Kai moved forward and touched him lightly on the shoulder.

"The people who carved the *lanti* spread stories too," he said. "Tales of horrors in their forests, things that would eat you up unless you knew the rites to propitiate them. When the Ashir grew strong those people retreated into the trees and then *they* became the monsters. But they died out long ago. There hasn't been anything to fear in these trees for a thousand years."

The young man's face brightened. Kai smiled at him.

Moments like that were among the better things about being the servant of the Bearded God. Better than the endless ceremonies and sacrifices, or the awestruck crowds, filled with men and women who held their children up to see Kai as he passed by. To see the *kamachi,* more truly, the role rather than the man. Certainly better than dealing with the *kura* every day, now he thought about it, with their endless supply of pinch-lipped solemnity. Still, Kai could almost hear Salali make a wry aside about the young warrior, and he very nearly

13

turned to share a smile with Matlal before walking on. He shook his head. There might be time to grieve later, if the gods were kind, but there wasn't now.

The sun was well to the west by the time they emerged, behind them and to their right. The trees gave out suddenly, as though afraid to go higher up the slope. The band had been climbing again for the last couple of hours, working their way up an incline so gentle it was hard to notice, except for the slowly spreading ache in thighs and knees. Here the slope became a mountainside between one step and the next, thick with tough grass and patches of scrub. The band gathered there, standing in silence with their heads craned back to look at the skyline.

"You have got to be joking," Evain said.

A flight of massive stairs ran straight up the side of the mountain, each step twenty feet long and five deep. Tufts of grass poked out from the sides, but nothing grew on the bare stone. The edges were worn by wind and rain, and perhaps by feet too, though almost nobody came this way any more. Not since the makers of the *lanti* had died, or moved into their last refuges deep in the forests. Why they had chosen to live here at all was a mystery to Kai. The peaks were windy and cold, and the valleys covered with forest so thick it was almost impossible to clear. Even then it grew back with ferocious speed, like a predator eating every scrap of open land it could find, and never able to satisfy its hunger. Life here must have been a constant struggle to hang on, and in the end, it was a struggle the builders lost.

But they had known how to build, even before Viraca came. The cut stones that made the steps fitted together without a join, nowhere for grass or weeds to sink a root. And their town was still there, or what the mountain elements had left of it. Small stone houses peered over the top of the scarp like tumbled teeth, above slopes cut into terraces where food had once grown. Pujyu was a place of ghosts, but it offered shelter for the night, even with its cracked walls and tumbled roofs. Trees didn't grow on the heights, which meant the *alqo* and trapdoor spiders didn't go there either. It would be enough.

It was only a mile away, up that long flight of steps. Over a thousand feet above their heads.

"No joke," Burru said. He scratched irritably at his jaw. "Either we camp at Pujyu or we go back through the forest, and I don't much like the idea of sleeping with the spiders tonight. I want to wake up tomorrow."

"What do we have to do tomorrow?" Chinita asked. "Leap gorges and climb above the clouds?"

"Only half of that," Kai said.

Her jaw dropped, and Achachi roared with laughter. He might have been worried about his knees, but of them all he seemed to have the most energy left, and not for the first time. Kai's legs hurt just looking at that stair. He thought about urging the band on, and decided not to just yet. A few moments' rest wouldn't go amiss, for him as much as for them.

"Everyone's heard of the Left-Footed Trail," Achachi said when his laughter subsided. "Hardly anyone knows where it is, because the priesthood keeps that secret close."

"Not close enough, apparently," Kai said. "The *kura* didn't manage to hide it from you, old man."

Achachi only grinned at him. "All of us are lucky to be here, and walk along these steps. Tonight, we'll sleep in the ruins of a town of the Old People. Tomorrow we'll be higher than Makisapa ever climbed. We'll look down on soaring eagles and walk above the clouds, where the air is so thin it rasps in your throat and burns your lungs. The day after that we'll cross the Apachita, the highest pass in Apusuyu, where in winter lightning splits the rocks every day. And then we'll drop down thousands of feet in a few hours, and we'll be in the valley of Kuska."

"Kuska?" Suchi turned to stare at him. "The Place? Where the first man and woman were formed from the mist?"

"So the stories say," Achachi agreed. Most of the Ashir looked stunned, as though not quite able to believe what the old man had said. "Maybe they were, at that. But what matters now is that the sorcerer could search Apusuyu for a hundred years and never find us there."

It was a sanctuary, Kai thought. The valley was the safest place he could think of, mostly because so few people knew it existed. But the route in and out was hard to find and harder to remember. If another one of the Thrain decided to try to return to his own people, he'd never find his way out alive.

Besides, even if Terzian did somehow learn of it, and brought his army, he still had to find the Left-Footed Trail and follow it through. It was easy to get lost in the forest, and hard to find your way back again once you had. Men would fall from cliffs, lose themselves in tangled gorges, make camp in the forest and be bitten to death in their dozens by spiders and *tanqa* beetles. The Thrain army would be torn apart.

Perhaps Terzian would find his way through, with his magic. Kai's hand stole to the *cizin*, still tucked under his coat.

"We're never going to win here," Evain said softly. "The Thrain, I mean. Not if you have places like this."

Catori was leaning against a tree, massaging one foot, but he looked up at that. "Your sorcerer could destroy it in an hour, from what you say."

The soldier nodded. "Less, I expect. But what then? Your Blessed Land is vast. There must be a thousand places like this, where a handful of warriors could hold an army at bay for months. I wouldn't want to force my way into a town like this. So Terzian would have to come and destroy it, and then move on to the next one. But he hasn't got enough men to leave a garrison, and as soon as he leaves you could just move back in."

"Deer warriors might do that," Catori admitted. "We're good at sneaking. But Puma and Eagle would be offended by the mere suggestion. They prefer their enemies in front of them."

15

"Most soldiers do." Evain's lips quirked in a half smile. "But here, in Apusuyu, we Thrain don't know which way to face."

"Then why did you come?" Catori challenged. "Why attack us at all, if you thought you couldn't win?"

"Because we didn't know," Evain said. "We never guessed Apusuyu could be this huge. We thought all we had to do was capture your king and your capital and the land would be ours. So we came here, and everyone we asked pointed us south towards Hatun, but no matter how long we marched and how many mountain ranges we climbed, we never seemed to get any closer."

"Hatun," Achachi said. "I'd like to walk those streets again, before Supay takes me to his Halls."

Catori gave him an exasperated look. "Is there anywhere you haven't been, old man?"

"The coast," Achachi answered with a grin. "I've seen the ocean, but only at a distance, from the tops of mountains. I'd like to walk along a beach someday. Why? Do you want to keep me company?"

Ignoring the byplay, Kai kept his eyes on Evain. "And you? Why did you come here?"

"To retire," the solider answered. "I've been a mercenary most of my life. I fought when asked, for whoever paid me the most, but I turned forty with hardly a coin to my name. I kept meaning to save money, but there was always something to spend it on, and saving could wait another day." He shrugged. "So I was desperate, and when Terzian promised officers a piece of land of their own, and a title to go with it, I jumped at the chance."

"That's *our* land," Catori muttered, just as Achachi said, "Title?"

Evain chuckled. "Tell you what. I'll explain about land and titles over supper tonight, and you can tell me how long it took to carve these giant's stairs up the mountain. But for now, I want to save my breath. We still have all those steps to climb, don't we?"

He started forward, leading his horse by the reins. Several of his men followed, surrounded by Ashir as always, which left Kai and Achachi to exchange wry looks by the trees.

"Decisive, isn't he?" Kai observed.

Achachi nodded agreement. "I wish I understood more than a tenth of what he says, though. There's something new all the time with that man."

"There would be with any Thrain," Kai said. "Well, standing here won't get us any nearer camp. Can you manage the climb?"

"I always have before," Achachi shot back. He turned away and set off towards the steps, tapping the ground with his cane as he went. Kai followed, trying to ignore the ache in his legs, and not to let the others see his weariness. He didn't dare look up at the old town on the peak. If he took one step at a time, and thought of something else the whole way, it might not seem so hard.

It was hard from the start, and by the time he was halfway Kai could hardly force his legs to straighten with each step. All around him people would climb ten steps and stop to catch their breath, then climb ten more and pause again. The men with the horses whispered and stroked them, cajoling them up one step at a time, so concerned with the animals they didn't seem to notice the ache in their own legs. As Kai neared the top a breeze began to blow, cooling him but also snatching breath away just when he needed it most.

By the end Kai could only climb two steps before he needed to stop. When he reached the top his legs were burning from hip to ankle, and his chest felt so tight that it hurt to breathe in. He flopped down on a patch of tough grass, waiting for the black spots to fade from his vision. Panting men were slumped all around. Two of the Thrain sat together, their faces tinged with grey and their hands shaking. Someone was coughing repeatedly, hard enough to choke on his own lungs.

They had emerged onto a flat summit, perhaps three hundred yards from side to side. Tumbledown buildings covered all of it, except for an open plaza in the centre. On three sides terraces climbed down the slope in overlapping rows, cut through in several places by water channels and pools. The town must only have held two hundred or so people, but even so there was no way enough food could have been grown there to supply the populace. The terraces might have been ceremonial, or perhaps just aesthetic. The builders did seem to have loved the sight of running water.

They had built all this, in the years before Viraca came to teach the Ashir civilisation. But it had already been here. Architecture, farming, even art. Kai wondered how he could have missed it before.

Burru and Chinita began leading the horses to the square. The animals had managed the steps easily enough in the end, if slowly, and the people who'd stayed with them seemed fresher than the others. Burru himself was the most energetic after the long climb, though old Achachi looked about alertly from his seat on a convenient rock. There must be good mountain stock in that family, Kai thought, deep chests and wide veins. Himself, he hardly felt able to move. The tightness in his chest was easing though. If he stayed where he was for a little longer, he might feel he could stand.

"*Kamachi?*" Taruka came over on unsteady legs. Breath whistled hoarsely in his throat. "One of the outlaws… he can't stop coughing."

"They're not outlaws," Kai said. His voice was whispery, like a spider's leg rustling across cloth. "I gave them my blessing. Remember that."

"Uh, yes, *kamachi.*" Taruka shuffled his feet. "Anyway… Suchi had a look at him. It isn't good news."

A tired sigh escaped him. "The red plague?"

"Yes. Evain told me his people call it scarlet pox." He hesitated. "He says there's no cure."

Suchi said the plague was killing hundreds in Chakanay. It had done the same north of the Uma Mountains as well, and likely would spread south in time. It would reach the high peaks and the coastline, the valleys and plateaux and hills, and wherever it went people would die by the thousand. More would

17

be killed by the red plague than the swords of the Thrain. Kai had a sudden, nightmare vision of a triumphant Apusuyu, the invaders driven out, slowly crumbling from the inside until nothing was left but stones and trees, and the wind.

Perhaps in ten thousand years new peoples would happen by, and marvel at the temples they found across the land, and the towns, and wonder who had built them and why. Kai pushed himself to his feet. Black spots flickered before his eyes again, but he ignored them.

"Take me to him," he said.

3

Several of the men couldn't stand. If they tried their breath shortened and they felt dizzy, and had to sit or lie down again. It wasn't just the Thrain. Ashir flopped on the floors of broken houses and lay like the dead.

"It's the altitude," Achachi said. "Air on the heights is very thin. By morning they should be used to it a little, but until then, they could kill themselves if they move too much."

"I know," Evain answered. "There are mountains in Thrasin. Not as high as these, though."

"Then you don't know what it's like," Achachi said. "There are people who've lived on the plateaux for generations. They have very deep chests, like barrels. It helps them breathe."

"And they're still Ashir."

"Like everyone in the kingdom," the old man agreed. "They speak their own languages but they speak Ashir too. They worship their own gods and build temples to Viraca as well. Same as the coastal folk do, and the highlanders in the south."

"Because of Kai."

Achachi nodded. "They've produced *kamachi* before. They're bound together with ties they can't break."

"Where is Kai from?"

"I don't know. Neither does he. The priests took him when he was a baby, and raised him at the Retreat."

"I'd find out, if I was him."

"No *kamachi* ever knows," Achachi said. He smiled, turning his face into a mass of wrinkles. "But a lot has changed this spring. Maybe he'll go looking, when the war is done."

Three cook fires had been lit in the plaza, on the eastern side so the wind blew smoke away from the buildings. The houses were still strong, despite their age. The builders of this village had meant it to last forever. Times had changed, but perhaps a *kamachi* had been born here too, so long ago that nobody remembered anymore.

Evain could smell boiling chicken, and the richer flavour of chilli and maize. His stomach rumbled. He'd developed a taste for chilli, if in small quantities. Some of the Ashir dishes used enough of it to burn the skin from the roof of his mouth.

In the nearby houses someone was whispering, or several someones, though Evain couldn't tell which house it was. He wished they'd stop. It was grating on his nerves.

Most of the women were with the horses, rubbing them down awkwardly with handfuls of coarse grass plucked from the higher slopes. The animals were too tired even to snarl at them, as warhorses sometimes did with strangers. They stood with their heads down and their legs trembling, as weak and breathless as the men left lying in the house. Two pails of water stood not far away. The horses were desperately thirsty, but they would be sick if allowed to drink before their sweating and shaking had stopped. One of the soldiers, a southerner named Saivar, moved between the women offering advice in broken Ashir.

Evain's lips quirked. They were learning, all of them, Thrain and Ashir alike. It was a strange road they found their feet on, but once walking, there was no choice but to see it through to the end. Saivar believed so, at least. He'd been walking with Umiar when the fool made a run for it in that narrow valley, and Saivar hadn't even tried to follow him. He had too much sense. Anyone with a brain knew what greeting Terzian would give them.

"We can trust you now," Achachi said.

The captain frowned at him. "Do you read minds?"

"Don't be silly. I read faces." The old man shrugged. "You can tell a lot about someone by seeing what he looks at, and how his expression changes. Our peoples are the same, in that much."

"It's strange," Evain murmured. "Every time I think about it, I can name a hundred important differences between Thrain and Ashir. Our religions, our politics, our farming and our cultures themselves. We live in such different worlds, and yet here we are, finding common ground in the least little things." He shook his head slightly, trying to shake off that incessant whispering. "But yes, Achachi, you can trust us now. And you know it." He gestured back down the mountainside. "If for no other reason than that forest. We'd never find our way through without getting lost. Which I think is why your *kamachi* brought us here."

"True," Achachi agreed. "But it's not what I meant. I think we can trust you because of *you*. All you Thrain have thrown your lot in with us now. Maybe you had no choice, but it's the deed that counts, in the end."

Evain snorted. "The Church teaches us that the means count for more than the ends. Although it also teaches that the path to damnation is one of good intentions."

Achachi chortled. "Our *kura* are like that. They tell us to help the poor and unfortunate, and then cast people out if they can't pay their way. It's why people become outlaws."

"Common ground," Evain said, "in the least little things. Anyway, you're right. You can trust us."

The horses had calmed a little, and at Saivar's gesture one of the women went to fetch the water pails. The sight of women with weapons made Evain slightly uneasy, and what was worse, it seemed they had been outlaws until recently. There was something strange there, because apparently their former lives were not to be spoken of, as though they had never happened at all. Kai was tied up in that, of course. Stranger yet, those peculiar fighting women were part of the ramshackle force which had beaten a full patrol of Thrain cavalry. Every single officer Evain knew would laugh himself hoarse if he heard about that. Evain might have laughed himself if it had happened to someone else, but now it didn't strike him as funny. The ambush had been cleverly laid, but still, it was embarrassing to lose to *women*.

Women with bronze weapons, no horses, and armour of quilted cotton or leather, much of it worn through in ragged patches. Hardly the stuff of elite soldiers. Sometimes it was difficult to look at them without sneering, whether they were women or the crested, tattooed men. The Ashir were primitives, in so many ways. But there was always something to change the way Evain saw them. The beauty of their gold figurines, their sculpture, or the sheer scale of the roads and steps which criss-crossed the country and leaped over mountains. They were not primitives, however they might appear to the casual eye. They were simply different. That was the first mistake the Thrain had made, when all this was being planned, and it might be the one that killed most of them.

Evain's gaze came to rest on Kai, seated beside on of the campfires and deep in conversation with two other men. One of them was Burru, the outlaw leader who now had never been an outlaw, somehow. A cynical man, Evain judged, but one whose eyes glowed whenever he looked at Kai.

The *kamachi*. The greatest mystery of them all, in this strange land. A man with no lands or titles, no power, no servants, and yet able to raise armies and forgive past sins. Able to defy a Qapac, beyond doubt, should he choose to. Much of the power in Apusuyu rested with the priesthood, and Kai stood at the heart of that. Born with a plum-coloured snake twined around his left eye like a badge, like a banner around which society rallied, as one man had been in every generation for hundreds of years, if the legends were true. Evain had once been quite sure they were not. The warriors tattooed society markings on their arms. Why couldn't a priest tattoo a snake around a baby's eye?

That was what Draivan and the other Examiners said. The priests of Apusuyu were frauds, peddling their ridiculous gods with lies and deceit. Their Servant was no more than a fiction. Evain had never been a man to place much trust in the clergy, but in this he'd been sure they were right.

And then the worn bronze sickle Kai carried had cut right through Ramian's breastplate in the tunnel. It should have been impossible. The best steel in Thrasin sliced apart like a cobweb, when it was made to stand up to the impacts of crashing swords and hard-swung maces. Impossible.

Evain had seen that coiling snake up close now, several times. He didn't think it was a tattoo.

He shook his head. Someone was still whispering not far away, though he couldn't see anyone, and it set such a tickle inside his skull that he gritted his teeth in annoyance. He spoke just to drown the sound out. "Will tomorrow's road be as hard as today's, Achachi?"

"Harder." The old man grimaced at the prospect. "After a few miles through the forest we start climbing towards Apachita, and that's one of the toughest trails in the Blessed Land. It's so rough that nobody ever tried to build a road

21

there. It's just a track, muddy in places and rocky in others, and overgrown as often as not because it's hardly ever used. I wouldn't wish that trail on anyone."

"How will we get the horses through?"

"I don't know, lad. That's your problem." The old man flexed his hands until tendons popped. "But you'd better hope they're well trained. The pass at Apachita is above the clouds. Some days you can see all the way to the ocean, and the air is so clear you might even be able to pick out the sails."

"That's impossible," Evain said. His mind struggled to cope with the pass as Achachi had described it, so he lighted on the one thing he could be sure was false. "The ocean's seventy or eighty miles away."

Achachi cocked an eyebrow at him. "I'm not exaggerating. You likely won't enjoy the view much, because it'll be all you can do to breathe. Then we climb back down the other side, four thousand feet of switchback trails and gullies, and into Kuska. I'm looking forward to that," he added wistfully. "I haven't seen Kuska since I was a boy."

"Catori was right," Evain said, smiling. "You really do seem to have been everywhere."

"Not everywhere," Achachi snorted. "Apusuyu's too big for any one man to do that. I was born in the Uma Mountains, and I know pretty much every village and trail and byway within fifty miles of them, but I've never really been further than that. This is just my part of the world, that's all."

"That's a large area to call home," Evain said.

"You don't understand." Achachi shook his head. "Apusuyu is my home. All of it. Even the parts I've never laid eyes on and never will. That's why I was so ready to leave my peaceful retirement and take myself back on the trails again, after years just sitting on my porch and watching the stars wheel by overhead. I used to be an outlaw, you know."

"No you didn't. Kai blessed you, and forgave you."

"Kai didn't bless me. I wasn't there." The old man's eyes were distant, seeing something long ago. "I'm not sure I want his blessing. It would make all I lived through seem like nothing."

"Even if it damns your soul?"

"I made my choice. I was an outlaw, and the warriors never caught me. Not many can say that. Thirty years a bandit, and I ended with a nice little house and a bit of land, and no chance of being spitted like a squirrel on a stick. And now this." He made a wide gesture with one hand. "I'm back on the trails again. All the Blessed Land is my home, and I'll fight for it."

Evain looked at him. "Because of Kai."

"Yes," Achachi said, his voice almost as soft as the incessant whispers. "Maybe you do understand after all. The *kamachi* is what makes us one people, from coast to mountain peak, and from one end of the Pasqa to the other. One people, and one country. Without Kai, and those before him, there would be no Ashir. Only tribes in valleys and villages. Just ghosts and stones and memories, with nothing to make Apusuyu into a *land*."

22

The campfires crackled. People gathered around them as the food was served on wooden platters, some talking but most too weary to do more than sit and chew. Kai was handed a plate, by a figure made so shadowy in the gathering twilight that Evain couldn't tell if it was a man or a woman. Burru and the other man were gone now, leaving Kai alone at the edge of the firelight. Ten yards behind him Chinita sat, her eyes reflecting flames as she watched him.

"Well," Achachi said. "Conversation always makes me nearly as hungry as climbing. I think we should eat."

"I think we should," Evain agreed. He let himself study Kai for a moment longer before he moved though. *One people, and one country.* Everyone within the borders of Apusuyu named themselves Ashir because of the men like Kai, all the way back to the Teacher God who was said to have raised their ancestors from among the beasts. You had to go back to the men who had carved the stone *lanti* and built Pujyu, so long ago that their name and language were forgotten, to find people who were not united by the *kamachi*.

Except that now the Thrain had come, outsiders by geography and much more so by culture. Perhaps they would never be accepted here, whatever Kai said, whatever he asked.

Or perhaps they would, *because* he asked.

4

Once on the south side of the old town Kai let himself down on to the stepped terraces, where a stream had once flowed down a channel of smoothed rock. Water must once have emerged on the top of this steep-sided peak, by whatever trick of geology. It was just too unlikely that the builders had carried water all the way from the valley a thousand feet below. Now foliage had encroached on either side of the stream bed, and covered what had once been farmed terraces with tough bushes and long, coarse grass. He went down again, onto a third tier, and then he eased himself past a couple of shrubs and sat with his back against the fitted stones and waited for the tears to come.

And couldn't cry. He sat there in silence, watching the forest below and the pinwheeling stars above, and could find no tears willing to creep from behind his eyes and fall. A whispering came to him on the breeze, soft and unceasing, though he was alone. He couldn't really remember being alone anymore. There had always been Matlal.

It was very cold. He put his hands in his armpits and watched his breath form sparkles in the air.

"You can weep," he said, his lips hardly moving. Breath puffed, faded. "Blood and bones, you can weep for him. For them both."

His grief coiled tighter in his chest, and refused to listen. He would have been able to let himself cry if Matlal was with him, he knew. If Salali was there the squirrel would probably have made a jest and changed the mood, so there was no need for tears any more. Kai would give – not his soul, but a great deal, a hand perhaps – to have either one of them with him now. Someone to talk to and listen, someone to trust. He sighed and rested the back of his head against the stones, willing to wait a while, and realised as he did so that he was not alone after all.

Someone was walking down the path of the old stream, the same route he had taken himself. Kai didn't bother moving. He listened instead, waited for the intrusive newcomer to take another step and move into view. He thought he knew who it would be, actually. For a long time that step didn't come, as though whoever stood there was watching or looking for tracks, but finally a figure emerged from behind the screen of bushes.

It was who Kai had expected to see.

"When you breathe out, the air from your lungs is warmer," he said. The figure jumped a little, as though surprised by the suddenness of something only half expected. "So it forms a kind of frost, in the air." He waved a hand through the silver of his own breath, so it vanished in swirls instead of simply fading. "Folk in the high mountains call it 'the whispering of the stars'."

"I know," Chinita said.

She moved towards him, skirting the bushes which had hidden her from view. In the darkness she was little more than a silhouette of deeper shadow, but she found him easily despite the gloom. She folded her legs and sat beside him, her hip almost touching his. Kai smiled a little.

"What brings you out here?" he asked, knowing the answer.

She shrugged. "I like to walk alone, some nights."

"No, you don't." He rested his head on the stones again. "I've never known you to do it before. So why now? Why here?"

That was actually a lie, because he *had* known her to wander at night, back when they'd camped by the lake in the Uma Mountains, ten or twelve nights ago. It felt as though years had passed since then. But Chinita didn't know he'd heard her that night, so Kai maintained the fiction. She didn't reply for a long moment, and when she did her voice was almost as soft as the endless susurration of whispers all around. "I'm… worried for you. We're all worried."

"I know that," he said.

Worried for him. He supposed he should appreciate that, now of all times, when he was choking on sorrow. It was so hard to remember though. Sometimes it was hard to care.

Achachi would be livid if he knew Kai had let himself sink so deep into his own misery. No doubt he would have words to say about the suffering of others, men and women who needed Kai to be there for them, and to ease their pain. Now of all times, he thought with a sardonic twist to his mouth, when they were choking on sorrow. But grief was allowed. Even for him, for the *kamachi*, it had to be allowed, or what would he become?

"And you?" Chinita asked. "What brought you out here?"

That twist of his lips became a lopsided smile. "I like to walk alone, some nights."

"No, you don't," she said.

He turned to look at her. It was difficult to make out her face, but her eyes caught a glint of starlight and threw it back, and Kai could understand half a person's life from one glance and a handful of words. His gift, if such it was, from Viraca. He stared at her, not speaking.

"You had friends you liked to walk with at night," she said, "Kai, you're allowed to cry."

He snorted a laugh, incredibly. So much for his vaunted intuition. He had missed this altogether, had simply not seen it coming, and couldn't quite decide how. Yet Chinita understood why he went away alone sometimes at night, away from the snores and the stares. She must have been watching him, and he hadn't seen it. There was probably a valuable lesson in humility in all this. Nata would certainly say –

Nata would *not* say so.

"I know that," Kai replied, for the second time.

"Do you?" He thought her smile was sad. "You never have, though. You loved Matlal. You can grieve for him."

25

His throat tightened. "And Salali, too. I loved both of them. And I sent them to their deaths."

"You sent neither of them to anything," she answered gently. "They did what they chose to do freely, because they loved you as much as you loved them. They loved *you*, Kai. Not the *kamachi*, not an abstract heavenly servant, but you, for yourself. Can't you see that?"

Of course he could see that. It only sharpened the needles in his heart. Sala and Matlal had trusted him, had faith in him, and had died because of the things he had asked them to do. He couldn't think of a way to say that without sounding as though he was whining like a self-indulgent child, and the thought made him frown. What if he really was whining?

"Blood and bones," he said with sudden savageness, "I can't stop thinking, and analysing, for long enough to *feel*. Sometimes I think I'm not a very good *kamachi*. I can't seem to meet the expectations."

She laughed in the darkness. "You don't meet your own, that's all. You more than match the expectations of everyone else."

Kai blinked at her, and then smiled. "Including you?"

"I might not be the best person to ask." Her amusement was gone already, but she didn't look away. "My... opinions of you aren't exactly... detached."

There it was, the thing he'd missed. Kai hesitated, then reached out and found her hand, and wrapped it in his own. Her fingers were like ice. He made sure his voice was as gentle as he could make it. "This isn't a good time to fall in love, Chinita."

"Is there a good time?"

He had to concede that. "Probably not."

"Love happens when it wants to," she said shakily. "Not when we might prefer it to happen. Viraca taught that it was our hearts which made us what we are, do you remember?"

"I remember."

"I feel as though you're walking around with part of me inside you. Sometimes I stop to do something, and I know you're walking behind me, without having to look. It sounds foolish, even to me. No, don't speak, Kai." She placed the fingers of her free hand against his lips, while the other tightened its grip on his own. "Our hearts make us what we are, but in their own way. Isn't that strange? And none of us can help it. Not even Viraca, I expect."

"I don't doubt it," he said when she took her fingers away. "Viraca loved us, all the Ashir. How strange is that?"

"And it doesn't even matter that you don't love me," she went on. He might as well not have spoken at all. "I know you don't, Kai. You would have said by now, if you did."

Something inside Kai seemed to break loose, and the needles in him sharpened and grew softer at the same time. He had to clear his throat to speak. "Chinita, I don't know what I feel. I'm..." He tailed off, but she'd been honest

26

with him, which must have taken some courage. The least he could do was be open in return. "I'm in pieces inside right now. I can't think about this."

"Blood and bones," she said, "maybe you should stop thinking. Just for long enough to feel."

"Oh, very clever." He meant the words to snap, and was surprised when he realised he was smiling. His tone changed. "Very clever indeed."

She tightened her grip on his hand again. He could feel her trembling, though her voice was steady and calm. "Outlaws are used to loved ones dying, Kai. We tell ourselves we can avoid feeling too close to someone, because we know any of us could die, at any time. The truth is that most of us are terrible at it. Like my grandfather. He pretends, but nothing more than that."

"Your grand –" Kai broke off, studying her as best he could in the night. "You knew all along, didn't you?"

"I *thought* he'd told you," she said, sounding satisfied. "All right, then. We'll wait until the Thrain are gone, and if both of us are still alive we'll sit down and talk about our future. Not before."

"Our future?" he repeated, blinking. "And you're going to be alive, at least. You want your women's warrior society to be riders, remember? So you have to stay and learn."

"I go where you go." Her tone left no room for argument. "And there's the red plague, anyway."

"What does that have to do with it?"

"I could stay away from battle and take no risks," she said, "and still die. Disease doesn't care who it touches."

He nodded. "True."

"Quilla's mercy, I wish that whispering would stop." She let go of his hand, pulling her legs up under her chin. "For the first hour up here I kept turning around to see who was behind me."

"It's the grass," Kai told her absently. "In the breeze the blades rub together to make a sound like people whispering, and up here, there's always a breeze. You'll stay in Kuska with the horses, Chinita."

She gave him a look that he recognised, even in the dark. His words had been heard, and she was going to do what she wanted in spite of them. Women were good at that look. "None of us will be leaving Kuska any time soon, I think. Not until we know who will come down with the red plague and who won't. What's the point of taking twenty warriors back over the pass if most of them will be dead before they can find the Thrain?"

That was true, unfortunately. The band needed to rest in any case, after two weeks in the mountains and then a battle, followed by a mad rush through some of the steepest valleys and peaks in Apusuyu. Besides, there was something Kai wanted to do before he left Kuska himself. He studied Chinita for a moment and then shrugged mentally. She was going to stick close to him, no matter what he said. He might as well trust her.

27

"I want to send out scouts anyway," he told her. "Spies, really. This plague has decimated the message Runners, but I want those who remain to bring me word of where the Thrain are, and what they're doing. Someone will have to go out and find the Runners first. Then I'll have them summon the town governors and village headmen, from one end of the Blessed Land to the other, to gather their warriors ready for an attack at autumn equinox. I won't send them where the sorcerer is, he'd cut them apart. As soon as he appears our people will have to scatter, just flee so he doesn't have a target to aim at. But if any of the Thrain are found without him, I want them killed. Singly or in numbers, they have to die, and quickly. A job for the Snake society," he added, "and for the women riders, if there are enough of you."

"And if more come?"

"Then we fight them too," he said, but he couldn't keep despair out of his voice.

Chinita heard it, and she studied him in the dark. "You've thought of something, and it's got you worried."

"More worried than I have been, you mean?" He laughed under his breath, though it wasn't funny at all. "I keep thinking about Thrasin, and mercenaries. Men there fight for anyone who will pay them. If the sorcerer manages to send our gold back home, as his son was trying to do, there might be ten thousand soldiers on the ships when they return. Twenty thousand, or fifty. We don't know how big their homeland is, and we can't guess how many men they have. But we can be sure that if they send an army, Apusuyu is finished. Even another ten thousand of them might be too many for us to deal with. We have to finish this quickly. Autumn is as long as we dare wait."

"None of that matters if we can't get rid of Terzian. We…" She tailed off, still watching him. "You think you've already found a way to deal with the sorcerer, don't you?"

"Maybe," he replied. An insanely risky way, but… maybe. He'd been thinking about it for two days. Magic against magic. "What does Terzian want, more than anything else?"

"His son back," she said at once.

Kai shook his head. "He must know he can't have that. Our gods never brought a dead man back from beyond the grave, and I'm sure theirs hasn't either. He wants something simpler than that."

"You," she said. Her eyes gleamed in the dark. "That's what you mean. You're going to make yourself into bait."

"And when he comes after me," Kai said, "it will be in the mountains and gullies, with forests wherever you turn and a hundred ways for a careless man to die. Yes. I'll make myself bait." He put a hand under his coat, just to make sure the *cizin* was still there. "And Terzian will come for me."

5

"Five *karwa*? For a slice of filled bread?"

"It's good bread," Jarawi said. "Squirrel or pork, your choice, and only the finest. You'll find no rat in my bread."

The customer, a farmhand in from the fields to judge by his plain, grimy clothing, was not mollified. "For five *karwa* I'd expect a blessing from the Bearded God and the love of three beautiful women."

Jarawi shrugged. He'd had this conversation several times today already. "What can I tell you? Half the traders won't come to Chakanay while the Thrain are here, and half the rest have died of the red plague. It's a wonder I've got any meat at all, let alone good pork and squirrel."

The man hesitated, then looked around as hooves clattered on stone. People had grown used to that sound already, knowing it meant soldiers were nearby, and Jarawi had seen that sidelong glance more than once today too, as riders passed by. People were becoming good at looking from the sides of their eyes without seeming to.

The Thrain sorcerer and a thousand men might still be somewhere to the north, but the number of patrols hadn't dropped. Whoever was in charge in the Precinct now was determined to keep a tight lid on trouble.

"Oh, *no*," the farmhand groaned as the horsemen came into sight. "Not that howling monkey again!"

"Blood and bones," Jarawi growled, "keep your voice down, will you?"

He wasn't going to sell to the farmer now. Jarawi watched as riders filed into the plaza, the sun glinting off their red-and-black shields. In normal times they would have had to push their way through thick crowds, and past stalls crammed so close together that their bright-striped awnings overlapped at the edges. These were not normal times. Two thirds of the stalls were missing, and of those which remained few boasted full stock. Grocers struggled to sell wrinkled tomatoes and chillies, and squashes that had sat unclaimed for so long that they had begun to turn soft. Clothiers called in desultory voices for buyers to at least view their rolls of linen. Shoppers moved between them with lowered heads and quick steps, eager to buy the minimum they needed and head back to their homes.

Several of the citizens shot bleak glares at the Thrain, and then simply turned and walked away. The soldiers didn't seem to notice, though behind the side plates of their helmets it was hard to be sure. They walked their horses between the stalls, staring down at anyone who came too close, hands always near the hilts of their swords. There was a tension about them since Terzian had gone north that hadn't been there before. It made Jarawi nervous.

But the soldiers weren't what had caused the farmhand's groan. Amidst the riders walked a man wearing the brown of a Thrain priest, with a thick book clutched in his hand. At a glance his face was serene and composed, though Jarawi thought he saw tight anger underneath that calm. No wonder. He could see citizens streaming away from him and out of the plaza, the way they did whenever they saw him mount the steps at the southern end of the square.

One of the traders gave the Thrain a flat stare, turned his back, and began to pack up his boxes. The insult couldn't have been plainer, and a muscle jumped in the brown-clad man's cheek. He gave no other sign that he'd noticed though, and the soldiers stayed in their cluster around him as they moved towards the steps.

"It's disgusting," the farmhand muttered. "That they should do this in front of the Temple of Quilla sickens me."

It sickened Jarawi too, but not as much as the broken pillars and remnant walls which were all that remained of Quilla's shrine. The Thrain had looted it of all gold and gems and then smashed the walls looking for more. They were crazed for gold, insane with lust for it. Jarawi didn't understand. Copper, tin, even lead was more useful.

He made sure not to look at the ruin. "Are you going to buy my bread or not?"

The farmer glowered and moved away. That was one customer who wasn't likely to be back very soon.

Well, one more buyer lost didn't count for much, with half the town dead or dying of ague, or else away visiting relatives. It was almost funny, how many people in Chakanay had suddenly discovered the urge to visit nephews or cousins they hadn't seen in years.

The Thrain priest reached the steps and began to climb, while the sixty soldiers spread out in a double line at the bottom. Halfway up the priest stopped, by the wide plinth on which the golden statue of Quilla of the Moon had once stood. The Thrain had melted it down two days after they took the town. Further up, at the top of the wide steps, fallen masonry formed a jumbled and fire-blackened heap. Jarawi felt his lips tighten. He was looking at the ruins after all.

"Children of the One!" The priest's voice rang across the plaza: he might be an invader and a fool, but he had the lungs of a puma. His voice was nearly as harsh as a puma's too, and that and his accent mangled the words so badly that Jarawi struggled to make them out. "I am Draivan, chaplain of the One God. I come to save your souls from darkness.

"You have been misled by evil men." Bright blue eyes swept the plaza, seeming not to notice that every face was turned away. "You have fallen into the worship of false idols and demons, and if you do not turn from them your souls will be damned. There is only one God, and He is a jealous god. Obey Him and you will all be brothers, united in faith. Fail to repent, and you will scream in the fire for eternity."

It was the same speech as always, with almost the same words every time. Draivan and his colleagues seemed only to have the one lecture to offer, one bottle to sell, and nothing else. Perhaps they learned it by rote. What it amounted to was that their god tolerated no other gods, and he didn't much like anyone who didn't worship him either. One of the *kura* had told Jarawi, long ago, that

30

when the Blind God came to Apusuyu he threatened death and suffering to those who refused to abandon Viraca. This Thrain deity sounded enough like that to make Jarawi's skin crawl.

He glanced around, trying to distract himself, and his eyes fell on the whorehouse with its characteristic, yellow-striped windowsills. The shutters of the upper rooms were closed, of course, even in the pale sunshine of a spring afternoon. Trade would slow with the Thrain in the plaza, but a prostitute's business was mostly done in the evening, and not much could stop a man passing coins to a woman anyway. Rumour in the town said you couldn't catch the red plague if you'd been to a prostitute in the past week. Jarawi wondered if the whores had started that whisper themselves, and scolded himself for his cynicism.

"You look hungry, my friend," he said to a passing shopper. "I have real pork here, and for just four *karwa* a slice." He wasn't going to sell it at five, and besides, he wasn't really here to make money. Not today. Still, there was no point in letting the bread go to waste. "When was the last time you tasted pork, eh? Who knows when the next time will be?"

The man hesitated. "You swear it's pork?"

"I'm Jarawi," he said. "Maybe you've heard of me. I always sell proper meat, my friend, and this would oink if it could."

Another moment of doubt, and then the man dipped into his pocket and came over to the stall. "I'll have two, then. My wife would skin me if I didn't bring her something back too."

"Oh dear," Jarawi said, letting sympathy into his tone in great spoonfuls. "The women of Chakanay are the most ferocious in Apusuyu, I'm told."

"But there is hope yet!" Draivan trumpeted from the steps. "The Lord forgives all those who come to Him with open hearts, may He be praised for all time. You are His children, and you need only turn from your false idols and step into His Light to be redeemed. Bathe in His presence, and your sins will be washed from you, and you shall be left pure. The Holy Book says, 'No man is so blessed as one who has seen the Light of the Lord.'"

"Ferocious?" The man grimaced. "It's my own fault. I saw her mother before I married Tehua, and there's a woman to give you cold sweats and nightmares. I should have taken the hint."

Jarawi began to wrap the bread in dried reeds. "My friend, if I'd taken a few hints when I was a young man, I can promise you I wouldn't be standing in an empty plaza selling bread."

"But the people of Carian refused to heed the word of God!" As the plaza emptied, so Draivan's voice grew louder still, until the paving stones seemed to tremble. "They turned their faces from Him and worshipped their terrible, false gods, and the Lord said to his servants, 'I shall visit torments upon them, that they know my wrath." His voice tightened. "And first of these torments shall be frogs.'"

Someone laughed, as someone always did, every time the priest spoke of frogs. Jarawi and the buyer exchanged grins, but furtively, so the soldiers wouldn't see. Across the plaza a man howled with mirth, doubling over to clutch his belly. His clothes were worn but had been expensive once. There hadn't been enough time for that to happen since the Thrain arrived. This man had fallen on hard times all by himself.

"Frogs," the buyer snorted.

Jarawi handed over the bread. "Doesn't sound *very* tormenting, does it?"

"Maybe that god of theirs isn't all they say he is."

"Maybe not," Jarawi said, voice bland.

The man frowned for a moment, as though puzzled by the noncommittal response. Then he seemed to decide it didn't matter, and with a nod he stowed the bread in his bag and walked away. The fellow who'd laughed was staggering out of the plaza, still clutching his belly and almost choking on stifled howls of mirth.

"The second torment shall be insects in the fields, which eat the corn," Draivan boomed from the top of the steps. "Should you yet resist the Lord, the third torment shall be black boils on the flesh."

Jarawi's smile faded. Apusuyu had its share of pests, worst of them the *akatanqa* beetle that devoured its way through crops. Now it had plague as well, though the pustules were red and not black. Still, if those threats really came out of the book Draivan held, they were an eerie premonition of the present. *Maybe their god isn't all they say he is,* Jarawi thought. *And then again, perhaps he is. And may our ancestors have pity on our souls if that's true.*

Draivan's Ashir was improving though, despite his thick accent. But he wasn't perfect. At one point he said that an unbeliever had once been converted to worship of God by a talking bush, but that must have been what he meant, because Draivan didn't correct himself. The chaplain spoke for more than two hours, mostly to a plaza empty except for traders and a few morose shoppers. Jarawi stayed where he was, on the corner by the whorehouse, while his bread grew stale in the cart.

Finally evening began to steal over the plaza. He decided to leave then, unwilling to make himself obvious by standing out. If word hadn't come by now it was probably not going to. Maybe tomorrow –

"Four slices of squirrel filling, please," someone said.

Jarawi looked round into tilted dark eyes, framed in hair sewn with silver beads. "Qula!"

She grinned. "Caught you just in time, did I?"

"I thought it was too late," he admitted. He looked her up and down, from her mane of black hair to shapely legs exposed to above the knee, and several interestingly curved places in between. Qula never minded when men admired her, and they usually did. A lot of them just looked at her with their jaws hanging. "Four, you said? I think I've got that many left."

She snorted, and still managed to look lovely doing it. "You've sold two slices in the last hour. *I* think you've got enough left to feed all the craftsmen in town from now until the Festival of Masks."

"You might be right." He darted quick eyes past her, to where the Thrain were escorting Draivan away from the plaza again. It brought them uncomfortably close to his stall, too close for him to speak openly. "And your business, Qula? Have you seen young Fala recently?"

"He was just in," she said. "Insisted on seeing me, of course. He always picks me. He'll even wait if I'm with someone when he comes in. The other girls don't like it." She pouted, letting the Thrain see. "When are you going to come visit me yourself, Jarawi?"

Fala was back. He'd only been gone a few days, but it had seemed an age. Jarawi's heart thumped, but if the soldiers noticed they'd think it was because this stunning woman had just offered herself to him. "I don't dare, Qula. My wife is largely why Chakanay's women have such a reputation for ferocity."

"But you're not married."

"Well no," he conceded, now with a lecherous grin. "Now you mention it, I'm not. Wait until trade puts coins in my hand again, and I'll be right in to visit you. Here. That's sixteen *karwa*."

She handed him a clinking cloth bag, took the bread, and swung her hips as she turned back towards the whorehouse. "Now you have coins in your hand again, master Jarawi."

"I think I'll need a little more than this," he said, looking at the meagre coins in his palm.

"To afford me, you will," she agreed, with a smile over her shoulder. "But you promised, and I won't forget."

"You'd better not," he called after her. He could feel something else in the bag apart from coins. His hands felt clammy.

Ten minutes later he was out of the plaza, pushing his cart along a wide boulevard which would have been thronged on a normal day. Too few people were left in Chakanay for anything to be normal, and those who did remain were often indoors, hiding from the storm. He didn't see any funerals though, for a change. Lately they had come so thick and fast that Jarawi had wondered if anyone would be left alive in all Apusuyu by the time the plague died down. Maybe that would be the end of this struggle. Everyone would be dead, and the world would be as it was before men and women were made from the mist in Kuska, a land empty except for pumas and howler monkeys screeching in the trees, and vultures high above.

He turned off the boulevard and on to a narrower lane, all but deserted. Planks laid side by side made a bridge over a drainage channel, and there he turned right and shoved through the battered back door of Tumay's *machana*, into the familiar smells of *chicha* beer and peach brandy. A hum of low conversation came from the front room, four or five people talking in soft voices over their beer. Tumay would be in there as well, of course, chatting to the customers. Making everything seem normal. Jarawi wanted a drink quite badly, but it would have to wait. He went upstairs.

Salali was waiting in one of the guest rooms, leaning back in a chair, apparently asleep. Ilari sat across the table, his face a grey mask. His eyes were bright though, feverishly so in that pallid face. Dyani perched on the window ledge with his feet propped across from him, a man at his ease, but when Jarawi came in his whole body went taut.

"Sala," Jarawi said. He tossed the bag across the room.

Sala opened his eyes and picked it out of the air with a casual hand. He looked at it and then opened the drawstrings, shaking its contents out on the low table. Battered coins spun and tinkled, some falling to the floor. In amongst those on the table was a set of knotted cords tied together, tassels of red and blue and green. Sala ignored the coins and picked up the quipu, holding it to the light. For a moment nobody moved.

"Ah," Sala said, very slowly. "Well, then."

Jarawi felt he was going to burst. "What? Don't keep us guessing, man. What does he say?"

"Tonight," Salali said. Ilari sighed like wind escaping from a tomb. "Chimalli will be here two hours before dawn, with four thousand warriors. Fewer than we'd hoped. But it might be enough."

It was half what they had hoped. Sala had expected warriors to have gathered away from Chakanay, waiting for a chance to strike back at the invaders, and he had been right. But there weren't many. Perhaps there hadn't been enough time. It was only two weeks since the Thrain had arrived, just ten days since the slaughter in the Precinct. That seemed incredible. It felt like far longer.

It felt like the two thousand years when the Blind God had ruled, the land clutched in his clawed hand.

"It will be enough," Dyani said from the window. "With the men we have in Chakanay, it will be."

"The sorcerer isn't here," Ilari added. He rubbed his hands, his fevered eyes gleaming. "And without him the Thrain die like anyone else. It's time they died. Time they all died."

"It is," Salali agreed. He gave Ilari a cautious glance, as though the artisan had turned into a poisonous *binchuka* and was ready to sting. "With the red plague still killing people the way it is, I'm half surprised Chimalli managed to gather as many warriors as he has. The plague must have ravaged them, too." Sala threw the quipu back to the table and looked at Ilari. A smile flickered around the corners of his mouth. "So. Tonight."

"You're giving the order?" Jarawi asked. He realised he was grinning. "We can spread the word?"

Sala nodded. "Tell the men. But they are *not* to spread the word to anyone new. A man who's ready to join us will do so soon enough once the fighting starts. Our people are to act normally. Meet in houses or shops, but stay out of sight and do nothing to make the Thrain suspect. No crowds in the streets, not so much as a thrown stone until my signal. Make sure everyone understands that, all of you."

"We'll tell them," Ilari said.

"And the signal?" Dyani stared at Sala, hungry-eyed. "When will you blow the horn?"

"When Chimalli is due," Sala told him. "Two hours before sunup."

Dyani swung his legs down and stood up. "We will, Salali. Trust us now. We were warriors once, and we know our work." He stopped, one hand going to his hair. "Jarawi, does your friend Tumay have scissors, and a razor? I haven't had my hair in a crest for twenty years, but I think I want it tonight."

"Warriors again," Ilari said.

Sala looked from one man to the other, and reached into his pocket to produce a pair of scissors and a long, straight razor. Evening sunlight gleamed off the bronze blade.

"I was never a warrior," Sala said. "But if it doesn't offend you, I might crest my hair tonight, too."

Dyani's answering grin would have made a puma cringe.

6

Torches lined the sides of the courtyard, guttering in the breeze. Kisain's squad waited in four lines, their cloaks drawn tight against the night's chill. High above, the moon played peek-a-boo behind scudding clouds, outriders of the darker mass of a spring storm moving in from the west. Kisain could feel its approach in the thickness of the air. There would be thunder and rain before dawn. Just his luck to be on patrol.

He stood on the platform atop a newly built wooden tower, rising ten feet above the wall to one side of the bronze doors. The Precinct had been a temple, now it was a fortress and barracks. A pair of archers stood under the eaves of the slanted roof at the front corners, peering into the empty plaza below. Usually townsfolk straggled to and fro all night, either heading home from a late drink at a *machana* or working, but not today.

"It's quiet," Traive said. "I like that."

"I don't," Kisain said. "It makes me suspicious."

"Better than a riot."

He wasn't sure about that. In a riot you could see the trouble and deal with it. When the streets were empty you had nothing except guesses, and a guess was usually wrong. He shook his head and moved to the front of the platform, for a better view of the plaza below.

"Looks like you're going to get wet," one of the sentries said. "That looks like a nasty storm to me."

"Show some respect to an officer," Traive growled.

Kisain suppressed a sigh. Everyone was feeling strained at the moment. With Terzian gone and rumours flying that his son had been killed, the whole army was on edge. Kisain knew the truth of that, of course. The prince was terribly maimed at the very least, and almost certainly dead. Kisain hadn't told anyone though. Enough whispers were flying anyway, one of which claimed that Terzian had been killed too, and a vast horde of Ashir warriors was gathering to the north. Kisain doubted that, but even so the possibility made his hands start to tremble if he let himself think about it. If it was true the remaining Thrain were as good as dead, cut off deep in a hostile land, and surrounded by enemies with murder on their minds.

He pushed that aside and gave the archer a smile. "Berain shows respect when it counts. "I know. He was at Morind Gap with me."

Traive scowled. "I wasn't there."

"I know," Kisain said again. That was why he'd mentioned it, to put Traive in his place. "Berain was. That's what matters."

The archer gave him a quick smile. "And we don't forget."

"Never," Kisain said.

Every soldier who'd fought at the Gap remembered it, usually in nightmares that woke them gasping and soaked with sweat. Awake, they did their best not to think about it at all. Eight hundred mercenaries had been hired by the Church to protect labourers while they built a fort east of Thrasin, in the hills beyond which the steppe horsemen teemed. Invasions had come from that direction often enough, from one tribe or another, most recently a bloodthirsty horde calling themselves the Galan. A series of forward forts seemed a sensible precaution. Except the Galan didn't see it that way, and decided not to wait until the forts were finished before they did something about it.

"They came out of the grass," Berain said. He shuddered. "Just like that, as though they were coming out of the earth. Thousands of them. Half the men in my squad ran like frightened chickens."

Kisain nodded. That was how he remembered it too. A calm summer day, and then all at once the wide valley sprouted horsemen like a field bursting with corn. The patrol disintegrated in moments. Kisain barely made it back to the fort alive. Some two hundred soldiers hadn't been so lucky. The rest found themselves trapped a hundred miles from home, in an unfinished fort and with just enough food to last them for a week. All the Galan needed to do was sit outside the walls and wait.

"I would have run as well," he said, "except there was nowhere to run to."

The Galan hadn't waited. Their first assault on the walls came immediately, while the last soldiers caught outside were still fighting for their lives in tight circles amidst the throng. The second came before nightfall. No Thrain was left alive outside the half-finished walls by then. It seemed that none would be left inside soon either, but the defenders held for a day, then two. Their arrows ran out, so they took shafts from the piled corpses of dead Galan. They replaced broken chainmail by stripping their own fallen, tossed aside shattered blades and seized others, or fought with wood axes and smiths' hammers. Two more days went by. Men slept on the walls and ate when they could.

By then almost every man was carrying an injury, some of them severe. All of them spoke final, absolving prayers to God every hour. Five days, then six, and finally on the seventh morning the sun rose over a plain empty of Galan except the dead.

Kisain still didn't know why the horsemen had left. Maybe their losses were too great, or maybe they just thought they'd made their point. In any event, Morind Gap wasn't the only half-built fort attacked, they all were. It was just that the Gap was the only place where soldiers survived. The forts were abandoned, of course. The whole episode had been a folly, a too-ambitious plan with no chance of working. Even if the forts had been secure, the Galan could still have butchered anyone who tried to travel to them. There was no way the plan could have worked.

Of course, the men who'd dreamed it up survived to invent new follies. It was the mercenaries who died, as usual. Of more than six thousand men, only a hundred and twenty survived, all from Morind Gap, and of those more than half were too badly maimed to ever serve as soldiers again.

It was always the same. Great men made plans, and mercenaries died for them. That was what they were for.

"This reminds me a bit of the Gap," Berain said after a moment. "Being here, I mean. We're cooped up here, and there's no way home."

So it wasn't just Kisain's mind playing tricks on him. Berain felt it too, the oppressive weight in the air that was more than an approaching rainstorm. Part of the reason for it was that Terzian was gone, leaving the soldiers without his magic to defend them. Another part was that Kai had finally struck at the Thrain, the *kamachi* they'd heard so much about, and who the Ashir seemed quite certain would leave nothing of the invaders but bones before he was done. Soldiers were a superstitious lot, and the presence of an unseen ghost ready to swoop on them was bound to put a chill in their blood at the thought of him.

And part of it was just the air, full of the weight of foreboding.

Kisain made himself smile at the archer. "I don't think it's as bad as all that, Berain."

"Not yet, it isn't," the other man agreed. His tone was grim. "Let's see what happens tomorrow."

"Nothing will happen tomorrow," Traive said with contempt. "Or afterwards, come to that. Terzian broke the Ashir the day we arrived. I doubt there's a warrior left with the guts to face us now."

Berain grinned humourlessly, showing teeth. "Terzian broke them, you say. Say you're right. What if the Ashir know that? They'll feel safe attacking now he isn't here, won't they?"

"So what? We still have our horses and steel, and one of our soldiers is a match for three warriors anyway."

"And what if the Ashir *don't* know they're broken?" Berain went on, ignoring that. "If they still have fight in them? Then we'll need to be three times better than them, and more."

"Enough," Kisain broke in. "The patrol is coming back." He couldn't see them yet, but he could hear the sound of hooves on stone. "Time you went to your horse, Traive."

"Sir." The armsman saluted before he scrambled on to the ladder. The platform trembled as he descended.

"Your friend's an idiot," Berain said when Traive was too far down to hear. The wind had risen further, making the tower creak from side to side. "Too much hot blood in him, I think."

Kisain nodded, deciding not to mention that Traive wasn't really his friend. "Let's just hope his blood *stays* in him, and in all of us."

"The Lord willing." Berain crossed himself, then gave the captain a sideways glance. "Some of the lads are talking about going home. They don't think it's going to work for them here any more."

"Because Ramian's dead?"

The archer frowned. "That's official, is it?"

38

Kisain cursed inwardly, furious that he could make such a clumsy slip. The second's delay in his reply was a second too long: Berain nodded to himself, eyes hooded in thought. Best to move on as quickly as possible. "If it was me, I wouldn't say a thing like that to Terzian when he gets back."

"Aaaah," Berain said, almost a sigh. "So it's true. Ramian's dead."

The incoming patrol began to make its way into the plaza below. There had still been no sign of a single Ashir though, not even a drunk veering across the roads on wobbly legs. That was starting to make Kisain nervous. Something in Chakanay wasn't right. He remembered what Berain had said: *We're cooped up here, and there's no way home.* It had the sound of a prophecy.

"He's dead," Kisain said at last. Berain had been at Morind Gap. He deserved the truth. "Or dying, at the least. This *kamachi* gutted him, and then cut out his eyes and tongue."

"As good as dead, then." Berain grimaced. "Not a nice way to go. Why did the *kamachi* do that to him?"

"Religious reasons." Mimiteh had explained as much, once she'd calmed down after her staring match with Terzian. The woman had more courage than a whole pride of lions, and less sense than a rock. He smiled slightly just thinking of her. "Ramian's escort was wiped out."

"Redeemer protect us," Berain said softly. "And the gold's lost, too? We'll get no reinforcements, then."

"No reinforcements." Kisain swung his feet on to the ladder. "Just us, Berain, whichever way it goes in the end. Tell your friends that. If they want to live through this, their best chance is to stick by Terzian and hope he can kill this *kamachi* before the whole country blows up in our faces."

"I'll tell them," Berain promised. "I'm not sure it'll do much good, but I'll tell them."

"It had better do some good," Kisain answered grimly. "The only way we're going to get through this mess is by staying loyal to Terzian. And it wouldn't hurt to pray, either."

He knew could trust Berain – he'd been at the Gap, after all – but those last words were spoken mainly for the benefit of the other archer in the tower, the man who'd just stood there in silence while the others talked. Some soldiers were always ready to run to the commanders with tales of disloyal words and treacherous thoughts. Traive, for example, who'd betray his own mother for a chance at promotion. He wouldn't be the only one.

Kisain went down the ladder. It wobbled under him, just a little. The tower had been a quick build, thrown together to allow sight over the gates, but it would have been stone if time allowed. Or bolted to the wall, at least. Now it looked sturdy but was fragile, just like the Thrain grip on this huge, absurd country. Or so Mimiteh would say. Kisain wasn't going to say so. In the army it was best to think before you spoke.

But nothing could stop men thinking, whatever words of loyalty were on their lips. Kisain had been doing some thinking of his own. He took his reins

39

from Traive and swung into the saddle, and his gaze went to a window on the third floor of what had once been the Qapac's residence. Mimiteh's room.

She wasn't at the window, but just as Kisain began to look away with a pang of disappointment, he caught a flicker of movement in the shadows. She *was* there, then, but preferred to watch without being seen herself. Doing some thinking as well, he thought wryly. He knew how that went. There was a good deal to think about.

The bronze doors swung back to allow the incoming patrol through. The captain raised a hand to Kisain, but didn't ride over to talk, which meant there was no trouble to warn of. Kisain lifted a hand in reply.

Mimiteh.

It had all started with her because Kisain wanted to learn about the Ashir, the strange and wonderful people Ramian was to rule over. Partly that was common sense: the first rule of soldiering was *know your enemy*, a lesson even more important than *know the terrain* or *make the enemy come to you*. The other part was simply that the country was so fascinating, so rich in many more things than gold and gems. The Ashir made lavish tapestries, created wonderful frescoes and sculptures, and told myths of bewitching originality and power. They believed such strange things, not least the story of their origins, when Viraca the Teacher God came across the sea to them on a raft made of living snakes. When he told Mimiteh how unlikely that sounded her dark eyes had flared with heat.

"It happened," she said, her voice flat. "And if you want to talk about what's unlikely, how can your one God be both light and dark? Both good and evil, purity and sin, night and day? A single god can't possibly represent both sides of one coin." She pushed on before he could speak. "How can he know the name of every one of his worshippers? A farmer doesn't name the seeds he plants. Why should a god be different?"

"It's not the same," he protested.

Mimiteh ignored the interruption. "But if you doubt the tale, Kisain, think of the *kamachi*. One boy child a generation born with a snake around his eye. Sometimes there are two at once, one old and one a child. Sometimes there are none – but another is always born. Always one child, and another, as one age becomes another, and another. For three thousand years that has been true. We have the proof of Viraca's love. Where is the proof of your god?"

Which had floored him, of course, because you couldn't prove the existence of the One God. The chaplains always said that proof denies faith, and the Lord wishes his people to show their love for him through faith alone. It was how the worshipful were sorted from those who only pretended. He tried to explain that, but Mimiteh's scorn was plain on her face.

"My fear," she said later, hesitating before she continued, "is that your One God will prove stronger than all of ours together. Sometimes I wonder why Viraca never taught us how to work iron. He showed us bronze. Why not this writing you use? Didn't he know of them? If that's true…" She tailed off, then looked him in the eye. "If that's true, then Viraca was a minor god, and yours might be stronger than he could ever be, however strange and unlikely he is. And for just thinking that, I might be cursed to eternal blindness in Supay's halls when I die." Her voice dropped to a whisper. "I don't want to be blind."

The truth was that she was terrified, as all the Ashir must be, frightened to their blood and bones that their world would fall. Or worse, that their gods had never been more than bit players, insignificant outside the borders of the Blessed Land, and broken as soon as another god turned his eyes to them. Mimiteh was trying to face that fear, but it was hard for her. It must be almost paralysing for the mass of the people.

"If Viraca *did* know these things," she'd said, another time, "then why didn't he teach them to us? Were we not worthy? We've always believed we were the god's chosen people, his favourite in all the world, but now it seems he didn't think us good enough."

That was their dilemma, then. Either Viraca had never known of the skills the Thrain knew, in which case he was a poor and feeble god, or he'd known but never thought the Ashir deserving enough, which made them poor and feeble themselves. Each possibility was a blow at the foundations of their beliefs, the things that defined them, more serious than any sword blow could ever be. They had already suffered one shock when they found there were other people in the world after all. They couldn't sustain more.

They had one hope to cling to, one rocky haven in a stormy sea: Kai. The *kamachi*. It all came down to him, all the hopes and fears of Ashir and Thrain alike. Kisain's fears, too. Because Mimiteh was right. The Ashir did have proof of the love of their gods, in the shape of the man born with a snake coiled around his eye, once in each generation. A week ago Kisain would have scoffed at the idea. Now he wasn't sure any more. That was a heresy in itself, because the Church taught there was only one God, indivisible and all-powerful, tolerating no rivals.

If Kai was the chosen of another god, and if that god proved to be the stronger, here on his home ground... then everything the Church taught was a lie. Kisain shivered at the thought. *I don't want to be blind,* Mimiteh had said, but the Ashir were not the only ones who feared their souls being damned to torment forever if their god proved false.

"Sir?" Traive reined his horse closer and lowered his voice. "Are you all right? You look like a ghost just walked over your grave."

"I'm all right," he said. The incoming patrol had cleared the doors. "Time we got moving. It seems quiet tonight, but I don't trust it. Tell everyone to keep their eyes open. I want to get back without losing a man."

Traive nodded and called the orders back along the lines, repeating them word for word. When he was done Kisain heeled his stallion forward, through the doors and into the plaza beyond. There was still no sign of any Ashir making his way home. Every window was dark. Chakanay might have been deserted.

Mimiteh. It had started with Kisain's fascination with the Ashir, but in a week it had become something more. Something he could scarcely credit, and

41

hardly knew what name to give. Or hardly dared. But she kept intruding into his thoughts, on patrol or in the mess hall, in the stables and his own room, and when she did there was a queer feeling in his stomach. Of all the things he'd thought to find in this conquest, love had not been one of them.

He felt the first fat drop of rain splat into his arm. He grimaced and crammed his helmet on his head. Apparently his entire duty was to be completed in the coming storm. Perhaps, he thought wryly, God was punishing him for allowing his faith to waver.

7

It was still raining, though not as hard as it had been two hours before, when thunder rattled windows and the mountains flashed with lightning. Spring storms were usually fierce, but they spent their anger quickly and faded into cold drizzle that could last for hours. The rain probably wouldn't stop before midmorning, perhaps not until the afternoon.

Below Mimiteh's window, in the courtyard of the Precinct, a drain had backed up, blocked by straw and fragments of broken stone. Five soldiers waded through knee-deep water as they struggled to clear it, before the flood climbed all the way into the stables. So far they hadn't succeeded. An officer watched them from the shelter of a doorway, arms folded across his chest.

Kisain was still out in the town, doubtless soaked to the bone and cursing the bad luck that had put him on patrol during the downpour. The thought made Mimiteh grin to herself. He had a wry sense of humour that came out when he felt hard done by, and his not-quite-serious grumbling always made her laugh. Not that the situation was funny, when she thought about it. She was halfway in love – more than halfway, probably – with a Thrain, one of the hated invaders, and she couldn't imagine what Suchi would say about that.

It didn't matter. Love chose its own path, sweeping men and women along with no regard for what they thought they wanted. Certainly with no regard for what made sense. Mimiteh couldn't sleep when Kisain was on patrol any more, which was why she was standing by a window and watching the rain patter down, waiting for him to come back safe.

Suchi was going to go *berserk*.

A horn blew somewhere in the town, and thoughts of Suchi blew away like seeds in the wind.

Mimiteh knew that sound. It was a warrior's horn, its harsh call like the coughing howl of a puma on the hunt. A summons to battle. She stood frozen, hardly daring to move.

"Now?" she whispered. Sala hadn't said a word to make her think his attack was imminent. "Tonight?"

Another horn sounded in reply, then a third, and suddenly the night rang with warrior calls. Mimiteh stood frozen as the howls rose through the town.

Kisain.

"I love him," she said out loud.

She whirled and went to the bed, where she'd thrown her cloak. She grabbed it and ran for the door, trying to put on the cloak and clip it as she moved. Her heart felt tight. Kisain was out there.

He might love her, and he might not. His expressions were strange, his tone of voice hard to read. That didn't matter either.

The buckle close at last and she wrapped the cloak around herself. It might keep her dry for a few moments, at least. As she burst into the courtyard and the

43

rain she cursed Salali's name for not telling her about this. She had saved his *life,* and this was her reward. Kai's friend or not, she would have his hide when this was over.

She pulled the cloak over her head and began to run.

*

"What in the name of the God was that?"

Kisain twisted around in his saddle, trying to find whoever had blown the horn. In the dark and the drizzle it was hard to see much of anything more than forty feet away, so it was wasted effort really. He wiped water from his eyes. Across the street was a *machana*, its heavy door shut tight and chairs piled neatly under an overhanging veranda. Kisain would like nothing more than to shelter there. Just long enough for his undershirt to dry.

"I don't know," he said. "Did you see anything, Traive?"

"Not in this murk," the under-officer answered. He turned his horse in the street, peering up at nearby rooftops. Several of the other riders did the same, their hands resting on sword hilts. All of them were drenched and bedraggled, but that didn't mean they had lost their wits entirely. "But it didn't sound very pleasant, that's for sure. Like an angry animal."

"That was no animal." Kisain paused, trying to decide which direction the sound had come from. "All right, we'll go down to the market square and then head west. I think that noise was –"

The howl rose again, much closer this time, and before its echoes had died another broke the night like a scream. It really did sound like an animal, a large wolf perhaps, and in pain. More answered, howl after howl climbing from roofs and windows and streets, until the steady drum of the rain was all but drowned out. It was hard to tell what was a new horn and what an echo, reverberating down the streets. Kisain licked his lips.

"This is bad," he said, and broke off. Metal rattled nearby as bolts slammed back. The door of the *machana* swung open and men began to spill out, most of them better than forty years old, paunchy and balding or grey. Aged they might be, but their hair stood up in narrow crests, and every one of them held a weapon.

Wooden clubs, or table legs. One man carried what looked like a flatiron. But there were bronze maces too, and axes, and chips of obsidian in the clubs glimmered in the rain.

"Form lines!" Kisain bellowed. Hooves clattered as his men rushed to obey, but Traive simply sat his horse and stared, white-faced. "Armsman! Stop gawking and get in line!"

More men were pouring out of the tavern. Several wore sleeveless shirts that revealed the tattoos of warrior societies, though most of the arm holes were ragged, as though sleeves had been torn from a coat to make an impromptu warrior tunic. Jewellery sparkled on wrists and fingers, and threads of red or

44

gold were woven through their hair. Warriors beyond doubt, then, and inside Chakanay, where warriors weren't supposed to be. Kisain didn't think they'd slipped past the patrols. These were former fighting men who'd been working as traders or builders, any of the ordinary occupations which made a town run from day to day. They might not have fought for twenty years, but they had seen blood before, and they knew the appalling damage even a wooden club could cause. Kisain did too, and he swallowed.

He heard a rush of feet and wheeled around to see another knot of men hurrying out of an alley behind him. They carried the same motley of weapons, axes kept as mementoes of fighting days, or else clubs and kitchen knives. A few carried spears, not quite straight and tipped with wooden points or flakes of obsidian. Not an army, but there were a lot of them, and more every second. Men kept emerging from houses or out of the sheeting rain, one here and two there, gathering into a mob.

"This was planned," someone said. Another voice, further along the line, called out, "God protect us!"

Kisain snorted. God was all very well, but only steel and courage would protect them now. He wished like *hell* that Terzian hadn't gone away. "Stand as you are! Be ready!"

"Stand as we are?" Traive repeated incredulously. "But we – sir, we have to break them! One charge and –"

"Shut up," Kisain said savagely, "or I'll strip that braid from your shoulder and kick you into the gutter."

Traive shut up. He didn't understand. The street was already packed with Ashir, and the mob was still gathering. But it was a hard thing, to take that final step and rush into combat. The throng might scream and hurl stones, and yet not quite dare to come close. Best to play for time.

"Stand firm," he called again.

Still Ashir came out of the dark, weapons in their hands and bucklers on their arms. Most didn't have the crested hair of a warrior, but many did. Too many for comfort. The voice in the ranks was right, this was not an isolated ambush. This was a full-scale uprising.

As though to prove that, shouts erupted from somewhere across the houses, coupled with the rattle of charging hooves, and almost immediately men began screaming. There went playing for time.

A lot of his men would die if it came to fighting. He might still be able to avoid it, if he was brave enough, and lucky. Or if the Redeemer really did smile on him. Kisain let his stallion edge forward.

"Go back to your homes!" he shouted. He had to yell, over the rain and the din of battle from a few streets away. A few feet ahead of his men he felt horribly exposed. "If you fight here tonight many of you will die, and for what? Go back to your homes."

The crowd muttered, but nobody moved. And then one man did, stepping out from the mob with complete calm, as though he was walking through a meadow

45

in the summer sun. His hair was crested, and he carried a mace with long ridges of bronze running along its length. The handle of another weapon stuck out of his belt, but in the rain Kisain couldn't see what it was. He could see cuts on the sides of the man's head though, where his hair had been cut into a crest. He looked again, and his breath caught.

"Salali," he said.

The *kamachi's* ally had crested his hair like a warrior. Kisain knew then that it was Sala who had orchestrated this revolt. Maybe Kai had even sent him here with that in mind. He seemed to have been a step ahead of the Thrain from the start.

And Terzian was not in Chakanay. Kisain cursed and put a hand on the hilt of his sword.

Salali didn't react to his name. He lifted his mace and pointed straight at Kisain, and he began to smile.

"Tonight you go to Supay's halls," he said. His voice was soft, barely audible over the rain, but then he raised it to a shout. "Kill them!"

He flung the mace without warning. It whipped end over end through the air and struck an Armsman full in the face, smashing his nose and cheekbones and pitching him off the back of his saddle with a shriek. The crowd roared and surged forward, coming from all sides. Kisain drew his sword and dug his heels into his stallion's flanks. "Squad, charge!"

There wasn't enough room to get up to full speed, but a warhorse was still formidable even at a canter. Kisain spurred forward. His horse crashed into the onrushing throng with a shock that sent two men flying backwards, one of them with the vivid red mark of a hoof arching across a shattered jaw. An instant later the rest of the patrol hammered into the Ashir, flinging more men away like broken toys. Steel swords began to fall. Kisain blocked a blow from an axe and slashed at an angle, opening a deep gash across his assailant's chest.

"Push forward!" he bellowed. There had to be five hundred Ashir in the street, far too many for a single patrol to overwhelm or disperse. "We have to break through them! Push forward!"

Break through this mob? Not likely. But then, the odds against them had been huge at Morind Gap as well. You did what you could and you prayed. Sometimes it was enough.

Beside him Traive felled another axeman and drove his horse into the gap, screaming wordlessly in the rain. Kisain let him go, taking the chance to look right and left along the line of riders. One was down already. A second toppled from his horse as Kisain watched. The mob closed on where he had fallen, there was a flurry of movement, and then the Ashir moved away. But the cavalry were pressing deep into the Ashir now, forcing them back by sheer weight all along the line. They were going to break through. An Ashir screamed and fell almost under the hooves of Kisain's mount, blood gushing from his shoulder.

A roar whipped Kisain's head around. He was just in time to see Salali in the midst of a knot of townsfolk, crashing into the right flank of the Thrain from

46

near the door of the *machana*. Two riders went down at once, one of them lifted clean out of his saddle on the point of a long spear that had slipped through his armour under the armpit. His thrashing legs caught a third soldier and knocked him sideways; his sword waved wildly, and an Ashir darted forward to smash a hammer into the side of his horse's head. The animal screamed, a horrible sound that ripped at bones, and fell to its knees. One breath, and the crowd swarmed over it, dragging the rider down and breaking through the line.

It had happened too fast to stop. Battles swung in moments, as brief as the time between life and the killing blow. Kisain wheeled his horse and spurred towards the breach, yelling a warning to Traive.

There was just time as he turned to see more Ashir behind his patrol, a tide of them pouring up the street. Every one of them wore crested hair and tattoos, and they chanted a deep rolling chorus that rolled ahead of them as they came. Warriors then, men in the prime of life and pride. Kisain had only a second to wonder where they had come from before an arrow struck him just above the elbow and he cried out in pain.

Then the warriors struck like a storm. They crashed into him and the whole of his line, and then Kisain was slashing desperately and just trying to stay alive a little longer.

"We have to get out!" someone yelled beside him. There was no time to glance across to see who it was. Kisain took a heavy blow on his shield and wheeled his horse with his knees, so the stallion could bring his hooves to bear. The warrior dodged back, but still absorbed a massive blow that splintered his wooden buckler and left him staggering in shock. "Sir, we have to get out!"

"I know!" he shouted. He wished he could see a way to do it. Ashir filled the road, well over a thousand of them now, and there was no time to form lines or even gather men together. He changed a downward cut into a thrust straight ahead and took a warrior through the throat. "Get to the side of the road! We need our backs against something. Hurry!"

To one side Traive was fighting alone, surrounded by swarming Ashir. His sword flashed rapidly as he cut left and right, but even as Kisain looked, a warrior hefted his mace and threw it from behind the under-officer. It struck Traive in the back of the head. He lurched forward, the sword dropping from loose fingers as blood began to run out from under his helmet. Somehow he stayed upright, and even grappled at his belt for a knife, but there was no time. An axe bit into his leg, another into his stomach, and he toppled into the throng.

No time for regrets, and it was always a regret when a soldier died. Even if he was a fool. But wise men died as easily as idiots, and Kisain didn't want to die here, not today. Not without seeing Mimiteh again.

A big warrior ducked under Kisain's sweep, going to one knee in the road. Half out of the saddle, unbalanced, Kisain grunted as his horse began to turn, pulled sideways by his frantic attack. The Ashir waited, looking up in perfect calm, and when the stallion was side-on to him he spun the axe in his hand and drove it into the animal's front leg just where it joined the chest.

The stallion shrieked, stumbled forward, and then went down with his teeth bared and his good foreleg pawing at the air. Kisain didn't fall with it. The moment he saw the blow land he kicked his feet out of the stirrups and pushed himself backwards, something he had practised many times in training. His life depended on getting it right this time. He landed on both feet and his boots slid in rainwater and blood. He put out an instinctive hand to steady himself.

His sword hand. The Ashir who'd killed his horse was rising in front of him, axe raised for the killing blow.

The axeman screamed and stumbled as the stallion's flailing leg caught him in the back of the knee. Even so he managed to bring the axe down, in a wild sideways attack that was hardly a proper blow at all. It came underneath Kisain's arm and struck him on the hip, below his breastplate where only a thin coat of mail protected him. He felt bone crack and bit down on a scream. Stumbling, with agony a white sheet in his hip and leg, Kisain launched a scything riposte that opened the man's throat and almost took his head off his shoulders. He collapsed in a spray of blood.

A rider shoved between Kisain and the Ashir. A moment later another unhorsed soldier caught his arm to steady him. "Sir, it's hopeless! We can't get out!"

"The buildings," Kisain managed. The arrow in his arm hurt badly enough, but his hip grated like broken glass whenever he moved the leg. Putting weight on it would be torment. He looked at the distance to the door and flung a prayer at the sky. "Get into the buildings. Forget about me!" he snapped when the soldier began to help him along. "You can't afford to slow down!"

"Sorry, sir." The man stopped, deflected a mace with his shield, and then half-turning he thrust his sword quickly into the Ashir's belly. Two more men joined them, their blades red with blood. "Didn't quite hear that in all this noise. Tell me again when we're inside."

Kisain ground his teeth. The soldier on the horse gave a yell and his animal went down, scattering Ashir and pitching the man forward on to the paving stones. He slid into the throng and axes flashed as they fell. Glancing around, Kisain could see pockets of fighting along the street, but no riders still in the saddle. None. His patrol was gone. He swallowed hard.

"Here," the soldier supporting him said. He pushed a door open with his foot and helped Kisain through it, into a small room packed tight with tables. The smell of maize beer hung in the air. Kisain pushed away from the soldier and sat down with a groan, then immediately tried to stand again as his hip screamed in protest at the weight. He managed to half-stand in the end, clutching the table for support. Pain made a haze behind his eyes as he looked around.

"We need to get upstairs," he said. "There are too many ways into this room." He could count four, a pair of windows and two doors. Four entrances, and five soldiers, at least one of them badly hurt. There weren't even bolts on the door, though it wouldn't have helped much if there were. Upstairs they would be rats in a trap, but Kisain didn't see any choice. "Quickly. Help me."

One of the other men slung Kisain's arm around his shoulders and hauled him upright. Blood from a deep gash in his cheek dripped on to Kisain's shoulder. The stairway was barely wide enough for them to climb side by side, and it was agony even with help, so by the time Kisain reached the landing he was shaking with effort. Glass tinkled downstairs.

"They've broken the window," one of the men said unnecessarily. He helped his captain into a room and set him down on the edge of a bed, with surprising gentleness. Kisain struggled to remember his name through the waves of pain, but then it came to him; Naraid. It was only two years since he joined, and he'd never seen a major battle. He seemed to be coping with disaster as well as anyone, though. "Do you want me to pull that arrow, sir?"

Grimacing, Kisain reached up and snapped the shaft. "Leave it. I'll only bleed worse, and I don't think there's any point."

Naraid looked at him and nodded. There wasn't much more to say.

8

"Talk to me," Sala said.

Dyani rubbed his chin. "There are eight or ten of them, I think. Some wounded, some not. I saw at least one archer."

"We can root them out," Tumay put in. The stout man was breathing hard, and kept rubbing the bulge of his belly as though he could wish it away. "No doubt about that. But we'll lose men doing it."

"A lot of men," Dyani agreed. "And we might need an hour to do it."

Sala grimaced. "I don't have an hour."

"Then it will cost even more lives."

"Never mind what we lose," Ilari snapped. Darkness and rain made his hollow face look like a parched skull, with blackness inside. "As long as we kill them, we win."

"But at what cost?" Dyani asked.

"Never mind the cost, either."

Ilari was bent on obliterating the Thrain, no matter how many Ashir died in the process. The loss of his family had blinded him to everything but that. Do it his way, though, and the stairs up to where the Thrain had taken refuge would be choked with bodies. Sala was no warrior, but he knew how hard it was to take a defended position.

The trouble was that Ilari was right. It didn't matter how many died here. The Ashir could lose a hundred men for each Thrain they killed, two hundred, and still win the war. But that would take time, and Sala didn't have it. He needed to be at the Precinct soon, now in fact, to lead the assault there. Take the old temple and Chakanay was won. After that perhaps no one else would have to die, and warriors old and new could go home to their families and tell tales of this night and their glory.

Kai would not send men to useless deaths. Not for any reason. And there were only eight Thrain here, too few to be much of a threat. Sala wiped rain out of his eyes and looked at the warriors crowded around him.

"Who's wounded?" he asked. A dozen hands were raised and he sighed. "Blood and bones, don't waste my time. I've got a lot to do tonight and a lot of ground to cover. Anyone who can't keep up is useless to me. Now, who's wounded?"

Twenty hands went up, and then slowly another ten. Sala could see blood on the clothes of men who'd kept their hands down, and some of those men limped or winced when they moved. But he'd take what he could, and say nothing about the rest. There wasn't time.

"Better, he said. "You men stay here. Ilari, you're in command. I want those men up there dead, but you're not to waste lives doing it. Take time. Burn the building if you must, but don't make any stupid attacks up the stairs, understand? I'm trusting you here."

"I'm going to the Precinct."

"I need you here."

Ilari shrugged. "I'm going."

Kai never had this problem. One word and people fell over their own feet as they hurried to obey. "Have it your way. Tumay?"

"I'll do it," the stout man said. "But I'll do it fast, Salali. We'll bar the doors and throw brands through the windows. Burn them like rats in a prairie fire. The flames won't spread in this rain."

"I can't let you do that," someone said.

Sala had become aware of the crowd opening a moment before, and he was already turning. He knew the voice too. But he still stopped and stared in disbelief at the slight figure who stood in front of the warriors, her hair plastered to her head and water pouring down her blue robe.

Mimiteh.

*

"What?" Dyani said.

"You destroyed their patrol. Go on to the next one."

"Some are still alive," Ilari grated.

"But they can't hurt you anymore," Mimiteh said. "Go on, now. There's still a war to win."

"They deserve to die."

"No one deserves to die," the priestess said. She stood there in her drenched robe, facing five hundred warriors with her head high. "Sometimes warriors have to kill, but we should always mourn the need."

"Mourn? For them?"

"They're men just like us, Ilari. They have families, and dreams, and fears that keep them awake at night."

"They're monsters! They are *ichiri,* the destroyer that comes in the dark to maim and kill. They must die!"

"Not monsters. Just men."

"Priestess," Tumay said. "Forgive me. But these men murdered a whole village at Ayllu."

"And burned the people!" someone shouted. "Burned them alive!"

The crowd rumbled. Sala shook his head so that water sprayed, trying to make his brain start working.

Mimiteh waited until the growls faded, and then asked, "Should we be murderers too, then?"

"It isn't murder!" Dyani cried. "They came here to kill and conquer us. We have the right to defend ourselves."

"Yes," Mimiteh said. "We do. But slaughtering a handful of men hiding in a room isn't defending ourselves. They are weak, and wounded. We're not Thrain. Spare them."

51

"They're animals!" Ilari shouted. "We must kill them all!"

Mimiteh didn't reply to that, and Ilari's words seemed to hang in the silence. *Animals. Kill them all.* That might have been what the Thrain said, when they crossed the border of the Blessed Land, or when they rounded up women and children at Ayllu. *These Ashir are animals. They do not even know the word of God, or the grace of the Redeemer. Killing them will leave no stain upon your soul.*

Killing always left a stain on the soul.

There was something else though, something Sala knew but couldn't quite place. He was too intent on the battle for Chakanay, too wrapped in his plans and fears. He made himself pause, breathing deep of the night air, and it slid into place in his mind.

"You don't want to save them," he said. "You want to save one of them. Just one. Don't you?"

Mimiteh hesitated.

"Kai always says love is rogue," Sala said. "It comes when it will, and not even gods can control it. I expect he heard it in the Retreat. Kai wouldn't know love if it bopped him on the nose."

"Love?" Dyani repeated softly. The crowd was quiet. Shouts still came from across the town, and the crash of metal, but the street was silent except for the drumming of rain.

"Yes," Mimiteh said. Her chin had come up again and she faced them squarely. "The captain. Kisain."

"You love one of... them?"

"Yes."

Sala gestured at the bodies littering the street. "He's most likely dead. If this was his patrol anyway."

"It was his. That man," she pointed, "was called Traive. A thug and a brute. I won't mourn him."

"And your captain?"

"I don't see him. I think he's upstairs."

"Kill him," Ilari said again.

Mimiteh moved to stand across the doorway. "It would be murder, and I won't let it happen."

"Killing armed men isn't murder," Sala said. He was fighting the urge to laugh. The situation was ridiculous though, an army of warriors held still by a single priestess in love with one of the enemy. He didn't have time for this, but she held him too.

"Then give them a chance to lay down their arms," Mimiteh said. When he hesitated she took a step forward. "I smuggled you out of the precinct, Salali. I saved your life. You owe me."

He did laugh at that, the sheer audacity of the woman. "Yes, that's true. I owe you. Are you calling in the debt?"

"I am. Spare them."

52

Sala was still laughing. "Kai taught me to understand, and you're teaching me to have a conscience. Who'd have thought that?"

"You'll agree, then?"

"Yes, I'll agree. We'll spare them – if they lay down their arms."

"What!" Ilari almost screamed. "They are *Thrain!* We need to wipe them from the land!"

"No, we don't. I'll tell you one thing, Ilari; Kai is certainly trying to bring some Thrain over to our side. He'll be trying to learn from them. We might as well do the same."

"Learn from them!"

"If they betray us we'll come back and kill them later," Sala said. "But for now Mimiteh is right, and besides, there's no time to linger anymore. Leave it now, Ilari. Mimiteh and I are going up to talk with these men."

Ilari scowled and stalked away. He didn't go far, just pushed into the crowd and waited with his arms folded. Sala doubted he'd go far. There were still Thrain to kill.

Thinking of which… "Tumay, if I don't come back down, do what you planned and burn them out. Even if Mimiteh and I are still inside."

The stout man went grey. "I can't do that. You'll have no body in the next world."

"You'll do what you need to," Sala said. He went to the door where Mimiteh stood and pushed it open, being careful to stay out of sight. No arrow flew though, no sword whistled past where his head might have been. He peeked quickly round and saw an empty room.

"Come on," he said to Mimiteh. She followed him into the building. Both of them turned towards the stairs at once, making sure they didn't offer a target to an archer crouched at the top. Once they were by the wall at the bottom step Sala paused.

"It's up to you now," he said.

Mimiteh nodded. She eased past him, so she was right at the corner of the wall, and called, "Kisain?"

There was a silence, and then an accented voice said "Mimiteh?" in a tone of utter disbelief.

"We're coming up," she said. "Tell your men not to shoot."

"What? Who's *we?*"

"Just don't shoot," she said, and began to climb. Sala thought about praying, decided he'd done all right so far without any gods to help him, and went up behind her.

*

The Thrain were waiting in the largest upstairs room, where parents might sleep in normal times. There were only five of them, not the ten Dyani had predicted. Two were badly hurt, one seated and leaning over to the side

53

to keep weight off a hip, the other slashed across the face. He'd pressed a folded piece of bedsheet over the wound and tied it tight, but it was already soaked with blood.

Mimiteh turned towards the seated man as soon as she was through the door. The smile which lit her face was clear even to Sala, who was half behind her and not really watching anyway. His attention was beyond her, to where an invader stood with his bow half drawn and an arrow on the string.

"Going to shoot us?" Sala asked.

The man with the wounded hip said something, then turned to Sala. "He won't shoot. Don't be concerned."

"I'm not."

"I am," Mimiteh said. She put her hands on her hips. "Look at you. I thought you could take care of yourself."

He smiled, though exhaustion never left his face and his eyes were dark with horror. He wore the shoulder badges that showed rank among the Thrain. That made him Mimiteh's captain, and the leader of the patrol. ""So did I. It makes us both fools."

Her turn to smile. "We've got a much better reason to call ourselves that."

"I suppose we have," Kisain said. He looked at Sala. "We should have killed you in the Precinct."

"It wouldn't have mattered. There are other men who would have led an uprising without me."

"Not other men who know the *kamachi,* I think. That's what allowed you to do this so quickly, isn't it?"

"Great," Sala said. "I finally do something worthwhile and Kai still gets the credit for it. But I don't have time to talk. You're alive because Mimiteh asked me to spare you. I'm going to leave some of my men around this building. If any one of you puts a foot outside before dawn, you all die. Is that clear?"

""Yes," Kisain said. "Thank you."

"Thank her," Sala said. He could see Mimiteh's heart in her eyes when she looked at Kisain, and it made him want to laugh and weep at the same time. Laugh, because love was just so ridiculous; and weep because they were on opposite sides in a war, and grief lay ahead of them whatever they did.

Well, they were both adults, and it wasn't his problem. He had Thrain to deal with. Sala went back down the stairs.

Rain was fading to drizzle as the storm passed. The motley band of townsfolk stood in doorways and under the *machana's* veranda, watching the rain fall into the eyes of the dead. A few warriors from Chimalli's newly-arrived band were scattered among them. Two men picked their way through the bodies to meet Sala as he stepped through the door.

"You're going to let her do it." Ilari's voice was thick with anger. "You're going to let them live."

"Yes," Sala said. Tumay pursed his lips.

"I don't understand. You brought us to this fight, Salali, and now you turn away from it? You know what those men did at Ayllu. You know what they did to my daughter." His mouth twisted. "Why, man? Why do this?"

"Because there are more important battles tonight," he said. He wasn't really sure of the answer himself, but as he spoke, he realised these *were* his reasons. Somewhere on the far side of town shouts erupted, faint in the hissing rain, and then the clash of metal. Several of the men turned to look, as though they could see through houses. "Because it would be murder, and Mimiteh was right. We're better than that. And because she loves him."

"He's a killer. A murderer!"

"But we are not," Sala reminded him gently. "We're not, Ilari. And there's a need for love, on a night like this."

Ilari didn't reply. Beside him Tumay looked up, surprise etched on his face before he gave a slight smile. He understood, at least. Ilari was too blinded with hate to do so, at least for now, though he might realise it in the morning. If he lived to see the morning. There was a good deal more fighting to be done yet. As for Sala, he thought Kai might be proud of him.

"The plan's the same," he said, more loudly now. "Those of you who were staying to assault the house can now stay to guard it. Nobody comes out, nobody goes in. Understood?"

"Can't we come with –"

"No, you can't. I explained this. We'll need to move fast, and the Flayed God alone knows what we'll find when we start. I can't afford to dawdle because hurt men can't keep up."

The man grimaced, then nodded reluctantly. He had a long gash down his left leg, the kind of wound a boar might make if it didn't quite manage a direct hit. He limped as he moved towards the *machana*. A score of others followed him, most of them hobbling too. Sala hid a smile. He'd ordered twenty, but twelve would be enough, and he thought they'd obey his orders and leave the Thrain upstairs alone. There was no time to argue in any case.

"If all they'll do is guard, then I'm coming with you," Tumay said.

Sala nodded. "Fine."

"You remind me of my cousin, you know."

"How do you mean?"

"Huem was always dancing with the girls with a cup of beer in his fist. He knew how to charm, did my cousin."

"Sounds like a man I could like," Sala said.

Tumay shook his head. "Not any more. He died pulling villagers from a burning barn. He wouldn't stop going back to find more survivors."

Sala's smile faded. There was enough death around tonight without the stout innkeep invoking more. "Come on. I want to find Chimalli."

"He went to the Precinct." It was one of the warriors, a very tall man whose face seemed to be mostly scars. "Our best chance is to pen the Thrain inside, he says, and then burn it down around them."

"Then it looks as though we'll see fire tonight after all," Sala said.

"The fire began when the Thrain crossed the border," Ilari answered.

"It probably did," Tumay agreed. He kept hefting his mace, as though to reassure himself of its weight in his hand. Rain had washed the ridged bronze clean, but blood still clotted under his fingernails and in the creases of his knuckles. "Tonight might be when the burning ends."

Ilari's teeth flashed again.

Thunder boomed to the north, over the Uma Mountains, as they set off. The drizzle thickened to proper rain again as though in answer. Dawn was less than an hour away, but in the murk under lowering clouds there was no sign of it. Sala could see the buildings to either side, and the road for thirty yards ahead, but nothing more than that. The Blind God himself could be stalking the streets, vultures flapping through the night behind him, with no one any the wiser.

Water splashed under the band's feet. There were still ninety men around Sala. The rest had plunged off to find another fight while he spoke with Kisain. Maybe they'd decided not to trust Sala anymore. At any rate, a quarter of those who'd stayed were warriors and the rest townsfolk carrying whatever weapon they could find. Some, like Tumay and Ilari, had been warriors in their youths, and held old maces or axes kept as souvenirs from their youth in the societies. Others, never fighting men, clutched cleavers or meat hooks, sickles or long knives. Several held thick staves in their left hands, to use as makeshift shields when fighting came. A motley band indeed, but they had seen off a full Thrain patrol, sixty big men on horses in full armour. They moved confidently now, searching for another target to pull down.

Turning right along a narrow, twisting alleyway, they had to clamber over a pile of household furniture, tables and chairs packed together in a rough barricade. Beyond it bodies were strewn in heaps, many of them Thrain. One rider with protruding eyes lay with his feet still in the stirrups, though his horse had no head. The soldier himself seemed unmarked until you looked at him from behind; then Sala saw his skull had been smashed in. That explained the bulging eyes.

There were dead Ashir too. Men with missing hands and great cuts across their faces, like the claw marks of the god of eagles. Fathers with spear shafts sticking out of their chests, sons and brothers with hoof prints on caved-in

56

foreheads. Sala's heart cried out. The fight had been savage, but he supposed that was inevitable. Both sides were fighting for survival now.

"Clever," Tumay said.

Sala frowned. "What is?"

"The ambush. Oh, of course. You weren't a warrior." The tavern keeper brushed water from his forehead. "Someone built this barrier, and then drove the Thrain to it. When they couldn't get through the alley they had to turn and fight, but in this tight space their horses wouldn't be much use. The rooftops are low on both sides. Men could lean down from them and crush heads."

"Looks like they did," Sala muttered. Tumay had deduced all that from the tight packing of bodies, had he? Sala hadn't thought of the stout man as especially bright, but maybe he should have done. Men had many layers, most of them hidden deep, out of view. Kai would have known within moments of meeting the man, of course. Five words, and Kai would have understood Tumay's greatest fears and highest hopes, all without even trying.

Beyond the alley was a wider street, running east-west across Chakanay. To Sala's right the sky was a fraction paler, away in the distance where the heavy cloud cover broke up. The storm would clear soon, then. Turning left, he led the band deeper into the town. Another few minutes would bring them to the Precinct, where Chimalli would be leading the assault.

Sala didn't want to be part of it.

He'd orchestrated this, planned the Rising as best he could, though a lot had to be left to chance and the gods. Probably that was always the case. Back then he'd meant to be there at the finish, close enough to see the last Thrain's eyes roll up as he died. But he'd seen battle now. Things had changed.

War had a *smell*, something made of blood and fear and stale sweat. He hadn't really understood that until tonight. He wondered how Kai and Matlal had coped, after their ambush in the mountains. Neither of them was a warrior either, and they'd have had no more idea what it felt like to fight than Sala had done. Though now he thought about it, Kai wasn't likely to have fought. The others wouldn't let the *kamachi* risk himself in –

"Listen!" Ilari threw up a hand for quiet. "That drumming noise…" He hesitated. "Is that thunder?"

"That's horses," Tumay said after a moment. The paving under Sala's feet had begun to tremble. "Horses!"

"Spread out!" Sala shouted over the drumming rain. "Get up against the buildings and stay –"

With that the riders came, a long line of them stretching right across the street. The red of their shields was oddly bright in the darkness. Sala saw it like a splash of blood, saw spears coming down as the Thrain spotted men ahead of them. Someone shouted an order in the alien, guttural speech of the invaders. Ashir scattered towards the sides of the street, but Sala's feet seemed locked in place. His eyes searched the Thrain line, found a man with gold badges on his shoulders.

"Salali!" Tumay bellowed.

It was too late to run. Sala threw his axe.

He missed completely, of course, but the flying haft struck the man next to the captain on his chin, and he jerked backwards so hard that his horse half-reared and pulled left. Sala saw blood flower under the cheek guards of the man's helmet, fifteen yards away. He laughed.

Something moved near the paved stones, something long and narrow, and hard to see in the gloom.

And the horses went down as though cut off at the knees, one moment a line of charging riders, the next a mass of fallen men and screaming horses. Sala sprang backwards as a soldier was flung ten feet into the air and twenty forward, crashing down on the street right where Sala had been standing. His head twisted half over his shoulder with a wet crunch. A second rank of cavalry tried to pull up, to avoid the thrashing carnage of their comrades. Some even made it. Most went down in the ruin of the squad, kicking free of stirrups, tucking in their shoulders to roll as they landed. Some managed that, too. Behind them there was chaos as the horses which had stopped were crashed into from behind by their comrades, creating a tangled, kicking mass as riders struggled to break free.

Sala grabbed for the knife in his boot. Several of the Thrain were climbing to their feet. One was halfway up when a screaming horse kicked him in the temple with its one unbroken leg; he went down bonelessly, without a sound. Others drew their swords. Even stunned they began to group together at once, looking quickly around to find the new threat. Half a dozen of them turned straight to Sala, standing alone in the middle of the street. He grinned at them, not knowing why.

"Come on then," he chuckled. He felt dizzy, exhilarated. "Are you afraid?" He spread his arms out to either side and laughed in the darkness. "This is my country, so if you want to take it *come to me!*"

"Kill them!" Ilari bellowed, somewhere in the night.

Ashir swarmed out of the darkness, two hundred of them, coming at the Thrain from all sides with spears jabbing and axes slashing down. The invaders might have steel swords and gleaming armour, but they were dazed, and some looked to have broken arms and ribs in their fall. Ilari was among the first to rush past Sala with his face twisted into something grotesque, hardly recognisable any longer. He reached a Thrain struggling to stand and kicked him in the head, knocking him to his back on the stone. Then, lunging forward, Ilari smashed the axe straight into the soldier's face. Teeth and bone flew in a wild fountain of blood. Ilari laughed shrilly, hauling the weapon free.

"Mother save us," Sala murmured. He no longer felt dizzy. Every muscle in him seemed to be trembling.

"What did you think you were doing?" Tumay seized his arm and pulled him around until his nose was in Sala's face. Someone behind him shrieked, as high and clear as a girl. "You just stood there like a fool. You could have been killed!"

He didn't have a good answer, so he did what he always did, and grinned. "I just laughed in the Blind God's face, my friend. Weren't you watching?"

Tumay's hand sprang off Sala's arm and the tavern keeper stepped back, his face suddenly white. Sala blinked in surprise.

"You're insane," Tumay said quietly after a moment. "I've seen battle fever, but this… you're asking for death. Welcoming it."

"I'll die when Supay is ready for me," he answered. It was no answer at all, really, but it would have to do. Whatever strange mood had seized him was gone now. When he thought of himself standing in the street, taunting the soldiers scant yards away, his legs turned to water and his insides felt loose. "And if you want to see battle fever, look at Ilari."

Tumay glanced over at the artisan, but the fighting was already over. Ashir moved among the dying, spears and axes ready. A Thrain voice rose in what sounded like a plea for mercy, but only for as long as it took an axe to fall.

"What happened?" Sala asked. "We had ninety men. Where did these other warriors come from?"

"We were already here," a new voice said. Sala turned to find himself facing a warrior with the tattoos of the Snake society down his forearms, under spatters of blood. "My name's Aranka. It's good to meet you, Salali."

"And you," he said politely. Good manners seemed almost surreal here. "What did you do?"

"This is the quickest road out of town to the west," Aranka said. "It seemed likely the Thrain would try to move along it at some point. So we ran a hemp rope across the road, in one of the water channels so they wouldn't be able to see it. When they reached it we pulled it tight." He broke into a grin. "You appeared just in time to draw them into a charge. Made the plan even better."

Sala gazed across the street. All the Thrain were down, sixty more of them sprawled in puddles of rainwater and their own blood. He could only see three Ashir among them. Tumay was still watching him with cautious eyes, probably in case Sala went crazy again and began to gibber. "Do you know what's happening? Or where Chimalli is?"

"Last I knew, six patrols had been destroyed," Aranka answered. "It might be more. It's hard to be sure in this storm. But Chimalli is waiting for you at the Precinct. He wants you to be there for the assault."

"That's very kind of him," Sala said, "since he knows I planned it that way from the start."

Aranka shrugged, and water danced on his shoulders. "He's a chief of the societies and you're not, Salali. He'd have been well within his rights to take command of this rebellion the moment he arrived. Making allowance for you *is* kind."

"Maybe," he muttered.

"Anyway, the old Auk spoke admiringly of you. You were with him at the start, I've been told. When the Thrain first came to Chakanay."

"I was there," Sala admitted. The Auk had *admired* him? Was this how stories began, then? Sharing a jest with poor Pusaq on the way to the Thrain camp became something more significant, as days went by with disaster built upon disaster, and tales went whispering from mouth to mouth. Sala snorted to himself. All he'd done was be where he was needed, and even that had made him so scared that he traded jokes with Pusaq simply to keep from thinking about it. Most of the time he'd felt like a leaf in a river, caught helplessly in the middle of something he couldn't control. And some hero he made, sick with the red plague, smuggled out of the Precinct in a cart of dirty laundry, and finally hiding in the back rooms of an artisan's house to avoid capture. It was hardly the stuff of legends. Mind you, he might enjoy being a hero. Heroes were given all sorts of things.

"Then we'll go to the Precinct," he said. They'd been heading there anyway, but it was good to know Chimalli was waiting. "Are you staying here, Aranka? I don't think the plan will work twice, with dead horses and soldiers all over the road. You and your men can join the assault, if you like."

Aranka grinned. "I wouldn't miss it."

Away to the west, the sky was definitely clearer. It wasn't the light of dawn, not yet, but stars glimmered through breaks in the cloud, promising an end to rain. Sala should have been glad of that, but he just felt tired. Maybe he was ill. He wasn't light-headed any more, and his muscles no longer quivered like a girl on her wedding night, but he was... drained. As though all his blood had leaked out of him, through cuts he didn't know he had.

He might suffer those cuts for real before the sun came up. For some reason the thought made him feel better.

"Then let's go," he said.

*

Chimalli had made his base in a whorehouse. Sala was bowed through the door by a raven-haired woman wearing a few straps and a pleated skirt. "Salali. I'm pleased to meet you."

"I'm *extremely* pleased to meet you," he said, pausing. She looked to be nineteen, at most. "What should I call you?"

She was all smooth curves, even in the gloom of the night. "I'm Cuxi."

"Cuxi," he smiled. "Would you like to go dancing with me when this is over, Cuxi?"

"We are here," Aranka said gravely, "to meet Chimalli. Not to flirt in doorways while the rain splashes in."

That was true, unfortunately. Cuxi had the mischievous look of a woman Sala would like to know better. Intimately, you might say. But that would have to wait. Still, she put a hand on his wrist as he turned away, just for a moment, and he grinned to himself.

Everyone in Chakanay was in this fight, it seemed, no matter what they did in their daily lives. Or nightly ones. But the whorehouse was a good choice of base. The yellow-striped windows faced across the plaza to the bronze doors of the Precinct, shut and barred now of course, with the Thrain inside.

It was ironic that the end should come like this, with the Ashir besieging their own sacred compound. No doubt the *kura* would make something of it, at any rate. Well, Sala didn't much mind, as long as the tale finished with the last Thrain dying in his own blood.

His lips quirked. Who would have thought there was such bloodthirstiness in him? But then, he'd never expected to have to find out, even when the first uncertain rumours came south of strangers in the Blessed Land. Matlal had come to roust him out of a *machana* in Hatun, so they could go and roust Kai out in turn from his sanctuary in the mountains. How Matlal had known where to go, Sala didn't know. But the big man was like that. What Kai knew from instinct, or the god's strange gift, Matlal learned from watching and working. He never seemed to rest.

That had always annoyed Sala.

He couldn't really remember why, now. It would even be good to see Matlal again, when this was over. But back then the appearance of strangers had been shocking but not alarming, except in a spiritual sense, and Sala had never wasted much time worrying about the gods.

Every man and woman in Apusuyu walked a different road now, whether they'd laid eyes on the Thrain or not. Their world had changed, and there was no way to put it back as it had been. Innocence once lost is lost forever. Strange roads indeed, and no way to tell where they led.

"You think a lot," Aranka said. "You're a deep man, it seems."

That made him laugh. "I know some people who would disagree. Including me. I'm a shallow man in deep water, that's all."

"Perhaps," Aranka said after a moment.

The main downstairs room of the whorehouse was where the women showed themselves to customers, displaying just enough bare flesh to tease and never enough to satisfy. It was very large, taking up most of the ground floor, and it was filled with wounded men. They lay along the walls and in rows down the middle of the room, tended by women more practised at ministering to different needs of the flesh. They worked efficiently though, sewing wounds with quick if ugly strokes; Sala saw a gash down one man's thigh that was barely held closed, and would leave a horrible wide scar. Still, it would heal, which was what mattered. Quick and ugly was good enough sometimes.

He barked a laugh before he could stop himself. In a whorehouse, quick and ugly still cost you a penny.

"Sala?" One of the wounded men raised himself on his elbows, shooing away a woman's attempts to stitch him. A savage cut ran from hairline to chin, barely missing one eye, and hitched the side of his face up to leave him with an odd lopsided look. "I thought that was you. Glad to see you made it."

61

"I nearly didn't," he answered. Tumay grunted under his breath as he followed Sala in, with Ilari and Aranka bringing up the rear. Sala had to study the man for a moment before he realised who it was. "You'd better let her see to that, Dyani. She seems quite upset."

The woman glared at him, but Dyani only chuckled. "Nothing she can do to make me handsome again, is there? And I'm not the only one hurt. Jarawi took a sword point in his shoulder, though he insists he's fit enough to fight. Oh, by the way, Chimalli wants to see you. He's in the back with the chiefs."

"I'll show you," another woman said. This one was stunning, with a fall of ebony hair and huge eyes deep enough to swim in. She drove Cuxi right out of Sala's mind with one flick of eyelash. "I'm Qula. And you're the famous Salali, I gather."

"And getting more famous by the moment, it seems," he grinned. Pretty women always made him grin. "Though I must say, I wouldn't expect such beauty to concern itself with the likes of me."

Qula pursed her lips. "Well, you have a gift for flattery, though I've heard better. Another time I might be intrigued. Follow me."

Feeling rather punctured, Sala trailed her across the room. *Another time,* she'd said, and with wounded men in the room and dead ones in the streets, he supposed she had a point. He just hadn't considered it before. Sala was doing his best not to think about death, and innards spilling everywhere, even though his clothes stank of other men's blood. If he dwelt too much on dying he wasn't sure he'd have the courage to go on. Battle was *awful.*

Qula pushed open a door and gestured Sala through. Beyond was a largish parlour, dominated by two tables pushed together in the centre. On them someone had scratched an outline of the Precinct and the bigger buildings inside it, probably with the knife which stood upright beside them, its point driven into the wood. Other buildings were marked by scratches outside the Precinct walls, though with less care. Five men were hunched over the makeshift diagram. They stopped talking as Sala led the other three in.

10

"Glad you made it," Chimalli said laconically. The Puma really was a massive man, much bigger than Matlal. Smaller than most of the Thrain, though. "I thought you might have got lost."

"Chimalli." Sala reached out to grip the other man's forearm, trying to mimic his dry tone. "I arranged this dance. It would be impolite to miss it."

"There's plenty of fun for us all," Chimalli answered. He spoke like an educated man, unusual in a warrior. Now he studied Sala with critical eyes, taking in his ruined clothes, and smiled a little. "You've had a tussle of your own, I take it?"

"One or two," he said. Rain drummed on the tiles of the roof. "We got through them well enough."

The Puma nodded. "You got here, which is what matters. Now." His voice became serious. "The Thrain tried to break out through the laundry gate half an hour ago. We were building barricades outside to contain the cavalry, but they weren't finished, which I expect is why the Thrain attacked when they did. We outnumbered them and managed to drive them back inside, but it turned into a mess. Both sides lost over five hundred men."

"Glad to hear it," Sala said, and then frowned to himself when he realised how that must sound.

Chimalli gave a tight smile. "Yes. If we kill one for every one we lose, the battle's ours, and the war with it. So, with the Thrain we killed on patrol, I think we've dealt with over eight hundred of them now. Perhaps a thousand."

"Then there are two and a half thousand left."

"And all trapped in the Precinct," Chimalli agreed. "We have about six thousand, as near as I can tell. If we can keep the Thrain in the Precinct, where they can't use their horses, I think we can take them. All of them."

One of the chiefs scowled. He was a big man too, if not so much as Chimalli, with the tattoos of the Eagle down his forearms. "Half our men left the societies twenty years ago, if they were ever in them in the first place. Either they're old or they're inept. We can't rely on them."

"The Blind God take your bones," Ilari growled from the doorway. "We've done our share so far."

"Quiet!" Chimalli snapped. "Both of you." He stared at the chief. "But the man's right, Suwak. Anyone who's come this far has proved himself. And I'll take the help I can find in any case."

"So you plan to break in," Sala said. He moved closer to the etched plan of the Precinct. "How?"

The chiefs exchanged worried looks.

"I'm getting to know that expression," Sala said lightly. His stomach had begun to churn again. "You want me to do something dangerous, don't you?"

"Everything tonight is dangerous," Suwak put in, before Chimalli silenced him with a glare.

"Yes," the big Puma said simply. "Sala, I can't storm the walls. I don't have enough men, and certainly not enough time. One of my men suggested building wooden towers, then pushing them against the wall so our warriors can jump straight on top of the Thrain, but the sorcerer will be back before we could do that. We might be able to force the laundry gate, but not if the Thrain are waiting for us there, and they almost certainly are."

Sala didn't understand, but Aranka saved him from admitting as much. "You need a diversion."

"Exactly." Chimalli put his finger on the diagram, just outside the wall. "This house is used to accommodate visiting nobility, sometimes. Families without the rank to stay in the Precinct itself. I stayed there myself once, as a boy."

"You're a noble's son?" That explained the educated voice. "What are you doing in the societies?"

"I'm a noble's *fourth* son. That's what I'm doing in the societies. My two eldest brothers learned how to wield power in Hatun, and the third went into the priesthood and learned to use *their* power. I was surplus to requirements, and I don't think I was made to be a *kura*, do you?"

Sala couldn't help smiling. "Not really, no."

"Then let's go on. Because nobles stay there, that building is allowed to be higher than any other around the Precinct. Its roof is exactly level with the top of the wall. There's only a narrow alley between them, which can be bridged with planks. And inside," the finger moved, "the Qapac's apartments are built close to the wall as well. Men could jump that gap quite easily."

Sala's heart had begun to beat faster. The rain went on pounding at the tiles. "I'm no expert, but if the Thrain are waiting there too, won't they pick us off like farmers cutting maize?"

"Yes," Chimalli said. "They will. But they don't have enough men either, Sala, and they can't cover every weak point. If they send men to the apartments they'll weaken the laundry gate, and we can force it. If they don't, you can break in that way."

"Blood and bones, that's a risk."

"What isn't, tonight? Suwak is right about that. But it's my bet the Thrain have concentrated on the laundry gate. Anyway, they've only been here a little more than a week. They might not have realised there's a way in over the roofs."

"And you want me to lead the attack there."

Chimalli nodded. "Yes."

"They'll have seen the danger of that roof in about three seconds, Chimalli. They might be monsters, but they're not stupid."

"No. But they *are* few, and they're afraid, and they make mistakes like anyone else. The *kamachi* showed that in the mountains."

"Yes, but he's the *kamachi,* you see."

Chimalli was smiling, just a slight lift at the corners of his mouth. "Are you reluctant to do this, Sala? You arranged the dance. Wouldn't it be impolite to miss it?"

His own words, used against him. Kai did that sometimes, with a little smile of his own that was very different to the one Chimalli wore.

But the point was a good one. This was Sala's uprising, a revolt he'd planned in back rooms and cellars through Chakanay. It was difficult though. He was no warrior, but he could imagine the Thrain putting men inside the apartment building, waiting for men to drop through the windows. If they had it could turn into a slaughter very quickly. He hesitated. He could easily lead men to a bad death here. Come to that, he might go to a bad death himself. And he didn't want to fight again.

But this was a chance. It might be the only chance, or the best chance, the Ashir would ever have to deal the Thrain a mortal blow. They couldn't afford to miss it.

"Afraid?" Chimalli asked softly.

"Terrified." Sala took a deep breath. "But it has to be done. All right. How many men do I get?"

"Three hundred," Chimalli said. "Get in, fight your way down to the ground floor if you can, and fire the building. The basement would be best, where the laundry is done. Then get out before too many of the Thrain come after you. They won't know if your attack is the main assault, but they'll have to divert a lot of men against you just in case it is, and even more to fight the fire. That's when I'll launch my assault through the laundry gate."

Sala looked over his shoulder. "Are you coming?"

Tumay nodded, and Ilari bared his teeth, which Sala took as agreement. He began to turn back to Chimalli.

"I think I'll come as well," Aranka said. "My warriors would skin me if I let them be left out of this."

Sala frowned at him. "Are you sure?"

"It wouldn't be right to send townsfolk and no warriors." Aranka laughed suddenly. "Besides, this is what Snake are good at. Tricky fighting, where Puma fall over their own huge feet and Deer don't have room to slip away." His smile faded as he looked at Sala. "And if Supay learns my name tonight, I'd rather he found me at the heart of things, not skulking at the edges."

"You're a madman," Sala said. He almost winced at the near-echo of Tumay's words to him earlier. Maybe battle took normal men and made them a little mad, and maybe you had to be mad to do it in the first place.

Suwak cleared his throat. "I think I'll go, too. We should have a chief there," he added when Chimalli turned to him. "In any case, there might be heavy fighting. We'd best send some Eagle, or the Snake won't have anyone to hide behind when it gets rough." He gave Aranka a thin smile.

"Good idea," the Snake said. "We can show you the way out if you get lost on the stairs."

"Very well, then." Chimalli looked at them in turn. "I'll give you half an hour to get into place. When I send a runner I want you ready to begin." He

65

hesitated, then sketched a sign of blessing in the air. "May the Blind God never see you, and Supay not know your names."

Half an hour. Ancient men lying on their deathbeds had more time left in the world than that. Sala reached forward to clasp Chimalli's arm again, trying not to let his fear show.

"The rain's stopped," Tumay said.

It was true. Sala hadn't noticed, but now it was mentioned he couldn't hear the beating of water on tile any more. He managed a broad smile. "Well, that could be a good omen."

"It is for somebody," Chimalli said.

*

"The roof is slanted, but it's not very steep. Normally it wouldn't be hard to stand on the tiles, but the rain will have made them slippery, so be careful of your feet." Sala let his gaze rove across the men crammed into the hall. A hundred Snake warriors, a hundred Eagles, and a hundred artisans and labourers, more or less. Most of them either slightly wounded or not proper warriors, and none of them needed for the assault on the gates. "The eaves are solid stone. You'll be able to get a good grip and then swing yourself down and through the windows. The pole men will see to that."

A knot of eight or nine men by one wall nodded vigorously. All of them held long sticks, to be used knocking the windows through while men swarmed over the wall. Some of those poles had previously held up washing lines, or been used as scythe handles and railings. Amazing what could become a weapon at need.

"Once we're inside, we'll have to get down to the basement quickly. If there are too many Thrain, or they come too fast, then just set fire to what you can." It felt strange, talking to warriors as though he had a right to command them. Perhaps he'd earned the right, now. "We're trying to draw them away from the laundry gate, remember, so we want to draw attention to ourselves. If you hear me blow my horn, make all the noise you can. Bang your axes on tables, smash windows, anything you like. Bring the Thrain to us."

"How do we get back out?" someone called from the back.

"Same way we got in," Suwak said. He stood half a pace behind Sala, with Tumay and Aranka beside him. "Climb on to the roof and jump back. The fires should stop too many Thrain giving chase."

If the fires had been set, they would. And if the Thrain didn't respond too fast, and weren't waiting in the building anyway, and... Sala didn't want to think about that. One miscalculation, one piece of bad luck, and the Qapac's old residence would be a charnel house, with all these men trapped inside and fire blazing up from the basement. And he might be one of them. Would be, most likely, if it all went wrong. His palms felt damp.

"We're a diversion," Sala said. He swept his gaze across the men again, trying to find the words to inspire them. "But don't think that makes us unimportant. What we're about to do might, just possibly, be the act that turns this war against the Thrain forever. Aranka said it right, back in the whorehouse. This is the heart of things. What would you prefer to be doing tonight?"

"Dancing with a pretty girl," someone shouted. There was a ripple of laughter. Suwak nodded as though pleased about that, though Sala didn't know why he would be. Fighting men needed to be focused. Or so Sala had thought. Maybe he was wrong.

"You're a man after my own heart," he said when the laughter faded. "But think about tomorrow. Think what people will say about men who dared to walk into the Puma's lair, and seized it by the tail." He grinned at them. "What will the pretty girls do when they hear about that?"

The men chuckled, and several slapped their comrades on the back. Aranka gave them only a moment to enjoy the prospect. "All right. Get to your places. Snake, we're first in, so I want you by the back windows and ready to climb. Move, warriors, and may Quilla smile on you tonight."

They did move, talking in quiet voices as they flooded towards the stairs. A dozen of them carried unlit torches, their heads made of cotton wrapped tight and then soaked in sesame seed oil. Braziers were already burning in the back rooms of the house. With luck, Sala thought they could set the fires before the Thrain knew anything was wrong. Even with that luck there would still be fighting to do. It wasn't enough to start a blaze and leave. The invaders had to be drawn into the Qapac's building, fooled into thinking a major attack was coming out of that house, at least until the fires took hold. In the smoke and chaos they might not realise they were wrong until it was too late.

Aranka and Suwak stayed with him, waiting in the hall for Chimalli's runner to tell them to begin. Everyone else went upstairs. Sala could hear the floorboards creak as they moved, and there was a soft murmur of conversation, but that was all. Not enough to give them away. He sat down, but stood again almost at once and went to look into the street. His hands were still damp with sweat.

"I can never relax either," Aranka said when Sala paced back across the room. "But the waiting is the worst of it, believe me. Once it starts there's no time to feel nervous."

Sala's lips twitched in sardonic amusement. He'd been in battle now, and knew that was true. Tumay had called it battle fever. Perhaps this wasn't a good time to mention that. "I'd have thought dying would be the worst of it."

"Who knows?" Suwak leaned against the cold fireplace with his arms folded, the only one of them who seemed at ease. "Nobody's ever come back from dying to tell us what it's like."

Aranka made a warding sign with his fingers. "It's bad luck to speak of dying before a battle. Draws the Blind God's eyes to you."

"The eyes of the Blind God have been on us for weeks," Suwak muttered. "Ever since the day these cursed Thrain crossed the border into Apusuyu. Maybe since the day they heard of us."

"I know his eyes were on *me*," Sala said. "I had the red plague, remember? The sorcerer healed me so he could force me to tell him about Kai. He might come to regret doing that."

In truth, he wasn't concerned about feeling nervous once the fighting began. Aranka was more right than he realised. Sala remembered that strange, vibrant feeling that filled him as the cavalry plunged along the street, and didn't like the memory very much. He'd never expected to feel *joy* in the prospect of battle, and maybe death. Sometimes killing was necessary – the gods knew the Thrain had to die, come what may – but a man wasn't supposed to take pleasure in it. Only pumas and vultures actually liked the flow of blood.

He wondered, again, how Kai was coping. The *kamachi* wasn't a violent man, had never fought in his life except in games at the festivals, when there were contests with staves or wrestling matches. That was very different from real battle, as Sala had found out tonight. Kai would have discovered it three days ago, in his ambush of the Thrain patrol that ended with Ramian dying in his own blood. Sala wished he knew exactly what had happened there. From what Mimiteh said it seemed Kai was alive, and none of the Thrain were, so it must have been a clear victory. Sala only hoped he could be part of such a triumph tonight.

He became aware that Suwak was murmuring under his breath, and turned his head to listen.

"Poetry?" he said. This hardly seemed the proper time.

Suwak stopped his recital to look at him. "It just came into my mind. 'Comes the Puma'. I always liked it, even when I was a boy."

"Warriors often do," Aranka smiled. "And it does seem apt." He spread one hand out wide, mimicking the declamatory pose of a singer. "*Comes the moon; through the night; over the highlands; with fingers of light; full and round; comes the moon.* The moon is still up, isn't it?"

"It's still up. But that isn't the stanza I was thinking of, actually." Suwak turned from the fireplace to face them. "*Comes the wind; through the night; across the highlands; with mouth wide open; shouting, wailing; comes the wind.* It always made me think of battle, and vengeance."

Sala could see how it would. He didn't say anything though. The exchange had made him realise, with an almost physical shock, exactly how much danger he was putting himself in when he went over the wall. His heart was suddenly thumping hard. He had to work moisture into his mouth before he could swallow. Perhaps he shouldn't have agreed to this.

Trotting feet sounded in the porch. A moment later the door was thrown open and a tall man stood in the frame, a message Runner with white feathers braided through his hair. Almost all the Runners were dead, claimed by the red plague they had carried across the country, but evidently Chimalli had found one Runner the disease had missed. He caught the door with one hand as it bounced back off the wall.

"The Auk says it's time," he said. With that he was gone again, vanishing back into the first glimmer of sunrise. Sala turned to the warriors.

"When did Chimalli become Auk?" Suwak muttered. "You don't become leader just because you say you are."

"Never mind that," Sala said. His heartbeat slowed, eased. He was ready. "Quilla smile on you both, and Inti light your path forever. All right. Let's get it done."

He turned towards the stairs. As he climbed, the end of the poem drifted into his mind, both a salutation and thankfulness for life;

Puma and moon
wind and ice
beautiful enchantment
night in the highlands
thus am I fed.

Aranka hurried ahead, going to join his Snake warriors for the first wave of the assault. He was almost dancing on his toes, eager for the fight. Sala drew a deep breath. He seemed to have done that a lot tonight.

"Good luck," Suwak said. Then he was gone too, striding down the corridor to where his Eagle waited, and Sala was left alone. His hands were shaking again.

"Thus am I fed," he muttered. He went to join his men.

11

Someone shoved a hand against Sala's backside to boost him through the window and on to the roof. He bumped against another man before he found his footing. The slope was very gentle, but rain had made the tiles slick and treacherous, and his boots slid as he turned towards the wall.

Dawn had turned the sky grey, with fingers of pink in the east. Clouds streamed away west with tatters trailing behind them. Ahead of Sala was a gap to the wall of the Precinct compound, then another space to the roof of the Qapac's house. Snake warriors had begun to run across planks laid from the eaves to the Precinct wall, then jump over the second gap. Fifty or more were already across.

Another jumped, fell a little short. Hands scrabbled for grip on the slippery tiles, couldn't find it, and he went over the edge with his fingers flailing at air. He didn't cry out even as he fell, and landed in the alley with a cracking noise that made Sala flinch.

More Snake had slipped along the wall itself, and the crash of breaking glass sounded as they thrust with their long poles. Aranka swung down from the Qapac's roof and through a broken window, legs first, to land inside. Warriors followed him in, agile as spider monkeys leaping through high branches. There didn't seem to be any fighting yet. Maybe the Thrain had been caught by surprise after all.

That wouldn't last long, Sala realised as another window was smashed. He hadn't considered the noise glass made when it broke, and fell thirty feet on to stone. As though in response to the thought shouts sounded from deeper in the Precinct, voices calling in the harsh Thrain language.

"Torch bearers forward!" he called. "Quickly, now. Get inside as fast as you can!"

The Snake were across. Sala slithered down the tiles and ran across a plank, not pausing as he reached the wall. The gap was wider than he'd expected, but not too wide, and he leapt to land on hands and knees on the far side. For a moment he slid again, but then his boots found grip and he turned, reaching for the eaves.

"Me first," Ilari said as he pushed ahead of Sala. The artisan gripped the gable and swung his feet out over empty air, flipping himself into space. He swung around the pivot of his hands and in through the broken window with ease. Sala grimaced and followed, though without the grace. He had to lower himself over the eaves and feel for the window sill with his feet. Someone trod on his fingers and he muffled a cry of pain.

"Sorry," Tumay said above him.

Sala's boots touched stone, and then hands caught his waist and hauled him inside.

He reached back and up, groping until a torch was placed in his hand, and then turned into the room. Warriors called to each other in the corridor, Snake already spreading through the building. A glance outside showed the last of Sala's townsfolk streaming over the makeshift bridges, and behind them Eagle warriors clambering on to the roof of the town house. How Eagle would manage that flip from the roof, Sala didn't know, but that was their problem.

"They know we're here," Ilari said. He moved towards the doorway, pulling his axe from his belt.

"Of course they know." Sala leaned out of the window, caught a man's coat, and pulled him into the room by main force. He got a kick in the shoulder as he did so. "That was the plan, remember?"

"Time for them to die," Ilari said. He didn't seem to have heard Sala at all. "Time for all of them to die."

That definitely was *not* the plan, at least as far as this attack was concerned. It was Chimalli who would destroy the Thrain, after they had been distracted by this little foray over the wall. The task was difficult enough without Ilari getting battle fever. Sala didn't want to see that again, having felt it himself. "Stay calm, Ilari. We're here to confuse them, not to win the war."

"What does it matter, as long as they die?"

He rolled his eyes and said nothing. If anyone had reason to hate the Thrain it was Ilari, and Sala doubted anything he could say would change the other man's mood one jot. He reached back out to help another man through the window, and knew just by the stocky torso hanging down that it was Tumay.

"Thank you," the tavern keeper said. He took the torch from Sala and set off towards the door. "We'd better hurry. One of the others saw soldiers coming this way, and fast."

A dozen men had gathered in the room now, enough that it was becoming crowded. More were still swinging down from the roof. Sala pulled his axe free. "Let's get moving."

They went into the corridor in a tight cluster, Ilari shouldering his way to the front with Sala behind him. The artisan led them left, in the direction the Snake had taken. Their voices drifted faintly up the stairwell, like disembodied echoes. Outside a Thrain officer shouted an order, and boots stamped. Faint light showed through the windows now, as the clouds blew away and let dawn come through. Niches along the corridor stood empty, their statues and filigreed vases stolen by the invaders. Melted down, probably. A mural of stylised faces above the stairs was still intact, though. They were nothing but a few quickly-drawn lines with no discernible features within them, old and abstract, and of no value to the Thrain. Sala glanced at the faces as he went past. They were only outlines, faces without souls.

Shouts came from below when they were halfway down the stairs, and then the ring of steel on bronze. A voice cried out. Something overturned with a crash and then everyone was screaming, fear and fury mingling in each voice. One man gave a bubbling scream, and crockery smashed.

"Left!" Sala shouted as Ilari reached the bottom of the stairs. "The basement is to the left!"

71

Ilari must have heard him. He was only three feet in front of Sala, easily within earshot even in the sudden din, but the artisan turned right and began to run. Sala grabbed for him and missed, his fingers scraping along the back of Ilari's coat. "Blood and bones, come back, you fool!"

Ilari kept moving. Sala cursed and waved for Tumay to go back. "Let him go! We have a job to do."

"Let him go?" Tumay repeated. "Alone?"

"To the Halls of Darkness with that," another man growled. He pushed past them and set off after Ilari, raising an ululating cry as he went. Three others went with him, and Sala swore so savagely it was a wonder paint didn't blister on the walls. He scanned the corridor quickly, his gaze finding a pair of tall windows draped on either side with eight feet of green cotton.

"Oh, by Tezcata's poisoned balls," he muttered. "Tumay, you and three men stay here. If you're attacked, fire those curtains and get out, all right? We have to set a fire. That's the whole point."

"You want me to fire them with you still in here?" the tavern keeper said doubtfully.

"Blood and bones, is everyone going to argue with me today?" Sala pointed his axe at the other man. "You just do it. The rest of you, come with me!"

He set off after Ilari, trotting down the corridor towards the sounds of fighting. By a turn in the corridor they passed a single man, a Snake, sprawled against the wall with his hands folded peacefully in his lap. He might have been asleep apart from the arrow in his throat. Beyond him the corridor turned again, and as Sala approached the corner a Thrain staggered into view, walking backwards and tottering on his feet. Both hands were pressed to his chest, trying vainly to stop blood gouting between his fingers. One of the townsfolk backhanded him with a casual sweep of his mace and the soldier went down without a sound.

Sala turned the corner and found himself in a large room with windows all down one wall, probably a dining room in normal times. Now it was full of fighting men. It was hard to see who was who, in the struggling mass. He would have to be closer, and with that thought he plunged into the battle.

Somehow things had turned around, or maybe they had started this way, though Sala couldn't see how that was possible. For whatever reason, the Thrain fought in a thin line with their backs to Sala and his band of five, struggling to hold back a gaggle of Snake who darted and weaved around flashing swords. The two forces must have crept past one another before the fighting began, unlikely though that seemed. Both were vulnerable to an assault in the rear because of it, and by good fortune Sala and his band had arrived first.

Close to one wall Ilari was fighting a stocky Thrain in bloody armour. The artisan slipped sideways as a blade cracked plaster where he had been standing, and twisting around he swung his axe and opened his opponent's throat. The man dropped his sword and tried to scream, but managed only a wheeze before Ilari hit him again. Then Sala was in the fight, his axe crashing into the shoulder of a Thrain before the soldier even knew he was there. The man was unarmoured: evidently at least some of the Thrain had been surprised. The axe sheared through flesh and snapped the collarbone, and with a grunt the man stumbled sideways. A Snake in front of him thrust a spear into his middle and he folded up, blood coming from his shoulder in a great river. The Snake grinned bloody thanks at Sala. Then he twitched, opened his mouth, and spat a great gobbet of black blood on Sala's knees as another Thrain soldier dragged his blade out of the Snake's back.

More of the invaders had appeared, behind the first Snakes. After that everything was a frenzy.

Sala blocked thrusts and ducked slashes, unable to do more than stay alive, and that barely. One blade sliced across his forearm, while a blindingly quick stab from another man put an inch of sword point into his bicep. The man who did that went down before he could pull the sword free, felled by a blow from Sala's axe that that split his helmet in two and split his forehead in two. There was time for a gasped breath before another soldier came at him, this one screaming like a skinned monkey, his eyes so wide they seemed all whites. Sala backpedalled, boots slithering in the blood, until Ilari came howling in from the side with a Thrain spear in both hands. He spitted the man at a dead run, hurling him against the wall with the ferocity of his charge. The man didn't even scream. He bared his teeth, and hanging a foot off the floor he brought his sword down.

Ilari jerked spasmodically. His hands loosened on the spear shaft. He turned, and Sala's stomach roiled. Half Ilari's face was gone, cut away, hair and ear and cheekbone sliced clean off. His eye rolled as though about to fall from its socket. He staggered and then he fell, but before he hit the floor Sala thought he began to smile.

"Got them!" someone was crowing. It took Sala a moment to recognise Aranka's voice. "Twenty of them, killed!" Snake warriors bellowed in response, more howls than words.

"The fires," Sala croaked. He was shaking, with exhaustion more than nerves. He'd heard before that warriors could never tell how long a fight had lasted, and now he believed it. This one must have been mere moments, yet he was weary to his bones. "Are they set?"

Aranka gave him a quizzical look. The Snake was blood all over, his face streaked with it. Some of it was his own, and still flowing from a cut high on his scalp. "Can't you hear them?"

Sala frowned, and then realised he could. He could smell smoke too, over the blood and urine of dead men. He just hadn't realised it before. "Good, then we can get out. The gods know this must be enough to draw the Thrain here. If we're quick we can get most of – what?"

Aranka was shaking his head, a queer smile on his face. "You go, Salali. Take your men. They've done their part, and more. But this is not over. The Thrain need to believe this is a real assault, so we need to do all we can to draw them. This is a dance I won't run from."

There were growls of assent from the warriors around the chief. Sala stared in disbelief. "You're crazy."

"I am Snake," Aranka said, his voice full of pride. The men around him bellowed again, shaking weapons in the air.

"Well I'm getting out of here," Sala said. He made sure he didn't look at Ilari. Poor Amaru was going to die of grief. "Right now."

Footsteps rattled on the floor behind him, and he turned to see Thrain running into the room. They saw the Ashir and hesitated, then began to spread across the room. More pushed in behind them. Sala felt breath leave him.

"Welcome to the dance," Aranka said quietly. He lifted his bloody axe. "We are Snake!"

The warriors roared, and then they surged forward. They went past Sala like a storm from the mountains and he was swept up with them, borne straight into the waiting Thrain. Surprise showed on the soldiers' faces. It lasted only a moment, but that was enough for the Ashir to be on them. Axes hammered into chain mail, maces crashed against helmets, and swords flickered frantically in reply. Men went down in both lines, some in silence, some screaming the name of a god, or a lover. Aranka hammered a soldier aside, hacked through another's arm and plunged into the Thrain line, making straight for the officer behind it.

Sala fought with axe and elbows, knees and feet and desperation. Something slashed along his thigh as his axe shattered on a soldier's cheek guard, crushing it into the man's face. The Thrain screamed and stumbled backwards. Sala thought he might be as young as sixteen, with faint fuzz on his chin and his good looks ruined forever. A quick blow with the axe handle smashed his windpipe so he wouldn't have to worry about that. Sala scrambled on the floor for a weapon, found a fallen Thrain sword. He started to rise, holding the unfamiliar weapon in both hands.

He looked up through wisps of smoke, saw a soldier's blade descending, and knew he was dead.

The blade clanged into something. An axe, blocking the blow. Sala thrust upwards into the Thrain's groin and a torrent of blood gushed out. The sword ground on bone as Sala yanked it free and the man went down, clutching himself and shrieking like a girl. Then Sala was up, back on his feet. The man who'd saved him, a town man he didn't know, laughed at him through a face smeared in blood, with a long gash down one side that had taken out an eye. He didn't seem aware of it.

Ahead, Aranka staggered away from the officer. He bared his teeth and swung the axe again, but there was no strength in the blow, and the Thrain leaned aside as it drifted past him. He struck twice. Aranka collapsed like a torn shirt.

Something in Sala broke at the sight. He lunged through the line with a cry, slashing with an overhand blow made awkward by the sword. It was the stroke he knew though, if dealt before with an axe, and it met flesh even as the officer turned to face him. The other man's sword darted at Sala's midriff, a fraction too

74

slowly. Half a heartbeat, to decide life or death. Sala's blade cut into the officer's neck and he lurched sideways, steadied himself, and spat a torrent of furious words. Then he toppled over. Sala dragged the weapon free with a snarl. Part of him thought *battle fever* but it was distant, a voice too faint to hear, and he turned to find another enemy.

Only to find the battle was over. Three Snake remained on their feet, and two of the townsfolk, including the man with one eye lost to a horrible gash. All the Thrain were down. There were at least seventy dead men in the room, more than half of them Thrain, so it was hard to find a place to stand without putting his feet on a corpse. Sala's frenzy drained out of him like spilled blood. He sucked a deep breath, then another. He couldn't seem to get enough air.

He looked down.

"Oh," he said.

The officer hadn't been too slow after all. *Half a heartbeat*, Sala thought, with peculiar detachment. Blood was spilling through his shirt. Quite a lot of it, and he couldn't feel his feet. He put his free hand over the wound without thinking, as though believing it wouldn't be real if he couldn't see it.

From the courtyard a roar went up, hundreds of throats raising a battle cry, and hard behind it came the crash of weapons. Chimalli had launched the assault. The diversion had done its job.

"Oh, dear," Sala said, and sat down hard on someone's back. Whoever it was didn't move.

"We can carry you," one of the warriors said. "We can...."

He tailed off. They might be able to carry him, if they didn't meet any more Thrain, but how were they going to get him up on the roof? Or across the gap to the wall? And if they somehow managed all that, he would still die, because this was a wound beyond any healer in the Blessed Land. He thought the lumps trying to ooze out of him might be intestines. It still didn't hurt, but every movement had become difficult, too much effort to make. He managed to look up though. His head felt very heavy.

"You get out of here," he said. His tongue was too thick to shape the words clearly, but one of the Snake nodded anyway. "Tell the *kamachi*... tell him what happened. Tell Kai."

"I will," the warrior said. He bent and touched his hand to Sala's head. "Quilla smile on you, Inti bless you with his light, and Supay welcome you home, Salali. Go in beauty." He straightened, and nodded once. "You were never in the societies, but if my shade should know yours in Supay's halls, I would be honoured to walk in the sun with you."

"I look forward... to it," Sala whispered. "Get out, now."

He waited until they were gone before he tried to move. He couldn't stand, but he did manage to push himself to his knees, still holding his guts in with one hand. Men could live a long time with a belly wound. It was what warriors did to outlaws when they caught them, and staked them by the road to die. Not a pleasant thought. But it gave him the chance to see the sun come up, if he could

75

make it as far as the windows. One more sunrise, to warm his soul on the journey to Supay's halls.

He'd always thought Kai would be there to bless him, when he died. As long as Kai didn't hold Sala's drinking and jokes against him, anyway. It was strange, but here on the edge of death it was the *kamachi* Sala wanted to see, more even than Quilla herself, or Inti with the gift of his light.

"You see, Matlal?" he gasped. "I do... believe."

The big man had always doubted it. Sala would rather have a *chicha* beer than go to prayer, rather dance with a pretty girl than tell a priest he would try to be a better man. But he'd always had faith. Still, thinking of pretty girls reminded him of Cuxi, waiting at the whorehouse for the heroes to come home. Sala wouldn't be among them.

Shame, really.

He couldn't make it to the window. When he fell, sprawling half-upright against the remnants of a shattered table, he could see the edge of the glow of sunrise, if not the sun itself. That would have to be enough. Sala smiled, and closing his eyes he let the warmth of dawn fall on his face.

12

Warriors ran past Tumay, back the way they had come through a corridor filling rapidly with smoke. Several limped or clutched wounds in hip or side, where the Thrain liked to strike with quick stabbing thrusts from their swords. Ashir warriors were used to overhand blows with axe or mace, not these darting attacks lower down. They didn't know how to defend them, and most of the men were wounded. Only limps and groans told Tumay who. Every warrior was streaked with blood, hurt or not.

The sounds of battle still echoed down the corridor from below, metal clashing on metal and men screaming in challenge or pain. The Ashir down there would be cut off by the fire if they didn't hurry back. It was probably too late for most of them already, in fact. Tumay hesitated, trying to look past the fleeing warriors to the rooms beyond them.

"Get out!" a hulking Eagle yelled, right in his ear. "More soldiers are coming. Get out now!"

"Salali!" Tumay bellowed. Fire crackled below, followed by the crash of falling timbers. He inhaled smoke and doubled over, almost choking, before he could call again. "Ilari!"

Black smoke billowed up the stairs from the ground floor. Orange light flickered angrily behind it, and heat washed against Tumay's face. He hesitated once more, reluctant to leave his friends now, but time had run out and he didn't have a choice. The three men with him were shifting their feet, eager to run. Tumay thrust the torch he held into the curtains, barely waiting for them to ignite before he tossed it to the floor. "Let's go."

They ran back up the stairs, bending low to find clean air. Smoke rose from below in a steady stream now, not just the tendrils of mere moments before. Somewhere below weapons clashed again and men shouted, their cries faint against the growing roar of fire. Even in the blaze warriors and Thrain still fought, it seemed. Tumay hoped Ilari wasn't among them, that he'd come to his senses and got out before the fire trapped him below. For Amaru's sake, mostly. The girl had lost her mother and sister to the red plague. It would be cruelly unjust if she lost her father as well.

Suwak stood in the upper room, shoving warriors through the broken window and up to the roof. Most were wounded and needed help, a push from below while others dragged at them from above. Suwak turned from the last as Tumay and his companions stumbled in with their eyes streaming. Coughs hunched them over like old men. By the Bearded God, Tumay *was* an old man, certainly too old to be running around with a mace in his hand. War was for young men, still full of hot blood and glory, not those with grey in their hair and more fat than muscle on their bones.

Still, he'd done a warrior's work today, in the streets and then here. He wasn't even wounded. There might be time to revel in that, but not now, with smoke choking his lungs and his muscles trembling with weariness. He stumbled and Suwak caught his shoulder to steady him, then slapped Tumay on the back so hard he thought his lungs would come right out through his throat. "Where's Salali? Did he make it?"

"Don't think so," Tumay croaked. His lungs felt better for that thump, but his spine stung from it. "Didn't see him, anyway. Nor Ilari, or Aranka."

"Pity," the Eagle chief said. "They were good men. Can you climb to the roof now?"

Tumay nodded. He'd better be able to climb, since the choice was to stay here and be roasted or choked. The three warriors with him had already scrambled out, he realised. Well, they were younger and fitter, and didn't have to drag bones that ached in the cold. He stumbled to the window and clambered on to the ledge, reaching up for the eaves.

His fingers had barely found them before Suwak shoved him upwards. Tumay gasped and grabbed at the stone with white knuckles. For a moment his fingers scrabbled for a grip and then they found it, and hands caught his wrists and pulled. He shot up onto the tiles like a frog leaping up a tree, which started him coughing again. He forced himself to stop, and to breathe evenly, just as Suwak slithered lithely up beside him. The last thing he needed was another great smack on the back.

"What are you lying there for?" The Eagle dragged Tumay to his feet. "Come on. There's work to do yet. We should get back to Chimalli and find out where he wants us next."

Next? What Tumay wanted next, what he needed, was an hour in a quiet room with a damp cloth laid over his eyes. Every muscle in his body ached. He gritted his teeth and launched himself across the gap to the wall, knowing that if he stopped now he wouldn't be able to start moving again. He barely made the jump, knocking away one of the plank bridges and sliding on his stomach before his wildly grappling hands found a purchase. He dragged himself atop the wall and lay where he was for a moment, trying to catch his breath.

"Will you get up?" Suwak landed beside him. "Hurry, man!"

"May maggots eat your balls if you don't shut up," Tumay gasped. The Eagle laughed, not at all put out by the insult. Tumay got his hands under him and levered himself to his knees.

He froze there, staring past the Qapac's house to the wall to where the laundry gate ran into Chakanay.

"Blessings of the gods," he whispered, and then raised his voice to a shout. "He did it! Suwak, look, *Chimalli did it!*"

The laundry gate was broken. Shattered remnants of wood hung from their bronze hinges, with the rest a splintered mass scattered across the stones of the passageway. What looked like the trunk of a moderate-sized tree lay discarded there as well, amongst the broken bodies of Thrain and Ashir. *A ram*, Tumay thought with a grin that stretched his smoke-blackened skin tight across his face. Closer to him, deeper into the Precinct, a double line of Thrain on foot struggled to hold back a surging, howling mass of warriors, mostly Puma and Eagle to

78

judge by their size. Another large group of crested men stood outside the gate, bright and proud in the pale light of morning, waiting their chance to enter the fray.

And the chance would come, Tumay realised as he watched. Already the Thrain were being pushed back, to where the passage that led from the laundry gate began to widen into the main courtyard of the Precinct. More and more Ashir would be able to reach them then, stretching the Thrain line thinner. Tumay turned to look the other way, searching for signs of more soldiers, and through the smoke he saw a solid mass of cavalry standing in long lines. They knew as well, he realised, and were ready to counter the breakthrough when it came, as Snake would do for the Ashir.

There weren't enough of them. He knew it at once, with a soaring in his heart. There were too few of the Thrain to matter, even taking account of the horses. Perhaps six hundred were fighting to hold the line, and half that number waited behind in their saddles, but a thousand Ashir already pressed them and more, far more, stood in the streets. Tumay laughed out loud, forgetting the smoke and his aching muscles.

"We beat them!" Suwak yelled, and pounded Tumay on the back until his eyeballs rattled. This time he didn't mind in the least. "We did it, by Quilla's light! They're finished!"

Grinning, Tumay grasped the Eagle's offered arm and pulled himself to his feet. The Thrain below were pushed back another step, leaving more of their fellows to litter the floor of the courtyard. Ashir were falling too, more of them than Thrain, but the warriors could afford their losses. The alley was widening where they fought. Another five yards and they would be in the courtyard proper, able to spread out around the soldiers. The cavalry would have to charge before that happened. Tumay's gaze went back to them.

The warriors waiting by the laundry gate began to turn suddenly, all of them in the same direction with their heads craning backwards. Tumay twisted to follow their eyes, still smiling.

Soaring above the streets was a silvery speck of... something. Squinting, trying to focus, Tumay thought at first it might be a flake of ash, or a feather caught in an up draught. It moved too slowly though, and too smoothly, like a very slow arrow in flight. He couldn't seem to focus on it properly.

"What are they doing?" Suwak wondered aloud. "Chimalli must be able to see the Thrain are breaking. Why doesn't he attack?"

The warriors began to scatter. Tumay glanced at them, and just as he did so the speck flashed searing white at the edge of his vision and plunged into the street.

"Get down!" Suwak yelled, but Tumay was already throwing himself to the wall with his eyes squeezed shut, half blinded by that flare of pure light. Even so, he was barely down when a wall of air struck him with a deafening roar and he was shoved sideways, flailing for a grip on the stones. *Hot air*, he thought as his legs swung over the edge. His skin, already dry, seemed to crinkle in the

79

blast, but there was no time to wonder what had done it. He had a sudden, sharp vision of the paving stones, thirty feet beneath his dangling boots.

Cool air rushed back in just as he found a grip and steadied himself, and he realised he could hear screaming.

"I can't see!" Suwak bellowed. "I can't see! What in the name –"

"Close your eyes tight," Tumay gasped. He dragged himself back atop the wall, his shoulders creaking with the effort. "Keep them shut until your vision comes back."

Jagged lines of white zigzagged across his own eyes. If he hadn't glanced away when he did he might have been blinded, but as it was those jittering white lines made him feel nauseous. He tried to ignore it, and lying on the wall once more, he peered down at the warriors by the laundry gate.

To where they had been. Men lay broken in a wide circle, their limbs twisted at grotesque angles, or else missing entirely. Bodies were piled against walls and under shattered windows, and all were burned. Smoke rose from charred clothing, from staring empty eyes and flesh, from the paving stones themselves. There were fifteen hundred of them, more. Two thousand warriors snuffed out like mice in a fire.

In the middle of the street a crater had appeared, five yards across and two deep, in which flickers of flame danced and died.

Struggling men had fallen in the Precinct itself, knocked from their feet by that wall of heated air. They fought on as Tumay watched, stabbing one another even while they tried to rise or grappling on the floor. He shook his head, unable to understand. Had the fire spread, somehow? Flames might have reached a keg of sesame oil, he supposed. But that didn't explain why the explosion had happened in the street, or what that soaring silver fleck had been.

"Quilla's mercy, I can see," Suwak said. The Eagle was still flat on his stomach, clinging to the wall with both hands. "Colours, anyway, and I think I can see you, Tumay. What's happening?"

"They're dead," he said. His voice was distant, after the roar of the explosion. "All of them."

"Dead? That's impossible, they weren't enough Thrain. Nothing could have killed…" Suwak trailed off. Colour drained from his face, and half-blind or no, he turned slowly to stare down at the gate.

Thrain rode into view, dusty but unbloodied. Scores of them moved to block the alley, then hundreds of them, but Tumay hardly saw. In their midst rode a figure without weapon or armour, grey-haired and unremarkable. Tumay stopped breathing. He had never seen the man, but he knew him.

"The sorcerer," he said hoarsely. He could smell roasted flesh, thick and sickly. "The sorcerer is here."

In the Precinct, the cavalry moved at last. The few Ashir still alive were caught in the charge and crushed, most of them vanishing beneath trampling hooves before they could strike a blow. Tumay looked away. His throat felt tight. Victory had been theirs, it was won, and now it had been snatched from their hands. He was afraid he was going to be ill.

"What do we have to do?" Suwak muttered beside him. The chief's eyes were unfocused, and his hands groped blindly on the stone. "Have the gods turned their backs on us? Perhaps we're fated not to win this war. Perhaps Tezcata has cast his shadow over us again."

Tumay thought of Ilari, dead somewhere in the burning building. And Salali too, the man who'd organised this uprising and never lost faith in the *kamachi*. Dead, in the burning building. He shook his head.

"I won't accept that," he said. "And if it is true, if we are forsaken, I'll still keep fighting, until someone sticks a spear in me." It had been that way once, for generations, when Tezcata was lord here and the memory of Viraca's love grew fainter every year. Those who clung to his teachings had been driven to hide in corners and the high mountains, hiding from the hunting dark. For two thousand years life had been bleak, but still the *kamachi* had been born, one in every generation. There had been hope. There still was.

He glanced back at the courtyard. The sorcerer rode forward, over the sprawled bodies of the dead. With him came the senior officer, a man Tumay had seen before but whose name he didn't know, and behind them hundreds of soldiers. It wasn't the fighting men who mattered. Only the one man was important, and there was no way to fight him.

"Come on," he said. He took Suwak's arm. "I'll guide you over the planks. It's time we were gone."

They made it to the road without incident. Twenty warriors lay scattered across the street outside the town house, or what remained of warriors. It was hard to be sure how many there had been. Bits of them were strewn across the stones, limbs and pieces of torso ripped apart and flung in every direction. Tumay had heard of the same thing happening in the Precinct when the Thrain first arrived, but at the sight he still stumbled back through the door and threw up. Too many horrors too fast, he supposed.

"Supay welcome you home," he said. The end of the farewell to the dead, and all he could manage right now. He lifted three middle fingers and drew a sign of blessing in the air. "Go in beauty."

There would be no beauty for them after this. In the next world they would be maimed, or else bodiless, forever. Tumay had seen battle in his days as a Snake, and plenty of death, but this had not been battle. This was evil at work, inchoate darkness, and under his nausea he felt the touch of fear burn cold in his bones.

"Hurry," Suwak said. He squinted across the street. "I can see better, but I still need your help."

"Be glad you can't see this," Tumay said. He wiped his mouth and took the Eagle's arm again. "Let's move, and quickly."

They went across the street with rapid steps, Tumay taking care to ensure they didn't walk over any of the… pieces. Suwak wouldn't see them until he

81

tripped. When they made it into a twisting side alley Tumay allowed himself a sigh of relief, but he didn't stop. They went past an angled corner and over a covered drain, its water stained with eddies of crimson, as though a dyer had been careless with his pots. They stumbled across and on past a row of houses, Suwak trusting him without a word spoken. Down another twisted alley they came to a house with its door hanging open, its occupants likely dead or fleeing, and Tumay ushered his companion inside and collapsed against a wall with his chest heaving.

"We should be safe here for a while," he said when his heart had slowed somewhat. "Not for long, though. The Thrain will come looking for revenge now their *binchuka* leader is back."

Suwak chuckled in the shadows. The doorway and window faced west, away from the rising sun, and the room was still mostly in darkness. All Tumay could see of the warrior was a vague form, sitting against the far wall.

"*Binchuka*," Suwak said. "I like that. A poisonous beetle." He coughed, then spat a great gobbet of phlegm to the floor. "It'll take a week to get that smoke out of my lungs."

"You should live so long," Tumay muttered. "The Thrain will kill you on sight, you know. As soon as they see those tattoos on your arms you're as good as dead. Me too, for that matter."

"Everyone dies, my friend. We knew the risks before we went over the wall tonight, and nobody ran away rather than face them." Suwak's teeth gleamed in a smile. "I'll take one or two of them with me, at least. And you know, tonight wasn't all a disaster."

"No." He had to admit that, despite how it had ended. Despite the bits of bodies in the street, and despite the dead friends. Ilari most of all. Quilla's mercy, how was he supposed to tell Amaru? He ought to fetch her before he fled Chakanay. There was danger in delay, but some things had to be done, if you wanted to look at yourself in still water and see the face of a man looking back.

Things like rebellion, when the chance came. However it turned out. But this would not be a good town for an orphan now. Not good for anyone.

"We bloodied them," Suwak said. "Oh, we bloodied them, sure enough. Chimalli thought we'd dealt with a thousand of them before we attacked the Precinct. We must have got a few hundred more there."

"And lost as many," Tumay pointed out.

"Yes. But we have enough men to lose." The chief shifted his weight. "They had barely enough men to hold Chakanay even before last night. They might even have to go home now."

Tumay laughed without humour. "On the wall you were sure we were forsaken by the gods, and doomed."

"And now I'm not," Suwak said. "I can see enough to move, I think. More blurs than details, but well enough to manage. Shall we go on?"

He wanted nothing more than to lie down and sleep, but Tumay pushed himself to his feet with a groan. Something in his back popped with a stabbing pain that made him gasp, but he found he could move more easily afterwards. "We best had, I think. West? Any warriors who got out will probably be heading that way, back to Chimalli's camp in the hills."

"West," Suwak agreed. He wobbled slightly as he made his way to the door, holding his side with one hand. "As fast as we can. We have plans to make, while the Thrain are wounded."

"I have to pick someone up on the way," Tumay said. He was prepared to go to Amaru on his own if the warrior demurred, but Suwak only nodded. A trickle of blood ran between the fingers pressed against his side. "You're wounded. Why didn't you tell me?"

"Because it isn't serious, and it wouldn't do any good," Suwak snapped. "I can manage. Now let's go."

13

The streets bore scars. For the most part it was barricades, piles of furniture and debris thrown together to block off an alley or entrance. Sometimes there were bodies though, Thrain and their horses jumbled together with dead Ashir. Tumay could read the story of each fight. Here a place where the invaders had been ambushed and hemmed into a corner of the street, then slaughtered. There the site of a more direct clash, corpses sprawled in piles in the middle of the road, Thrain among many more Ashir.

Once they passed a scene like the ambush Aranka had sprung, a rope across the street and Thrain strewn across it. Men and horses made a tangle of bodies and blood. Thirty of each, Tumay thought, assuming none had got away. It didn't look like any had.

People slunk through the carnage, skirting the dead and the wreckage of smashed windows and masonry. They stayed close to the edge of sight, little more than shapes like ghosts, hard to pick out clearly. Tumay didn't bother to try. They weren't Thrain, and that was enough. Besides, with the streets clear he and Suwak could move quickly, or as quickly as the wounded chief could manage. It might be enough.

There was no clatter of armour, no clop of hooves on stone. The Thrain were staying in the Precinct. They might have been bloodied worse than Chimalli thought.

Tumay led Suwak through the wreckage.

There had been a time when he could have run all day and fought a battle in the evening, then slept on the ground for an hour and run all the way home again. He'd been a Snake then, as strong and hard as any man in Apusuyu. But those days had passed, and regret did nothing to bring them back. Now his thighs were turning to water and his back ached, hurts due not to injury but to age.

His face felt brittle too, where the sorcerer's wave of heat had passed over him. Tumay kept wanting to scrub the dried skin off. It made him feel unclean, soiled somehow. Nonsense, of course. But telling himself so didn't make the loathing go away.

"There," he said at last. There was still no sign of the Thrain. "There. Ilari's house."

Suwak didn't reply. He claimed his wound was minor, but the chief was grey in the face and stumbled on the steps. Tumay knocked and went in without waiting for a reply. "Amaru? It's me, Tumay. Are you in your –"

He broke off. Amaru was seated at the kitchen table, staring at him with her good eye suddenly wide. She wasn't alone.

Across from her sat a young woman in the blue robes of the *kura*, and a blood-streaked man with his back to the door. His shock of blond hair had never belonged to an Ashir. A moment later Tumay saw the uniform, red and black for all the dirt, and he began to snarl.

"It's all right," the priestess said. Tumay had to search his memory before her name came to him: Mimiteh. "Come in, both of you."

"I will," Suwak hissed, "when he leaves." He drew the axe from his belt. "Or dies."

Mimiteh stood up. "He will do neither."

"He's the man you saved earlier," Tumay said. He stumbled to a chair and slumped down, too exhausted to bother arguing. "The one Salali said you're in love with."

"Salali was right." Her jaw was set firm. The soldier looked at her; only that, but something clear and shining bloomed in his eyes. "His name is Kisain. He is changing sides."

"I've already changed sides," the soldier said. He was sitting awkwardly, with most of his weight on one hip. "I changed when I realised I'd rather be with you than my own people."

"How convenient," Suwak snapped from the doorway. "And will you kill your *own people* now, then?"

Kisain shook his head. "Not that. The men of my patrol, those who survived, went back. I can't blame them, and I won't kill them."

"Then what use are you?"

"Enough," Mimiteh broke in. "Chieftain, either come in or go away. It's a long story, and I don't intend to tell it now, so you'll have to have faith in me. You know the *kura* have always deserved your trust."

"Until Nata," Suwak snapped.

The priestess flinched at that, but her eyes remained steady. "He paid for that, and the price was no more than he earned. Now. We're leaving Chakanay as soon as Ilari gets back, so I suggest we go together."

"He isn't coming back," Amaru said. Her voice was a bare whisper, but it silenced the room. She watched Tumay across the table, her face expressionless. "He's dead, isn't he?"

"Child," Tumay said, and stopped. He looked at the floor.

"I think I knew," Amaru said, still in the same soft voice. "I knew before he left last night. Part of him wanted to die, I think."

"Oh, girl, no –"

"Part of him did. He couldn't see how to live without Mother," she added matter-of-factly. Her voice trembled for the first time. "That's why I told Salali he had to let Daddy fight. He needed to do something. He couldn't have lived with himself if he hadn't."

"Salali," Tumay began. He broke off again. Shook his head. He didn't really know how to deal with this girl-woman, half child and half adult, with all the maturity and understanding that brought. "Salali is dead as well. They were both lost in the Qapac's house in the Precinct, when they led an assault over the wall. Suwak and I were there. They were heroes, Amaru."

"I know they were," the little girl said.

"We nearly won," Suwak said. He came fully into the room at last, his fists clenched at his sides. "We *would* have won, if the sorcerer hadn't come back. We only needed a little while longer."

Kisain's face paled. "Terzian's back?"

"He threw some sort of firefly and a thousand men were burned to death," Tumay said. "I can promise you, he's back."

"Then we have to leave right now," Mimiteh said. She took Amaru's hand. "And we have to move quickly."

"I don't think I can," Kisain said.

"Then we'll leave you for the vultures," Suwak snarled. "I don't want you along anyway. Your presence disgusts me!"

Mimiteh laughed. "I saw you limping when you came in. How fast can you go?"

"I am Eagle. Pain doesn't stop me.'""

"Chieftain," Amaru said. She still hadn't spoken above a murmur, but he turned to her anyway. "I've accepted Kisain into my father's home. I think you might accept him as well, don't you?"

Suwak stared at her with an expression Tumay had seen many times before, when adults spoke with Amaru. *Half child and half woman,* Tumay thought wearily. People found it hard to reconcile the pretty little girl with the adult words coming out of her mouth. Suwak frowned, started to speak, and then folded his arms and glared at her. Obviously he couldn't decide how to treat her, so he settled for the most dignified silence he could manage.

"Good," Amaru said, as though Suwak had agreed with her. She turned to Kisain. "You're much taller than my father, but I think his clothes will serve you better than your uniform. As long as you wear that, your people will recognise you from a mile away, and come for you."

"My former people," he said. Brightness shone in Mimiteh's face at the words, a light of love clear enough to hurt. Suwak snorted, but under his breath, and he darted a glance at Amaru as he did so.

"Mimiteh knows which room is Daddy's," Amaru said.

The priestess went to Kisain and helped him out of his chair. He stood slowly and with awkward care, trying to keep his right foot off the ground, and muttered in his own language as she helped him towards the corridor. Tumay thought the words were oaths, by their tone. Amaru rose too, going to the cupboards to begin collecting food. Her movements were stiff and precise, unnaturally so, but Tumay could think of nothing to say.

"We're going to be butchered," Suwak said once Mimiteh and the soldier were out of earshot. "If the Thrain catch us we're dead, and with him along, our own warriors might chop us apart."

Tumay shook his head. "I doubt it. That would be murder, and we're better than that." He rubbed his face. If he got out of this alive he was going to sleep for a week. "And there's a need for love, on a day like this."

Salali's words, more or less, from early in the night. They had struck him as important then, a reminder of a time when life had been normal, and love could bloom without fear of death. Perhaps a promise as well, of a time when that would be true again. It was hard to imagine.

Love was the greatest of Quilla's gifts to mortals. The *kura* said it survived even death, so shades walking in Supay's Halls could remember a little of who they had been, in the passion of life.

"He'll slow us down," Suwak muttered. "We'll be caught."

"I couldn't go much faster than him anyway," Tumay said. He rested his head on his folded arms. "And right now, I'm too tired to care."

*

The rain was back.

It fell as drizzle, so fine it was more like mist than rain. But it was enough to wet skin and clothing, and soon to plaster Tumay's crested hair to his scalp. He's borrowed a poncho from Amaru and wrapped it around himself, knowing it wouldn't do much good. It had been her father's, though. He would not throw it away.

They were an odd little band. An injured chieftain, and an ex-warrior running to fat with his head newly shaved. A half-blind child, a priestess, and a Thrain who could only walk with Mimiteh wedged under his right shoulder to keep his weight off that side. Rain darkened Kisain's hair, and in a striped poncho he looked almost like a native, at least from a distance. Tumay hoped nobody would come close enough to learn better.

Small chance of that.

The streets were no longer empty. Trickles of people flowed through the rubble and the dead, staying as close to the buildings as they could, ready to duck out of sight. All the walkers headed the same way. The people of Chakanay were leaving, before the Thrain emerged again to wreak whatever vengeance they would wreak. Ayllu was still fresh in the memory, where the Thrain had burned the innocent to leave them bodiless and mute in the afterlife.

"We must go faster," Tumay said.

Mimiteh didn't bother to look at him. It was Amaru who nodded. "Go then, innkeeper. Don't wait for us."

"You should come with me."

"We'll catch you up," she said.

Tumay ground his teeth. She was like an itch under his skin, this strange orphan girl with the violet eye. But he waited while Kisain rested, and admitted to himself that Suwak needed the pause nearly as much. The chief sat hunched on a low wall, head down and hand pressed against the bedsheet wrapped around his middle as a bandage. He didn't look as though he'd last much longer, but then again, Eagle were tough.

87

He might need to be. A knot of warriors saw them and one strode over, a man whose face was mostly one livid bruise. Kisain came to a halt, turning his body towards the man as though sensing a threat.

"Amaru," the warrior said. He was a Puma, all muscle and power. "May we join you?"

Tumay blinked.

"Of course, Khuno," the girl said. "Though you should know, we have a Thrain with us. He's on our side now."

It was the big man's turn to blink. "Strange times we live in. You trust him?"

"I wouldn't walk with him otherwise."

"Well, we've learned to trust your judgement," Khuno said. "There are six men with me. All of us together are safer than the five of you alone. Where are we going?"

"Out of town. To Chimalli's camp, if we can."

"As good a plan as any. Lead on, *hamawt'a.*"

Tumay frowned in the rain as they started off again. *Hamawt'a* was the name for a community leader, a person of wisdom, usually a man. Always an adult, as far as he knew, yet the Puma had given the name to Amaru and she accepted it as though from habit. Tumay wondered how that had happened. She must have impressed a lot of warriors since the Thrain had come. Well, he ought to have expected that. Amaru impressed everyone.

And unsettled them, too.

So the band grew to eleven, then to fifteen. The trickle of refugees had thickened to a stream by then. Near the edge of Chakanay Tumay threw his axe and killed a dog that was sniffing at corpses. Next thing it would have begun to nibble, and from there it would have been too feral to trust again. He picked up the body and gave it to one of the women. "For supper tonight."

"You want us to eat a scavenging dog?"

He gestured at the clots of people heading out of town. "I want us to eat. How much food do you think this lot will leave?"

She scowled at him, but she slung the dead animal over her shoulders with the legs hanging down. It would bleed on her poncho, but the rain would wash it clean at the same time anyway. Sunlight threw the woman's cheekbones into relief as she turned away.

Except the sky was solid clouds, and the sun lost above them. Tumay turned to look back at Chakanay and saw flames there.

14

A gesture from Terzian had been enough to extinguish the flames in the Qapac's old quarters. Heat still lurked below the surface though, smouldering into little fires that broke out here and there on cloth or through cracks in stone. Men worked with buckets to douse it. Smoke still curled out of corners though, no matter how much water was thrown down.

That wasn't the worst.

Bodies sprawled in corridors and made grotesque carpets in some of the rooms, jammed from wall to wall. Bodies and bits of them, overlaid with spatters of blood and flesh. Soldiers never quite grew accustomed to such sights, no matter what they might say. Gavair knew he never had, and he'd seen the aftermath of two dozen major battles and countless skirmishes since he signed up, over thirty years before. You knew, looking at the split skulls and chunks of brain, the severed limbs and blood, that it could very easily have been you. Next time it might be, and your friends would have to carry your corpse out to the pyre and try not to let your gizzards fall out of the holes.

Then there was the stench. Gavair stopped to smear a thick layer of honey under his nose. It didn't quite hide the stink, but it did mute it, at least a little. Until he reached the laundry room.

A soldier leaned on the doorjamb with his back to the carnage, swallowing over and over. His face was white and taut, as though the skin had been stretched and was about to tear open. Smoke trickled out of the room, above his head. Gavair patted him on the shoulder as he went inside.

It was hard to tell how many bodies there were. A layer of black soot coated every surface of the room and ran in thick swirls across the ceiling. A heap of corpses mounded up below the high window, where men had struggled to get out as the fire spread. The door must have been blocked, or cut off by the flames. Thrain and Ashir were tangled in that pile, distinguishable only by their size. Clothes and flesh had melted and run in the heat, leaving bodies too burned for recognition. Men who had been fighting must have abandoned their battle to scramble for the window, only to struggle again as they jostled to escape, clawing at each other in desperation and then agony. Nobody had made it. The window glass was still intact, somehow. Funny how fire could rage across a room and leave one corner untouched.

There was no point trying to identify the dead here. Gavair walked back into the corridor, where the soldier clung to the doorway and tried not to throw up.

"What's your name, armsman?"

"Berain." The soldier gulped and managed something close to a salute. "Berain, sir. Third Company."

"Where were you when this began?"

"On – on the tower, sir."

"Lucky for you," Gavair said. Hardly a man from the patrols that had been out when the uprising began had made it back alive. Dead men littered the streets of Chakanay, more Ashir than Thrain, but there were more than enough of the latter. Far too many of them, in truth.

There had never been enough soldiers. It was easy to see, now. For all the months of planning, all the careful questioning of merchants and travellers with their stories of a fabulous land in the south, Terzian had never understood the size of the task he'd set himself. The merchants simply hadn't known enough. They'd heard rumours and whispers, all second or third hand. Snippets heard from traders or tribesmen in far-off ports, men who wore bones in their noses and couldn't wait to cheat you. The stories had seemed to add up. Terzian had heard the same claims over and again, and he'd believed that consistency made them likely to be true.

But the merchants had been telling the stories they heard from each other. The tales were similar because they were the same tale, told by a different mouth. Another thing that was easy to see now, when it was too late. None of those traders had seen the Blessed Land for themselves. Or if they had, they'd only come as far as the coastal towns, perched on the shore with the desert behind them. Nobody had gone deeper, into the wide plains and bands of mountain, or the high plateaux. Nobody had known how *huge* Apusuyu was.

Terzian had come prepared to conquer a little land of fishermen and villagers. It was a misjudgement. The Blessed Land was too big, too populous, and too strange to be easy prey. The army had begun to realise that on the march south, through a land which seemed never to end, towards a capital city that never seemed to come any nearer. With every mile they put behind them they felt a little smaller, a little more lost, like men swallowed into the belly of an enormous whale.

Misconceptions, he thought, letting his mind wander. They understood so little of this land, and the people they came to rule. The Ashir were peculiar in ways that had never occurred to Gavair, or to anyone else. How could a whole culture place no value on gold, except as decoration? How could they build such a sprawling empire without iron or writing, or even pack animals, and cover it with roads and monumental buildings? How could they maintain it, when they actually *elected* a new Qapac when the old one died? None of the Thrain had even considered such questions. They knew the Ashir had no writing, no iron, and assumed they must therefore be primitive. The truth was they were not.

Terzian's original plan was to capture the Ashir king, kill his sons – if any – and marry his eldest daughter to Ramian, tying the invaders into the Ashir royal line. Later she could be made to convert to the One God, which would encourage others in the nobility to follow suit, and then the peasants. With that would come control, in the end. By the time Terzian died, leaving the Thrain without the power of his magic, the control would be enough.

But it turned out there was no Ashir royal line, and the plan collapsed. If Ramian wed a noble's daughter the Ashir would simply choose another patrician to be Qapac, negating the whole point of the marriage. That had been the second setback, after the sheer size of the country. It was a minor one compared to the catastrophes of the past three days, but the early problems were always important. Later misfortunes tended to stem from small beginnings.

"I understand you spoke with Captain Kisain before he went on patrol," he said. It was time to stop maundering and deal with what he could.

Berain nodded. "Yes, sir. He came up to wait for the other squad to return."

"What did he talk about?"

"The weather mostly, sir." Berain's brow creased. "And Morind Gap, too. We were both there. He remembered me from the battle."

Morind Gap. That had been a disaster in its own right, and part of a wider nightmare of misjudgements and bad planning. Gavair had been fortunate to miss it. He believed, privately, that while the soldiers of the Thrain armies were the finest in the world, their leaders were usually idiots. It was astonishing how often brave and skilful men were sent to their deaths because someone hadn't bothered to make basic preparations.

Gavair pursed his lips, trying once more to banish such pointless thoughts. "Kisain said nothing else?"

The soldier hesitated. "Well, sir, he said our best chance of living through this was to stay loyal to Lord Terzian. I'd heard rumours that Ramian was dead, sir, you see. Some of the others…" He licked his lips, seeming more nervous now than nauseous. "Some of the lads were talking about heading home, sir, begging your pardon. They're not sure about staying any longer."

Well, that was inevitable, Gavair supposed. "What are you sure of, armsman Berain?"

"I'm sure Kisain's in trouble for something," Berain said. "And I'm sure he didn't tell me what it was, sir. Not a word."

"That's a very good thing to be sure of," Gavair said dryly. "And the rest of it? Do you want to turn for home?"

"If I thought I had a chance of making it back, I'd be gone already." Berain met Gavair's gaze levelly. "But I wouldn't make ten miles. I'm staying, sir, just the way I did at the Gap."

The man was probably too honest for his own good, but he was clever as well. "You hold on to that thought, armsman. Hold on tight to it. Now get this room cleared out. Tell an officer I want a full squad on this duty, and I want all the dead buried by sundown."

"Sir? What's Captain Kisain done?"

Gavair looked at him. "By sundown, armsman. Carry on."

He turned back down the corridor, picking his way between bodies and pools of sticky blood. Berain would find out about Kisain soon enough – soldiers were worse than sailors for gossip and rumour, and far worse than whores – but there was no reason to let him know beforehand.

Desertion. There could be no doubt of it, given what the soldiers who had returned to tell of it said. Gavair wouldn't have believed it, and certainly not of a man who had fought at Morind Gap. And done for love, of all things, like a star-

91

crossed hero in the romantic plays that had women in Thrasin swooning all through theatre season.

In a way, the whole invasion was in the name of love, and for its memory. Terzian had lived through the death of his wife and was determined not to do the same over his son, regardless of what he needed to do to prevent it. Had been determined, anyway. Ramian was dead, left on the floor of a tunnel with his eyes and tongue gone, and his innards slopping over the cold stone. Only Terzian had actually seen that, thankfully. The sorcerer had pulled the tunnel down to make a tomb for his son before the cavalry caught up with him.

"I couldn't reach him in time," Terzian said as Gavair rode up. The rest of the men waited a hundred yards down the broken road, allowing them privacy. Half the mountainside was gone, tumbled into the gorge below. "I tried, Marshal. Oh, I tried. I filled my horse with magic and ran it here at a gallop. It keeled over as soon as I dismounted." He gestured to where the animal lay. "But I felt my son die. I was still an hour away when I felt him die. A father should be there when his son needs him, don't you think?"

"Of course he should," Gavair said through bloodless lips. "You were, my lord. Always."

"I wasn't here, when he needed me."

"Sometimes," he said, wondering if he would die for these words, "the hardest thing a father can give his son is freedom."

"I am going to kill the kamachi," Terzian said. His voice was calm, almost detached, and yet in his tone dreams froze and stars died. He got up and went back down the road without another word.

In that mood Terzian was lethal, apt to kill without thought, and Gavair left him alone on the ride back to Chakanay. He had been a loyal retainer all his life, and remained one still, as his father and grandfather had been before him. None of that made him stupid.

His duties meant he had to speak with Terzian now, and Gavair found his lord waiting in the Qapac's building, among the spilled lives and the burning. There was still smoke in the air, and the smell of the last fires smouldering in tiny pockets, but that suited Terzian just now. Gavair went up the stairs, careful not to slip in the blood.

He knew too many of the dead. A captain from Thrasin itself, born almost under the shadow of the Royal Walls, lay with one hand clamped around what remained of the other. Both were drenched in his blood. In the corridor a soldier named Orain, from the slumdog streets of the eastern ports, slumped against a wall with the top of his head caved in and one eye grotesquely misshaped. Gavair knew without checking that the last letter from his betrothed was folded in his pocket. An under-officer sprawled on his stomach with his head twisted around so he stared at the ceiling, a surprised frown still fixed on his features. He had always enjoyed an illicit game of dice in a back room, sometimes even when he was meant to be on duty. He'd have been a full officer years ago if not for that, and might have avoided this butchery.

Gavair let his eyes rove over the dead, but he refused to allow his mind to truly see them, and certainly refused to think of them. If you did not see them, or acknowledge them, you could not grieve. It was a poor epitaph for the fallen, but the only one a soldier could allow himself, if he wanted to hold on to sanity. Once you saw the fallen, really saw them, you would imagine your own face on each of the dead and terror would freeze you forever.

Too many boneyards, he thought as he stepped around the bodies. There had been far too many, spread over too long a time. Gavair had already known that, actually, back home. He was forty-nine, iron-grey at the temples, but not quite so steely in his heart as before. Those slaughterhouses caught up with a man, in the end. Only his loyalty to Terzian had persuaded him to forego a deserved retirement, fishing from the gnarled banks of the river and brewing cider in the old milking shed. He'd never liked cattle, even as a boy in the country. An apple orchard was easier to manage, and he much preferred the smell.

Well, done was done. He was here now, in this strange and fantastic land where feathered warriors danced and even servants wore jewels on their fingers, and the only way he was likely to get out was by sticking close to Terzian. The banks of that river had never seemed so far away.

He heard voices a moment before he stepped into a large, squarish room, with long high windows running down one side. Bodies were everywhere, two deep in many places, scattered amidst broken furniture and discarded weapons. In the middle was a heavy table, one end collapsed and the oak broken and pitted all along its length. The copper stink of blood was sharp in the air.

He knew this room. But the complex mosaic on the floor was hidden under bodies and blood. Like all Ashir art it was abstract, made up of swirls and spirals. Gavair couldn't remember the details, now.

"– can find them, the rebellion will collapse," Draivan was saying as the Marshal stepped through the doorway. The chaplain's brown coat was ripped and stained with blood, but he didn't have any obvious injuries. "I'm sure of it, my lord. Find those two men."

Terzian stood in the middle of the room, hands clasped behind his back and facing away from Gavair. He looked neat and calm as far as Gavair could see, as though he was waiting to enter church in the morning, not up to his knees in dead men. A leader had to appear cool under stress, of course, but Gavair's scalp prickled. He halted a pace inside the door, not sure why he'd done so.

"Marshal," Terzian said without looking around, and Gavair jumped. "I'm glad you could join us. What is our situation?"

Well, that was clear enough. Gavair started forward again, deliberately not looking at Draivan. The priest made his knuckles twitch. Sometimes there was a brightness behind Draivan's eyes that made Terzian's silver irises seem comfortingly familiar. "Not very good, my lord, I'm afraid. I don't have an exact count yet, but it looks like we lost around half our force last night."

"Half," Terzian said. His voice was very soft.

"Yes, my lord. We have something less than two and a half thousand men remaining, and one in three of those is wounded. Many seriously. We'll need at least a week before we can move from here." He came to a stop again, not far from the battered table. Terzian had still not turned to face him. "Some men holed up in cellars and have made their way back from the town. A few more might do so."

"But only a few."

"Yes, my lord." He was aware of his heart thudding. "If we had been an hour later reaching Chakanay, there might have been no garrison here to meet us at all. Perhaps just half an hour later."

"Or less," Draivan put in. He fingered the rip in his coat. "I had to fight for my life right next to your men, Marshal."

"Most admirable," Gavair murmured. He forbore to wonder whether it was the first time the priest had ever fought. Aloud, anyway.

"Draivan tells me the uprising had two leaders. Or so our captives say." Terzian pushed a dead man's head back with the toe of his boot, studied the pallid features, and then let it fall. "Some see me and start babbling their secrets. The chiefs were a warrior named Chimalli, and Salali."

"That's what I've heard as well," Gavair admitted. He had to stop to moisten his lips. "My lord… I know how Salali escaped from the Precinct, the first night we were here."

"Oh?" The sorcerer turned to him for the first time. His face was shockingly white, almost bloodless, and his silver-black eyes gleamed in that pallor like polished stones. "Do tell."

"The priestess smuggled him out. Mimiteh. I assume she's been passing information to Salali ever since."

"I would suspect that's true," Terzian agreed. Suddenly his voice was almost jaunty. "She spent a good deal of time with Captain Kisain, if I recall. We should have been more careful."

Gavair swallowed. This was ridiculous; he *never* waffled around when there were plain words to be spoken. He made an effort to firm his voice. "There's more, my lord. Four of Kisain's patrol survived the night and made it back to the Precinct after we arrived. It seems their lives were saved by this Mimiteh. After which, Captain Kisain abandoned his oaths and went with her."

"He deserted?"

"Yes, my lord. He did."

"And that is how you know it was Mimiteh who smuggled Salali out," Terzian observed. He pursed his lips. "Well, well. How very unexpected. She was rather plain, I thought."

Gavair shifted his feet. He'd expected a verbal lashing at the very least for bringing that news, and he was hardly unhappy to be wrong, but Terzian's mood was beginning to unsettle him. There was something brittle about the sorcerer, an air of icy splinters that flashed in the light, ready to cut. He opened his mouth and then closed it again.

94

"And now?" Draivan apparently had no such compunctions. "What do we do now?"

"We find the *kamachi* and kill him," Terzian said. "These other men are not important. I want Kai."

We don't know where he is, and this is a large land. Words best left unspoken, for now. Perhaps for ever. Terzian's silver eyes flashed to Gavair as though he'd heard the thought though, and his white lips stretched in a smile. It was grotesque. Gavair shivered.

"Nothing else matters," Terzian said. "Nothing. I want Kai found, and I think I know —"

"The Church matters," the chaplain broke in bluntly, "and you should not forget it."

15

Gavair stared at the priest.

Draivan must have a death wish. Before today Gavair would have said the cleric was a coward, too afraid to fight with the men. But he'd done so, and now defied Terzian with the sorcerer in this black mood. That went a long way beyond brave. Utter stupidity described it better.

Terzian's lips thinned until they were barely visible. His hands behind his back clenched once, then relaxed. "Does it?"

Draivan smiled tolerantly, a father indulging a child's careless word. "You don't mean that. Of course the Church matters, in the name of the God it serves. We came to spread the Word of the Lord here."

Gavair wished he could find an excuse to leave. He wished he dared speak.

"You may have come for that," Terzian said at last, his tone silk over steel. "I came for other reasons."

"You thought you did," Draivan said. "Perhaps your own goal was even part of it. But God works through us all, my lord, and the Redeemer He sent to save us. All things serve the One. And the Church deals with affairs beyond the realm of the mundane, my lord. Our concern is with eternity, not the transient concerns of the moment."

"My son's death is not *mundane.*"

"But it is transient," Draivan said. "Faith is not. "I was sent to bring God to these heathens, and with Heaven's blessing, that I will do."

"Then that you may do," Terzian said. A muscle jumped in his cheek, stilled, then twitched again. "As best you can, cleric. But I go to kill the *kamachi*, and my soldiers go with me."

Again Draivan smiled. "I will have to inform the Basilica. I doubt they will be pleased."

"They can scream themselves into fits for all of me," Terzian said. His tone was still calm, but ice crept across the words like frost on a window. The muscle in his cheek jumped again, and a tic twitched below one eye. "Nothing matters but the man who murdered my son. Nothing at all, in this world or the next. Are you insane that you don't understand that? That you taunt me?"

"Taunt you?" Draivan shook his head. "No, my lord. But there are greater things than our lives on this world. And as for the rest, what have I to fear? I am armed and armoured in the Lord." He bowed slightly. "With your permission, I will leave you now. I have a letter to write."

He turned and walked away. Terzian actually took a step after him, hands trembling as he raised them as though to throttle the priest from across the room.

For a moment Gavair was quite sure Draivan was about to die. He had never seen Terzian lose control that way before. The man was almost as disciplined as a soldier. Then Terzian stopped, and his hands came down again as he mastered himself. Draivan reached the door and was gone.

Gavair let out a breath. He had no idea which of these two men was closest to insanity right now, but he didn't think there was much difference.

"And you, Marshal?" Terzian kept his back to him. "Have you turned against me now as well?"

"No, my lord." His mouth was very dry. Gavair wished suddenly that he had retired after all, and was sitting now on the bank of a river with his feet trailing in the water, and his rod lying idle in the grass. Anything to not be here, with this suddenly unpredictable man. "My family has served yours for three generations. Nothing has changed."

"Thank you," Terzian said softly. "Thank you, Marshal. Of course, I have a problem now."

"My lord?"

"This Kai hides in the wilds," Terzian said. "And in this vast country there are a lot of wilds. We could have a hundred thousand soldiers here and still never track him down, if he wanted to stay hidden. Instead we have barely two thousand. There is only one way we can find him."

"Make him find us," Gavair suggested. It didn't take a great leap of imagination, to be fair.

"Exactly," the sorcerer said softly. "And I believe I have thought of a way. But I will need your help."

"Whatever I can do, my lord."

"Find out where he was when we arrived," Terzian said. "The sanctuary, in the mountains somewhere east of here. Find it. The *kamachi* likes to winter there, and from what I have heard, it is a place of great religious importance. He won't let it be destroyed."

That made sense. Gavair was tired of waiting for Kai to appear, tired of chasing up and down mountains and wondering where he was, or when he would strike. It was time to bring the enemy to them for a change, as a good commander should. "Will he believe you'd destroy it?"

"I'm going to make sure of it," Terzian said. He strode to the windows, and at a gesture the glass shattered and blew out. Cool morning air rushed into the room, sweeping away the sour miasma of death. Gavair followed after his lord, mostly so he could enjoy that fresh air. "The Ashir tried to start a burning here, Marshal. I'm going to show them what burning is."

He stretched out his hands, and in the room behind them something bloody opened its eyes.

*

The pain was gone, surprisingly. Sala didn't understand that. In its place had come a sort of lethargic lightness, seeping through every muscle and turning it to clouds and feathers. He supposed this must be how death felt, and it wasn't so bad. When he opened his eyes there would be nothing to see but half-glimpsed

97

forms, shadows drifting through the gloom of Supay's Halls, and perhaps now and then a distant shimmer that might be sunlight.

Still, it wasn't so terrible. In a way it was even quite pleasant, which he hadn't expected at all. He could deal with this, even for eternity, as long as the pain didn't come back. That had been very bad. Who would have thought there could be so much pain in one body?

Then something flashed beyond his eyelids, followed almost at once by the roar of tumbling masonry, and Sala's eyes slid open.

He couldn't see very well. His left eye wouldn't open all the way, stuck by blood most likely, and he lay at a lopsided angle where he had fallen across toppled bodies. Something thick was lodged in his throat as well. But he could see, in a hazy red-blurred sort of way, and the sun was shining on him. Inti had given him a last glimpse of the dawn before he went –

That wasn't the sun. That was flame. Sala lifted a hand to rub at his eye, the fingers floating through air much thicker than it ought to be, and looked again. He was staring out of the window of the room where he'd fallen, across the plaza into a blazing mass that had once been houses. Two figures were limned against the inferno, one with an arm raised to shield his face, the other with both hands thrust out before him. They came into focus and then became blobs again, dark shapes against the fires, but Sala knew.

The sorcerer. Ten feet in front of him. Hardly further than Sala's feet, really. With his back turned.

His lips skinned back from his teeth.

This man was the reason Sala lay here, in all this blood, a marinade of his own torn flesh. The reason he was dying. He thought of what he'd said to the warriors before the attack: *what will the pretty girls say when they hear about this?* Sala felt a stab of loss, surprisingly bitter, at the thought of all the pretty girls who would never smile at him, or let him dance with them. He liked to drink *aqha* from little pottery cups. Sweet-talk a woman into walking to the barn for stolen kisses, and maybe more. All gone now.

This man's fault.

Not taking his gaze from the two Thrain, Sala reached out a careful hand and felt around the dead men beside him. Once his fingers delved into something sticky and soft, but then they closed on the hilt of a sword. It was broken, the blade ending in a splinter of steel after just a foot, but it would do.

This was going to hurt. He didn't dare close his eyes, but he sent a quick prayer out to Inti or Quilla or any other god who might be listening, even Tezcata himself; *spare me the worst of the pain.* He wrapped his left arm around the hole in his middle. Bits of him would fall out if he wasn't careful. Slowly, so delicately, he put the shattered point of the sword against the floor and used it as a lever, pushing himself to one knee. Something in his stomach slithered sideways and his mouth gaped in silent pain. He would have shrieked, had there been air in him.

Another building roared. Light washed across the room as stonework cracked and tumbled.

His vision cleared again. He didn't think it would get any clearer. Sala got to his feet. The effort left him swaying and he had to lean back against the remnants of the table, fighting to straighten up with stomach muscles that had been sliced in two. After a moment a lance of red agony shot through his abdomen and hunched him forward. A hiss of air escaped through his teeth, and he thought he'd bitten off the end of his tongue trying to hold it back. He couldn't feel it though, a minor mercy. Maybe one of the gods had heard his prayer. Quilla, he hoped.

Blood ran down the back of his throat, but the men by the window didn't turn. There was too much noise for them to hear him gasp.

Sala took a step forward. His eyes were fixed on the sorcerer's back, as though held there by invisible pins. Something like a fat worm slithered over the hand at his middle and hung there. A second step. The sorcerer was three yards away, no more than that.

His heel slithered in blood, and Sala was falling. There was no chance to save himself, no way his poor mistreated body could stop the slide. The sword slipped from his hand. He watched it fall, knowing the rattle as it landed would give him away. He fell too, though oddly slowly, and then he was down, with his cheek cushioned on something soft. His eyes were still open, for what good that did. All he could see was a haze.

In it something moved.

It resolved into a figure, taller than anyone he had ever seen, more slender than an old man's hope. His fading sight couldn't make out the face, but the figure was wrapped in shrouds, and that named him. Sala felt his lips curve in a smile.

"Oh, Supay," he whispered, and the figure took him in its arms.

*

"Dead," Gavair said. He let the man's head fall back. "He should have been dead already, with that tear in him."

Terzian stared at the body for a long moment. If the shock of finding an armed man collapsing behind them had rattled him, the sorcerer gave no sign of it. He simply stared, his silver eyes unreadable.

"That's Salali," he said at last.

"Is it?" Gavair studied the dead man. Through all the blood it was hard to tell. The man wore his hair in a crest, which Salali never had. And for some reason he'd died smiling, which did at least seem apt for Salali. "He wasn't a warrior. Or was he, and we never knew?"

"He wasn't a warrior," Terzian agreed. "Until tonight. That's why he cut his hair. I wonder if all the Ashir men will become warriors, to fight us?"

That was a chilling thought. Gavair glanced up at his lord, wondering if he was serious, but Terzian's expression was as lifeless as those of the corpses.

A moment later Gavair jumped backwards, his boots slithering, as Salali's body twitched. *Still alive* was his first thought, incredible though that might be. Then there was a blast of heat and Gavair threw up a hand to shield his eyes. Through his fingers he saw Salali's flesh blacken and peel away like old skin, only for the flakes to then shrivel to nothing. There was a glimpse of skull and bones and then they crumbled. For an instant ash and dust remained and then it was burned away.

Gavair swallowed, trying not to vomit.

"Let him spend eternity with no voice," the sorcerer said softly, "if that is what they believe. And no body. Let him howl unheard, while I burn his world." He turned back to the windows. "He will have company soon enough."

He stretched out his hands, and power crackled between them.

16

They found the horse near the bottom of broken scree, screaming and trying to stand on a shattered foreleg.

"Threw a shoe," Evain said, after he put an arrow in its throat. "Then panicked, and ran."

He saw their quizzical looks. "Horses wear iron shoes on their hooves. No, really. See for yourself." He lifted the dead animal's maimed leg, showing them the hard hoof, then did the same with the other leg. That one bore a curved band or iron. "The horse lost a shoe on those rocks. He was already short of air and close to panic. This pushed him over the edge."

Well, they were all short of air.

Nobody had run after the horse. They all felt the same way Chinita did, as though cords had been wrapped around their chests and tightened, then tightened again. The trail behind them – where there was a trail – was strewn with Thrain and Ashir sitting on rocks, grey-faced and trembling. The pass at Apachita was *high*.

They'd hit the first patch of snow when the summit was still a notch in the mountains above them. It was ankle deep, melting into rivulets that ran away down the stones. Half a mile further they hit a deeper drift, and then the trail was swallowed by ice that took an hour to cross. Winter was stubborn here, clinging on while spring flowed over the lowlands. There might even be more snowfalls in the nights.

If the travellers were still this high when darkness fell, they'd die. All of them. Chinita didn't need to be told that.

Just below the pass someone fell. A warrior, still wearing no fleece over his leather vest. Chinita could see the blue tattoos of the Eagle society as he scrabbled for a handhold. He was called Hanapo, Hapan, something like that. She'd talked to him once.

Mamani threw himself down, sliding on his belly to grasp Hanapo's hand. An outlaw, risking himself to save a warrior. Their fingers brushed and then Hanapo was gone, over the edge of the cliff and all the way down. The walkers all stopped, staring at the place where he fell.

"Eagles are… clumsy," Taruka said at last. "Need Deer… for this kind… of thing."

They moved on. The horses were struggling worst of all now. Their Thrain handlers moved them a little way and let them rest, whispering in their ears, then moved them a little more. Then they reached the pass, a narrow slash in the mountain piled with packed snow, and movement all but stopped. Men moved back and forth cutting the ice with their axes, breaking it up enough for hooves and shoes to grip. They got the horses across then, between lots of slips and pauses. On the other side Kai was waiting for them.

"Don't lie down," he said, just as the first men had begun to do just that. "Don't even sit down. It will be like dancing with the Blind God when you try to get up again. Now listen."

He pointed down the trail ahead, what there was of it. A track that appeared and vanished again, even without the spills of snow that sometimes lapped across it. "That's the way to Kuska. And we have to be there before sundown or we'll die. The night time winds on this mountain can freeze llamas in an hour. You won't last half as long.

"And noon is long past." He indicated the sun, a high brightness which gave no heat. Not this high. "I know you hurt. You throats burn and your chests are wrapped in stone. But I will not let anyone die here, so get up and get moving. One last effort, and you can rest."

The men who'd laid down got up again.

*

They had their first view of Kuska late in the afternoon, with mountain shadows already stretching across the valley.

The temple was tiny with distance, and still far below where the band had paused. It was more like a village than a place of worship, though built as a single structure. Interlinked buildings climbed the gentle slope of the valley in a series of steps, each storey a little higher than the one below. They were divided by walled gardens, in some of which trees grew. Fields spread out around it all, some ploughed, some home to animals like specks of colour.

"It doesn't look much like a temple," Chinita said.

"It's not," Kai told her. "Not the way you mean, at least. People pray, but the men here are already *kura,* and they talk to the gods all the time. They don't need the usual rituals."

Chinita was weary beyond words, but she wasn't too tired to miss the implication of *that.* "Just men?"

"All the *kamachi* have been men," Achachi said. "Ninety-nine of them. Some of the senior priests say if that's how Viraca wanted it, then we should follow his example."

Izel had come to join them, pale with fatigue. Or with anger. "So women are pushed out again."

"Not all the way," Kai said. "Women can be *kura.* Besides, you have your women's warrior society. Would you have me change the whole world in a day?"

"Much of it," Izel said.

Achachi laughed, the rasp of a throat coarsened by thin air. "There are thirty priests here. That's all, girl. And even the *kura* of the towns don't know what happens at Kuska. This is an exception, not the rule." He caught Kai's eye. "If the stories are true, that is."

102

"Not many of the stories seem to be true," Catori noted. He had stayed close to the front of the straggling line of men and horses all day, as far from Suchi as he could get. "Not any more."

"Don't you think so?" Kai asked. One hand had strayed inside his coat, where the *cizin* nestled against his chest. That happened a lot now, and it worried Chinita. "It seems to me they're as true as they ever were. For we Ashir, at least. I couldn't really say what might be true in the Thrain lands."

Catori frowned at him. "But that's the point. The Thrain exist, so the old stories can't be true. Apusuyu is not the whole world."

"And the Thrain have iron," Achachi wheezed.

"So? We learned a few stories the wrong way. Maybe we misunderstood, or the legend changed over time. Or perhaps somewhere a priest changed it, deliberately or by accident. It doesn't mean Viraca lied to our forefathers, or that he loved us any less." He shrugged. "I'm still here."

He moved away, further back along the line to share a word or two with others in the little band. Just by being there he lifted spirits. Watching him, Chinita saw that he was limping a little after all, and there was a split running out from under the sole of his right boot. It didn't seem to bother him.

I'm still here.

"You know," Catori said after a moment, "the gods and all the little spirits know, I'm glad that man's with us."

"Then do what he wants you to do," Achachi croaked, "and get down this cursed mountain before dusk."

They did get down, reaching the valley floor with startling suddenness just as the sun touched the western peaks. The ground went from steep to flat between two steps. Chinita's knees groaned. She wanted to sink to the grass and wouldn't let herself. Kai was off to her right, helping Thrain and Ashir who had collapsed back to their feet. Shafts of sun came between two mountains to light him in gold. Gods alive, he was beautiful.

Still, if he came to her blankets at dusk and offered her a night of love like Quilla and Inti themselves, she would tell him to amuse himself with the llamas and leave her to sleep.

Sleep. Oh, Quilla, she needed to lie down and sleep for two days, and not wake up unless the house was on fire.

"And this is the only way in or out of Kuska," she said. She looked back up the precipitous trail and winced as a muscle in her back creaked. "I'm surprised anyone ever bothers to come."

Catori grinned at her from a pale, drawn face. "I thought you fighting women said you were tough. Could run down mountain goats, and still have..." he paused to suck a lungful of air, "still have enough energy to carry them home. And likely cook them on a spit, besides."

"I thought you warriors said you were tough," she said. Her voice was hoarse and weak, the harsh crackle of an old woman. "Could chase down stags all day and fight a battle in the evening. And boast about it, besides."

He managed a wry smile, which she returned. The warriors were just like everyone else, really, once they forgot they hated you and gave you a chance to get to know them. Some were idiots of course, but most were decent enough. The same as any group, in any walk of life. They didn't look ready to fight a battle any more though. Three aged grandmothers with brooms could sweep the whole band away if they attacked now.

"Priest coming this way," Waki called. The stocky man had actually jumped on top of a rock to see better, as though he hadn't done enough clambering about for one day and more already. "He doesn't look happy, *kamachi*."

Kai grinned at him. "I suspect he looks ready to commit murder, in fact. Am I right?"

"Now you mention it, I believe he does." Waki looked down at him. "Is this a problem?"

"Not for you," Kai said. "I'm not letting some *kura* cause any problems at all for *my* band."

He went off to meet the priest, leaving the others to exchange weary grins. Ususi actually reached out to slap a warrior on the back, her bow lying forgotten on the ground. The warrior snorted but gave her a smile in return: *we're the* kamachi's *band*. Chinita could see a glimmer returning to eyes, a hint of colour to ashen cheeks. Two men who'd sat down despite Kai's instructions levered themselves to their feet again. The second of them coughed with a loose rattling from deep in his chest, and Chinita's smile faded. That was the red plague. Everyone knew the sound of it now, that racking noise that started down in the belly and worked upwards from there. She thought the coughing man knew it too, unless all the greyness of his face came from tiredness and thin air. The man who'd been coughing in Pujyu lay under a high mountain cairn now, but it seemed the disease wasn't finished with them yet.

Suchi walked unsteadily past her, heading towards Kai and the white-haired priest, fifty yards closer to the temple. For her to have arrived so quickly, she had to have been close enough to hear Kai dismiss priests as irrelevant. Chinita debated following her, and decided to rest her aching knees instead. A knot of blue-robed *kura* waited by the river, chattering in obvious excitement and often pointing to the band, as if to say *they're still here!*

Suchi was still short of the two men when Kai and the priest started back towards the warriors. When they reached her she spoke to the white-haired man, he gave a brief reply, and then all three came on until they reached the edge of the band. Everyone turned to face them. The priest, a bony-looking individual, glanced at Kai and coughed into his hand.

"It seems you need, humph, a place to rest," he said. "In the most sacred place in Apusuyu. Humph."

"It isn't the most sacred place," Kai reminded him in a serene voice. "The Retreat is. Kuska is merely holy."

"Holy. Yes. Of course." The priest coughed into his hand again. Coughing made Chinita nervous these days, but she thought in the old man's case it was

104

nothing more dangerous than a habit. "Well, it is most unusual. Most unusual. I never heard of such a thing before."

"And yet change is part of life," Kai said, still in that tranquil tone. "Only stone never changes."

The old priest looked at him from the corner of his eye. White eyebrows like hairy caterpillars twitched and wriggled. "We have known this since Viraca taught it to us."

"Indeed we have," Kai said.

"And yet you think I need reminding," the priest said testily. "Yes, well. Humph." He turned to the band. "I suppose I must welcome you, then. I am Paqu, the senior *kura* here. The Good Goddess knows where we'll find beds for so many, humph, but we'll do what we can."

"Thank you," Kai said. "We will need food as well, my friend. And fodder for the horses."

"Food, yes. And the… horses." Paqu stared for a moment, then gave himself a shake. "Horses. Are they, humph, real?"

"They are. A number of things are real," Kai said. "Including some that never used to be."

That made Catori grin. Kai cut his eyes towards him, but kept facing the temple and not Paqu, who was frowning at him. After a moment the old man muttered, caterpillar brows twitching. "Come on then. I'll show you where you can, humph, sleep for a while before suppertime. Um. Where do the… horses sleep? Do they sleep?"

"Evain will tell you what they need," Kai said. The big Thrain nodded and stepped forward, at which Paqu's eyes went wide and he trembled all over.

Stuttering and unsure he might be, and he certainly hated having such guests as these on his holy ground, but Paqu kept his word. After three hours of blissful sleep Chinita was woken by the smell of meat cooking, and stumbled into her clothes with the ragged end of a dream in her head. Something to do with Kai, and a stream, and moonlight. Never mind. Her stomach rumbled as she pulled on a coat.

She managed to stagger to the outdoor kitchen the priests had set up, roasting strips of llama meat, which they laid across thick slices of bread and then piled with chillies and beans. It was a simple enough meal, but Chinita wolfed her portion and went back for more, and then a third helping. Most of the band did the same, washing the food down with water fresh from the river that tasted of snow-covered slopes, and fizzed icily on the tongue. A simple meal indeed, but nothing had ever tasted better. Chinita went back to bed, wobbling on blistered feet but warm and full, and she fell instantly back into her dreams.

She woke not long after dawn, as she'd done for all her adult life, and limped down to the kitchen to see what she could scavenge. A young priest there gave her more meat and chilli and two peaches, both still damp with dew. He also gave her a long-lipped leer that made her think he'd been here at Kuska for far too long, and wasn't really suited to it.

Then she went looking for Kai. It was him she had dreamed of, after all. These days – these nights, she supposed – it was nearly always him. She found him on the far side of the river, standing alone in knee-high grass with his face turned towards the south.

17

Chinita started towards him. She was thirty yards away when someone spoke behind her.

"You're not for him," Suchi said, and Chinita jumped. She hadn't heard the smaller woman behind her. "Nor he for you. A monkey should know not to fly with eagles."

Something inside Chinita opened angry red eyes at that. A lost temper was never good for an outlaw, it could kill in fact, but that was a lesson she'd never quite mastered. "But a monkey can dream, priestess, and you hate that. What did you ever dream of?"

Blood darkened Suchi's face. "You are an outlaw. A murderer. Do you think a few words of blessing can take away what you've been? Things will be as they were, when the Thrain are gone. Every word you speak will be counted against you, when you're taken to the side of the road."

It was hard to breathe, and not because the air was thin. *When you're taken to the side of the road.* Chinita thought of her mother, screaming for a day and a night before she died.

"You defile the *kamachi* with your presence," Suchi said. "You endanger Viraca's love for us, so flee. While you can. You'll be hunted down when the Thrain are gone, but you'll live a few more weeks if we have to root you out of the mountains."

Chinita laughed. She was furious, livid to her bones, but it was the laugh and not her anger which wiped the thin smile from Suchi's face. "I risk Viraca's love? After all these years, all these Servants, the god will abandon us over one woman's closeness to the *kamachi?*"

"You don't underst –"

"Warriors disembowelled my mother," Chinita said. "I may die screaming before this is over, but it won't be that way, *kura*. Because Kai has changed everything for us, and for all your words you can't change a bit of that. That gnaws at you, doesn't it? So you will try to go on as you *kura* always have, hoarding your power, waiting for times to change so you can put your hand over us all again. Not in love, like Viraca, but for love of power, which means so much more to you than the gods, or the people you know nothing of, and never truly cared for."

"I know the people. It's the people I'm thinking of."

"You don't even know love when you see it."

Suchi opened her mouth and then closed it again. Her hands worked, forming fists and opening, only to clench again. She didn't speak. Her face had begun to take on a purple tinge.

"You teased Catori and then spurned him," Chinita went on, biting the words. "Because he's not what you want, is he? Or what you ever wanted. It was enough for you to know you could make him come when you crooked a finger, and once he'd done so you could toss him aside. Because you only spread your legs for women, other priestesses, don't you? People who already agree with you, or who you can control. That isn't love."

"It was love!" Suchi snapped. "It is love!"

"It's something dark and repulsive," Chinita said. Her temper was cooling now. This twisted woman wasn't worth the effort of rage. "Two women in love can do as they please; it's no business of mine. But for you it's about power, and control, and the Blind God basks in it."

"It is not –"

"I love Kai," Chinita went on, meeting the smaller woman's eyes. "I'll give up my skin to fly with him, even for a little while. Even if I can't do more than fall from a mountain like Makisapa. Because it's better to fly in the sun for a day than live for years on the ground. And you don't understand that at all."

Suchi stood there for a moment and then whirled, striding back towards the tiered temple with her fists still clenched at her sides. She didn't notice the llama that peered down at her over a hedge, and when it spat, the gobbet caught Suchi on the side of her face. She flinched sideways, cursing in words no priestess ought to know, much less use, and Chinita couldn't help laughing.

When she turned back to Kai it was to find him already looking at her, a thoughtful expression on his face. Surely he was too far away to have heard the conversation. Probably he was. Chinita was suddenly sure she and Suchi must have been shouting, but a glance around showed nobody at doorways, or staring in shock.

Still, Kai seemed able to deduce the truth from a single word, or sometimes to pluck it from the air like a conjurer. Well, if he knew, he knew. Chinita gave the one-shouldered shrug that was more characteristic of her than she knew, and started towards him.

The river flowed rapidly, but not strongly enough to drag Chinita from her feet. She waded across, up to her knees in icy water, then crunched over the stones and scrambled up the bank. By the time she reached him something inside her had begun to quiver, like thin glass tapped by a fingernail. He smiled and the quivering became a chime, ringing bright and clear as sunlight.

"Good morning," she said. "Admiring the scenery?"

His smile gave way to a chuckle. "Hardly. Cursing the fact that we have to climb over it all again when we leave."

"We've had one night in proper beds," she said with mock despair, "and already the man speaks of leaving. You're a monster." Quilla Mother of All, he was beautiful. Not merely handsome: what would handsome matter? He was gorgeous. Even the way he *stood* made her palms tingle. Oh, Gods, she was already lost. She might as well throw her heart and fortune, such as it was, at Kai's feet and beg him, weeping, to take her in his arms.

Except for her pride. Blood and bones, she'd always been proud. It was part of her. Achachi liked to say she was made of sharp-edged rocks and shards of ice, enough to cut anyone who tried to come too close, and that was true. If Kai pushed her away she would sob for a month, and then likely go looking for a high cliff with rocks the whole way down, but she wasn't going to beg. Not even for him… but gods, he was gorgeous.

"More than speaks of it," Kai said. His eyes seemed strange, as though they were looking inwards rather than out. Nice eyes though, beautiful eyes in fact; *oh Quilla, he's already tied my heart on a string and I'm helpless.* Just looking at him made her insides chime once more. "We're going to have to leave. Soon."

She stared at him. "What's happened?"

"I don't know," he said. His gaze drifted away from her, to the towering snow-capped mountains to the south.

He plucks truth from the air like a conjurer, she thought again. Kai's hunches were good, and since she'd known him had always turned out to be right. They had planned to stay for three days. But listening to Kai now, Chinita doubted they would stay in Kuska that long. Nobody else had come into the valley, bringing news. But something had changed, and Kai knew it.

"You're hearing the god," she said. The thought awed her. *That* was the secret of his uncanny intuition, then. "Viraca is speaking in your mind."

"Not that," he said, and then hesitated. "Not exactly that, at least. I've never heard the god, in truth."

"Matlal wouldn't have agreed."

Kai looked at her. "You talked about me with Matlal?"

"Sometimes. When we were bored."

Her smile at the jest faded when Kai's expression didn't change. "You're right, anyway. Matlal did believe the intuition is the Bearded God speaking to me. He said I just wasn't listening closely enough."

"Maybe he was right," she said.

"Maybe," he agreed. "In which case I've been wrong, all my life."

He was still watching her, his face unreadable. Sweet mercy, his lips were… she shook the thought away, trying to remind herself to breathe. "And your intuition is telling you something now?"

"It tells me that we don't have time to wait," he said. "We have to leave, and soon. The scouts will have to go out tomorrow, however tired they are. Time is pressing, and it won't wait for us."

"It never does."

"No," he agreed, and without warning leaned forward a little further and kissed her gently on the lips. He didn't press hard, and after too short a moment he drew away, but Chinita's lungs didn't seem to be working and she couldn't focus her eyes. His hand rested on the nape of her neck for a moment and then that was gone, too. Chinita managed to draw a breath.

He had brushed her lips, no more, and given her the best kiss of her life.

"You may have been right," he said mildly. "It seems I have come to love you, after all."

She could feel tears welling in her, and she could hold those back, but she couldn't stop the great idiot grin that spread itself across her face. A dozen chimes were ringing in her now, but she would not beg. Not ever. "I might need to think about that for a while."

Something changed in his expression, usually so carefully guarded and blank. For a fleeting moment something else showed, a flicker of loneliness and need. It was so brief that she might have been wrong, and then his face was bland and shielded once more.

"Something about you," he said. "I'm slow to trust, Chinita. Too many people see only the Servant, not the man."

"I see you," she said.

"I know you do."

"But I can't be Matlal for you," she went on. *Rocks and shards of ice.* "If you want someone just like him, you need to keep looking."

"I don't want you to be Matlal. I want you to be you." A smile flicked at the corner of his mouth. "Chinita, you'd find it impossible even to pretend to be anyone else."

She was aware, then, that perhaps she couldn't hold back the tears any longer. *You're not for him, nor he for you. A monkey should know not to fly with eagles.* She was flying with them now, or her heart was. She wasn't sure her feet were still on the ground.

"Oh, Chinita, no," Kai said. He reached out to wipe a tear from her cheek. "I'm sorry, so sorry. I should have waited –"

"If you'd waited any longer I would have kicked you," she said through her tears. "I'm happy, you idiot!"

He grinned, an open smile of simple pleasure, and then his arms went about her and his mouth came down on hers. Chinita, who prided herself on her strength and independence, clung to his shoulders and let him curl up her toes and put a tremble in her knees. She felt him move a hand to the back of her head, his fingers twined in her hair. It could have been made to fit there.

He pulled back, but didn't move his hands. For a long moment they just looked at each other. Chinita didn't think she could speak.

"Don't turn around," he said, "but three priests are watching us. They look rather scandalised, in fact. The rumour of this is going to be all over the temple in ten minutes. At the most."

She reached up to trace fingers down the side of his face, over his jaw, back up. Oh, gods, he was so *unfairly* gorgeous!

"Huniy kuma," she chuckled. "Let them gossip."

"What did Suchi say?"

"She told me to stay away," Chinita began, before she really realised what she was saying. When she did her smile faded. She reached up and took his hands away.

"Don't do that to me," she said. "Ever again. I'm never going to like being controlled, Kai."

He tilted his head. "All right."

"You promise?"

"On my heart," he said.

"Good," Chinita answered. "Then Suchi told me to stay away from you. That I defile you, and the god's love for the Ashir."

"Did she, now."

"I don't want to talk about her," Chinita said. She reached up to kiss him again, short but fierce. "The priests can say what they like and so can she. You're sure we have to leave soon?"

The sudden change of subject made him blink. "No. But I think it's true. It feels that way."

"Then do what you have to do today," she said. "And we can have tonight together. In a real bed."

"That will give the priests fainting spells," he said, and she couldn't help laughing.

18

"We should have got some sleep," Kai said.

Chinita laughed in the back of her throat, like an amused puma. "Wasn't I enough to satisfy you?"

"The first time." He grinned at her. Moonlight spilled through the window to brighten her body, silvering the hollow of her lower back, where his fingers traced. "The second time I'd rather have caught some rest."

"I *see*," she said, stretching languidly under his hands. "You're bored of me already, then."

"Not that," he chuckled. "But there was a priest watching us."

"Was there?" Chinita stretched on top of the blankets, half-turning so someone standing outside the bead curtain of the door wouldn't *quite* be able to see... what he wanted to see. She was astonishingly beautiful underneath her forest clothes. More muscular than any woman Kai had known before, but still long-limbed and supple, smooth and soft and sensuous.

There hadn't been many other women. No barmaids in villages to tell lurid stories about what the *kamachi* liked in bed, or to sob on shoulders because he had taken her love and then walked away. Once there had been a priestess in a town by the sea, and later a widow on the plateau, trying to hold her late husband's llama herd together. A couple of others. All strong women, independent, not quick to gossip.

Kai was careful, always. He watched moonlight play across Chinita's buttocks as she stretched.

"For a little while there was," he said. "Then he dashed off as though he'd been bitten." He examined his fingers. "Which I have been. Several times, it seems."

"That's to mark you," she told him, and stretched again. "I've never been watched before."

"You mean you didn't save yourself for me?"

"As though you did, for me." She turned to face him through a fall of black hair. "I would have waited. If I'd known. But nobody could have guessed the *kamachi* would find me, or love me."

"Or that you'd love me."

"Loving you is easy," she said. "You've given me a new life and a reason to live it. You've put flowers in my hair and chimes in my heart. I'll be with you, Kai, wherever this road takes us, and beyond."

He stroked a hand down the curve of her back. She had a round scar below one shoulder blade, left by an arrow he thought. Another long-healed gash ran from her stomach over her left hip, to peter out halfway down her thigh. That was either from an axe or a knife, and whichever, it had come within an inch of killing her. It might have been dealt by a warrior in a battle, or by another outlaw, or maybe even by a farmer trying to keep his barn from being raided.

Kai didn't know and didn't ask. Such confidences came in time, if they came at all. No reason to demand everything at once.

Still, he looked forward to discovering other scars, other marks on her body, in the nights they had to come.

"I can't imagine," he said in the moonlight, "how I have lived so long, without you, and called myself content."

"Oh, I can make you much more than content," she said. She moved her hand down his belly.

"I'm sure you can." He caught her hand, laughing, and brought it to his lips. "But not that, not now. Dawn's coming."

"Already?"

"Already," he agreed. "As you'd have noticed, if you weren't being so... persuasive."

She snorted laughter and bit his shoulder.

Persuasive was hardly the word. Kai had been given scant time to follow Chinita into his bed chamber before she was pulling his clothes off, and kissing him hard, while the beads of the door curtain still rattled behind him. He was somewhat taken aback. Women didn't behave that way.

Sprawled on his back in the bed, a few minutes later, he decided that sometimes they did. Especially this one. She reached back, naked, to untie the cord that held her hair in a tail down her back, and shook her head to free it. Moonlight framed her face and breasts, faded to darkness as it ran over her flat belly. Kai stretched out a hand to stroke her skin.

She slapped it away. "*I* am in charge here, master *kamachi*."

He couldn't help laughing, though that stopped quickly enough when she began to touch him. Whenever he reached for her she pushed his hands away, so he could only lie there and let her move slowly up his body. His memory grew a bit blurred after that, though he did remember her straddling him. He remembered his hands on her hips as she moved. He remembered her biting his finger, hard, and leaning forward to kiss him and then bite his neck, too. Then they were lying together in tangled blankets, Chinita half across him so her weight held him down. He could feel the heat of her breath on his throat, slowing, cooling.

"Good?" she asked.

"Very good." He could only manage a croak. He felt like an *ikaku* bird singing for a mate: *listen to me, look at my plumage, see my careful nest*. Any female who came might choose to mate, or not, but one would in the end and by early summer there would be eggs in the nest for her to warm while the male went foraging. By autumn, when the chicks could fly themselves, the male was so exhausted by his labours that he died, his beautiful song reduced to weary cries in the trees.

The *ikaku* built its nest of thorns. Kai thought he knew how it felt, now, with Chinita in his bed. Thorns wherever he turned.

113

They had dozed a little, after, wrapped together for much more than warmth. Now the night was over, the moon slipping down behind the steep peaks of Apachita and the sky to the east beginning to turn grey. Dawn was near, and another day, with all the ravelled cares it would bring.

Crossing Apachita again would be hard, as before. Harder than before in fact, with muscles still weary and lungs sore after the first ascent. After that the travellers would face the hilly country east of the plains, not quite in the mountains but not entirely out of them either. It was known to be rough going, largely rocky tors and forests, spotted with marshes in bowls. Kai couldn't remember a single proper road there, just rock-strewn tracks that wound between villages and valleys. At the end of it, with luck, they would face the sorcerer himself, drawn into the wilds where he might be vulnerable. Somehow. Kai didn't know. It had to be tried.

"Your face has changed," Chinita murmured into his chest. "You look cold. Distant. The way you were when I first saw you."

He frowned at her.

"I can tell," she said. She lifted her head to look at him. "You're getting ready to shut people out."

She was right, of course. It was what he always did, to give himself room to breathe so he did not suffocate under the sheer pressure of people's need. She was right, but he knew what she needed to hear, and perhaps that gift really was the god speaking in his mind, after all.

"Not you," he said.

Chinita's smile came suddenly, brighter than the shining moon. She crawled up his body and kissed him, not with the hunger of before but with simple love, soft and undemanding. "Let's get dressed."

They did so, lighting a lamp so they could hunt for the clothes so hurriedly discarded the night before. Searching for his sleeveless vest, Kai caught sight of Chinita wandering the room in one stocking and her shirt, and all the thoughts in his head crashed into one another and he stopped. When she noticed him watching she straightened her shoulders and began to strut, which made Kai collapse laughing on the bed wiping tears from his eyes. By the time he recovered she was dressed, and she handed him his boots with a raised eyebrow.

"Thank you," he managed. His right boot was fraying, the upper coming away from the sole on the outside. He'd have to find a cobbler at a village somewhere. It would do for now though. He stamped his foot into it and tied off the laces, snuffed out the candle and followed Chinita out of the room. He almost walked into her when she stopped a pace beyond the bead curtains, on the step into the next room.

"I'm told you've ordered me to stay and oversee the prisoners and the horses," Burru said as he rose from his chair. "While my daughter goes into danger again. Let her stay here with me."

Kai had sleep in his eyes and his mind, was still early-morning sluggish, but here was his first problem of the day. Not even a pace outside his bedroom. He wished he was still asleep, or better yet, that he was in bed with Chinita, and *not* asleep. He opened his mouth.

"I go where he goes," Chinita said. "And you're needed here, father. You and the women of the society, and most of the warriors."

"Yes," he said. "Someone is needed. So you stay too. Learn to ride those horses, like Ususi and the other women."

"She goes where I go," Kai interjected. That won him another shining smile from Chinita, but Burru scowled. "It's dangerous, I know. But it has to be done. And we brought the red plague with us, Burru. We could all die of it right here, sitting in a high valley where the Thrain will never find us. There's danger everywhere."

"You love her?"

Kai met his gaze. "Yes. Much to my own surprise, and at the worst possible time, but yes. I love her."

"And I love him," Chinita added.

"And I loved your mother," Burru said softly. "I can't lose you as I lost her. Just make sure you come back."

"As sure as I can," she said. She pecked him on the cheek. "I'll be careful, Father. But I have to go."

Burru studied her for a moment, then sighed and turned to Kai. "All right. I'll guard your horses and babysit your prisoners for you." He levelled a finger at the smaller man. "But bring her back to me, *kamachi*."

"If I can," he agreed.

The outlaw leader strode out of the room, leaving Kai to exchange frowns with Chinita.

"It seems we were quite an attraction last night," she said. "My father must have sat there watching the priest watching us."

Kai grinned. "I doubt that. If he'd seen the priest Burru would have split his leering lips."

"That's my father," she agreed. "Shall we join the band?"

They stopped to wash on the way. Kai pulled off his shirt and was surprised to see Chinita do the same. Apparently having her with him was going to bring a lot of surprises, and maybe even more temptations. He concentrated on splashing himself awake. There was enough to worry about already.

They were all there, waiting in the Court of Thorns by the light of several lanterns posted to the walls. The women had been delighted to find the place, seeing in it a good omen for their new warrior society. But it was just a cloister, turned into a hidden copse by tala trees with yellow-blue flowers peering under spiny branches like eyes. Among them the men waited, thirty or so of them in clusters between the trees. Chinita saw them and wondered, a sudden morbid thought that lodged in her mind, how many of them would be dead before this was over.

Achachi, her grandfather, sat on a stone with his feet in a flowerbed and hands clasped on his stick. He looked too frail to walk on his own, though under

115

his wrinkled skin he was all gnarled roots and stubbornness. Evain stood not far away, easily the biggest man there and wearing his long shirt of iron mail.

Taruka and Catori leaned on a wall to one side, with a small gaggle of warriors and outlaws just beyond them. Waki stood at the front of those, the scouts Kai had asked for the night before. Beside them was another person, half-hidden until Chinita stepped fully into the Court.

Suchi.

"I'm told," Paqu said, "that you intend to leave your men, humph, here. In Kuska. With the… horses."

The little priest was angry. He might appear diffident but there was a thread in his voice, a crease by his eyes, which gave him away. Kai doubted anyone else would notice, and it didn't matter. There were other things to deal with. He could see Suchi, standing by the trees.

"That's right," he said.

"But it's ridiculous."

"I don't have time to explain all my reasons to you," Kai said. He looked weary already. Chinita supposed she shouldn't be surprised, given how they'd spent the night. "Leave it, Paqu. The horses stay."

"But we *kura* won't, humph, get any work done at all."

"You have thirty priests here who have little enough to do at the best of times," Kai said. "A few days of hard work might be good for them, and a few missed prayers at need won't make Kuska any less holy. Now leave it be." He turned to the assembled men. "Are you all ready?"

"As they'll ever be," Taruka agreed. He'd found time to shave the sides of his head, where the skin gleamed as though freshly oiled. It probably was. "They could all use a bit more rest, but it's not us setting the steps of this dance."

"And you, Waki? I didn't realise you were much of a runner."

"I'm not," the stocky Snake answered. "But half the band have got blisters on their blisters, and half the others are coughing. It might be the thin air, or it might be the red plague." He shrugged. "I'm what you've got."

Kai had asked for scouts, men with the wit to avoid Thrain patrols and sniff out information, and the speed to bring it back as fast as possible. His band was safe here, but Apusuyu still writhed under the hand of the sorcerer. He needed to know where Terzian was, and what he was doing, if he was ever to change that.

Six men stood in the scouts' group. If there were so few, the red plague must already have seized the band and was spreading like dust on the wind. The Thrain were the main danger, the one Kai could fight, but this disease might leave nothing of the Ashir but memories if it went unchecked.

Suchi was staring at him, eyes aflame. In turn Chinita's glare was fixed on the priestess, but Suchi didn't seem to notice. That was a small problem, compared to the others, but it was one Kai could solve.

"Very well," he said to Waki. He had been uncertain of himself, back in the Uma Mountains above the great road, but confidence had grown in him since then. Some of that he owed to Chinita, and some to Achachi. Most, though, he owed to the god. Viraca had chosen his Servant, and in the past days Kai had, for the first time, begun to understand why.

Time to act like a *kamachi*.

"I hope you've all said your goodbyes, because it's time for you to go," he said. "I need you back here in eight days, with whatever information you have. It means two more crossings of Apachita and I'm sorry, but there's no help for it. I won't order you. I'll only ask."

"That's all you have to do," a skinny rake of a man said. Kai only had to think for a moment to remember his name; Mito. One of the warriors, though they were all warriors now.

Kai nodded, then turned a little. "Suchi."

She was still looking at him, eyes still angry in a too-calm face. "Yes, *kamachi*."

"Have you joined us here because you want to go with the scouts?"

"They might have need of a *kura*," she said.

"They might," he nodded. "If she is a good one." Paqu looked up sharply, catching something in Kai's tone.

"What does that mean?" Suchi demanded.

"It means this," Kai said, and suddenly his words were chipped obsidian. "Burru and his followers are now counted among our people. This is done. My blessing was freely given, and it cannot and will not be taken back. Things will *not* be as they were, priestess, not ever again for these men and women, and you *will* accept that or I will strip your blue robe from you myself and kick you down the mountainside. Is that clear to you?"

The Court of Thorns was silent. Nobody moved, but there was a sense of drawing away from Suchi, to leave her standing alone. The priestess went first red, then white.

"I asked if that was clear to you," Kai said softly.

"It's very clear to me," Suchi said. Her teeth were gritted. "But it isn't acceptable to me."

Taruka gave a start. Beside him Catori went very still. "What? We've fought with them through –" He stopped when Kai flung up a hand.

The priestess's hands gripped her robe, the knuckles white, but her voice was steady. "What are you fighting for, *kamachi*?"

He smiled a little. "The Blessed Land."

"And yet you give away what we are," she said. "You bring invaders among us, and spend your time pondering what makes them better than us, wiser then us, stronger. The truth is, we Ashir are better than them." She jerked her head towards Evain. "Why should we learn their ways? Killers, despoilers, who would unmake what we are." She swivelled to stare at Chinita. "And you invite bandits to join us. Murderers, not fit to live among decent people. I wonder, when you have finished saving this Blessed Land, whether you will leave a Blessed Land at all."

"We survived Tezcata," Catori said. "We will survive this too."

"But as what?" Suchi demanded. "You're such a fool. We endured through Tezcata's darkness because we clung to what we were. To what we *are*. We preserved our beliefs, our way of life, in the face of everything the Dark God threw at us. And now, today, the *kamachi* tells us the way to survive is to

118

abandon all that, to adopt outsider ways and transform ourselves into something we have never been." She shook her head. "He abandons our history."

"He abandons nothing." It was, surprisingly, Taruka. "He only adds to what we have been."

"He changes us," Suchi shot back savagely. "He changes what we are, and makes us into something we don't wish to be."

"And what," Evain asked, "would you have him do? Against iron and horses and magic, come against you from a world you never dreamed existed, what would you have him do, priestess?"

There was a silence. An *ikaku* bird sang from among the trees, a male calling to attract a mate to the wonderful nest he had built for her, out of twigs and leaves and desperate hope. He cried once and was quiet, as though waiting.

"I would have him defend what we are," Suchi said at last. "I would have him protect what our gods gave us to protect, and what our ancestors guarded for so long. I would not have him betray us from within, until nothing we have ever believed matters any more."

Chinita had taken Kai's hand. He didn't remember her doing so.

Once he'd stood on a bridge with Matlal and waited for a bandit chief to come to him. He'd felt then that he knew what needed to be said, and what Burru would say before the other man spoke the words. All the steps of the dance, laid out before him like a gift, a tapestry of understanding. He felt the same now. He knew what to do.

"You don't want us to change," he said. "But we always have. Our ancestors changed even before Viraca came among them. You know the quote, Suchi. *Viraca took his wisdom the length and breadth of the land. To the highest peaks he went, and to the low places where the sea laps against the shore.* He walked between those places on the Pasqa. The road was already there. How was it built, before Viraca taught us to work stone?"

"The peoples of those days were Lost," Suchi answered. *"Chisqa.* Those who built the *lanti,* or the roads, vanished because they would not listen to Viraca. A warning to us."

The expected reply, the riposte she was always going to make. Kai smiled a little.

"But the Lost knew things," he said. "They knew how to build, how to carve stone. They farmed; you can still see the terraces they cut, on hills where nobody lives anymore. One people in the forests, others on the plains and in the hills. Perhaps they thought they would last forever, but change came to them. As it always changes."

"Not for us. Viraca made it so."

"And at what price? Perhaps we could have had iron, like the Thrain, if we hadn't been so sure that bronze was what the Teacher God wanted us to use. We could have had it a thousand years ago. Are we primitive because we saw our culture and were satisfied, and never wondered beyond it?"

119

"Now you blame Viraca?" she said, her voice rising. "Do you think those Lost peoples were as good as us? You might as well say the god showed us nothing, and gave us only dreams."

"No," he said softly. "No, Suchi. He gave us the *kamachi.*"

Still the courtyard was silent.

"The *kamachi*," Kai repeated. "A line of us, all the way back through time to the day Viraca stood on the beach beside his raft of living snakes, and gave us a way to remember his love. Now there's me. The ninety-ninth Servant. Until now I haven't done much except open festivals and speak the words of consecration in a new temple somewhere. Most of the time that's all a *kamachi* needs to do. Except simply be there."

He let his eyes move around the circle, meeting every gaze. "But sometimes it's different. It has to be. When Eyota fought in the war against the Shore People, or when Adsila stood on the steps of the Hallows and denounced the Qapac as a fool, and forsaken. Or right back in the beginning, the days of the earliest *kamachi*, when nobody truly knew if the snake on their faces was a sign of the god's love, or just a strange mark on the skin."

"You betray their memory," Suchi said in a low voice.

"Betray them?" Kai looked at the little priestess. "Do you think I would act as they did, in their time? Or they in mine? Eyota's Blessed Land was different from ours, and the Shore People were outside it, but they were brought inside the border and Apusuyu changed. And Adsila's Blessed Land was different again, just as it will be different in the future, with or without the Thrain. Because Apusuyu *does* change. We only think it doesn't because the changes are so slow." He shook his head. "Suchi, you're fighting to defend a dream that was never real."

"I'm fighting to preserve the land I love," she snapped back.

Kai nodded slowly. "And you won't change your mind?"

"I will not," she said. Her chin was high.

"Then you are no longer welcome among us," Kai said. It would cost him Taruka and Catori, he knew. They would go with her but he couldn't help that. It was the next step in the dance. "Go now."

"Wait," Paqu began, starting to rise from his seat, and Kai levelled a finger at him and said, *"Shut up."*

Suchi stared at him. She was breathing hard, and her hands still had a death grip on her robe, but she didn't move from beneath the trees.

"I will go," she said at last. "But you will hear me again, Kai. From the Temples of Hatun you will hear me, when the Thrain are beaten and the land is ours once more. And when your bones are cold underground Apusuyu will still be as it was before they came." She looked around the group. "Some of you must know this. Who will follow me?"

"I will," someone said. He moved forward from the crowd, a lean man with rough tattoos on the sides of his neck. An imitation of warriors, unusual in an outlaw. His name was Yurac. "I'll go."

"What?" Burru exploded. "Why, in Quilla's name?"

"Because the priestess is right. And I don't trust him," Yurac said, with a nod towards Kai. "What's to stop him having us killed like bandits, when the Thrain are gone?"

"He wouldn't."

"Are you certain?"

"I am," Chinita said. She was still holding Kai's hand. Nobody else spoke. Suchi looked around the group again, until finally her gaze was went draggingly to her brother. For a moment they looked at each other.

"Oh, Goldfish," Taruka said, and turned his back on her.

A surprise, Kai thought. He saw Suchi's face crumple and for a moment her heart was visible there, twisted with pain, and then her hands came up to cover her expression. She started to turn and Catori said, "Wait."

He turned to Kai. "I'll go with her."

"I know," Kai said.

"Someone should. She deserves a friend."

"Yes. She does."

Catori glanced the other way. "And you, my brother? Do you understand?"

"No," Taruka said. "I don't. The fight is here and you're going to walk away from it. You're no Snake."

Around the courtyard breath was drawn in. Catori just looked at his friend though, huge brown eyes unperturbed, and then he turned away. He went to Suchi and Yurac and the three of them walked out of the garden, leaving silence behind them.

"I'm sorry," Kai said to Taruka.

The warrior nodded, still facing the trees, and didn't speak.

Kai drew a breath. "If you want... Taruka, you can go with her. I wouldn't force you from your sister."

"No," the warrior said, his voice thick. He straightened, visibly squaring his shoulders as he turned to look Kai in the eyes. "No. I'm grateful, but I stand with the *kamachi*."

"Thank you," Kai said again. His fingers tightened around Chinita's, but he gave no other sign of tension, or grief. "All right. Time to go, Waki."

They went to watch the scouts depart, from the steps at the front of the tiered temple of Kuska. There was no sign of the three separatists. Chinita kept hold of Kai's hand, unwilling to let it go. As they walked she leaned close and murmured, "Suchi's wrong. You can be sure of that."

"Can I?" he asked, even more softly. "I don't hear the god's voice, Chinita. I'm guessing here, and if I'm wrong then I will be guilty of everything Suchi says, and Apusuyu will be lost because of me."

They were at the steps by then, and she had no chance to reply. Ahead of them llamas still peered over the hedge at the idly grazing horses, but with less unease than before. The strange can become normal very quickly. The priests were less relaxed, standing by the doors and watching the horses as though waiting for them to attack. Chinita found herself smiling at that. Horses had become normal even to her. A little, anyway.

The small band waded across the river and started up the gentle, grassy slope that led to the pass. Chinita craned her head back to look at the twisting peak, and the notch just below. It looked too high for even eagles to manage. She could scarcely believe they had crossed it.

But there was work to do, however much she might wish to sit and rest, and with a smile for him Chinita let go of Kai's hand. "Master Evain, will the horses be rested enough for us to train with them?"

The big Thrain nodded. "As long as we don't push them too hard. A little light trotting should be fine."

"Then we'll train," she said. Izel nodded reluctantly, but Ususi and the rest of the women grinned. "Before that, though, there's something else we need to do, if we're to be warriors." She turned to Taruka. "Do you have scissors, and a razor? We need to crest our hair."

Even Izel grinned at that, and after a moment Taruka nodded.

Tukuchiy   the finishing

20

Chimalli had brought her a black eye patch, with a cord that was almost invisible against her ebony hair. On it was sewn the outline of a puma's head seen from the front, mouth open in a scream of rage, in real thread-of-gold. A warrior who wore it would look fearsome, which Amaru knew she didn't, but she liked the gift anyway. It was much more comfortable than wearing a stained bandage wound around her head, and prettier too.

"Had one of the Snake make it for you," Chimalli said when she asked where he'd found it. "He was wounded in Chakanay and can't walk – he nearly lost his leg at the knee – so he was going insane with boredom. Making this kept him busy for a few hours."

Almost every warrior in the camp was wounded in one way or another, including Chimalli. A livid burn emerged from under his tunic to crawl over the left side of his jaw and up his cheek, stopping just beneath his eye. He'd put a salve on it, but the coating was too thin and trickles of yellow-stained blood had leaked through. There wasn't enough salve, of course. There wasn't enough of anything, from bandages to food, and certainly not enough hope.

She knew Chimalli thought he'd been lucky to escape Chakanay with only a burned face and shoulder. Probably the man who'd made the eye patch felt the same, maimed leg or no. Amaru wondered whether she should visit him, and decided it was wiser not to. Warriors seldom liked to be bothered when they were recovering from a wound. "Would you thank him for me?"

"Of course I will. You know, pumas have the best eyesight of any animal in the world, except maybe a hawk. Perhaps a little of that will rub off on you. Help you see from that eye again."

"I don't think that will happen," she answered politely. She wished she could believe it would. It was awkward, not being able to see anything to her left. She kept tripping over stones or tufts of grass she hadn't seen. She'd already begun to develop a habit of cocking her head a little to the left, so her one good eye could see to both sides ahead of her. "There isn't an eye there to see from, after all. But I do thank you for the concern."

"It's nothing. And if you need anything else, just ask. There are plenty of men here who'll be glad to help." He looked at her steadily, when so many people hurried to glance away, as though by not seeing her wound they could make it disappear. "In war the people who suffer worst are the ones left to live with their hurts. We all think of you, Amaru. We care about you."

It was very hard not to cry. These men were wounded and desperate, and yet with everything lost still they found time to think of her, and care for her. But she knew tears would only upset Chimalli, so Amaru managed to smile instead, touching the eye patch with one hand. "It doesn't hurt much any more, Chimalli. Anyway, I might actually see better, now."

He frowned. "How?"

"There's less to distract me," she said. That earned her a baffled look, though it was no more nonsensical than Chimalli's comment that the puma eye patch might help her see better from the empty socket. He left her soon after, saying he had duties to attend to, and while that was true Amaru knew perfectly well that he could have stayed a little longer, if he hadn't been bemused by her. She did wish adults wouldn't behave like that so often. She was a child, not an idiot. Her father had never forgotten it. Neither had Salali.

And *that* was the real hurt, the pain she still felt; the loss of her family and home. Only Tumay was left, like an uncle she barely knew. He'd never been a regular visitor to her home, before the Thrain came. In a short time Salali had become something close to family, a loyal man with a smile always hovering behind his lips, but now he was gone too. She wished he wasn't.

She wished her mother wasn't gone, and her sister. Most of all she wished Father was here, with his pride in her and his calm, easy comfort. So many people were lost to her. It was as Chimalli had said. The greatest hurts were saved for those who survived, and were left to find a way, if they could, to live their lives in the aftermath of grief. But she thought it would seem selfish to cry, when so many were dead or permanently crippled, and all she had was grief for those she loved.

She thought that perhaps Quilla had turned her eyes from Amaru, and everyone she came to love would be taken away.

*

They halted at a farmer's rough cottage, one of a dozen clustered at the edge of the plain, thirty miles south of Chakanay. The settlement was too small to be called a village. It was a hamlet at best, a random cluster of huts at worst. Most had been abandoned when the refugees arrived, with seventeen fresh graves in a field to one side even though there was no sign of violence. The red plague had reached even here, a tiny community too poor and remote for even a narrow road. The survivors had left, probably in search of safer parts, and taken the disease on with them.

Chimalli sent scouts across the fields towards Chakanay to give warning if the Thrain moved. There were only a few of them, picked from whoever was fit and uninjured, and so far it had been a waste of effort. In the five days since the rebellion the Thrain hadn't moved at all. Even Kisain couldn't explain why.

"From what you've told me," the big man said, "there can't be more than fifteen hundred soldiers left alive. Perhaps two thousand. That isn't enough to conquer any more of Apusuyu than they can camp on, but it *is* enough for a punitive raid. Terzian's sorcery makes it enough."

"A raid?" Chimalli asked. "Against whom?"

"The *kamachi*," Mimiteh said. "For killing his son."

Kisain nodded. "Perhaps. It depends on whether Ramian really is dead."

"He's dead."

125

They were gathered in the main room of the cottage, a cramped space that served as kitchen and dining room alike. Two pinched little bedrooms huddled against the back wall, both of them windowless. The front room was so tiny that Kisain's chair had to be pushed into one of the doorways, beside which Mimiteh crouched on her heels like a watchdog.

There were five of them, including Amaru. The last was a gnarled old warrior named Uchu, who Amaru thought might have last picked up an axe when Viraca was a young god with big ideas. He had almost no hair left, and that white and scraggly at the back of his head. His skin seemed made entirely of scars and wrinkles, though he claimed most of that was the result of years fishing along the coast, and nothing to do with fighting. His arms were marked with the tattoos of the Snake society though, one of them marred by a pucker of white flesh that could have been left by a spear thrust which must have nearly cost him the arm.

When word came of the Thrain he'd abandoned his boat and nets and set off inland, carrying his battered old axe on one shoulder.

"I'm in no more danger here than I am at sea," he'd said, laughing a cracked laugh, when Chimalli asked doubtfully how much use the ancient could be in a fight. "Besides, there are things in the deep seas that would turn your hair as white as mine, boy, big lad though you are. I'd like to see you fight for your catch with a *quch'aqway* and live to talk about it."

"What's a *quch'aqway*?" Chimalli asked.

The decrepit man grinned toothily. "A great fish that lives down deep, so it can swim underneath its prey. Then it aims upwards and rises as quickly as it can, which is very fast indeed. I've seen them leap right out of the water, their mouths wide open. As big as five llamas, they are, and they have teeth that would make a puma turn tail and flee into the forest."

"I've never heard of it," Amaru said.

"You're plains-born, little girl. Folk by the sea all know the *quch'aqway.*" His teeth flashed again. Old he might be, but he still had his own fangs.

Uchu could tell stories of his fanged fish for hours and never repeat himself once. He had reached the village one day after the refugees, and two after the failed uprising, and was still colourfully angry about that.

"Perhaps Ramian is dead," he said now, in the vulture's croak that was his voice. "I would quite like to be sure. I always used to say that you could never guess what the other chief would do next, unless you knew what he knew."

Chimalli frowned at him. "The other chief? Did you command warriors in battle, Uchu?"

"I might have done," the ancient warrior grinned. When he smiled his skin wrinkled up so much that his eyes became mere points of light amidst the folds. "Here and there."

"Don't mess me about," Chimalli said wearily. "I've found myself in charge of this band within a week of being made a chief, and I'm making it up as I go along. I keep expecting someone more experienced to come and take over, and it might not be a bad thing. I could use some help."

"Oh, I'll help," Uchu said. "I want my chance at these *binchuka* outlanders, however late I was getting here. But the command is yours, Chimalli. You've done all right up until now, and besides, I'm too old to want to chivvy headstrong young idiots any more."

"How old are you?" Amaru asked, not thinking until the question was out. "Oh. I didn't mean to be rude."

"You can be as rude as you like, girl." He reached out to ruffle her hair. "Let's put it this way. I gave up my society some twenty years ago, but my first battle as a chief," he turned back to Chimalli, "was up in the north-west, when the Tihuac decided they wanted a king of their own."

The big warrior stared at him. "That's impossible. That was forty years ago, at least."

"Bit more than that," Uchu said. "Those Tihuac knew how to fight, but let me tell you, their warriors were cowering in caves and their women weeping long before we were finished with them. And if we could beat *them*, well, I reckon we can see off these *carajo* Thrain, as well." He gave Amaru a wink.

She looked up at him in awe. Uchu had worn his tattoos before her father was even born, and yet here he was, ready to throw his leathery old body into battle one more time. He looked capable of it, too. One of the Thrain was likely to have a nasty surprise if he took this bony old man for granted.

"If we could stay with what is important," Mimiteh said in a strained voice. She was strained a great deal, since Kisain had abandoned his life to come with her. Anyone who gave the soldier so much as a slanted look found himself the target of an eruption of rage that left him white and shaking. "I have no doubt that Ramian is dead, but the Thrain are still just sitting in the ruins of Chakanay."

"Not just sitting there," Chimalli disagreed. "They send out foraging parties every day."

"Can we kill them?" she asked. Kisain winced, and the fierceness melted away from Mimiteh's expression all in an instant. She put a hand on his leg and earned a wry smile in return.

"Only with heavy losses ourselves," Chimalli said. "I tell the men to spread out, so the sorcerer can't kill more than a few at a time even if he appears, but that leaves my warriors very vulnerable to horsemen. Especially in the open fields, where there's nothing for them to hide behind." His gaze rested on Kisain. "What would you suggest we do?"

Mimiteh flashed to her feet. "Show some respect! Those were his friends. You can't ask him that!"

"I must ask him that," Chimalli said wearily, "because warriors are dying out there, priestess. *My* warriors, men to whom I have a responsibility. What, would you have me watch good Ashir men die while he sits here in silence?"

"It isn't fair!" she snapped.

127

"Hush," Uchu said from his place by the wall. His croaking voice was quiet, but it stilled them all despite that. "The man is right, Mimiteh. Your soldier here made a choice, and I for one respect him for it. But now it's time to pay the bill. What's fair and what isn't won't save a single life."

"This is true," Kisain said. His tone was bitter, but he met Chimalli's gaze evenly enough. "I won't raise a weapon against my comrades."

"I won't ask you to," Chimalli said. His hand came up to rub the raw burn on his neck, before he controlled himself and put the hand back down again. "But I do need advice."

Amaru looked at him, and then at Kisain slumped on his chair. He was very pale, still in considerable pain whenever he moved, and under much more strain even than Mimiteh. If it was difficult for many of the Ashir to accept his presence among them, it must be a hundred times harder for him. Amaru wished she could help him, and that was a difficult thing as well, to want to help one of the men who had caused your father's death, and to feel guilty for it.

"All right," Kisain said at length. "Though you've already said most of what matters anyway. Don't bunch your warriors together. If that makes them vulnerable in the fields, don't send them there – at least not in daylight, when the soldiers are gathering food. Send them in at night and destroy the crops. Raze every field you can reach, and drive the animals away, if any are left. That will force the Thrain to move in search of food, and when they do they'll have to spread out to find it. That will be your chance."

"They'll just go to the granaries along the Pasqa," Chimalli said. "They'll know where those are by now."

Kisain shrugged. "So? You know where they are too. Burn the stores as well, or move them away."

"The Qapac can have you put to death for that," Chimalli said. He frowned as he heard the words coming out of his mouth. "All right, there isn't a Qapac any more, but you see what I mean. Those stores exist to help people if the harvest fails. Besides, burning them wouldn't be honourable."

Uchu snorted laughter like a ripping curtain. "Honourable? My friend, if I found myself behind a man in a fight, I used to knife him in the arse with no hesitation at all. Depend upon it."

"Besides which," Mimiteh said reluctantly, "the Thrain have shown no honour to us. No, Kisain, it's true," she said when he looked at her. "They burned villagers at Ayllu, and now they've burned Chakanay too. Thousands of Ashir have gone to the Halls of Darkness with no bodies, to suffer forever. And your people will keep doing this if they can, until all Apusuyu is aflame from one end to the other. Chimalli, you asked for Kisain's advice. I think you ought to take it."

"It won't do you any good," Kisain broke in, before Chimalli could answer. "You asked what I would do, and I told you, but military strategy doesn't count for very much in this. Terzian changes everything. I keep telling you, and telling you, but I don't think you're listening. You can't defeat him. You can't challenge his power or negate it. He's going to stay in Apusuyu, and he will go on burning and destroying until he finds your *kamachi* and kills him, no matter how long it takes or how many people he has to kill. Whittling away at his forces won't bother him in the slightest. If it comes down to Terzian and one wounded cavalryman, he'll stay, until Kai is dead. Maybe even after that."

"Then we have to kill him," Uchu said.

Kisain laughed. "How? He protects himself against arrows and blades. If you collapsed a building on top of him he'd walk out without a bruise. Back in Thrasin the King himself, with all his soldiers and court wizards, didn't even dare try to kill him. It can't be done."

"There has to be a way," Chimalli muttered. "I'm not about to let him kill Kai. No *kamachi* has ever been murdered. If I allow Kai to be, my soul will wander the Halls of Dust and never see the sun."

"Then try, if you must," Kisain said. "But I'd suggest you stand off as long as you can. Use bows and spears to pick off soldiers when they go foraging," he swallowed hard, saying that, "but stay away from Terzian until you have no choice."

"You told us he can't heal a heart," Amaru said.

"That's true. But it doesn't matter if you can't hurt him there."

There must be a way, though. Any weakness could be exploited. It might be hard, even seem impossible, but if the vulnerability was there it could be done. Amaru was about to say so when shouts erupted outside, and the two warriors spun towards the door as their hands dropped to axes.

21

"Stay here," Chimalli said. He took one step towards the door before someone rapped on it from the other side and he stopped.

The door opened. Behind it stood two warriors, with more milling about behind like angry bees. Between the pair stood another man, head shaved into a crest but so covered in mud that it wasn't possible to say much more. Blood had dried in his hair and clothes. It lay think in a ragged wound too, running from hairline to jaw, that hitched up the side of his mouth.

"What is this?" Uchu demanded.

"He says he's come from Chakanay, chief," one of the warriors said.

"Since the burning?"

"I didn't ask."

"I wasn't talking to you," Uchu growled. "You, man. Have you news of the *kamachi?*"

The muddy man shook his head. "No. There's no word of him."

"But he fought."

"Well, he's disappeared again."

Amaru thought it was interesting that the warrior and stranger, both, addressed themselves to Uchu. There was an air about the ancient that made people want to respect him. Perhaps Chimalli was secure enough in his position not to see him as a threat. She was about to say so when something even more interesting happened.

"Mimiteh?" The filthy man peered into the hut, a smile cracking the mud on his face. "Is that you?"

She frowned. "Do I know –"

"Dyani!" Amaru shouted. "I thought you were dead!"

"I should be dead. Thousands are. But they let me go." He took a limping step into the room. "The sorcerer himself did it, the day before yesterday. He wanted me –" His eyes fell on Kisain, and he hissed through his teeth. "What's *he* doing here?"

"Helping us," Mimiteh said, "and if you have something to say about it, you can say it to me."

Dyani scowled. "Helping, is it? I suppose he gave you a good reason. Something convincing."

"The best reason of all," Mimiteh said. Kisain smiled at her.

"And he's convinced me," Chimalli said. "You look ready to drop, my friend, so let's have your news and then you can get some food."

"And a wash," Amaru put in. She couldn't stop grinning. "How did you get so dirty, mister baker?"

Chimalli waved a hand for her to be quiet. "The food's only a stew of maize and peppers, I'm afraid, but it's hot enough."

"Maize and peppers sounds wonderful," Dyani said. He aimed another frown at Kisain. "Oh, very well. If you say he can be trusted I suppose I'll have to believe you, though it smells all wrong to me."

Uchu cleared his throat. "Warrior, if you don't stop muttering and give us the news, I'll take you out the back and bounce you on your head."

Amaru smothered a laugh. She could just imagine Uchu doing exactly that. For all his age, he looked as hard as the roots of an old wayakan tree. He certainly had a more direct approach to leadership than Chimalli. Come to that, the big Puma was watching Uchu like a girl learning to weave at her mother's knee. He was going to get ideas before very long.

"All right, all right." Dyani leaned against the door jamb and rubbed his face, smearing mud around. "The sorcerer let six of us go, all in different directions. He wanted us to take word of what he plans to do." He looked around the room. "He's going for the Retreat."

"What?" Mimiteh was on her feet, her face ashen. "He can't – how does he even know where it is?"

"Jarawi told him," the filthy man said tiredly. "You mustn't blame him for that. The sorcerer burned the first man who refused to tell him. Just made him burn like a torch, right there in –" He broke off, wiping his mouth with the back of one hand. "Well, anyway, Jarawi told him. Then the sorcerer killed him anyway. Crushed his head like an overripe plum."

"Supay show him beauty," Amaru whispered, making a warding sign with hooked fingers. She felt ill.

"We can't allow this," Mimiteh said whitely. She turned to Chimalli. "We *mustn't* allow this!"

"I agree," he said. "Uchu?"

The wrinkled old man shrugged. "You're the chief, Chimalli. You choose where to aim the warriors."

"Yes," the Puma said. He sounded weary again. Kisain was smiling, a terrible expression with no joy in it at all. "Then rouse the camp. I want to get between Chakanay and the Retreat before the Thrain if I can, and if not I mean to harry them over every foot of ground, all the way to the mountains. Have we got any Message Runners left in camp?"

"One, I think," Uchu said.

"Send him south. He's to order any warriors he finds to the village under the Retreat. I can't remember its name. Mimiteh?"

"Hirka," she said.

"Yes, that's the place. Have the warriors stay as spread out as they can, but the Thrain are not to reach that valley. Go, Uchu."

The old man pushed Dyani aside and ducked out of the cottage. He started yelling for warriors before he was two paces outside the door. Someone his age should not have lungs like an enraged howler monkey. Dyani shuffled inside and sat on the window ledge, rubbing his face.

"You go and get some food," Chimalli said to him. "And get that wound seen to. You're lucky to still have the eye, but if you leave it like that any longer it'll never heal clean."

"Then it won't," Dyani shrugged. "I've come this far, chieftain. I think I'll see it through to the end."

Chimalli gave him a fierce grin. "You've earned that crest in your hair all over again. All right, you're in. Amaru –"

She had been waiting for this. "I've come this far, chieftain. I think I'll see it through to the end."

"You're not a warrior," he said.

"I wasn't as lucky as Dyani. I did lose my eye." She put a hand over the patch. "I think I've paid my fare for the journey."

"Half the men you'll send to fight aren't warriors," Mimiteh said, coming to Amaru's support. "Neither am I, come to that. And Amaru has as much right to be there at the finish as any of us."

Chimalli grimaced. "I don't have time to argue. But she's your concern, Mimiteh. I'll have all I can do keeping my warriors together. What are you smiling about?" he demanded of Kisain. "You already said you think it's suicide to face that sorcerer. I don't need to hear it again."

"You already *know* it's suicide," the soldier answered. "And from your own experience, not from any words of mine." He hesitated. "But I don't think I ever saw men with more courage than you Ashir. You know full well what's waiting for you, and still you'll go to meet it."

"That's what we do," Chimalli said. "We're warriors."

"Yes, you are." Kisain levered himself to his feet. "And at the least, you'll leave a name of glory behind, when the ground has cooled."

Chimalli nodded. "At least that. Are you coming, then? With your smashed leg and all?"

"How could I not?" Kisain asked.

"It'll be hard to keep up."

"Then it'll be hard," he said. "But I know what Terzian's like. He doesn't care about your gods, or your culture. If he's going for the Retreat then he must hope to achieve something by it. What do you think that might be?"

"The *kamachi,*" Amaru said, while the others were still thinking. "He's trying to find Kai."

"He's trying to draw him out," Kisain corrected. "And he'll come. To protect your sacred places, he has to. Terzian knows that, but he'll move slowly, to give Kai time to reach him. It looks like you'll find out where your Servant is after all, Uchu."

"If he comes," the old man said.

"Do you think he won't?"

Chimalli waved his hand again, dismissing the matter. "We need that man, but if he stays away we'll have to do this ourselves. Let's get to work. Time's wasting."

132

He strode to the door. Amaru followed a step behind Dyani, and she walked into the back of the mud-smeared man when he stopped dead a pace outside the door.

"Qula?" he said.

Peering around him, Amaru watched as a stunningly pretty woman let out a cry of delight and flung herself at Dyani, coated in filth though he was. She kissed him full on the lips without even bothering to wipe the dirt away. All the others turned back, Mimiteh frowning but Chimalli with a laugh that sounded strange in the sombre air of the camp.

"My favourite customer," the curvy woman said. "And how come you haven't come to visit me for so long, baker?"

"I thought you were dead," he whispered. He sounded as though he'd been hit on the head. "I thought you must be, for certain."

She grinned at him. "Not me. I know when to jump, and which way. When buildings started to burn I thought it was time to leave. There are things I want to do with my life yet."

"Would one of them be marriage?" Dyani said.

Qula gave him a slow smile, and linked her arm through his. "I like a man with a scar or two. Shows he has courage." She traced the wound on his face and then kissed him again. "Come with me, and we'll talk about it."

"Take me to a bowl of maize stew and I'll listen to anything you say," Dyani answered. Chimalli laughed again and turned away.

An hour later the whole war band was on the move, pouring east in a broad stream through the low hills. At least, those men fit enough to walk were moving. That meant several hundred left behind, but the warriors heading back to battle were a battered lot themselves. One man might have an arm swathed in bandages, another would be burned, and blood would seep from under the coat of a third. Dozens were limping. Three times before the sun went down, Amaru passed men lying half-conscious in the grass, their bodies unable to take them any further.

We're warriors, Chimalli had said. He was right where Mimiteh was wrong. Everyone in this band was a warrior, even those who hadn't had time to shave their hair into crests and weave it with scarlet threads. They were scarred and weary, most of them wounded in one way or another, but they were not beaten yet. And whatever Kisain believed, there was still hope.

*

They passed through villages of ghosts, abandoned by the living. Turkeys pecked in the streets while squirrels investigated empty houses, and both scattered when the ragtag army appeared. Weeds had begun to invade untended fields.

"It will take a generation to recover from this," Uchu said, "even when the Thrain are gone."

133

Twice Amaru passed a body in the dirt. Both times it was marred by pustules of the red plague. As if the Thrain were not enough.

Late on the second day the scouts came back to say the Thrain army was ahead of them, edging through the broken countryside. Chimalli ordered the warriors to keep their distance but sent runners ahead to Hirka, to warn of the danger coming their way.

The warriors knew there was hope. Amaru heard them talk, when they could spare the breath, and when she listened she heard some of their usual boasting, the easy arrogance which had been missing since the Rising. Partly that was just because they were moving, doing something instead of waiting for the sorcerer to act. But it was more than that too, a contagion that spread through the band from warrior to priestess, from fisherman to wife, in every brief smile and spoken word. That word was the same, on every lip, and it was *kamachi*.

22

"These are uncertain times. We face an enemy we never dreamed might exist. But there is a worse enemy.

"The Ashir were made by Viraca. When he came here our ancestors were disparate peoples, each lost in the midst of the others. He gave us one language, one identity. He taught us to build, showed us the quipu... you all know the stories. How he walked the land and bound us together.

"The greatest of those bonds is the *kamachi*. But any man, however holy, can be wrong. And I tell you now that the *kamachi* is a greater danger to us than the Thrain, or the sorcerer, or any other danger that may wait in the world we now know exists. They would take away what we are by force. Kai would take it away from within, like an *akatanqa* beetle already hidden in the crops."

She was good at the speech now. Catori had heard Suchi address four villages before, all much the same as this one. A scatter of small homes, made of frames covered with white adobe. A small temple, and several fresh graves. War hadn't reached this far. The red plague had.

Even the worst sicknesses left more alive than dead. Streets would be empty, after. Houses would echo only to the sound of birds nesting in windows, or rats that scuttled in the debris of the floor. But a generation would pass, and people would begin to move back in as the population grew. The Ashir would survive plague. They might not survive the Thrain.

Or Kai, if you listened to Suchi.

"Once before, everything we are fell under threat," she said now. "That was when Viraca left us, and the Blind God came in his place to bring terror and death. Those who kept the faith were driven to the mountains, to hide in the refuges and retreats. For more than two thousand years they hid, and fled when Tezcata's minions came to hunt them. But they survived. *Kamachi* kept being born. In the end Tezcata's time too came to an end, and the Faithful emerged from hiding to spread Viraca's love once more.

"Why should it be different this time? The Thrain are mortal. Their power will fade one day, or be broken. On that day we *kura* will still be here, with those we could save from the wreck. We will still remember the love of the Bearded God, and there will still be *kamachi,* Viraca's servants among his people. The Ashir will come into their own again.

"But not if Kai has his way. He plans to change us, to make us more like the Thrain and less like ourselves. He will save our country at the cost of our souls. When the Thrain are gone we will still be here, but we will be like them, pale shadows of something we were never meant to be."

There was no priest here. That might be because the hamlet was too small, so people called a *kura* from the next village when they needed one. Or it might be that the priest lay under freshly turned soil in his own graveyard, another victim of the red plague.

Suchi would see either possibility as a good thing. She was fixed on one goal, that of rallying support to defy Kai's changes. Nothing could distract her from it. Her mouth these days was a thin line, lips pressed tightly together, and hardly moving even when she spoke.

Except when she stood on a crate and roused villagers, speaking of fear to those who were already afraid.

"Join us," Suchi said.

Catori looked at her from the side of his eye, and wondered how far rage would carry her.

*

"Thank you for coming," she'd said, when he followed her and Yurac out of the courtyard at Kuska. "It was brave."

"You should have someone you can talk to," he replied. "Someone who knows you."

"I thought you didn't agree with me."

"I don't."

She frowned. "Then why are you here?"

"I just told you," he said, a little impatient. "You deserve a friend. I told Kai that, remember?"

"What about Taruka?"

"He told me I'm no Snake," Catori said. Snapped it, in truth. There'd been no reason to throw that accusation at him, and it would have to be paid for one day. He liked Taruka, but a warrior couldn't let abuse like that go by and still be proud of his crest. "He shouldn't have."

"No," Suchi agreed. "Well. Thank you anyway."

He shrugged. "We'd best hurry. We're not going to find much welcome here from now on."

They stuffed their belongings into cloth bags, not that they had much. Most of what they would carry was food and water. None of them had brought much from the wreck of Chakanay, and they'd had no chance to gather more.

Chakanay seemed a long way behind them.

"I'm surprised at you though," he said to Yurac. "The *kamachi* gave you forgiveness."

"I didn't ask for it," the lean man said.

"Even so –"

""Where was your *kamachi* when we were raiding for food? I've seen youngsters die, babies even, for lack of food. No fault of theirs, and none of their fathers' either. Apusuyu doesn't offer help to little people. If you're poor or weak, or just unlucky, the Servant doesn't mean much."

"But he wants to change all that."

136

"And if you believe him, why are you with us, and not standing by his side? Leave it," Yurac said when Catori tried to speak again. "You're here for your reasons and I'm here for mine. Leave it."

He let it go. He'd spoken of Kai's forgiveness, but there was still a part of Catori that thought of Yurac as an outlaw, no different from any man in a hundred other bandit bands across the Blessed Land. He didn't understand Yurac's reasons for anything. He didn't want the other man's enmity though, so Catori only hefted his bag. "Are we ready?"

They went out of a side door to avoid notice, but the valley wasn't wide enough for them to slip away unseen. Thrain were busy bringing horses out of their field and saddling them. They glanced at the three renegades without very much interest and went on with their work. But otherwise the valley of Kuska was empty. The scouts were tiny specks on the mountainside far ahead, clambering towards the dizzy peak of Apachita. There was no one else.

Catori hefted his bag again, and started towards the pass.

*

Three days later they came to Masma, the first of the flyspeck villages where Suchi would speak.

She spoke from atop a low wall, seeming almost surprised to find herself there. The words were halting, hesitant. Some of the dozen listeners began to drift away before she was half done. She finished with a despondent look. As she stepped down from the wall someone appeared from the shadows under a fig tree full of lilac flowers. An ageing man, his hair shot with grey in patches, like a badly bleached cloth.

Catori shifted his weight, ready for confrontation.

"I am Rimaq," he said. "I tend the people of this village. Not much news reaches us, here."

"The plague did," Suchi said.

"Yes. I suspect the plague will reach everywhere." Rimaq glanced towards the temple, where the fresh graves were. Then his eyes went back to Suchi. "Did he really do these things? The *kamachi,* I mean. Has he taken Thrain into his confidence?"

"He listens to them more than to his own people," Suchi said. "He will make us like them, if he can."

"I've no wish to become like the Thrain," Rimaq said. He pushed a hand through his piebald hair. "Tell me more of this."

He came with them when they left the next morning. Still unconvinced, or so he said. But he came, and he listened to Suchi's stories with an anger Catori would see increase from day to day. It was he who first began to call their journey *ch'uyu-karu,* or holy journey. A crusade.

Catori didn't like that. It reeked of confrontation, even more than Suchi's open defiance of the *kamachi.* That last could be healed, in time, which was

137

most of the reason Catori had come with Suchi in the first place. But a crusade against Kai... it was hard to see how that rift could be mended.

Suchi let the other priest use the term, though. Perhaps it was because Rimaq deferred to her, an older man allowing his junior to lead. Or else she just liked the sound of it. Perhaps she'd had *ch'uyu-karu* in mind all along.

Catori remembered her as a girl in Chakanay. He remembered the still slightly gauche woman who'd come back with the Qapac, short weeks ago. Suchi now didn't bear much resemblance to either of those people, and he realised he might not know her very well anymore.

"Join us," Suchi said. Catori looked at her from the side of his eye, and wondered how far rage would carry her.

One person did, a weedy-looking girl with pimples on a soft chin. The sort of person who might snatch at any chance to leave this forsaken backwater of a village, riddled with plague and promising only labour and toil. She was called Asisa. A pretty name for a plain girl.

"Be welcome," Rimaq said when she joined them. "This is the *ch'uyu-karu,* which will make everything right again."

Catori wanted to tell him not to make such claims. Nobody could make everything right, not even the *kamachi.* Not even the god who had sent him, if Viraca ever came to walk the land again. But Suchi let the old priest speak for her, take care of the little things, so Catori held his tongue. Again.

He wondered how Taruka and the others were, back in Kuska.

The little group went on. They slept that night in a store house by the road, a mile from the nearest house. The beds were shelves meant to hold sacks of grain, or potatoes carried down from the heights when crops failed here. It was an old place, long ago made obsolete by the larger warehouses along the Pasqa and its offshoot roads, but the roof was tight and it was dry.

Asisa snored like a sick llama. Catori woke from fitful sleep with a dull ache behind his eyes.

The first village that day was much like the others, small and poor, with new graves by the temple. Even the children were hollow-eyed, not with plague but with fear of it. The people listened to Suchi's speech and walked away, her passion no match for their weariness. They left, still heading south, and soon saw a man running the other way. He went past without looking at them.

"That was Waki," Catori said. "One of Kai's scouts."

"I know," Suchi answered. She'd formed the habit of speaking without turning her head, so it often seemed as though Catori was talking to an ear. "I wonder where he's going."

"Back to Kai, I'd think." He was careful not to say *Kuska.* There were people here who didn't know where the valley was, and it was best kept that way. "Come to that, where are *we* going?"

"Hatun," she said.

"All the way to the capital?"

"We can't change what Kai is doing from the villages. We have to go to the centre of power."

"What centre of power?" he demanded, driven beyond his patience. "The Qapac is dead, the Auk is dead. Nata was as senior as any priest and he's dead too. What power, Suchi?"

"The government is there," she said, unperturbed. "Most of the officials, and the senior *kura*. They are who we need to persuade."

"Hatun is a long walk, and the sorcerer is in our way."

"I know how far it is. I walked it when I came back to Chakanay. As for the Thrain, we can avoid them by staying off the main roads. Back trails worked for Kai and they can work for us." She did turn her head then, her lips as set as always. "Are you still with me, Catori?"

"Yes," he said. "To the end of the road."

She nodded, satisfied, and they went on.

They were chased out of the next village. The local *kura* did it, hitting Suchi twice with a broom before Catori took it from him. The priest spat rage as he struck, accusing Suchi of betraying the one thing that held the Ashir together, and gave them hope. They could have stayed and let Suchi speak anyway – the priest was harmless now – but several people had cheered him on as his blows landed, and Suchi didn't see the point.

In mid-afternoon they approached a little town. Nothing like Chakanay, hardly more than a village really, but it was twice the size of those hamlets put together. A thousand people, perhaps. From the earth road Catori could see men in the fields, and women stitching in groups along the streets. He saw a temple too, its square roof higher than anything else in the town.

"There are graves along the side of a field, there," Asisa said. Weak-chinned she might be, but her eyesight was fearsome. "The red plague must have reached this town too."

Of course it had. Plague didn't stop at town boundaries, or ignore everyone on the wrong side of a wall. Catori found himself travelling with idiots and pompous fools, and what did that make him?

"I am not afraid of plague," Suchi said. She started towards the town, not looking to see if her little band followed. They did, of course. Catori trailed along at the back.

To the end of the road, whatever came.

23

Slowing her horse to a trot, Izel turned and splashed back through the river. The animal tossed its head and veered to one side before she could control it, and then she pulled too hard on the reins and the horse gave a huffing snort of protest. Izel stole a glance at Evain and struggled to guide the animal back to the group waiting for her beside the small river.

"You sit the saddle like a sack of pork," the Thrain captain said when Izel came to a halt beside him. "I've told you over and again to keep your back straight and your knees in. And if you carry on hauling at the reins the way you do you'll chew the horse's mouth to pieces, and no animal will ever like having you on his back. Be gentle, and trust him."

"I do trust him," Izel said, as she half fell out of the saddle. "More than I did before, anyway."

"If that's all the trust you can show, you'll never make a decent rider," Evain said. "I know this is strange to everyone. But it's time you started to listen to the things I tell you." He pinched his nose with thumb and forefinger. "All right. Who's next?"

"I am," Ususi said. She led her horse over to the soldier and waited while he checked the girth straps. Evain insisted that each rider had to arrange her own riding gear herself, and he always found something wrong no matter how carefully they checked to make sure he could not.

Chinita watched without comment. She had already put in an hour's riding today, and while Evain never seemed satisfied with the progress the women were making, he had admitted she could make a rider one day. That was success, of a sort. Evain never actually praised anyone, so grudging words from him were worth a sparkling compliment from anyone else. Besides, her thighs were sore from gripping the horse the way Evain demanded. Chinita was content now to sit on the grass and study her sisters in arms. She might even learn more quickly that way.

So far she had learned that once the smell of horse got into her clothes, it was almost impossible to get out again. She'd learned that horse hairs could hide in fabric or skin and then pop out just when she thought the last of them were gone, and that horses produced a quite amazing amount of dung. But against all that, she'd learned from Evain's sparing comments that she could ride. Whatever knack there was to mastering these strange animals, it seemed she had it.

Kai was seated with his back against a pear tree, over by the temple building on the far side of the river. Chinita's gaze went to him from time to time, just to be sure he was still there. She didn't seem able to stop herself doing that, though it made her feel a fool. The man scrambled her wits just by being there, and somehow managed to make her glad of it.

It was eight days since the scouts had gone out, and Kai was becoming edgy. Twice already this morning he'd risen to walk down the valley to the foot of the pass, only to pace around for a few moments and then stride back to the orchard.

Both times a knot of warriors had gone with him, ambling along a little distance away and talking among themselves as though out for a casual stroll, though they didn't fool anyone. Nobody was going to let Kai take a risk he didn't need to, not now. He was all they had left. Any last hope of victory lay with him, and they knew it.

Taruka was lying in the grass not far from Kai, but the warrior had draped a cotton scarf over his eyes and dozed off in the shade of the trees. Tension never seemed to touch him, at least, or if it did he never showed it. He was a little quieter than he had been, before his sister had been sent away, but that was all.

Chinita's hand went unconsciously to the shaved side of her scalp. Another thing that never bothered Taruka was the idea of women as warriors. Some of the men still didn't like it, and muttered behind their hands when they thought there was nobody to hear them. Probably some would still complain ten years from now, or a hundred, but it didn't seem to matter to Taruka. Chinita supposed it was a small thing to him, given what he'd lost these past days. As for her, the exposed skin of her head felt strange. That made her laugh to herself. All the weirdness around her, and she was struck not by horses or writing, but by her own shaved hair.

"We've chosen a name," she had told Kai and Taruka, three days before. The two men had just emerged from the temple, where Chinita and the other women were waiting by the doors. "For our society."

Kai looked at her, then at the women ranged at her side, and finally nodded. "What did you decide?"

"We thought about Makisapa," she said, for Taruka's benefit. It had been his idea, to name their women's warrior band after the monkey who wanted to fly with eagles. "But we don't want our society to be forever seen as trying to be something it should never be. We thought about calling ourselves the Cats, or the Foxes, and decided against it. We wanted something different from the men's societies."

"Well?" Taruka said when she stopped. "I'm grinding my teeth here, Chinita. What did you choose?"

"*Kichka*," she told them simply. "We are the Thorns."

She thought it was a good name. The best animal names had already been used. Next to Eagle or Puma, calling the women's society something like Cat would have sounded feeble. There would have been no end of jokes about them doing nothing but purr at people. Thorn was different, unique enough to stand out, yet not aggressive enough to upset the men. Not any more than could be helped, anyway. Chinita didn't actually care whether male warriors were upset, but she did see the advantages in soothing their egos if she could.

"Very well," Kai had said, there by the temple doors. "The Thorns it is. Taruka can tell you more of how societies work than I can, but for you there's one extra rule."

"Why? Because we're women?"

141

"Yes. Because of that." He didn't blink as he met her stare. "No woman is to fight when she is pregnant, Chinita, or when she has a child to care for. If a Thorn wants a family she will have to choose what she wants, and if it's children, she must leave the society."

"We've already chosen," Izel said quietly.

Kai looked at the other woman, and Chinita knew him well enough now to see the flash of sorrow deep in his eyes. He didn't want women to fight. But he would allow it even though it caused him pain, because he had given a promise. He would carry that burden. It was all Chinita could do not to go to him then, to draw his head down to her shoulder and soothe his cares for a while.

Ten days ago, forming a warrior band had been all she wanted to do. Now she wasn't sure, not at all. If she had to choose between the Thorns and Kai, she thought she would let her hair grow out and go where he went, and never think to glance behind her.

"Very well," the man she loved had said again, and turning away he went with Taruka down the temple steps.

Chinita shook the memory away. By the river Ususi had mounted up and now flicked the reins to get her piebald moving. He stood there and twitched an idle ear, and she thumped her heels into his flanks with an irritated frown. The horse huffed and started forward. Chinita was beginning to think horses were cleverer than they let on. Certainly they knew the feel of an inexperienced rider, and rarely missed a chance to assert themselves. There was always the quirt, of course – Evain became quite irate when anyone called it a whip – but he didn't like the women to do more with it than flick the horse's flank. He became truly angry when they actually hit the animals.

"I thought I did quite well," Izel said. She flopped into the grass at Chinita's side, smiling broadly. "I was terrified of horses a week ago, do you remember? Now I think I'm starting to like them." Her nose wrinkled. "I would if I didn't have to clean up their dung, anyway."

"It's a good thing you are," Chinita said. Her gaze drifted past Kai again, still sitting under his tree with an arm draped over his knees. "You'll be spending a lot of time with them from now on."

Izel's grin widened. "Thorn."

Chinita smiled back at her, unable to help herself. Their new identity was still so new to them that it was impossible not to take pride in it, despite Chinita's secret new misgivings. She was sure that women would come streaming to join them, once the Thrain were gone and Chinita, Izel and Ususi led the Thorn into towns and cities for the first time. A lot of people would be horrified, or else would see the horses and hide under their beds with the doors locked and barred. But women would come, in ones and twos at first, and before very long. Women with no future except service in the temples or whorehouses, or else a bandit's life of fear and loneliness. Those forced to grub a living from society's leavings, clothed in rags and walking always with hunger at their side.

142

It would be a moment to savour, when the Thorn rode into the first town to lay eyes on them. Kai had promised to be there, and Taruka too, so nobody would be able to ignore the women or dismiss them as fools and upstarts. From there word would spread, the way rumour always did, like pollen in a high wind. Everyone in Apusuyu would know in less than a month, at least if there were any Runners left alive to carry the news.

They only needed to do two things to make that vision come true. One was to get rid of the Thrain.

The other, which for Ususi might be considerably more difficult, was to learn to ride. She jounced around in her piebald's saddle, unable to catch the rhythm of the animal's movements even at a slow trot. Worse, she held the reins in one hand and gripped the horse's mane with the other, more concerned with holding on than guiding her mount where she wanted it to go. Evain looked to be clinging to the last of his patience, his jaw tight with the effort.

"You're in love with Kai," Izel said.

Chinita looked at her in surprise. "So?"

"He says we'll have to choose. Between the society and a family."

"I'm in love with him," Chinita said. "We're not planning a brood of kids anytime soon."

"Fair enough," Izel replied. She nodded towards Ususi. "What if she just can't ride?"

"She'll learn. It might take her a long time, that's all. And we can't afford to turn anyone away."

"Good," Izel said. "We're going to have to think about tattoos, you know. So people can tell who we are."

"People are going to *know* who we are," Chinita answered. "You're right though, much as I hate to admit it. Fighting I can handle, but I don't like the idea of someone sticking needles in me."

"Neither do I," Izel agreed. Her grin returned quickly though. "How does it feel to be a chief?"

"Tiring," Chinita said. She'd never been responsible for others before, and the experience was wearing just as often as it was a thrill. She understood how her father had felt for years, now, knowing that any order he gave might mean the deaths of the men who trusted him. But she knew it was only a glimmer of the pressure Kai had lived with all his life, wherever he went, being forced to be what those who followed needed him to be. That was the source of the pain he carried, every day, that it seemed she could ease in him. Thinking that, her gaze drifted back across the river to the pear orchard, to where Kai sat and waited with Taruka sleeping nearby.

Except Kai wasn't there. She found him a second later, two hundred yards down the valley and striding swiftly towards the pass. Half a dozen warriors were hurrying along behind him, trying to look casual while managing a hasty walk. Something in his posture brought Chinita to her feet, scanning the distant slope where the pass from Apachita gave out. She had to squint in the sunlight, but finally she saw what he had seen before her. At the foot of the pass, a tiny figure moved.

"He must have eyes like an eagle," Izel murmured. "How in Catequil's name did he notice that?"

"Because he was looking for it,'" Chinita said. She didn't need to add, *as we should have been.* "Get the others, Izel. And wake Taruka. Tell him one of the scouts is back."

Izel scrambled up. "Are we leaving?"

"How by the Blind God's eyes should I know?" Chinita was already hurrying after Kai. "Just get them ready!"

She broke into a trot, splashing across the river where it broadened and flowed knee-deep over a bed of smooth stones. Kai was still well ahead of her, walking even faster than before, with the warriors now abandoning pretence to trot in pursuit. A llama eyed him as he went past, but didn't try to spit at him. Chinita gave the animal a wide berth even so, aware how temperamental they could be, and closing the gap she called Kai's name.

He paused and looked over his shoulder. For a moment he hesitated, but then he stopped by a thorny hedge. He lifted his right foot and studied the underside of the boot while the band of warriors went passed and fanned out ahead of him, and Chinita came up to him as well.

"I need to get that boot fixed," he said. "But it will have to wait. That's Waki up ahead."

With that he started off again, while Chinita squinted at the still-distant figure. She supposed it might be the warrior, though she couldn't be sure. "Did the Bearded God give you a gift of eyesight, as well as intuition?"

"Maybe he did." Kai didn't react to the jest. "He might have thought to give me calm nerves while he was at it."

The approaching scout stumbled and almost fell. He was weaving drunkenly as he began the long walk up the valley, seeming to catch his feet with every step, and his head hung down. Chinita didn't think he'd seen them yet. It *was* Waki, she saw now, and he was at the edge of collapse.

She felt suddenly uneasy. Waki was among the toughest of the warriors, which was why he'd gone out scouting when quicker men rested after the crossing of Apachita. If he was tottering now, he must have driven himself to exhaustion, and that could only mean bad news. She quickened her pace, but even so Kai was ahead of her, almost running now.

Waki lifted his head and saw them. Saw Kai, really. His whole body seemed to loosen and he collapsed into the grass.

144

24

"I came as fast as I could," Waki said. His voice was harsh. Chinita had heard vultures caw like that, when they were dying.

Kai unhooked a water flask from his belt and knelt beside the warrior. "Of course you did, and I'm proud of you. Drink now."

"There's no time."

"There's always time, if only a little. News can wait." He held out the flask. "Drink, Waki. Limit yourself to sips. You look as though you haven't drunk for days."

He noticed everything. That was the Teacher God's gift to Kai. He saw every detail, even those others missed, and those he wasn't really aware of himself. His eyes saw, and something in his mind read the scene like a Runner decoding the knots of a *quipu*. Something Viraca had put there. It had probably always been part of Kai, but since the Thrain came it had come fully awake in him, and it never slept.

"I last drank yesterday," Waki admitted. He propped himself on one elbow and took a slug from the flask, not a sip at all, and his eyes closed for a moment. Then he abandoned all pretence and upended the flask over his head, letting as much splash over his chin as went into his gulping mouth. "By the seven gods and their dearest dreams, that's good. I've done more climbing this last week than in my whole life before."

"Was it worth it?" Kai asked. Chinita laid a hand on his arm and he shook it off without looking at her.

Waki nodded. "It was worth it."

He had to stop to cough. Kai let him, sitting on his heels as patient as could be, but Chinita had heard the thread of urgency in his voice and knew it was just an act. One of so many Kai had performed in his life, day by day.

"I went through the spider forest," Waki said after a moment. "Turned south at the *lanti*. The path brought me into the lowland hills late on the third day." A pause, while he breathed slowly. "Next morning I heard word of an uprising in Chakanay. Artisans and old men who used to be warriors, and fighting men from outside the town too."

"About time," Taruka said as he came up. "Who led it?"

"A chieftain called Chimalli, of the Puma," Waki answered. "And the *kamachi's* friend Salali."

"Sala?" Kai repeated. A grin broke through his hard expression. "The Squirrel's alive? And he managed to turn himself into a warrior of sorts, it seems. Good for him. I never thought –"

"*Kamachi,*" Waki said. Kai stopped and looked at him. "Salali was killed in the uprising. He led an assault on the Precinct, and was trapped in a burning house. He didn't make it out. I'm sorry."

Kai stood motionless. He didn't speak. This time when Chinita touched his hand his fingers closed tight around hers.

"The sorcerer returned to Chakanay while the battle was still going on," Waki went on. He paused again, breath rough in his throat. "Our fighters were inside the Precinct by then, the Thrain cornered, but Terzian slaughtered us. Thousands of warriors were killed, and the survivors scattered."

"And the Thrain?" Taruka asked.

"They took losses too. There are fewer than two thousand of them left. Many of those are injured."

"What else?" Chinita asked when Kai still didn't reply. "There's more to come, Waki, isn't there?"

He nodded grimly. "The sorcerer destroyed Chakanay. Smashed it with his magic and set fire to the ruins. Hardly a building is left standing, except for the Precinct, and smoke still rises from the rubble. You can see it from the hills, in clear sky." Another pause. "Then he released Ashir prisoners to spread word of what he will do next. That's how I know this. I met one of his messengers on the road."

"Next?" Kai's gaze refocused on the scout. "What is it he plans to do next?"

"The Retreat," Waki said. "*Kamachi*, the Thrain left Chakanay four days ago, and are making for the Retreat. The sorcerer says he will do to the temples what he did to the town."

Chinita grunted as though someone had struck her in the belly. She felt Kai's arm go stiff. Someone behind her muttered a curse and she looked around to see Paqu puffing up to join them.

"*He will not*," Kai almost hissed. "Towns can be rebuilt, but I will not let him lay eyes on the Retreat."

"We can't stop it," Taruka said. "If the Thrain left Chakanay four days ago, they're already too far ahead of us. It would take us two days just to reach the other side of the spider forest."

"If we went that way," Kai said.

There was a silence.

Paqu opened his mouth, closed it again, and then snorted. "Are you going to break every taboo before you're done, *kamachi*?"

"If I must," he said levelly. "I am open to other suggestions. Do you have one, priest?"

"As it happens, humph, I don't." Paqu smiled thinly. "And I must admit, there are attractions to the directness of your approach. Humph. Although this would be insanely dangerous."

"Facing the sorcerer will be insanely dangerous," Kai said. His sudden fury had given way to renewed calm. "It seems everything is, these days. What does a little more hazard matter, here and there?"

"What are you talking about?" Chinita asked.

Kai and Paqu exchanged glances.

"Humph," the priest said finally. "Very well. There is another way out of the valley of Kuska. A secret path known only to the *kura*." His lips quirked. "Until now, anyway."

146

Taruka narrowed his eyes. "It must be south, then. Over the mountains."

"Yes," Paqu said.

"There's still snow on those peaks."

"Yes," the old man repeated. "Winds blow down from the mountains there, all through spring. Snow lasts on those ridges, humph, while it melts on others. Even in summer it's a hard journey."

"And in winter?" Taruka asked.

Paqu shrugged. "I would not know. Nobody's ever been stupid enough to try it."

"I never claimed to be clever," Kai said.

Taruka looked at him. "And on the other side we'll find the Retreat, won't we? Although it must be sixty miles away, maybe eighty, depending how straight the path is. A long way, in those mountains."

"The most sacred places in Apusuyu are all in the high mountains," Paqu murmured, as though people didn't know that already. "And the Retreat is the most sacred of all." He cocked an eyebrow at Kai. "While Kuska, humph, is merely holy, I am told."

"On the other side is the Retreat," Kai agreed. "There used to be a fair path across those peaks, a thousand years ago."

"What is there now?" Chinita asked uneasily.

"Now there is a trail," Kai said, in that serene voice he used when he was already certain of what he would do next. When the god was speaking to him, perhaps, somewhere in the quiet places of his mind. "A narrow trail, which at times runs across a ledge so narrow that you have to inch along sideways." He was smiling slightly. "We could be swept away, or find ourselves cut off, and starve to death up there. We could slip and fall into the gorges. As Paqu said, this is insanely dangerous. I won't ask anyone to come with me, but I am going to take the risk."

Taruka grinned. "You won't have to ask. You'll have company on the trail, *kamachi*. Could you doubt it?"

"I'll go," Waki began.

Kai cut him off. "You'll stay here and rest. You've done your part already, Waki, and you're in no condition to go further. I'll take no more than six people over the pass with me." He smiled ironically. "Seven of us, one for each of the gods. A lucky number, and we'll need every blessing we can get."

"One of the gods is a *goddess*," Chinita said. "You'd better include me, then. Or would you prefer a man to stand for Quilla of the Moon?"

Kai smiled at her.

"Also me," Paqu added. "If you mean to take unconsecrated men and women behind the walls of the Retreat, humph, you ought at least to have a *kura* with you, don't you think?"

"Then that's four," Kai said. "Evain will be the fifth, for advice when we meet the sorcerer. Who else?"

"Achachi," Taruka said. "That old man will come after us even if he's not invited. We might as well take him. Who's the seventh?"

Kai hesitated. Chinita saw it happen, saw him pause like a frog on a lily pad, taking just an instant while he assessed. "Viraca."

"What?"

"We need the god," Kai said. "Without him we'll all die. Let's leave a place for him to walk with us, if we still hold his love."

That brought silence. *If we still hold his love.* Chinita had never doubted it before the Thrain came. The weeks since had been different, shot through with terror and uncertainty. As Kai spoke she almost thought she saw a shadow on the ground beside him, the presence of another figure she couldn't see in the sunshine.

"All right," Taruka said. He looked at Kai. "I don't want to seem reluctant, but is this wise?"

"Wisdom has nothing to do with it," Kai said. "The sorcerer has left me no choice. I can't allow him to destroy the Retreat, and time allows me only one path. I must go to the Retreat by the shortest road, so I will take the high pass, and trust in Viraca to watch over me. Tell me, Taruka, what would a Deer do, if time left him just one road?"

"He'd take it," Taruka said.

Kai nodded. "Then may the gaze of the Blind God not fall on us, until we reach the other side."

"Or after," Taruka said.

"It might be wise," Paqu suggested quietly, "to offer a formal prayer for that protection, before we leave. Even for you, *kamachi.*"

Kai nodded. "Perhaps it would. But a quick one, Paqu. We can make good distance today before sundown."

"You mean to leave *today?*"

"I mean to do what has to be done," Kai said, "with my trust in the god and no fear of the danger."

Chinita felt a cold thrill at the words. It wasn't like Kai to speak so openly of Faith. That had been more Matlal's style, before. *He's changing,* she thought for the hundredth time, and then; *he's changed.* He wasn't the man she had first met, back on the bridge over the river Mayuma. His old friends were gone, and his tutor, all lost to the war. His innocence had been lost with them, and now he knew what pressure really was, and what it made of men.

*

"Didn't think we'd be facing this again just yet," Achachi said. He sounded almost cheerful.

Kai nodded. "Me, neither. But we're still not setting the steps of this dance." His hand went to his coat, to feel the weight of the *cizin* there. It had become a

148

habitual gesture over the past ten days, since the ambush at the tunnel. "Will Taruka be all right? About his sister, I mean."

"I know what you mean," he said shortly. They walked on a little way. The grass began to thin, then broke up into clumps broken by bare rock. Small, stunted trees grew in the few places where there was enough soil, driving their roots into the ground only to find stone a foot down, barren and cold. One of them supported the weight of a large boulder that had come tumbling down the mountain, shoving the trunk sideways and leaving a deep crack almost to the tree's heart. Somehow the tree had survived the blow. Its branches were still heavy with leaves, and one or two blossoms peered out from behind them.

When Kai lifted his head he saw a ridge ahead, streaked with snow on the heights. And beyond it another range, higher yet, and a third beyond that half hidden by clouds.

"He'll manage," Achachi said at length. "He's Deer. And when this is over he'll likely look for Suchi, and they'll find a way to make things the way they were. She'll help him, too."

"I hope they do," Kai said. "There's been enough pain already. But I don't think things will be the way they were, for any of us."

"Probably not," the old man agreed. "Still, we can make it close enough, with the gods' help." He threw weight onto his stick to help him over a step of rock. "Except for the outlaws, of course."

"Except them," Kai agreed. "I promised I'd find places for all who wanted them, and I will. And except for the horses we'll breed. Except the iron we'll forge, too. And the writing, and the ships we'll build, and –"

"All right, all right," Achachi grumbled. "I get the point. Nothing will be the way it was before."

"The important things will," Kai said. "We'll still have the love of the Bearded God, and *kamachi* will still be born."

"I suppose so. It takes some getting used to though. I'm an old man, and not very clever sometimes."

"You'll do well enough for me," Kai said.

Achachi snorted. "Given that you've got no choice, I'll have to. Meanwhile I think I'll walk with my granddaughter for a bit. Watch your feet on the climb. There'll be loose stones."

"I know there'll be loose stones," he said, but Achachi had already gone.

At the top of the ridge Kai turned to look back at Kuska. It was far below them already, and the figures standing at the foot of the pass to watch them go were tiny. He raised a hand. Someone down there lifted a palm in reply. Burru, probably. The former bandit wasn't happy at being told to stay behind, but he had agreed in the end. Kai wondered if warriors questioned their chiefs over every order they were given. Most likely they did.

A little longer, and perhaps he would be able to lay down the burden of chieftainship. One way or another. His hand stole to the *cizin* again, fingers brushing the bone handle.

"Do you need a rest already?" Taruka said as he clambered past. "I thought you said we were in a hurry. Come on, *kamachi*. Be careful of the loose stones."

Kai managed not to sigh.

The little party crossed over the lower shoulder of the pass just after midday. Kuska was a distant strip of green by then, often hidden by drifting wreaths of cloud. The path ran between patches of ice, vanishing here and reappearing there, sometimes easy to pick out but often lost as it coiled around rocks and bushes. Nothing worse than that.

Not yet.

Storms could blow up from nowhere in these high mountains, shrieking winds that drove sleet and hail almost sideways through the pass, and forced travellers to huddle in what shelter they could find until it blew itself out. If that happened in the next few days there was no way they could reach the Retreat before Terzian. It was in Viraca's hands, and the other gods'. Perhaps it always had been.

Ahead of them the path swooped into a shallow valley filled with stones and dust, and little else. After that it clambered up again, past tumbled showers of stones and looming rock walls, until it vanished into the mountains. Snow hid behind banks of clouds, higher yet, but all too close.

They paused to rest on a broad shelf where stunted bushes straggled in the cracks. Kai would have preferred to push on, but he knew that too much haste now would have to be paid for later, in shortness of breath and leaden limbs. On the heights, slow and steady was faster than quick and hurried. He made himself sit and relax, while the band left offerings to Pachacamac of earthquakes: a piece of bronze broken from a knife, a square of tattered cloth, a cup, a small string of beads. Paqu led them in another prayer, asking the god to bless them with a safe passage, though this time Kai didn't join them. He had made his plea in the temple at Kuska, all he intended to make, and he was the Servant of Viraca. If those things were not enough to draw the Bearded God's benevolent eye, then nothing would do so.

He stood and walked to the far end of the plateau, where the trail twisted away up a steep slope littered with rocks. Ice hid in the shadow of every stone now, and the wind was cold. There was nothing to see except clouds, and peaks peering between them, but the sorcerer was beyond them, somewhere. Kai's hand crept inside his coat to feel the *cizin*.

Made by the God's own hand, he thought, or so it was said. Kai had never truly believed that, until it had cut through Ramian's steel armour as though it was cotton. Now he thought it might be true, and either way, he would have an answer very soon. Events were running together now. The struggle would be decided on the far side of these mountains.

Kai had walked wide of the sorcerer from the start, guided by the unheard voice whispering just below the level of his thoughts. Terzian had stayed away from him too, though that was only chance, luck, the workings of fate…

150

whatever you felt was truest. But those days were over. It was time for them their dance to finish.

It would be the end of a long story, begun long ago. Years ago, and certainly before the Ashir knew there was such a people as the Thrain. Evain had explained it as best he could, though much of it sounded strange to Kai. Men talking in a room somewhere, full of the stories they had heard of a land beyond the mountains where gold flowed like rivers, and jewels lay on the ground for anyone to pick up. A land of primitives, without iron or horses, without even carts, hardly able to defend itself at all. A land of heathens where the One God was unknown. It might have been put there just for the Thrain to conquer, a whole country laid out just for them, rich and huge and wealthy beyond dreams. One man had thought so, listening as the merchants' tales flowed and the talk became freer.

In time talking had become planning. Men like Evain became involved, with no grand schemes or plans except a desire to find a decent bit of land to call his own. But behind it all there *was* a grand scheme, one that had come undone forever in a crush of shouting, sweating men in a tunnel in the Uma Mountains, when a Prince had died, and a friend.

He missed Matlal. He missed him with a deep, raw pain in his heart. Sometimes Kai would still turn and expect his friend to be there, half a step behind him, dour and grumbling as always. It was so hard to accept he was not, and never would be. Neither would Sala, with his insouciant smile and his jokes, shuffling a pack of cards or rattling the dice across a table. Death was so hard on the living. They had to go on, with nothing but memory to sustain them.

"What are you thinking?" Chinita asked. From half a step behind him, and a little to one side. Where Matlal used to stand.

"I'm thinking of beginnings," he answered. Strange, how that raw place inside was soothed at the sound of her voice. Memory was not all that sustained the living. There was hope, and love, and sometimes – just sometimes – they could be made to be enough.

She put her arms around him from behind, and after a moment Kai leaned back into her. She kissed his ear, but he didn't turn around. His fingers stroked the bone handle of the *cizin*, over and over, as he stared into the mist.

"I think" he said softly, watching the clouds swirl above his head, "that it's time for an ending."

25

The morning's rain had stopped, and a steady breeze blew the ragged tails of clouds back eastwards. Berain could pick out distant figures where they gathered around drainage ditches and small stands of trees, ahead and to the left. For days they had been scattered through the countryside around the Thrain, keeping pace with it at a respectful distance. Early this morning the force had paused on a ridge high enough to reveal the land spread out around them, and across all of it people moved in little groups, for as far as Berain had been able to see.

"See any food?" Naraid asked.

Berain shook his head, and the other man grimaced.

An hour after that someone found a cask of flour at the bottom of a dry ditch, below a barn that had been burned by the Ashir. The rest of the food was gone, but they'd missed this one barrel. It was damp and crawling with weevils, but the soldiers picked them out and baked flat pancakes of bread, the sort of thing an experienced man could make in the time it took for the next unit to catch up.

All Berain saw was a chicken coop, empty except for a few sad feathers, and that was hard on a man who hadn't eaten a proper hot meal for four days. All right, sometimes a soldier had to endure that, but it was still hard. His stomach was tight all the time now, and hunger trailed him through the days and gnawed him through the nights.

Lunch was pieces of cracker with the last of the cheese.

"If those bastards don't stop burning everything ahead of us, we're going to have problems," Naraid said.

"Shut up."

"We'll have to send out patrols."

"Shut up," Berain said again, and then laughed. "Why? Are you going to volunteer?"

"I meant the light cavalry should go."

He snorted. "Of course you did."

Anyone who left the main party was not likely to come back. They all knew that.

It had happened, a few times. Horsemen were sent out fast, galloping to catch a glimpse of the ground ahead, or to reach an outhouse that didn't look to have been fired yet. Some riders had fallen to archers who rose out of bushes or fired from perches in trees, and while the bowmen were killed, one for one wasn't an exchange the Thrain could afford.

But it had to be risked, because there was no food anymore. The Thrain were moving slowly, tending their wounded as they went. That was the official reason to dawdle, anyway. Most of the soldiers thought Terzian just wanted to give Kai time to catch up before reaching the Retreat. So here the army was, strung out on a road deep in hostile territory, ambling along like well-to-do merchants out for a stroll.

Half the injured had died, and been buried in shallow plots at the end of each day's march. Enough remained for Terzian to use as an excuse for tardiness. Not that anyone dared challenge him.

The slow pace meant that Ashir warriors had got ahead of them, and were now burning crops and driving off the livestock. Thrain patrols found fields of ashes and not much else. Gavair had ordered rations cut to two-thirds. Another day or two and they might be down to half.

"What's that?" Naraid asked, shading his eyes.

Something was moving ahead of them. A warrior peering out of a hole, maybe. Berain signalled for the archers to notch arrows but then kept his hand high, so they wouldn't shoot. The shape moved a bit but then came back on itself. The sun came out and suddenly Berain could see it was a pig, snuffling through the earth under a stand of trees.

He didn't have to tell the men to fire. Two arrows struck the animal and it fell squealing. It was up again in an instant, but one of the shafts had found its eye and as the pig tried to run it pushed the feathers into the ground and the point through its brain. It went down again, this time not moving. Someone let out a whoop.

"Spit that animal for tonight's supper," Berain ordered. Naraid and another man started forwards, both smiling.

"Hold where you stand," someone said.

Berain turned and his stomach sank. Striding towards them was a man dressed all in brown, with a net woven into his shoulder.

"That plunder does not belong to you," Draivan said in his harsh voice. "It belongs to us all. We will take it."

He motioned, and two junior priests moved past him. One took a spear from a soldier's unresisting hand, to spit the pig and carry it. Neither of the god-botherers looked capable of the task.

"We killed it," Berain protested. "It's ours by right."

"Your patrol cannot eat a whole pig."

"We wouldn't try. But we should be first to the feast."

"It will be shared among the soldiers, captain."

He could feel his temper fraying. "There are fifteen hundred of us, man! That's only one pig!"

"Nevertheless," Draivan said. It wasn't an answer and Berain opened his mouth to say so, only to be stopped by the chaplain's upflung hand. "Enough backtalk. You are new enough in your rank, *captain,* that it could be taken away on a whim. At a mild suggestion, let us say. Better to let us deal with it for you, don't you think?"

"And you'll feast on pork tonight," Berain said.

The words were out before he could stop them. He saw the priest's nostrils whiten but Draivan's eyes never changed before he turned away. In that moment Berain hated him more than any Ashir, more than an arrow in the dark. Hated every pinch-faced line of him. He fought the urge to swing out of the saddle and

153

beat the man bloody with the limb of his bow. The struggle took him some time to win.

"Move on," he said finally.

"But sir, the pig –"

"We'll get our share tonight," he broke in, though he didn't believe it. There wasn't a lot of trust in the eyes that weighed on him either. "But where there was one pig, there might be another. Keep your eyes open, because by the God, the next one is *ours!*"

That afternoon they saw the orchard.

*

It was outside a village away to the north. Berain's squad would have passed it if they'd held their course, but the army was marching five units wide, to keep everyone as close to Terzian as possible. Gavair's orders, not the magician's. It also meant they had more chance of finding any food the Ashir hadn't managed to burn or drive off.

That had paid dividends. Naraid was first to see the next two squads break into a trot. "They've seen something. But what?"

"There," Berain said after a moment. "That's an orchard. And – I can see fruit on the branches."

They looked at each other.

"Hurry!" Berain said.

The squad swerved left, leaving the road. The Ashir didn't bother with hedges, preferring instead to mark boundaries with posts or stones. It meant the soldiers could head straight for the orchard. As they drew closer Berain saw the trees were one of the local types, not familiar like apples or pears. He did know it though, a fat green fruit called lacanu or lucuma, something like that. Vendors had sold it in the market at Chakanay. Berain had found it dry, with an odd flavour a bit like maple.

His stomach growled and he pushed his horse to a canter. Behind them someone in the army was shouting at them to stop.

"Stop, hell," Berain muttered. The leading squad had already reached the orchard, with a second not far behind. Any delay and all the fruit would be gone. He could always claim he hadn't heard the shouts. Naraid must have decided the same; he galloped ahead of the squad and straight into the trees, laughing in relief.

Some of the men already there were eating so fast they'd begun to cough. Berain stood in the saddle to pluck a lucuma from the branch and missed it. He cursed, angling the horse for another try.

One of the coughing men went down on his knees, hands grappling at his throat.

154

"Stop!" Berain yelled. He came up beside Naraid and struck the fruit almost from the other man's mouth. Naraid swore and rounded on him. "What do you think you're –"

"It's poisoned," Berain said.

Naraid looked past him to the choking men, and went white.

A dozen men were down, wheezing in the grass. Their faces were turning black. The one closest held out a hand to Berain as darkness oozed across his throat and then over his jaw. He was trying to speak and couldn't. The inky stain reached his lips and he gave a rattling cough and pitched down on his face.

"Bastards!" Naraid screamed. He wheeled his horse to face the edge of the orchard. "Ashir bastards! You're cowards, murderers! Why don't you face us like men?"

Because Terzian cuts them into slivers every time they do, Berain thought. He dismounted, thinking in a vague way that he might be able to help, and then stopped. There was nothing he could do. The choking sounds were less now. Most of the men who'd eaten were dead.

"They painted poison on the fruit," he said.

More riders clattered into the orchard. Berain saw Terzian among them looking around at the dead with no expression at all. His silver-black eyes found Berain and stayed there. "You were ordered to stop."

"I didn't hear," Berain said.

"Others did, further away than you."

That didn't matter. A soldier never admitted blame, even when it was obvious. "Then I'm sorry, my lord."

Terzian scanned the orchard again. "How many died?"

"Twenty-seven," Gavair called. He strode into sight, and if Terzian's expression was blank the Marshal's was etched with rage. "They never had a chance. If this is the venom of that frog we heard about, they were doomed from the first bite."

"I could have saved them, if I'd been closer," Terzian said. "Poison is nothing. It's only the heart that magic cannot heal. But I can't save men unless I'm there." He looked around at the officers and raised his voice. "Take note of this. Your best chance to live is to stay close to me."

He twitched the reins and rode away. Gavair looked at Berain, seemed about to speak, but then mounted up and followed.

"Form up," Berain ordered. His voice was weak, colourless. "Let's get back to the road. Send someone to tell today's burial squad that there's work for them to do."

Nobody looked back.

*

155

Later that afternoon they rode past a chicken coop. Four birds pecked at the dirt, but none of the soldiers felt an urge to tuck them away into saddlebags for that night's supper.

"I hate them," Naraid said as they rode away. "The Ashir. I hate the stinking yellow guts of them."

Terzian called a halt on a low ridge, with level ground on every side. Figures still moved in the distance, Ashir warriors ranging around the army, too far away to be harmed. They'd close in as darkness fell, bows at the ready, waiting for someone to poke his head out from cover. Everyone knew it. Soldiers muttered to one another as they laid out the camp, the words too soft to make out.

The air seemed brittle, ready to crack.

Near sunset Draivan walked with another priest to the edge of camp and threw something heavy out into the fields. When they were gone Berain went to see what it was. He wasn't surprised to find the body of a pig, its throat cut but its skin still intact. Nobody dared to eat it now.

Before going to his blankets Berain prayed, for the first time in years.

The night was clear. Half a moon in a clear sky, so the fields were bathed in faint silver. That should have made Berain happy. It was hard for the Ashir to creep close enough to shoot.

Instead he remembered Morind Gap.

The nights had been clear then too, but even a full moon and rings of torches burning never made them clear enough. Falan tribesmen could creep through grass three inches high and never disturb a blade. They slid on their bellies like worms, impossible to see until their arrows were in flight, and then only for as long as it took them to vanish. Nearly always they hit what they aimed at. Barbaric they might be, primitive even, but the Falan were terrifying shots.

You couldn't even sally after them, because their archers were gone by the time your cavalry arrived. If you pushed on you'd run into another four bowmen, or another ten, all firing from concealment. Whole patrols had been lost that way until the Thrain stopped chasing. All they could do was stand guard, and hope the next arrow was aimed at someone else.

"We'll be able to see them coming this time," Naraid said.

"They won't come," Berain said tiredly. "Not yet. They'll wait until the early hours, when we're tired and don't watch as closely. They'll hope for clouds to blow in. But they won't come now."

"They're not that smart."

"Smart enough to brew that rebellion right under our noses," Berain said, but his tone was half-hearted. He didn't have the energy to argue.

The Ashir were clever enough to have killed seventeen men last night though, sneaking in close to fire arrows. Fifteen the night before that. It was a steady bleed of men from an army that couldn't afford the losses. Many of the guard posts had one injured soldier and one healthy man, because there weren't enough boots to fill the places otherwise.

Guard posts. That was another problem. At Morind Gap there had been a wall, not always finished, not often high enough, but a wall. Here the camp was guarded by a ring of hastily dug foxholes, with earth piled in front of them with two shields planted in it to make a barrier. That was all. One Ashir could wriggle right between them on a dark night, if he chose to. He'd never get out again, but he could kill a dozen men in their sleep before someone cut him down.

Berain watched dark shapes flit across the ground, much too far away for an arrow shot.

"There are more tonight," Naraid said.

There was no arguing with that.

A patrol had gone out during the afternoon, racing across the ground as fast as the horses could go. It was a gamble, of course. If the Ashir had been ready none of the men would have come back. But they hadn't been, and the patrol made it out half a mile to a small hillock, from which they could get a good look to the south. Something had been seen moving down there, and Terzian wanted to know what it was.

An army, was the answer. More warriors, hastening up the wide road from Hatun, the capital far to the south. The scouts hadn't waited long enough to make a proper estimate of numbers, but they didn't have to. Four thousand, ten thousand, it was all the same now. Terzian could melt their flesh or cut them into slices, but sheer weight of numbers would finish the Thrain the moment he wasn't there.

Two of the scouts had been shot by archers as they rode back. Nobody stopped for them. It would have been suicide to try. Berain tried not to think about it, but his mind kept circling back to the horror. No soldier ought to leave a comrade to die.

He was afraid he would have done the same, if he'd been there. From good sense, perhaps, but more likely from fear. He was deathly afraid now, all the time, like bile in his throat.

Those newcomers were not the only ones who now trailed the remnants of the army. A surprising number had followed from Chakanay, warriors and townsfolk who must have fought in the uprising or fled the burning that came after it. Naraid said they were supposed to have gone home. True, but they obviously hadn't gone far.

Berain thought they must have a competent leader among them, some high chief who had survived the slaughter at the Precinct and then escaped the rebellion's disastrous end as well. A lucky man, as well as an able one.

And every night the ground seemed to sprout new warriors, so the fields were slightly thicker with them each new day. Some of them had lapped around the army at night and now infested the fields and roads ahead, and though they moved aside when the army approached, it still felt to Berain as though the little force was surrounded. Tens of thousands of Ashir had died and yet still they swarmed around, their numbers inconceivable. They were worse than the Falan, more endless than grass on a prairie.

And there was still no food. At a stream this evening Berain had made sure not to be the first to drink, in case the Ashir had poisoned the water as they'd poisoned fruit.

"Movement," Naraid said.

Berain crouched behind the shields at once, peering over the top so he could scan the darkness. A sentry was no use if he cowered down and let enemies saunter as close as they chose. He saw nothing for a long moment, and then something moved low to the ground, perhaps fifty yards away.

"It's a rabbit," Naraid said with a brittle laugh. "A bloody rabbit! In God's name, I think I'm going crazy."

"You'd better not." Berain straightened up. "No hysterics allowed while on duty. Company orders."

The attempt at levity earned him a sniff. "And how many more weeks will we be on duty, do you think? We're heading east, into this valley Terzian is so

158

set on reaching, but there's no way out of this country over the mountains, and the Ashir are all around us."

"The Marshal says it will all change once this Kai person is dead." He tried to make himself sound confident. It would be better if he *felt* confident, but so much had gone wrong that Berain couldn't make himself believe it would be all right this time. "Once Terzian kills him."

"What if he doesn't come?"

"He can't help but come. It would be like the army in Thrasin standing by while barbarians sacked the capital."

Naraid grunted. "It would be nothing like that. These people believe they were conquered before, remember? By this dark god of theirs, whatever his name is, when the land was – "

"Tezcata."

"– Tezcata, yes, and the whole land was taken away from them."

"That's the point," Berain said. "They survived that because their priests held out at the Retreat, and when Tezcata was gone they emerged and spread their religion over the land again. That's what the Ashir believe, anyway. They won't let the Retreat be destroyed, because they can't."

"I'll believe that when it happens," Naraid said. "This whole expedition has been a disaster from the start. If I thought I could make it, I'd fetch my horse and ride like hell for the north, and not relax until my ship put in at a port in Thrasin and I could get drunk on cheap wine with cheap women."

He darted quick sideways glances at Berain as he spoke, obviously trying to gauge his reaction. Berain kept his face smooth and made no reply, though the truth was that he felt the same way. He wouldn't say so as openly as Naraid though, or say so at all in fact. If Terzian overheard him, or that snotty-nosed chaplain, Draivan… well, he didn't want to think too much about that. *If I haven't heard the complaint, I can't be blamed for it.*

But the invasion hadn't been a disaster at the start. It had gone marvellously well to begin with. Oh, there were problems, such as the so-called Blessed Land being about five times larger than even the wildest predictions had said was possible. But that was normal. Every expedition had to adapt as it went along, because nothing ever turned out the way the planners thought it would. They had Terzian, anyway, so nobody worried too much. For the most part, the army found what it had been told was here. A land of incredible wealth, inhabited by people with no horses and no steel, wallowing in a false religion of bizarre gods and crippled by their own ignorance. The soldiers moved slowly southwards, and then in a single day they overthrew the Ashir's military strength – such as it was – and captured their king.

And *then* it all went wrong.

It wasn't just because of Kai, whatever Terzian thought. The Ashir were amazingly resilient. Their king had been killed and their warriors butchered, exposed as the posturing braggarts they really were, and their remains carried out of the Precinct in pieces. Their temples were smashed, and yet within days

159

the Ashir gathered again to resist. When the uprising was crushed, amid yet more blood and slaughter, they rallied and came back for more, and this time they had learned. Their warriors stayed dispersed, denying Terzian the chance to cut them down in their hundreds. They burned fields and barns ahead of the Thrain army, doing a good job of it even in the rain, to leave almost nothing edible for the invaders.

Then there were the stakes placed to impale cavalry. The Ashir had never faced horsemen before, but already they'd found a way to deal with them. Sharp stakes planted at an angle could impale a running horse and send the rider tumbling. The Ashir had begun to ambush a patrol, driving it into a field or copse where the stakes waited under foliage. It was savage and very clever. Berain could almost admire them.

Kisain obviously had. The thought brought a frown. A soldier shouldn't abandon his comrades. Kisain had fought at Morind Gap, he knew that. And he'd been a friend. That made the betrayal worse.

Movement caught Berain's eye, away to his left along the ragged line of watch posts, and Berain half ducked before he realised it was Gavair. The Marshal stopped at the next post along, fifty yards from where Berain and Naraid huddled behind their shields. Berain could just make out a soldier in the shadow behind a pair of knotty trees, though if the man had a companion he was hidden by the night.

"That's either a very brave man, or a fool," Naraid said as Gavair started walking again. His voice was tight with tension but he still sounded awed. "Which do you think it is?"

"A brave man," Berain said, though in fact he thought the Marshal was an utter idiot. Gavair walked along as though on parade, hands clasped behind his waist and in no hurry at all, despite the possibility that an Ashir archer or sling man was taking careful aim at him somewhere in the dark. He looked like a gentleman taking an afternoon stroll beside the river. He must be completely mad.

A moment later Berain cursed and jerked his eyes back to the darkling fields in front of his post, which he'd completely forgotten to watch as the Marshal approached. That sort of carelessness would get a man killed here in no time at all. Half a dozen archers could have sneaked up while he was distracted. Naraid frowned at him, and then went pale and ducked lower behind the shields.

"You ought to keep a sharper eye out," Gavair said as he came up to them. No arrows had hissed out of the night, no stones had gone whirling past his helmeted head as he walked. Either the One God was smiling on him, or he had more luck than a whole room of gamblers. "You won't be able to see the Ashir coming if you huddle down like that, armsman."

"No sir," Naraid said. He still sounded tense, and no wonder. "But it's quiet at the moment, sir."

"It's usually quiet," Gavair said dryly, "right up until one second before the arrow lodges in your throat. Keep alert, armsman."

160

"Yes, sir."

Gavair's attention switched to Berain. "And how do you find the mood tonight? Does the quiet reassure you?"

"No," Berain said quietly. "No, sir, it doesn't. It reminds me of Morind Gap." His voice dropped. "And that scares me."

"As it should," the Marshal said after a moment. "It reminds me of Morind Gap too, armsman. And if you men keep alert, it may come to resemble that battle even more, because we may yet win."

"Do you really believe that?" Naraid asked suddenly. "I don't. I think our brave sorcerer will leave us here to feed the crows, and not care a damn about it."

Berain stared at his friend, hardly able to believe what he had just heard. Beside him Gavair seemed almost as stunned, though he recovered sooner. "I will pretend I didn't hear that, armsman. Now, I have other –"

The clink of hooves came softly to them, the sound of horses being led at a walk, and as stealthily as possible. Quite a lot of horses. Gavair turned to peer into the camp, which Berain thought was wasted effort. No lamps were burning, no fires lit, because either would give the Ashir bowmen clear silhouettes to aim for. The tents were blacker shapes in the night, and their shadow was inky dark.

But something was coming out of it now. At first all Berain could see was the glint of metal in one place, or the flash of white skin somewhere else, but gradually the glimpses resolved into a line of soldiers leading horses towards the sentries. Twenty of them, thirty, and still more came. All of them carried their packs, and full bags were strapped alongside their saddles. It was obvious what they were doing. Gavair stared at them with flat eyes, and some of the men wilted and fell back a little, but none of them halted until they had come up to the sentry post where Berain and the Marshal waited. Berain could see the horses' hooves had been muffled with strips of cloth, No wonder they had sounded so faint.

"I did not order a patrol," Gavair said. There was a terrible understanding in his voice, and Berain stole a glance at him and thought, *he knows.*

"We're leaving," Naraid said from behind him, and Berain's head whipped around in surprise. The other man pulled his shield from the ground. "Don't try to stop us, Marshal."

"Loyalty should stop you," Gavair said, "but I have no need to. You'll kill yourselves. You will all die out there, and you know it."

"We will die here too," someone in the crowd of soldiers said. Another two men joined them and were passed reins, and Berain realised they were the sentries from the next post along, where Gavair had stopped moments before. Horses had been brought for them, and for Naraid, which meant this escape had been well planned. "Terzian will kill us all."

"He will keep us alive," Gavair countered calmly. "He is the only hope for life we have, now. You men followed him here willingly enough when it seemed easy. Now it's hard, can you run away and still call yourselves men?"

161

"I can call myself alive," Naraid said. "You cling to your hope, Marshal. I wish you luck, truly I do, but you're a fool. You care more for Terzian and his family than you do for your men."

"I care for my men more than anything," Gavair retorted. "And that means keeping them close to Terzian, not leaving him."

Naraid shook his head and swung into the saddle of a big bay, settling his shield on his arm. "Are you coming, Berain?"

"No," he said immediately. "You won't get five miles, and it's as the Marshal says. Half crazed he may be, but Terzian's our only chance to live through this and see home again. Besides, I remember the Gap. We survived because we stuck together, and I reckon that's a good plan now as well."

"Not the phrasing I would have chosen," Gavair said, "but the sentiment is exactly right." He stepped aside. "Go on, then. None of you will live to regret this, but may the One ride with you."

"And with you," Naraid said. He glanced at the riders around him. "Are we ready, boys? Then let's ride!"

Nobody shouted to sound the charge, and no horn was blown. The horses' muffled hooves were curiously faint on the soft ground. Berain thought they sounded like ghosts already, men no longer wholly in this world the god had made for them. They drew together in a huddle, eighty men or more well used to their work, and gathering speed they hurtled into the blackness.

A spark of light drifted overhead.

Berain had one moment to turn his face up towards it before memory lit up in his brain and he flung himself down behind his shield. Gavair landed beside him, almost burrowing into the dirt. And then the night turned brilliant white, so brilliant that it lit up the inside of Berain's tight-shut eyes and he clapped one hand across them to shut it out. He could feel the hairs on his hand crisping in a sudden wash of warmth. His shield creaked as it heated suddenly and Berain fought back a scream. It kept rising in him though and he crammed a fist into his mouth and bit down hard, bringing blood from his own knuckles as he waited for the glare to fade.

It did, at last. Berain opened his eyes a crack, and when nothing blazed to blind him he clambered cautiously to his feet. He was surprised to find the camp bathed in a pearly luminescence that was barely stronger than moonlight, and he ducked without thought. Then he realised it was just a light, not killing magic, and the first thing it showed him was Terzian.

The sorcerer stood by the nearest of the tents, hands folded at his waist. His silver eyes shone oddly, like the sheen on oysters still wet with seawater. Around him men were blundering out of their blankets, some with swords gripped in their hands but most unarmed. This could not be anything the Ashir had done, after all. This was real power. Berain swallowed and slowly, dreading what he would see, he turned to look outside the camp, where the riders had gone.

The earth had been burned in a wide circle, its centre a hundred yards away from Berain's post and its edge lapping against his shield where he'd driven it

162

into the ground. If it had come any closer it would have killed him, and Gavair too. The Marshal stood and stared at the burned earth, breathing hard and no doubt thinking the same thing. Berain wondered if Terzian had cared about either of them.

Half of the deserting riders lay sprawled around the edges of that circle, and they too were burned. Many of them were missing limbs, and one had no head. A horse kicked feebly with legs that ended in bloody stumps. Across the circle two Ashir lay in a tangle of flesh and scorched shrubs. They must have been sneaking close, and happened to be in the path of the cavalry and thus, moments later, of Terzian's blast. The worst of luck for them, but perhaps good luck for Berain. One of them might have shot him, otherwise.

The other half of the deserters were simply gone.

One soldier stared upside-down at Berain with a single dead eye. The other was missing, lost in the fire-seared ruin that had been the left side of his face. What remained might have been Naraid, once. Berain turned away again, trying not to retch. He wondered suddenly whether Terzian had heard himself called *half crazed.* At the thought a bubble of laughter escaped him, and he had to hunch over to keep from laughing hysterically.

"So will I punish desertion," Terzian said into the silence. Power made his voice ring. "We are at war, and in a foreign land. I will not permit cowards to reduce our numbers with doomed attempts to slip away." His eyes were bright, but in his face no muscle moved. "We will reach Hirka in three days. Then this will be over."

He turned and went back into the camp, towards his tent at the centre. The soldiers stared at one another and then at the wide area of burned ground. Several stumbled away to throw up. A few, incredibly, rolled themselves in their blankets and went back to sleep. The pearly light faded, letting the night creep closer to the tents until it gathered once more across the camp, and nobody had spoken at all.

"Remain," Gavair began, and had to stop to swallow. He was very white, and his face was almost as rigid as Terzian's. "Remain at your post, Berain. I will detail other men to replace those who... were lost."

"They weren't lost," Berain said, unable to hold the words back. "They were murdered, Marshal, and you know it."

"Hush," Gavair said. He gripped Berain's arm with tight fingers. "Hush, now. What I know is that a careless word might get you killed, now perhaps more than ever before. Watch your tongue and watch your part of the perimeter, captain, and you may live to see the end of this."

Berain said nothing more. He went back to hunting for a flicker of movement in the darkness, trying to focus only on that so he wouldn't have to think. Another soldier came to join him a little latter, gagging at the smell of roasted flesh, but by then Berain had stopped noticing it. He stood and watched the darkness all night long, and he saw nothing move at all.

163

27

In the pale light of morning, not long after the Thrain had struck their camp and moved on, a small party of Ashir moved among the forgotten tent pegs and cooling breakfast fires, and stopped at the edge of the burned ground.

He has gone insane, Amaru thought. She stayed a step behind the others so she wouldn't have to see too clearly, but the stench of burnt meat turned her stomach over. *The sorcerer has gone insane, and what might a madman do with all his power, in the name of revenge?*

She looked sideways at Kisain and saw his face was pallid and still, almost sickly. Mimiteh took one of his trembling hands and held it in both her own. Beyond them Chimalli moved forward and stirred the ash with a toe. He was the only one to enter the burned area. One either side of it warriors streamed by in small groups, keeping apart to deny Terzian a target worth striking at, but none crossed the edge of the circle. Outside that clear line the grass grew green and fresh with last night's rain. Inside there was only death.

"They were trying to break away," Chimalli said finally. "That's what the light was, last night. They were trying to break away, to escape to the north, and the sorcerer caught them."

Kisain gave a jerky nod. Mimiteh raised his hand to her lips, her eyes soft as they rested on his face.

"The Thrain must be on the edge," Chimalli said. "One more push and their army might fall apart."

Amaru thought it was already falling apart. There was death outside the circle too, less horrible than that within, but perhaps more pitiable. The Thrain had built hasty cairns for the wounded who had died during the night. They were sacrificing lives with every day they went on. The sorcerer had killed those men too, Amaru thought, as surely as he'd slaughtered the soldiers inside the circle.

"Come," Uchu said at last, in his vulture's croak. He pulled his cloak tighter and turned away, and after a moment, they followed him.

*

The Thrain were idling. They had wounded to care for, but that wasn't enough to explain their slow pace. Eight, ten miles a day was all they covered. Amaru didn't understand it.

"He's giving your *kamachi* time to get here," Kisain explained. "It's no good burning the Retreat if it doesn't bring Kai into the open. That's what Terzian really wants."

"If you're truly one of us now," Dyani said sourly, "then he's your *kamachi* too."

Kisain nodded. "I suppose he is. But I'm a Thrain deserter, not a pretend Ashir. There's a difference."

"I can't see it."

"Then you need to look harder," Uchu said as he passed them. "Leave it now, warrior. Done is done, and bickering won't change it."

They pressed on, keeping as close behind the Thrain as they dared. Behind and all around, in fact. Warriors had encircled the invaders days ago, and begun to burn crops and drive off livestock ahead of the army. Lack of food ought to have made the Thrain move faster, but that hadn't happened. Chimalli didn't know why.

Even the daily crawl was too much for some of the wounded. It was nearly too much for Dyani, who needed to lean on the woman he'd asked to marry him back at the woodland camp. Qula, her name was. It seemed she'd been a whore. She hadn't accepted Tumay's proposal yet, claiming she was an independent woman and no man was going to tie *her* to a hearth, but Amaru thought it was only a matter of time. She had seen the quick glances Qula gave him when he wasn't looking, and the way her fingertips traced the ugly, half-healed scar on Dyani's face as she applied salve to the wound. The Blind God alone knew where she got the salve, or what she had to do to get it, but Amaru was sure Qula would marry him when this was over. If they were still alive.

That Dyani kept up was impressive, but that Kisain managed it was almost beyond belief. The former soldier walked with a queerly lopsided motion, pushing his left leg ahead and then swinging the right around in a half circle to plant the foot back down with a gasp of effort. All the time he leaned on a thick staff Mimiteh had cut for him, while sweat beaded on his brow and dripped from his nose. His skin had turned a permanent grey, like damp ashes. Amaru had heard several warriors murmur grudging admiration for him, and twice Chimalli had told him gently to stop, but Kisain shook his head and pressed on.

"I need to be there for the finish," he said the second time, pausing just long enough to gather the breath to speak. "You know I do, Chimalli. If the soldiers see me, they'll know they will be treated well if they surrender. It might make things easier. Save some lives."

"I thought," Chimalli said, "that you don't believe the soldiers matter any more." The burn along the side of his throat and face looked raw and angry in the sunshine. "Only the sorcerer."

"The soldiers don't matter to Terzian, is what I said," he corrected. "But they matter to me."

Kisain put a hand on Mimiteh's shoulder and pushed off, like a man launching a canoe, to start himself moving again. Off he went, step-swing, step-swing, while Mimiteh threw Chimalli a black look and followed after him. She took Kisain's arm and pulled it around her shoulders, leaning into him to take his weight. He muttered something Amaru couldn't hear and Mimiteh laughed softly, the sound strange and discordant in the heavy air.

It was midmorning when word rippled back that the Thrain had stopped. There was no reason for it. The weather was clear, the road ahead of the Thrain empty. It was only a splinter thrown off from the Pasqa, but it was ample to carry the traffic of a small army. Scouts couldn't explain the halt, except that it

165

was in a little village where soft beds could be found. No food, nothing to drink except the river, but a few comforts.

The pursuing Ashir stopped as well, and Chimalli began to snap orders.

"Get to those men who came up from the south yesterday," he told their one remaining Runner. The poor man was sickly yellow with exhaustion. "They're fresher than anyone else. Tell them they're to hurry on ahead and get to Hirka before the Thrain, or kill themselves trying. I want them through the village and on top of the cliff trail beyond. A hundred men could hold that track against the entire army until winter snows them in."

"Except for the magic," Kisain said in a voice like paper. This time it was Chimalli who threw a black look.

The Runner sped away, although Amaru thought *sped* might be stretching the truth somewhat. It was more of a stagger, not much faster than the sprawling band had managed all morning. Everyone else grabbed the chance to rest. Warriors sank down with their backs resting against each other, or simply flopped into the grass where they were. Several took their sandals off and rubbed at blisters, as though that would somehow make them hurt less. Amazingly, one gaggle of men produced a fistful of kindling and a small pot, and produced packages from various pockets. They began boiling maize and chopped squash into an impromptu stew. Sitting in the grass with her back against the trunk of a young tala tree, Amaru wondered where they found the energy.

"Shut up," Mimiteh said from nearby. The words might be harsh but the tone was tender, almost a caress. "I'm trying to help you here, and you're going to lie down in the end, Kisain. You can argue first if you want, but it isn't going to change a thing, so why bother?"

He muttered something under his breath again, but finally allowed the priestess to help lower him to the grass. Twice he hissed through his teeth, and as soon as he was prostrate he let out a long sigh that might have been a shudder, had it come from another man. Mimiteh at once began to probe gently at his bad hip with her fingers. Kisain closed his eyes.

"A tough man, that," Uchu cawed from Amaru's blind side, and she nearly climbed out of her skin like Makisapa with the shock. The wizened old man didn't seem to notice. "I've known seasoned warriors who would just have laid down the moment they took a wound like his."

"The Ashir are tough, too," she said defensively.

Uchu laughed his cracked laugh. "Of course they are. I knew one man, a young Snake, who was wounded in a fight with bandits in the mountains. He escaped, but collapsed later in the forest, just from blood loss. When he woke up a jaguar was watching him from the bushes."

"This is going to be one of your stories. I can tell," she said. "Are there any fanged fish in it?"

"Listen when I'm talking, you upstart girl," he said with a gap-toothed grin. "This man only had his belt knife with him, because he'd left his other weapons

166

behind when he fled. Silly thing to do, but when a man's wounded and scared, he's apt to do more foolish things than that."

"What happened, then?"

"The jaguar attacked him, girl," Uchu said. "That's what jaguars do, when they see you're weak. The warrior was weak right enough, and drenched in his own blood besides. He had to fight the jaguar off, one arm against two claws, and try to stab it in the belly before it could get its teeth into him. He did it, too. A week later he stumbled back into town. He was halfway starved, and blood and bruises all over, but he had that jaguar's head in one hand."

"That's a good story," Amaru said. "I don't even mind that none of it can possibly be true."

"Not true?" Uchu said. He pulled back the sleeve on his left arm, and scored among the tattoos on his bicep she saw a semicircle of white scars, the sort that might be made by teeth. He turned his arm over to reveal a similar pattern on the other side. Amaru felt as though her eye was about to come out of her head. That must have been a *big* jaguar.

"The Snake was me," Uchu said. He let the sleeve drop and ruffled her hair with gnarled fingers. "You see, some of us are tough as well, girl, just as you said. Too tough to slink away from a fight, even when we're so old we can almost remember when the mountains were young." His gaze wandered back to Kisain, "Young people think they have to be tough all the time, though. The truth is, you try not to need to be tough at all, if you've got any sense. And that outlander doesn't need to be here. He'd do better to rest while he can."

"He wants to be here," Amaru said.

"Of course he does. Young enough to try proving himself all the time, you see. But there's good gold in him, I think. He'll be a decent man one day." The ancient warrior grinned at her. "Now, did you say you wanted to hear a story about the *quch'aqway?* "

She smiled back at him. "No, I don't want to hear about your fanged fish, thank you, because none of it can possibly be true."

Uchu chuckled, a sound like old bark cracking. "Oh, I like you, girl. You've got as much courage as anyone here. But I'll tell you one thing about the *quch'aqway*. On the surface in your boat you can think everything's peaceful, all is right with the world. And then the fanged fish comes up from beneath you and throws your boat in the air, and that's the end of you more times than not. Now, does that remind you of anything?" He stood up. "Come along. The stew simmering over there smells just about ready to me."

It was, and the men gathered around the little fire shared were willing to share. There wasn't enough, but the stew was hot and welcome, and went down well with a heel of day-old bread. Amaru thought as she ate, watching Uchu gnaw his meal across the fire from her. He meant the Ashir were the fanged fish, of course, and the Thrain the unsuspecting boatmen. Probably it was all nonsense, a story invented to give her hope... but still, there *were* those teeth marks on his arm.

167

"News coming," Uchu announced croakily, just as she passed her bowl back. A ripple of murmurs passed back through the scattered warriors, and people began to stand and peer eastwards, towards the Thrain. Uchu tossed his bowl to a young man with a short crest of hair and cuts to his scalp on both sides. The youth must be one of those who'd become a warrior just for this fight, and had no tattoos on his arms or ornaments for his hair. He looked more frightened than fierce, but he was there, and that was what mattered. He nearly fumbled the thrown bowl, bounced it twice off his fingertips, and finally caught it just before it spun out of reach.

"Silly young buffoon," Uchu muttered as he and Amaru hurried back towards Chimalli. "He'll be a liability to everyone around him if he gets into the fight. All he's got is that heavy knife, and he's as likely to cut his own foot off with it as he is to scratch one of the Thrain."

"He's here," Amaru said. "And with that knife, he might kill a jaguar."

They reached Chimalli and the others just as a young man pushed through the warriors. He was hardly more than a boy, fourteen years old at best, but he had tied two raggedy white feathers into his hair. That was the ancient mark of a Runner, from the days when entry into the clique was gained by stealing tail feathers from the nest of an eagle. Nobody had done that for years. The boy's chest was deep, though ribs stood out against the skin.

"You're no Runner," Chimalli said as he looked the lad up and down. The big chieftain held a cup of what smelled like soup, and Amaru's mouth watered in spite of the stew she'd just eaten. "What are you doing here, boy?"

The youth's chin came up. "Bringing you a message, *old man*, if you're chief Chimalli. Do you want it, or would you rather spit insults at me?"

"He wants the message," Uchu interjected, before Chimalli could start shouting. "What is it, lad?"

"The Thrain are moving again. There were lights in the village half an hour ago. Don't know why. But they'll be on their way again soon."

"And the southerners?" Chimalli demanded. "Did they get ahead of the Thrain in time?"

"I doubt it," Uchu said in a harsh grumble.

The youth spared him a glance, and then another one, as though he couldn't quite believe someone so wizened could be travelling among warriors. A moment later his gaze fell on Amaru, and he fairly goggled at her in disbelief. His lips moved, and she thought they shaped the words *a little girl?* She felt her expression tighten before she remembered she'd just thought of him as hardly more than a child. She couldn't complain if he thought much the same of her.

"Well?" Chimalli demanded. "If you want us to treat you as a Runner, boy, then stop staring like a fool and answer me!"

The youth's head whipped back to Chimalli. "Uh… chief Otoron says he's already moving warriors ahead of the Thrain. He, um, also says he's never heard of you, and he, uh, is taking command."

168

"What!" Chimalli exploded. "He thinks he can come in here and just take over? You tell him –"

"Calmly, now," Uchu said, putting a hand on his arm. The big chief broke off, though his lips were thin and he glowered at the poor youth who'd spoken. "This Otoron is just throwing his weight around. He's come late to the fray and wants his share of glory, as every good warrior would. Someone needs to straighten him out, that's all."

"I bet you have someone in mind," Amaru said blandly.

He chuckled again. "Indeed I do. The lad here is too tired, after running here already, so I'll go. Mimiteh should come with me, if she's willing. A *kura* will add weight to your authority."

The priestess looked round. "I'm not leaving Kisain."

"You have duties," Uchu said mildly, "and no time to argue. Chimalli will look after your man until we get back."

"But –"

"*Now*, Mimiteh."

She hesitated a moment longer, then leaving Kisain she strode up to Chimalli and stared at him. "If he's hurt while I'm away, if he's even *scratched,* I'll have your hide for it. I swear I will."

Chimalli held up a hand. "He'll be safe, on my oath. Uchu, will this Otoron even listen to you?"

"I expect so," the old man cackled. "I taught him some skills, more years ago than I care to remember. If it's the same man. A big Eagle, more muscle than anything else."

"Like most of them," Chimalli said. "Go, then. He mustn't mass his warriors or Terzian will cut them apart."

"I know," Uchu said. He set off at a rapid trot. Mimiteh threw a final glance at Kisain, doubt still written in her eyes, and then turned to follow Uchu.

Chimalli raised his voice. "If you're cooking, pack up the gear. Get ready to move on my signal!"

Men raised hands to show they'd heard, and passed the order on. Chimalli peered eastwards, chewing his lower lip. "We need to know what the Thrain are doing. You can't guess what the other chief will do next, unless you know what he knows. But we can't get close enough to see them."

Amaru hesitated, and then with a shrug she stepped forward and said, "I have a suggestion."

The big chieftain glared at her. "Well?"

"I could climb that tree," she said, pointing. It was the one she'd rested her back against, before Uchu came to tell her about his confrontation with a jaguar and then inveigle a bowl of stew for her. "I bet from the top I could see right across the river. Maybe as far as Hirka itself."

"It's too dangerous," Dyani said from behind her. He'd come up with Qula at his side, as she nearly always was. Love seemed to be flowering, here in the midst of desperation and dread. "If the sorcerer sees you he could –"

169

"Yes, he could," she said. "But he's less likely to kill a little girl," she glared at the boy Runner, who flushed beet red, "than he is a warrior. If a warrior could even climb up there. I don't think those branches are strong enough to support the weight of a grown man."

"Amaru," the scarred man began, and was interrupted.

"Hush," Tumay said, coming to the edge of the group. "Hush, my friend. The girl is right."

Chimalli looked down at her with genuine concern. After a moment Amaru had to look away, almost afraid of the care she saw in his eyes. She was blessed beyond dreams of fortune to have found these people, just when those she loved had been taken from her, but it was hard to believe she would not lose them too. Perhaps before this day was done. Chimalli, Dyani, even Mimiteh and her weird outland man: they all loved her, she knew. She tried to swallow without them noticing. All in a rush she missed her father, missed him for all the years she would never hear his voice, and she fought back tears. If she cried now they would never let her go.

"All right," Chimalli said at last, his voice husky. Amaru broke for the tree at once, before her tears came and they stopped her helping the best way she could. She bumped off Qula as she blundered past, and had her hands on the tree before she realised she'd been followed.

"I'm sorry I called you a little girl," the youth with white feathers in his hair said. "I shouldn't have done that. My name's Chasqui." He linked his hands together and offered them to her as a step. "Help you up?"

"Amaru," she answered, for lack of anything else to say, and putting her foot on his hands she boosted herself up to the branches and began to climb.

She was still having trouble judging distances with only one eye, and clambering though the tangled branches of the tala tree was incredibly difficult. She learned quickly to set both feet and one hand before she moved the other, and then to grasp as tight as she could before moving again. Progress was slower than she liked, but she made herself breathe deeply and take her time. At last she emerged from the canopy and could see across the plain, all the way to where mountains reared against the sky, like the edge of the world the Ashir had once believed them to be.

She saw the Thrain straight away. Their armour glinted silver in the bright sunlight, making them easy to spot. They made a gleaming huddle just beyond the river, some two thousand men with horses trailed by a thin plume of dust, a little over a mile from the tree where she perched. The plume was aimed due east. Looking that way Amaru saw two outflung arms of the mountains with a valley between, receding into shadow.

Around the Thrain was a clear space half a mile wide in which nothing moved. Outside it Ashir swarmed in threes and fours, black dots crawling across the land. South and east of the invaders was a thick smear of movement, thousands of men moving in a mass across the fields. She squinted at the dark blob, trying to gauge the distance.

170

"Oh, *carajo*," she swore a moment later, an oath that her father would have been appalled to realise she knew. Then she was swarming down the tree, careless of the difficulty in her urgency. She sprang across a gap to catch a branch two-handed, swung once, and let herself plummet ten feet to the next one down. Someone below gasped aloud. Amaru reached for the next branch, missed it completely, and went tumbling the last fifteen feet to land on the grass with a thump.

"Are you all right?" Chasqui was kneeling beside her at once. "Amaru, are you hurt?"

"I'm fine," she said. She scrambled to her feet, pushing away the youth's hands. "I said I'm fine."

"Could you see anything?" Chimalli demanded. The group had come over to the tree while she was climbing, it seemed, and now waited for her news. "What can you tell us?"

"The Thrain are a mile ahead of us," she said. "And those men from the south are ahead of *them*. They're racing them to the valley, and they're all clustered together in one big group."

"That *binchuka* idiot," the big chief snarled. "How far are they? Will Uchu and Mimiteh reach them in time?"

"I can't tell," Mimiteh admitted. Her father had always said that it was best to admit it when you weren't sure, because then when you were people listened more willingly. "Maybe."

"We can't worry about that," Dyani said. The wound on his face was really awful, and it was going to leave a hideous scar, but Qula was still holding his hand and smiling at him. "We just have to push on, and hope."

"I'm not sure how much more the men can manage," Chimalli said.

"They can manage what they need to," Tumay put in. The stout man looked oddly shrunken, more than a few missed meals could account for. Horror and grief had done the rest, Amaru supposed. "It won't be for much longer anyway. One way or the other."

"One way or the other," Chimalli agreed. He lifted both arms above his head and turned in a slow circle, letting the scattered warriors see him. They began to clamber to their feet, some with half-stifled groans. The men who'd cooked stew kicked at their fire until it spluttered out in wisps of smoke, and the host began to move.

171

28

Kai led them out of the snow as twilight began to creep out from under the trees.

Led was the wrong word. He was at the front, that's all. But every step tore his thighs, every footfall rubbed blisters deeper and wider on his feet. He walked because to stop was to die. Even now.

"We did it," Paqu gasped, some distance behind. In the silence of a mountains his murmur might have brought an avalanche. "We came across. Now, humph, we can rest."

"Not yet," Kai said. The words rasped against his throat as he spoke them. "The night will be cold, this high. Too cold."

"We can light a fire," Evain began.

"I spend winters in contemplation above the Retreat, remember. I know the cold. This high, at night, it kills."

"We have to go on?"

"Yes," he said. *To stop is to die.*

They went on. The mountain was steeper here than before, falling away into a valley like a cut in the world, with a stream roaring in endless fury. There was no track, not even a trail worn by goats over thousands of years. Only thin soil and the snares of tree roots. Fall and you would roll a long way.

But nights were always warmer near water, and the stream was five hundred feet lower than this slope.

Kai started down. He heard the others follow.

*

They'd had one day. One day to cross the arm of the mountain, because if night caught you on the snow you were as dead as any of the lost peoples before the Ashir.

Kai had them moving before the sun was fully up. This high dawn came early, while the lowlands were still shrouded by night. It was one advantage, a single positive in a reckless enterprise. By the time sunlight flashed over the peaks his six travellers were already knee deep in snow, wading more than walking, using sticks to prod at the ground ahead before they moved.

Six travellers and a sevenths companion, unseen. He hoped. If Viraca didn't walk with them now they were dead anyway. Kai without the Bearded God's love was nothing, just another man, and the sorcerer would rip him apart with a flick of his fingers. Or keep him alive, screaming, through months and years of regret that he had ever killed the son.

He touched the *cizin* inside his coat. Chinita frowned at him and he took the hand away.

Up they climbed, taking turns to break the trail. Achachi was good at it, unsurprisingly. That old man could wrestle a puma if he wanted to. Paqu was less use, the priest more accustomed to devotions than to hard outdoor work. He took his turn anyway, giving the others a rest. When he led their progress was marked by mutters of *humph* every few steps, as though habit made him use the word even when he had nothing else to say.

They ate lunch on the move. Fruits and bread, with water from a flask. There was nothing to burn for a fire and they hadn't carried wood because of the weight. Kai couldn't feel anything below his knees by then. That was all right. Cold became a problem when you felt warm but shouldn't. Numb toes were welcome.

They crested the ridge just before noon, below a peak like a broken thumb sticking out of the ice. Going down was as hard as climbing, in these conditions. Harder, since they were tired now. Two hours later, congratulating themselves on making good time, they came to the cliff.

"… you're joking," Evain said.

He was the colour of old cheese. That was thin air and cold, not fear. The soldier was almost as tough as Taruka. But he studied the cliff and shook his head. "You want to walk on that?"

That was a wall of stone coated with ice, sometimes thin enough to see through, in other places curling into contoured shapes. A ledge ran along it, sloping down as it went. There was stone under there but ice had made the shelf wider, easily broad enough to walk on – if it would take a man's weight. Paqu shrugged.

"You wanted to take the mountain route, humph, to the Retreat," he said. "This is it."

"It's insane," Chinita said.

"There's no choice," Kai said.

"Not for you, perhaps," Paqu answered. "The rest of us could still go back."

"By all means," Taruka put in. "It took us more than half the day to cross that snowfield. If you think you can cross it again in what daylight is left, go ahead. I'll look for your body in the summer."

"Another way, then," Paqu persisted. "There must be a second path. There, perhaps."

He pointed to their right, down a wide snowdrift that might have lain undisturbed all winter. Kai couldn't see any marks on it, not even the tiny scratches of birds' claws. A mile away the snow levelled out, then began to rise again towards another peak.

"Humph," Paqu said.

Kai moved forward. "I'll lead."

There was enough space to walk normally, but the ice was smooth and his boots slid at every step. Kai moved with his hands placed against the cliff, more for balance than anything else. If he slipped there was nothing to hold on to. He would fall on the ledge or he'd fall over it, as the God and fate decided. He moved carefully, giving them every reason to spare him, but he couldn't be too slow. Sunset was coming and they were still on the snow.

173

It went on for a long time. A mile perhaps, before he rounded a corner and could see where the ledge gave out onto a slope again. Beyond that, down in the distance, he could see the green tops of trees. He called the news back to the others, strung out behind him.

The mountain answered him. Everyone froze as something high above them muttered, then rumbled.

"Avalanche!" Paqu shouted. "Flat to the wall!"

They pressed themselves to the cliff. It trembled under Kai's fingers, though his hands were so numb he hadn't felt anything through them for hours. The sound became a roar to his left, the way he'd come. Then the mountain was shaking and he fell to his knees, feeling them slide a little on the ice. Someone shouted. Kai couldn't make out the words or even who it was. Snow flurried over him and he couldn't see.

The roaring faded, died. Kai climbed back to his feet, aware he was the one trembling now.

"Are you all still here?" he called. His mouth was dry.

"Here," Taruka said, not far away.

"I'm here." That was Achachi. Paqu replied, then Evain. Kai's mouth was dry.

"Here," Chinita said, from the back of the line. Her voice was thin. "It missed me by twenty feet. I think the ledge is gone behind me. I've got a lot of snow down my coat, too. It's cold."

"Snow normally is," Taruka said.

Kai fought the urge to laugh, thought he'd won, and then burst into something close to hysterics. They were all laughing then, on hands and knees along the ledge, while snowflakes drifted down all around them. All except Paqu. The old priest watched Kai as he gained control of himself.

"A few moments earlier and that would have killed us all," Paqu said when they were calmer. "Earlier than that, humph, and it would have destroyed the ledge and forced us to turn back, and then the cold would have killed us in the night. You were right, *kamachi.*"

He hiccupped the last of his laughter. "About what?"

"The Teacher God is our seventh," Paqu said, "and he's walking with us in the snow."

His smile faded. "That's good."

He began to move again. Soon they were off the ledge, and two hours later they came to the end of the snow and were walking among trees, down to where water foamed between stones at the bottom of a valley like a cut in the world.

*

Morning found them crawling from the blankets they'd shared, huddling together for warmth. Chinita could hardly stand, and even that was beyond Paqu.

174

The three fighting men managed it, though all of them grimaced at popping joints and muscles that groaned in complaint.

Kai and Achachi were first to the banked fire. Wood had been left beside it last night, as much as could be gathered before exhaustion drove them all into sleep. Kai uncovered the embers and added a pile of thinner twigs. Cold air blowing off the mountain fanned coals into flames and the tinder caught. The two men sat on flat rocks, holding out their hands to the warmth.

"I need to ask you a favour," Achachi said.

"All right," Kai said.

Achachi held up his hands. Fingertips on both were discoloured, but Kai's gaze went to the last two on the left hand. That wasn't just bad colour, but black flesh. "Frostbite."

"If it's left, it might poison me," Achachi said. "I need the fingers cut off. Those two, for certain."

He was very tired, and his thoughts were sluggish. "Why me?"

"Taruka and I have axes, but they're no good for fine work. Too clumsy. Paqu and Chinita both have knives, of course. But with bronze you have to saw back and forth to sever a finger."

"Evain isn't armed. Bronze is all we have."

"No, it isn't," Achachi said.

It was a moment before he understood, and was startled into wakefulness. "You're talking about the *cizin.*"

"Will you do it?"

"I can't cut you with that," Kai protested. "I'd have to cut out your eyes and tongue as well. You'd have no voice in the Halls of Dust, for all time. You know that."

"I know much has changed," Achachi said, "and more will change in the future. And I know there are six of us in this frozen place, all of whom trust you, Kai. As I think you trust us. Will you do it?"

Chinita was coming to join them. This was her grandfather, the man who had raised her. Told her stories and wiped her nose, until she was old enough to join her father's outlaw band. There hadn't been much joy for her, even before her mother died.

And, yet. *Much has changed, and more will change.* New things had come to Apusuyu whether the Ashir wanted them or not, and some of them had to be embraced, if the people were to survive. Suchi couldn't see that, but her principles were true. Whatever could be kept should be. Kai should change as little as possible, to retain whatever of the Ashir's ancient identity could be saved. The culture must change, even the *kamachi* and his role. But the *cizin* had been made by the god.

Some things should be kept.

"What?" Chinita said beside him. She was looking from man to man, sensing the mood.

Kai exhaled. "All right. Put your hand on that rock."

175

Achachi did so, the first two fingers curled down and the last two laid flat on the stone. Kai took the *cizin* from his coat and Chinita's eyes went wide as he unsheathed it. He wasn't sure she was breathing. Back towards the blankets Taruka and Paqu stopped dead, Evain halting with them although he couldn't really understand.

"It's a holy thing we do," Kai said.

"No, it isn't. It's just a sickle." Achachi nodded at his splayed fingers. "Make the cut."

"It had better not be just a sickle," Kai said. He lowered the bronze blade to the older man's fingers, placed it, then pressed. It cut through with ease. Blood squirted and Chinita was there with a cloth, her paralysis broken as she wrapped it around her grandfather's hand. Blood stained it immediately.

"Get off me, girl," Achachi snapped. He pushed her away, then reached into the fire to pry out a half-burned stick. He touched the glowing end to the wounds and hissed between his teeth, the only sign of pain he'd given. A sweet scent of burning flesh filled the air.

The others came to join them. Kai put the *cizin* back in its sheath and under his coat.

"Next time you use that it will be against the sorcerer," Paqu said.

Kai nodded. "I suppose it will."

"Eat." Taruka was handing out packets of food, bread and fruits for the most part. Behind him Evain had set a pot on the fire. "We still have a long walk if we're to reach the Retreat today."

"We're not going to the Retreat," Kai said, and they stopped to look at him. "We're going to the top of the cliff below it, above Hirka. They call the place *jatun k'anchay.*"

"Where lightning strikes," Chinita said.

"That's right. It's sacred to Catequil of the Storm. He's as strong there as he is anywhere in the world, and it's where I'll face the sorcerer. With two gods standing at my side."

He could see fear in their faces. That was for Terzian, this foreign mage who could do things no human should be capable of. But there was awe too and that was for Catequil, for Viraca, and perhaps for Kai too, just a little. He didn't like that. Matlal and Salali had been able to see him as a man, not an avatar of the Bearded God.

"If the sorcerer wants to reach you he'll have to come up the path," Taruka said. "You'll be able to see him."

"That won't make a difference," Evain said. "I'm sorry, but Terzian can swat us all into oblivion with a wave of his hand."

"It makes the meeting on my terms," Kai answered, "and with my gods beside me. Anyway, I don't think he'll swat anything, not right away. He's going to want to talk first." He shook his head as they tried to ask questions. "Eat now. I'll explain later."

176

That quieted them, though there was one exception. There always was now, it seemed. Kai could receive obedience from a room full of warriors and priests and still Chinita would speak out.

"What did you mean," she murmured next to him, "when you said you'll use the *cizin* against the sorcerer?"

"That I have a plan," he told her, and would say no more.

29

"Warriors," Yurac said.

There was a note of unease in his voice, and no wonder. He carried a mace and belt knives and wore rough tattoos on his neck, and he carried himself like a fighting man. But he wasn't a warrior the societies would recognise. He was an outlaw, and word of Kai's amnesty wouldn't have reached out here in the plains of Apusuyu.

It only took Catori a moment to pick out the figures. Ten, fifteen of them, gathered around a cattle shed with a crumbling wall. When he looked further he saw more, dozens and then hundreds of them crawling over the fields. His heart leaped.

"Someone's brought the societies up from the south," he said. "Otoron? He had command last I knew."

"Who is Otoron?" Suchi asked.

"A chief. Eagle clan, I think. I don't know much about him, but Eagle are always much the same. Act now, think later."

She considered that. Suchi had been washing in streams, as they all had, but her blue robe hadn't been laundered for a week and was streaked with dirt. None of the others looked much better. Catori knew he must be crusted with mud too, but he was a Deer, and used to it.

"We must talk to them," Suchi said. "Come."

Her manner was more peremptory every day. Perhaps it was all Rimaq's talk of the ch'uyu-karu, the crusade to restore Apusuyu to what it had been before the Thrain. Suchi had begun to see herself as a saviour, coming to the rescue of her people. Taking Kai's role, in short. Doing the work he would be doing if he had stayed true.

It had been a mistake to join her on this journey. Catori had thought she needed a friend, but increasingly now she didn't need anyone. Suchi was holding herself apart. He saw it and mourned. But she had left him behind when she went to be a kura, and now left him again. He shouldn't be surprised, and any blame was his own.

"I think they've seen us," pimply Asisa said.

It would be poor warriors who didn't. A band of five people walking in the open through fields was not hard to spot. The warriors were looking at Suchi's group now. Some of them were, anyway. Others stared eastwards across the plain, and one took off like a white-feathered Runner towards the south, where presumably Otoron was.

"Others have seen us too," Yurac said.

"Everyone will see us," Catori told him. "They're warriors, and at war. Stay quiet, my friend. These men won't have patience for an outlaw."

The men pouring across the fields were laden, not with weapons but with food. Some carried sacks, others animals taken from coop or sty. One group herded a dozen llamas along a track. In the distance Catori could see tendrils of smoke, and for a moment he was afraid the sorcerer was there. But the fires were too small, and too far apart. These were blazes set in homes and barns. Ashir, burning their own land.

"I don't understand," he murmured, but too softly to be heard.

They came up to the barn, picking their way across a stripped field, and a warrior asked, "Who are you?"

"I am Suchi. Who leads here?"

"I do," a voice from the barn said. The man who stepped into view was small, a whip-thin weasel of a man with tattoos so thick they all but merged from shoulder to wrist. Snakes, writhing endlessly over his skin. "My name's Guayra. What are you doing here?"

"We are making for Hatun. But we must speak to you first."

"We're on a *ch'uyu-karu,*" Rimaq put in unhelpfully. Catori saw the leader's brows lower.

"A *ch'uyu-*"

"We need to speak about the Ashir," Suchi said smoothly, "and how we may survive."

"What?"

"I can make you see," she promised. "All of you, all you men here. Why do you fight the Thrain?"

"To kill them," someone said.

"To defend my home."

"For the *kamachi.*"

"Ah," Suchi said, nodding. "For the *kamachi.* But what if Kai is not fighting for you? What if he does not fight for Apusuyu, and for Viraca?"

There was a silence. The warriors were confused, Catori saw. They had thought they knew their jobs and now here came a grimy priestess to take away their certainties. Suchi had taken control of the conversation with a few sentences. When they reached Hatun she might become a formidable opponent for Kai.

He looked out over the fields again, trying to understand what the warriors were doing. Yurac was frowning too, but at least he'd kept quiet so far. More warriors had begun to head towards the barn, to find out what was happening there.

"We were made by Viraca," Suchi said. Her usual spiel, polished by practise and repetition. "The Ashir were many peoples once. Viraca made us one. He gave us our language, taught us to build and to farm. He walked every corner of Apusuyu and gave it all to us.

"The last of his gifts, the greatest, was the *kamachi.* A sign of his love to bind us together, however long the years, however dark the mornings. But Kai has lost any touch of the god he once had. He is a greater danger to us than the Thrain or their sorcerer, or anything else in the world that would destroy us by force. Kai, will destroy us from within, like an *akatanqa* beetle already hidden in the crops."

179

Another silence, shorter this time, and then Guayra said, "Get out of here." Suchi might not have heard him. "Everything we are fell under threat once before. When Viraca left, and the Blind God came with weapons of terror and fear. The few *kura* who survived fled into the mountains, to the retreats hidden there. They hid for two thousand years, but they survived, and when Tezcata's time ended they came out of hiding. With them they brought Viraca's teachings and his love.

"But they could have done nothing without the *kamachi*. Servants kept being born all through those dark years, and they kept the faith. While that remains true nothing can harm us. The Thrain are mortal, and they will fade to nothing more quickly than Tezcata did. On that day we will still be here, and our land will be ours again.

"But Kai would change that. He would change *us*, until we are more like the Thrain then ourselves. He will throw away what we are, what Viraca made us, in exchange for iron swords and horses. We will be pale shadows of what the Ashir once were."

"Get gone," Guayra told her again. "Take your poison and go, before I lose my temper."

Catori looked around at him. "Easy, Snake. You shouldn't threaten a priestess."

"Even when she spouts such lies? I'm surprised at you, *Deer*. You must have had honour once. What are you doing, slinking along with a woman who speaks evil like this?"

A good question, and it made Catori hesitate. He wasn't surprised when Suchi spoke into the gap.

"I have fought with the *kamachi* in the mountains," she said. "I walked with him in Kuska, where the first people were made. I know more of the truth than you can imagine, Guayra, and I tell you this. Kai has lost his way. He must be brought to it again."

They were surrounded by warriors now, fifty or sixty of them in a loose circle around the door of the barn. Beyond them Catori could make out the mass of a larger force, moving east on the road. He craned his neck, trying to see more clearly.

"What do you think the priesthood is for?" Suchi asked softly. "Do we exist just to lead prayers, do you think? To offer comfort to the poor? No. We are here to protect the people, all that we are, even when the *kamachi* has forgotten what he is. Then most of all."

"Has he really abandoned us?" someone asked. Catori was still peering at the road but the voice sounded very young.

"Worse," Suchi said. "He has betrayed you."

"This stops here," Guayra spat. "Speak again and I'll kill you myself, *kura* though you are."

Catori was beginning to turn, hand falling to his axe and a word of warning coming to his lips, when something in his mind clicked and he knew what the mass on the road was. He stopped dead.

"Those aren't our men," Asisa said. Her voice came from far away.

"We need to leave," Catori said. "Right now."

Guayra pushed past him. Normally Catori would never let a Snake treat him that way, or any other warrior, but he let it go. The other man went to the edge of the group and shaded his eyes to look west, towards the oncoming army. When he turned back he was smiling.

"Get ready to attack," he said. "Call everyone together. We'll hold them until the Puma get here."

"No. The sorcerer will slaughter you," Catori said. "You can't fight him. Spread out, strip the land so his army can't eat. That's what you're doing already, isn't it?"

"Some chief in the east ordered it. He was at Chakanay and thinks that gives him the right to command us. But we are Snake!" Guayra thrust an arm above his head. "We will fight! Call our men –"

He broke off. Men were craning their heads back, following the path of a glinting something as it rose into the sky from the enemy army. It was coming their way, arcing very high. Catori watched it climb.

"Lights?" Guayra laughed. "Is that it? Did he terrify you northerners with pretty lights?"

Catori didn't reply. The light had reached the top of its arc, seeming to hang in the air.

"Forgive me," Suchi said. She had come to stand next to him, Yurac on her other side. "Both of you. I've led you to your deaths."

"Death?" Rimaq asked. Asisa whimpered.

"There is nothing to forgive," Catori said. "You followed your heart and I followed mine. You always held it, Suchi."

"I know I did. I couldn't love you, Catori."

He snorted laughter. "I couldn't fall in love with an easy-going woman, oh no. Nothing so simple for me."

"What is this?" Guayra demanded.

"This is our deaths," Catori said.

With that the more of light flared brilliant white. For a moment Catori could see nothing but glare. Then it faded a little and his streaming eyes made out a streak of fire plunging down, straight at where they stood. He started to draw his axe to shake in defiance.

There was an instant of heat, and then nothing.

*

The bridge was broken. It had spanned a river that was deep and fast, but in several places large boulders had washed down from the mountains and now

181

squatted between the banks. Water rushed around them in foaming green and white. By the time she and Chimalli's little group arrived warriors had already begun to cross, leaping from stone to stone in ragged lines.

"Horses couldn't do that," Kisain told her when she asked. Without Mimiteh to help him walk the grey of his face had turned almost green, and his words came in gasps that seemed wrenched from him. "It's hard enough for them to walk up or down the steps you Ashir put in your roads. Their feet aren't built for that sort of thing. That's why Terzian had to do something else here."

They didn't know what the sorcerer had done, but a short distance downstream the earth was chewed up on both banks, just outside the cluster of houses. The villagers were all gone, probably in hiding, but a large number of people must have walked there, not long ago. The churned earth stopped abruptly a few feet from the edge of the water, only to reappear on the far bank.

"Looks like he made some sort of bridge," Dyani said.

Amaru thought he was right. Someone must have burned the old bridge, probably two days or more ago given that the remaining posts were charred but cold. Either Otoron's warriors or the village folk, trying to stop the Thrain from crossing. As though the invaders would have baulked at a stream, after coming hundreds of miles.

The Thrain did it differently. Some leaped from stone to stone, while others threw ropes across and tied them off. In moments rope bridges had taken shape. Warriors hung at intervals along them, using more hemp to bind the cross-ropes into place. Injured men would be able to cross more easily there than by the boulders, but it was still going to be torture for Kisain, and a few others. But then, mere walking was torture for them.

A light brought her head up. It was far ahead, a glimmer she could barely see, but she didn't need to be told to turn her head away. She waited for the flash to fade before she opened her eyes again.

"Another one," Tumay noted. "Those southern warriors must have gathered in a band again."

"They need to start learning," Dyani said.

"Would we have done, if we hadn't seen the sorcerer's power for ourselves?" Amaru didn't wait for an answer. She scrambled down the bank and crossed from stone to stone, slithering a little in someone's wet boot print. Tumay jumped after her, and then Dyani and Qula, while Chimalli crouched and let Kisain wrap arms around his neck. Then the big warrior sprang across in a series of impressive bounds, jouncing Kisain about but not hurting him seriously. He was still white-lipped afterwards, but that was better than dragging himself over the rope bridges.

"Not bad," Dyani said to Chimalli, and then added, "for a Puma."

The chieftain grinned at him. "It's not just you Deer who can march all day and still be able to climb mountains, you know."

"Of course it isn't," Dyani said.

"As long as you –"

182

"It's just," the scarred man went on, taking no notice, "that the Deer are better at it."

That made Tumay snort in amusement, Deer that he'd once been, and Chimalli laughed and clapped Dyani on the back. "We'll see soon enough, won't we?"

"Seems we will," Dyani agreed.

They pressed on. A mile beyond the river they came across the strewn bodies of warriors, sixty or seventy Eagles who had been smashed into the ground behind a low wall. Not by magic. Chimalli studied the carnage and decided the warriors must have thought the wall would give them some protection, but the Thrain cavalry had simply ridden over them and left only these mutilated bodies behind.

"Fools," Tumay commented, "who didn't believe a thing until they saw it for themselves."

They pushed on. Around them the Ashir moved, thousand on thousands of them pouring through the stripped fields. Their conversation was a distant low hum, fading in and out of hearing with shifts in the wind. Amaru's stomach had begun to grow tight, and not with hunger. She blotted her hands on her skirt, several times. Sweat pooled behind her eye patch and began to itch.

Just past noon they passed another group of abandoned Thrain soldiers, twenty-five bodies huddled together on a gentle ridge, by a stand of wayakan trees. All of them bore wounds, but it was the punishing travel that had killed them. They leaned haphazardly against one another, like sleeping spider monkeys crowded onto an uneven branch. The Thrain were dwindling before her eyes, men falling away from the army like flies from a desiccated corpse, and yet it hardly mattered. A few less soldiers made little difference. It was the hooded man they needed to see among the dead, the sorcerer, and there was no sign of that happening.

A hollow *boom* jerked her head around. Most of the warriors she could see had ducked for cover at the sound, but Chimalli and Tumay were already pushing through the copse so they could catch a glimpse of whatever had happened. She thought she knew already – so did Kisain, by the tightness of his jaw – but Amaru went after the two warriors anyway. Qula called something after her, but Amaru didn't stop. She wanted to see this sorcerer, just once; the man whose ambition had killed her father and her family. The least Quilla's mercy should grant her was the chance to look at his silver eyes and then spit in them.

When she emerged from the trees it was to see Chimalli and Tumay staring south and east, to where a black billow of smoke rose some two miles away. Something flashed briefly at its base, a light so bright it was almost blue, and then died. Moments later another dull rumble rolled over them. In its wake Amaru thought she could hear screaming, faint sounds like the whispers of the dead. The breeze seized the rising black cloud and began to push it sideways.

183

"That was the men from the south," Chimalli said after a while. "Again! Uchu should have reached them by now."

"Maybe they just didn't listen." Tumay glanced at Amaru. "They won't believe the sorcerer's power until they see it for themselves."

"We can't stop him, then," Dyani said finally. All around them warriors had come to a halt, looking towards the copse for instructions. "The sorcerer will reach the Retreat before us."

"Then we'll be waiting when he comes down," Tumay answered. Which wasn't the point, of course. The whole purpose of this desperate march across the plains had been to stop Terzian reaching the Retreat, to somehow block his path and then hope for a miracle. Being there to meet him when he came back was too late to matter and they all knew it. Chimalli still had his back to them, and was staring motionless across the fields.

"When he comes down?" Dyani sneered. "He'll have destroyed the Retreat by then, the last outpost of Viraca's love in the darkest of times, and what will have changed? We still won't dare gather in a group. He will still have his power. *How can we win, Tumay?*"

"By destroying the trail down the cliff, maybe. Or digging pits with stakes on the plain, and covering them."

"Pits with stakes," Dyani said, his tone corrosive. "Hidden, sharp sticks, against magic. Of course."

Amaru said quietly, into the silence, "*Kamachi.*"

Chimalli stirred, and twisting slightly he glanced over his shoulder at her. Kisain turned too, with the sceptical expression he always wore when Kai was mentioned. A few warriors who were standing close by murmured to one another, and Amaru heard her single word repeated and passed back.

"The *kamachi* gives us hope," Chimalli said at last, very softly. "But it's up to us what we do with that hope. I intend to make use of it, for as long as breath lasts, even if it really does come down to sharp sticks against all that sorcerer's magic. And you, Dyani? You've come this far, and earned yourself a pretty new scar. Are you going to give up now, and crawl away?"

The big Puma pulled the axe from his belt and set off, heading directly for the gap between the two outflung arms of the mountains. Directly for the Thrain. Dyani showed his teeth in what could not possibly have been a smile and started after him. Qula shared a glance with Amaru that said *men!* without a word spoken, and then she set off after him, Kisain limping along beside her. Another murmur spread among the surrounding warriors, and as Amaru watched the whole dispersed mass of them began to walk after the Thrain.

She was the last to move. Amaru couldn't quite believe what she was doing, that she was here among these brave men in the face of this evil, but she could feel a smile flickering on and off her face. Hope was still alive in her, despite the bleakness all around, despite all the death and loss and grief. Hope was still alive because the *kamachi* was still alive. She followed the warriors east, towards the

184

mountains, and as dusk drew down and the Thrain came to a halt in Hirka, on the top of the cliffs Amaru saw tiny figures looking down at them.

30

"There you are," Kai whispered.

He was standing very close to the edge. Chinita was a mountain girl to her bones, unafraid either of high places or the falls below, but the precipitous drop down to Hirka made her skin prickle. The cliff looked as though it would fall at any moment. It was simply too high, too sheer to stand for long. From this height the village seemed like a child's toy, grey-slated roofs over small huts, around which fields spread in rough circles. To her left a river splashed its way down the cliff in a series of spray-shrouded leaps, then hurried through Hirka between narrow banks.

Below, between the village and the edge of the trees beyond, the Thrain army squatted like a monstrous alqo beetle, red on black, waiting.

All this time, she thought. *All this time and now at last the sorcerer is here, and we must face him.*

Further away warriors were spread in a great fan, a plague of insects scattered across the land. It was hard to see them clearly in the gathering dusk, but from this elevation Chinita could pick them out by their long, grotesque shadows. They reminded her of Tezcata, twisted and deformed. It was an image she wished she could shake from her mind, but it lurked there and refused to fade, like a stubborn stain on linen. Campfires came to life as tiny sparks, most of them placed behind hills or stands of trees, out of sight of the Thrain. The enemy themselves lit no fires. The dark mass of their numbers began to blur into the gloom.

"What now?" Achachi asked from behind them, near the trees. He was sitting on a lightning-felled trunk, still pasty-faced and breathless from their passage over the lung-bursting trail from Kuska. Above the snow line arthritis had turned his hands into claws, and made his knees pop like falling stones as he moved, but it was his colour that worried Chinita most of all. She'd seen people with that dough-like skin before, and most of them had not lived long.

"We send him a message," Kai said.

There was no need to say who he meant, and a silence fell. The villagers of Hirka stood in the shadow of the wayakan forest, with a few of Otoron's warriors among them. The two groups had fled up here when the Thrain approached, never thinking to find their *kamachi* waiting. All of them knew what the sorcerer had done to prisoners. They had told tales of men burned alive, or torn to pieces by powers they could not see. They'd run from the mere rumour of the man now waiting with his army at the foot of the winding trail down the cliff. Now none of them moved.

Not even for Kai. Nobody wanted to risk eternity blind and voiceless in Supay's endless Halls. They avoided each other's eyes and shuffled their feet, and nobody moved. Chinita looked at them, expecting to feel disdain and finding instead she could summon up only a weary kind of pity. She came to a decision and stepped forward.

"I will –"

"You will not," Kai said, in his calm voice. As though he had known what she would suggest. "You go where I go."

The words should have thrilled her, in that secret place inside where Kai could make her feel warm and safe, simply with a smile. He hardly seemed aware of her though. His stare was fixed on the Tnrain below them with an unsettling intensity, leaving no room for anything else. She thought Catequil of Storms could walk down the mountain with the flayed god Xipe at his side, and Kai – if he noticed at all – would spare them no more than a glance.

"I'll go," Taruka said.

Kai turned away from the cliff to study him, where Taruka stood beside the others from Kuska. Paqu sat nearby, nursing an ankle he'd turned on a stone yesterday evening. An irony, to come through the snow without a mark and then hurt himself walking on grass. Achachi himself was that worrying pasty colour, and his left hand was swaddled in a makeshift bandage over the wounds where two fingers had been. The bandage needed a wash. There was no time for it now.

Neither of the older men could go. Kai couldn't, obviously, and sending Evain was out of the question. Taruka waited until Kai turned back to him and then smiled.

"Who else?" he asked.

"There's some danger," Kai said,

Taruka's grin widened. "Of course there's danger. Crossing the pass was dangerous too. Did you have a point?"

Crossing the pass had been appalling, and knowing what she did now, Chinita didn't think she'd have the courage to do it again, however great the need. Her vision had blurred, then begun to run together like colours in a pot of dye. The rocks first grew slippery with ice, and then vanished beneath layers of snow. Some patches remained clear, and there wind whistled and sang, sweeping snow away and tugging at the travellers' coats, this way and now that. The six of them skidded and slid. All of them fell at least once, and still they climbed and feeling bled out of their fingers.

Chinita didn't notice when they went over the top of the pass and began to descend. Her teeth rattled despite all she could do to stop them, and she tucked her hands under her arms to keep as much warmth in them as she could. That cost her precious balance, but if it was a choice between sliding and losing her fingers, she would risk the slide. But she couldn't feel her feet, and ice had begun to form on her eyebrows and make a crust in her hair. The air was so cold that it burned her throat. Fog filled her head, white and frozen.

But she would not stop. Would not. For Kai, and because she was *Kichka,* a Thorn, one of the first of that society. If she failed while old men went on she would shame every sister who came after her. She pushed on, but she might have walked off a cliff and not realised until she hit bottom, where she would shatter like a dropped glass.

Then Kai was there, as he always seemed to be when needed. He was nearly blue from cold, his skin glittering with a sheen of tiny crystals, and yet he found the energy to take her hands and rub them vigorously with his own. His voice when he spoke shuddered and shook like a palsied child's, and vapour puffed from between his lips and faded to wisps. "We're over, Chinita. The hard part's done. One more effort, and we'll be warm again."

Well, they were warm again, or as warm as you could be this high up. But Chinita's face still felt stiff sometimes, as though the muscles still remembered when they'd been frozen to her bones. She had blisters too, lines of them on her hands and feet. All the band did. They'd made the crossing, but it hadn't been easy.

"I will never," Paqu had said, "never, humph, do something as foolish as that again in my life."

Chinita thought he was thrilled, in secret. The priest had spent his days in calm, unhurried seclusion in Kuska, performing the rituals and tending his crops. It was a placid, orderly existence, one in which excitement happened to other people. But excitement had found him in his age, when the *kamachi* came striding into his valley with outlanders and strange beasts in tow. Paqu was in his element now, offering comfort and support to the villagers from Hirka, even though he'd never had to do such things before. He would have *blanched* at doing such things before, in fact. Chinita didn't have to have known him then to realise that.

It was strange, how the coming of the Thrain had liberated so many Ashir from the roles they had filled before. Bandits had become citizens, women were turned into warriors. Kai himself had been transformed into a battle leader, something no *kamachi* before him had ever done. Change had come to them all. It was the question of whether to accept it or resist, and how much of each, which had ended with Suchi driven away while her own brother turned his back on her.

"Of course there's danger," Taruka said. "Crossing the pass was dangerous too. Did you have a point?"

"I wish," Kai began, and then stopped. He glanced at the villagers, perhaps wondering how much he could say in front of them, and for an instant his placid demeanour cracked and he looked afraid. Chinita had time for one step towards him before his face became serene again. The man she loved smiled at her, but around the edges of his lips and eyes she could see the faint tracery of doubt amid the weight of the burden he bore.

"You wish what?" Taruka asked.

Kai's head came up. The doubt was gone, his expression calm. Evain must have recognised something in that look, for he began to smile a terrible smile, with no humour in it at all.

"I wish you to give the sorcerer this message," Kai said, and began to explain.

There was a long silence when he finished. Everyone stared at him, and Kai looked back calmly, but Chinita could still see that shadow of doubt in the deep places of his eyes. She took another pace towards him and then stopped. It was said to be bad luck to touch the dead, and he was dead, if this was his plan.

She'd thought he had something *clever.* A ruse, a trick, anything. But he had nothing at all.

He looked at her, one eyebrow raised. "What? Are you afraid Supay of the dead has one finger on me already?"

"I'm afraid," she said.

"This is *jatun k'anchay,*" he said. "Catequil of the Storm is stronger here than anywhere else in the world. His lightning strikes hard." He gestured at the stones around them, all cracked and broken into pieces. "And I'm the beloved of the Teacher God. The sorcerer has power. Here, so do I."

"I'm still afraid. What he does… it's monstrous."

"Yes. And it must be stopped."

His intuition was a curse as much as a gift. So it seemed to Chinita, anyway. How wearying it must be, to know the secret thoughts of others without effort. But he usually knew what choice to make, and when. He had brought them here out of trust in the God, and if Kai could put his faith in Viraca, she could put hers in him. She went to him and took his hand, bad luck or no, and as she did it seemed the group began to breathe again.

"Supay may want you," she said, "but he can't have you yet. You will not die today, my love. I won't allow it."

His grip tightened until it became painful, but suddenly there was nothing at all to read in his blank expression. Chinita knew she'd said the wrong thing, but she couldn't see how or why, and didn't understand. Then there was no time to ask, for Kai's gaze swept back to Taruka, still standing among the shattered stones in front of the little group from Kuska.

"You don't have to do this," Kai said quietly. "I will not blame you if you've changed your mind, my friend."

"I haven't changed my mind," Taruka said. He walked forward and knelt in the grass before Kai, his face upturned towards him. "But I'd ask you to bless me, *kamachi*, before I go."

Kai nodded and put his hand in the warrior's hair. He had to swallow before he began, but when he did there was no doubt in his tone. "In the name of Viraca, and by all the gods, I bless you, Taruka. May the glance of the Blind God never fall on you, until Quilla releases you and Supay takes you home."

"Thank you," Taruka said. He stood and brushed at his knees. "I think I can go now." He hesitated, then slapped his chest with his right hand in the warrior's salute. "Whatever happens, I doubt that any *kamachi* before you could have done better than you have. It's been an honour to walk with you, Kai, and with Quilla's mercy, perhaps we'll walk together again in Supay's Halls."

"I'd like that," Kai said. "If there truly is forgiveness, your sister will walk with us too."

189

Taruka nodded and turned away. As he headed for the head of the trail he gave Achachi a wave, which the old man returned with his uninjured hand. Taruka went round a stand of bushes and was lost from sight. For a while they could the rattle of small stones under his feet, and then that too faded into nothing.

"The sorcerer will kill him," Chinita said, very softly so nobody else could hear. "He'll kill him, and then he'll kill you too."

"Sometimes," Kai said, almost absently, "it's possible to die, and still live. And this is *jatun k'anchay.*"

That was no answer at all, of course. It was Xipe who died and yet lived, flaying himself every midwinter only to be reborn in spring, when life came back into the land and green things began to grow. But he was a god and Kai, Servant though he might be, was not immortal. If he died it would be once and forever, as it always was for the children of men.

Kai let go of her hand and moved over to the villagers, who watched him approach with a mixture of awe and unease. Perhaps they too thought he was halfway dead, and feared to stand too close to him in case they should draw Supay's eye themselves. Kai must be aware of it; he never missed anything so clear. But he gave no sign of it and began to talk. Gradually the villagers drew closer around him, as though they were cold and he a warming blaze.

Chinita turned back to the cliff. Taruka was somewhere below, following the trail down the precipitous descent, and out of sight. There was nothing to do now. She began to wait.

31

One of the younger soldiers handed Berain a platter. It held some sliced fruit and a chunk of bread, which one poke told him was stale. That was about what he'd expected. Rations had never been so bad.

The horn sounded as he moved the plate from one hand to the other, and he dropped it. Fruit scattered and the bread landed in a patch of mud. Berain cursed, but he'd needed the hand to draw his sword. He hadn't eaten all day, and now this.

"I hope you don't expect me to replace that for you," the youngster said sullenly.

Berain didn't bother to reply. He slammed his half-drawn sword back into the scabbard, pocketed a couple of bits of fruit that might still be edible, and headed for the alarm.

He couldn't see any Ashir. That didn't mean there weren't any. An archer could hide behind a bush or in a fold in the ground. But it did mean there weren't many, because a band would stand out in the empty land. Even the village had been abandoned, and stripped of food like everywhere else. There was nobody in sight. No danger that he could see.

The guard post was a gap in a fence, where a track ran through. Soldiers had blocked the opening with an upturned cart and crouched behind it for cover. More had begun to gather by the time Berain arrived, drawn in by the blast of that horn. Most of them had shields, which they held up to protect against an archer who might be lurking out there. Berain had his mail but no shield, so he loitered near to a pair of men who did.

"What's the alarm?" he asked.

The nearest man shrugged. "Beats me."

He was pale. Well, they all were, after so long with little sleep and no proper food. Berain shook his head and turned his attention back to the fields, which is why he was one of the first to see a patch of twilight shadows resolve into the figure of a man, hands held high and empty.

"Parley," the man called out, in the Ashir speech. Berain wasn't especially good with the alien language, but he was fairly certain that was what the newcomer had said. "Parley."

"Are you alone?" someone demanded.

"Alone," the man said after a moment. Probably he'd had to work out what the question meant. "Parley?"

"Parley granted," a light voice said, away to Berain's right. He glanced over and saw Gavair striding through the ranks. The Marshal's voice had always been gentle, and in the dark he'd sounded almost feminine. There was nothing womanish about Gavair though. The sight of his hard features and straight spine was all that had kept the army from panic, these last few days.

Less welcome was the presence of Draivan beside him, clad in his usual nondescript brown, with a silver net embroidered onto the shoulder of his tunic.

The chaplain had been all but insufferable since Ramian was killed. His sermons now were littered with reminders that a man's first loyalty should be to the One God, even if that implied disobedience to a senior officer. Or the brother of a king, Berain thought, and immediately squashed the idea. He had no idea if Terzian could read minds, but he didn't want to find out too late.

The figure outside the lines came closer, lowering his arms. It was an Ashir, of course, a tall lean man with the tattoos of a warrior down both arms. He looked ragged at the edges, as though he'd recently faced some hardship he'd barely survived. But the crest of his black hair was neat, sewn with corals and crimson threads, and his eyes were sharp.

An axe hung in his belt, and the rim of a wooden buckler poked over his shoulder, but he kept his hands out to his sides and away from them. Several soldiers put arrows to strings and half pulled their bows, even so. There was little trust left in the army, even for parleys.

"I am Taruka," the warrior said. He came up to the picket line and halted, looking at the assembled soldiers with no sign of fear. "I bring a message for the sorcerer, from the *kamachi*."

A murmur ran through the ranks. A few heads tilted back to stare up at the top of the cliff, where figures had been moving when the army reached Hirka and began to make camp. It was much too dark to see anything, but the thought was plain. Kai, the Servant who had proven such a bane to the invasion, was up there. They had run him down at last.

"You may give the message to me," Gavair said. It was odd, but Ashir words were even harder to understand when spoken in a Thrain accent. "I will see that it is given to Terzian."

Taruka shook his head. "I'm sorry, but no. My instructions are to speak to the sorcerer himself."

"I am the commanding officer of this army," the Marshal said sternly. "Anything you say to me will be passed to lord Terzian."

"I don't care if you're Makisapa's mother," the warrior answered. "You're not the sorcerer, and I will speak my message only to him."

"I could make you tell me," Gavair said.

Berain stared at his commanding officer in surprise. Until now the Marshal hadn't shown even the least sign of stress, but that comment revealed just how frayed his nerves must be. Gavair was often blunt, but rarely foolish. Even Draivan shot him a glance from lidded eyes, and the chaplain didn't notice subtleties until they jumped on his toes and shouted at him.

"I expect you could," the warrior said. He was outnumbered fifty to one, but he put his hands on his hips and looked at the soldiers down his nose. "No doubt you could burn me alive, as you have so many others. Do you think I'm such a fool that I never thought of that before I came?" His tone dripped contempt. "Go on, then. Do it, if you plan to. When my shade sees yours in Supay's Halls I will spit on you and laugh."

"There will be no need of that," a voice said from the deeper shadows beside the tents. Berain turned with the others and there was Terzian, standing cold and rigid behind them, wrapped in his grey cloak. He had come up in silence, drifting across the grass like a wraith. His hood was thrown back, leaving his head bare. His strange eyes glittered in the dark.

"My lord," Gavair said in greeting. "This man has come –"

"I heard," Terzian broke in. He stepped forward, coming up to the front of the semicircle of soldiers, and now Berain saw that the Ashir was afraid after all. His brown skin had paled, and his hands were clenched into fists at his sides. He didn't step back though, and Berain felt a reluctant admiration. Whatever else was true of these people, the Ashir were no cowards.

"So your great *kamachi* has stopped running at last," Terzian said. His voice was quiet, but it almost seemed to hiss. Berain shivered at the sound. "Well, then? What message does he send?"

"He invites you to meet with him at the top of the cliff in the morning," Taruka said. His voice quavered a little, but still he stood his ground, and his chin stayed high. "No attack will be launched on your army, either tonight or in your absence tomorrow, in token of good faith. But you are to come with no more than ten men. You will be watched as you climb the trail, and if you try to bring more, you'll find nothing at the top but the trees."

Terzian said nothing. He leaned forward to stare intently at the warrior and Taruka returned his gaze, though his knuckles were white. The silence stretched. Hardly any of the soldiers were watching for an attack. A group of Ashir archers could kill dozens of men now before anyone realised what was happening.

"Ten is not enough," Gavair said finally. "How do we know you don't have a horde of warriors up there, waiting to strike?"

"I suppose you don't," Taruka shrugged. "Though you've dealt with our warriors easily enough before, thanks to his magic." He nodded towards Terzian. "Even the swarm around you keeps its distance. With such power behind you, why would you need more than ten?"

"Why indeed?" Terzian said softly. His eyes gleamed. "But your Kai won't let the Retreat be destroyed. I could bring a thousand men, and he'd still try to bar my way. Isn't that true?"

"The relics kept there have been taken away," Taruka answered. "There are other holy places in Apusuyu, after all. Now all you can destroy at the Retreat is stones and mortar, and those can be remade."

Berain was paying close attention, and his nerve-heightened senses heard the warrior's words and at once screamed liar. If Terzian harboured doubts he gave no sign of it, merely staring at the man still harder than before. But Draivan stepped forward into the clear space between the warrior and the Thrain, and raised his voice as though declaiming from the pulpit.

"A holy place is more than merely the objects it contains," he announced. "All men know this. A church is holy because the spirit of the One resides there, if only in part. A glimmer of his radiance, when the full glare would blind our

193

eyes and sear our souls." He swept his gaze along the line of soldiers. "Should we believe that this Kai, this servant, would abandon his false gods?"

"Their gods are not ours," Gavair said flatly. Apparently this was one of the times he would be blunt. "The Ashir are not us, cleric. If there is one thing our time in Apusuyu should have taught us, it's that we err if we judge them by the standards of our own society."

"Would you judge them by their standards, then?" Draivan fixed the old soldier with a glare. "By the behaviour taught to them by their false idols? That comes close to heresy, Marshal."

Gavair arched his eyebrows. "It's no heresy to try to understand an enemy. I will do what I can to keep my men alive and in this world, and leave the welfare of their souls in the next to you."

Terzian ignored the interplay. He never took his eyes from Taruka, and still leaned forward as though about to seize the warrior and throttle him where he stood. Around him the semicircle of soldiers was utterly motionless.

"I agree," Terzian said at last. His voice was low and very soft, little more than a whisper. "But tell your *kamachi* I expect him to keep his word. If I come and he is not there, I will go to your capital at Hatun and burn it from wall to wall. This I swear. I will set fires throughout your precious Blessed Land, from the Retreat to the sea, and kill every man and child in the realm, if that is what it takes to bring the man who murdered my son to face me at last."

"My lord!" Gavair burst out. "I beg you to reconsider. This could be a ruse. If you leave the bulk of the army behind, who will protect them?"

Terzian made a casual flicking motion with his fingers. "They are soldiers. They can protect themselves for a time."

"But not without losses," Gavair protested.

"Armies always suffer losses," the sorcerer said dismissively. The Marshal opened his mouth once more, but Terzian rode right over him. "Well, warrior? Will you take my message?"

"I will," Taruka said. "And Kai will be there. Now, with your leave, I'll tell the warriors around your army to withdraw."

"Tell them what you wish," Terzian said indifferently. "You may do as you please, as long as you take my message back to your *kamachi*. Tell him I will come, and I will kill him tomorrow." He started to turn away, back towards his pavilion at the centre of the camp. "And do not forget what I said. The whole land will burn if he is not there to meet me."

"But with whose flame?" Taruka asked. He grinned at Terzian, possibly with relief that he was going to come out of the meeting unscathed, and melted back into the night.

*

194

"I count ten," Taruka said. He was lying at the edge of the cliff with his head poking over, so he could peer down the switchback trail and watch the Thrain coming up. "No, wait. Eleven."

"That's, humph, more than you stipulated," Paqu said to Kai. "It gives you grounds to abandon the meeting, if you wish."

Kai nodded and said nothing. He wasn't going to leave here without facing the sorcerer, not unless he had to. If Terzian had led a hundred men up the trail Kai would have taken his people and melted away, whatever threats the magician might make about the burning that would follow. All Kai had was his six friends, and forty villagers and warriors hidden among the wayakan trees fifty yards back from the cliff edge. A hundred soldiers would be able to overwhelm them even without the sorcerer's power.

Eleven was few enough that the villagers would be able to defeat them, if it came to combat. That would do. It meant events had come to a head, here at *jatun k'anchay,* among fallen trees and rocks split by the fury of mountain storms. He had stood here only weeks ago, with Salali on one side and Matlal on the other, and looked out over the expanse of the Blessed Land at the fading of the day. He had not expected the end to come here, or so soon.

He hadn't expected his friends to die, either. Matlal had always seemed close to immortal, big and imposing, and possessed of a passion in the gods that sometimes seemed to make him glow from the inside. And Sala, well... Sala was the type of man who could fall off a cliff and land in a hayrick. If he lost a copper *karwa* he'd find three in silver before the day was out. Or he would have done, before the Thrain had come to change the world. He was lost too, his soul wandering in Supay's Halls, searching endlessly through the gloom for a glimpse of the sun. Perhaps Kai would find out how he had died, one day.

Perhaps not.

"I will find you in the Halls of Darkness," he promised in a whisper. "Both of you. I swear it, and we will walk a ways together, you and I."

Taruka glanced back over his shoulder. He didn't speak, and Kai didn't look at him. He said, "But not yet," and moved forward to stand beside the Deer so he could see down to the trail.

"Nobody else in the camp has moved," Taruka said. "It's just the eleven of them, *kamachi.*" He hesitated. "One is wearing a hood, and another is dressed in plain brown robes."

"That will be the chaplain," Evain said. He was standing back from the edge with Catori and Achachi at his side. Somehow the three of them seemed to belong together now; warrior, bandit and Thrain, brought together by chance or the will of the gods, and now bound. "Draivan. He's an arrogant fool, but he'll only have come to gloat. You can ignore him."

It was he who had bound these men together, Kai thought. Not intentionally, but very little of what he'd done had been that. He had simply taken what steps he thought were necessary at the time, and things had added up. Along the way he'd become a chieftain of men, it seemed. In all the days of his life, he'd never dreamed he might become that. He'd never wanted to.

"And you?" he asked. "Will the sorcerer ignore you?"

The soldier smiled thinly. "He will have you in front of him. He won't spare a thought for me."

"I assume he's the hooded one," Kai said.

"Yes. Terzian hid his identity coming here, so his power came as a surprise at Chakanay. He wanted all your leaders to wait for him without fear, and be captured or destroyed. But disguising himself as a soldier won't gain him anything here, and he wouldn't do it anyway."

"He'll want me to see him as he is," Kai observed, "before he kills me."

Evain nodded. "Precisely."

"Except," Chinita said, speaking for the first time, "that he isn't going to be allowed to kill you."

Kai looked at her, and with a hint of irony said, "Precisely."

"That isn't funny," she snapped. "Kai, you're behaving as though this is a game, but that man is going to *kill* you."

"Quite possibly," Kai agreed.

"Then come away. Please, Kai, come away." She took his hand in both of hers. "Please. Don't do this."

He gripped her fingers with his own, and for a moment just drank in the sight of her. It was odd to think that he would never have met her, if not for the Thrain. Chinita would likely have been caught by the warriors one day, and left to die staked out by the side of the road. Either that, or she would have been killed in a raid, or simply have died from a minor wound that nobody among the bandits was able to treat. He would never even have known, never have given her a thought. Just another outlaw, dying with vultures at the roadside.

Instead she was the *kamachi's* lover, and leader of the new women's warrior society, the Thorns. As much a chieftain as he was, or more. Life was strange. Who could guess what was to come?

But for every blessing there was a curse. The Blind God's hooked fingers and mirrored foot, the opposite of the love of the Teacher God, and his smile. Hope and despair, eternally opposed. Kai had found Chinita, found love, but along the way he had lost both Matlal and Sala. There was neither point nor purpose in wondering if the love was worth the sorrow. It was done. Life was life.

"Please," Chinita said again.

"Think of this," Matlal had said, beside the fire with Salali on the day Kai left his contemplation at the Retreat. *"You are the living proof that Viraca still remembers us, and still loves us. That we're still blessed. You are the* kamachi, *and if you despair, we're all lost."*

Kai looked at Chinita.

"I never believed that Viraca spoke to me," he said. "I never heard his voice in my mind, as a *kamachi* is supposed to do. It's only now that I understand my

196

mistake. I was listening for words, for instructions, as though he was one of my tutors at the Retreat when I was a boy. It never occurred to me, not once, that he might give me insights instead. That he might speak without words. I understand things without knowing how I do, Chinita. Viraca speaks to me through instinct. Through hunches. Does that make any sense?"

"Of course it does," she said quietly. "And your hunches tell you to face the sorcerer here." Desperation crept into her tone. "But sometimes a hunch is just a feeling, Kai. Nothing says it comes from the Bearded God, and you might die for the difference."

"You need to have more faith," Matlal had told him, that day by the fire. He did. It had taken love to teach him that. He stroked Chinita's hands.

"If we are loved," he said gently, "if Viraca still knows and remembers his children, we will come through this." He put a hand under his coat and touched the *cizin,* which was resting now inside his belt. The bone handle was in contact with his skin. "The Bearded God is not merely a myth, or a memory. There have been *kamachi* before me, and there will be others to come, because we are loved."

Everyone was watching them. Achachi and Catori, with Evain between them; Paqu who hadn't left the valley of Kuska for decades before now; and all the villagers waiting at the edge of the trees. Even Taruka had turned his head, abandoning his study of the approaching Thrain. All of them were still. *Everything* was still; the forest, the sun overhead, even the air. There was always wind on *jatun k'anchay,* but there was none now, at the crux.

Catequil of the Storm was watching.

"I don't want another *kamachi,*" Chinita said. "I want this one."

"You've got him," Kai answered. He kissed the corner of her mouth, then stepped away from her. "Taruka. Where are they?"

"Better than halfway up," the warrior answered. "Everyone else is still at the camp."

"Then go to your places," Kai said. He touched Chinita's fingers again, but it was not for her that his heart skipped twice, unsettlingly. "It's time."

She didn't move, and when he frowned at her she said, quite clearly, "I go where you go. Remember?"

He couldn't help smiling, and knew the moment he did so that she had won.

32

She stood beside him and waited. Taruka was on her other side, and beyond
Kai stood Evain with his hands clasped behind him. The fingers writhed
constantly, like restless snakes. He had proved loyal to his word, but this would
be a perfect opportunity for him to escape, if he chose to take it. Chinita didn't
think he would, simply because Kai did not.

Viraca speaks to me through instinct.

She prayed, desperately, that the Bearded God had done so this time.
Otherwise they were going to die here, all of them. Kai looked perfectly calm,
except that his right hand kept dipping under his coat to touch the *cizin.* Perhaps
his instinct failed him where sorcery was concerned. Or perhaps Viraca's plan
had always been for the Ashir to come through all these years but then go no
further.

She *hated* that thought. It made everything they had done, through more than
three thousand years, seem like nothing. Children playing with stalks of corn
that would blow away in a breeze.

Her grandfather and Paqu were back with the villagers, in a rough line just
inside the trees. Achachi had been given command there, an authority he
exercised through gruffness and age. As for the *kura,* he was needed to soothe
nerves and lead quick, heartfelt prayers. The men themselves had very simple
orders; shoot down any soldier who attacked, but otherwise do nothing. They
were not to act against the sorcerer, and if Kai fell, they were to melt into the
trees and flee as best they could.

Achachi's breathing was better now. And she was distracting herself,
thinking of breath or villagers or Viraca's plans, anything except the terror
coming towards them up the cliffside trail.

She had sat by the cliff for hours yesterday, while the others sprawled on the
grass after the exertion of crossing the pass. It seemed she could see all the
Blessed Land from there. Hirka was below, and then a band of forest punctuated
by cleared areas in which villages huddled, like eggs in the nest of an *ikaku* bird.
Beyond that the fields spread and merged, then ran away to the great ribbon of
the Pasqa and the clusters that were towns, until finally distance turned
everything to a pale blue under streamers of cloud. It was beautiful. Or it should
have been.

Not far away, some five miles off at first, was the dark mass of the Thrain.
Sometimes a pike or breastplate would glint in the sun. And all around were the
marks of their invasion. Fields burned bare, and ribbons of black smoke that rose
and then curled away, blown in the wind. Clusters of houses with open roofs,
where the flames had come and gone already. Through that ruination a swarm of
figures crawled, warriors come to defend their homeland in spite of the horror of
what Terzian could do. More would still be on the roads, hurrying as best they
could from the far south or the distant coast. Too many, surely, for even Terzian
to face.

None of it would change what happened here today.

She clenched her fingers and then let them relax again. Her chest felt tight. Beside her the man she loved stood in apparent tranquillity, and she almost wanted to shout at him and demand whether he really knew what he was doing, or if he was just paralysed with fright, like a deer as the puma slinks closer. The urge to run was very strong. She took a deep breath and let it out slowly.

"Have they turned back, or are they dawdling?" Taruka wondered abruptly. "I'll go and see, if you –"

Stones rattled on the trail, and he broke off. Colour fled from his face in a rush. Chinita's mouth was suddenly as dry as the high desert, and then men came over the top of the cliff.

They were soldiers, clad in the red and black surcoats of the Thrain, worn over shirts of mail. Four of them came up, then six. Their eyes darted across the clear space between cliff and forest, and knuckles went white on their sword hilts. Several of them stared at Evain in open disbelief; one spat contemptuously near his feet as they fanned out. Evain met their glares, but behind his back his fingers writhed faster than ever.

Next up was a man in plain brown, with a net sewn into the fabric of one shoulder. That would be the cleric, Draivan, a pinch-faced man who looked at Kai with scorn. Then came three more soldiers, one with an array of gold badges on his shoulders.

"Gavair," Evain whispered. His lips barely moved. "Marshal of the army, and once my commanding officer." Kai nodded.

Somewhere in the forest a puma coughed, just once, and then was quiet. A moment later another man came over the cliff.

Terzian had thrown back the hood of his cloak, revealing light brown hair and a surprisingly youthful face. What caught the attention was his eyes though, unnatural silver irises set in black. Chinita sucked in breath and heard Paqu gasp too. The priest hooked his fingers in a warding sign against evil. No wonder people had thought the sorcerer might be Tezcata returned, back in Chakanay. Even now, knowing he was not, Chinita felt a chill of superstitious terror.

Those silver eyes did not even look at her. They went straight to Kai, and flared with an inner light. A muscle jumped in Terzian's cheek. Breath hissed through his teeth as he let it out. He moved slowly forward, soldiers hurrying to flank him on each side when Gavair gestured a command. For Terzian they might not have existed.

He came on, the alien mage who had brought ruin to half the land, until he stood a few short yards in front of Kai. Then he stopped. The two men looked at each other for a long moment.

"Did you think," Terzian said at last, "that you could murder my son and live?" His voice quivered with repressed rage.

"I did not know he was your son," Kai answered quietly. "Only that he was an invader."

"We came to save you," Draivan said. Brightness danced in his eyes too, hot and fierce. "For the salvation of your souls."

"Then you should have sent priests," Kai said, "and not soldiers."

"You would have killed them."

"No. We would have laughed a little, that's all." He didn't take his eyes from the sorcerer. "In pity for the fools with only one god."

"Archers in the trees," Gavair said quietly.

The muscle twitched again in Terzian's cheek. "Speak again and I will kill you where you stand, Marshal. Or you, cleric. Believe me in this." Terzian's voice was a rasp. "I am here for the man who killed my son. Neither the soldiers nor the god matter at all. Only him."

Gavair stared at the back of his lord's head. Neither Kai nor Terzian seemed to have blinked. Chinita swallowed against the tightness in her throat, struggling to tear her gaze away from those frightening silver-black eyes. She didn't understand how Kai could be so calm. He hadn't even reached under his coat since the sorcerer appeared.

"You meant your son to rule here," Kai said. "You meant to conquer us, and take our land away."

"Of course he was to rule here," Terzian said. "We would have taught you so many things. In a generation Apusuyu could have been great, a country to shake the world. You put an end to that when you murdered my son."

"You would have taught us," Kai said, and now a thread of disdain crept into his voice. "How generous of you. Just like throwing a bone to a dog. And you've spoken twice now of murder." His lip curled. "You come to our land with war. You slaughter our warriors with fire and sorcery, for nothing, and when your own blood is spilled you dare call it murder?"

Terzian's face went black, gorged with blood. He stepped forward. Two of the soldiers drew their swords, and an instant later Taruka snatched for the axe in his belt. Chinita pulled her long knife, and as she did so an arrow zipped out of the trees and struck a soldier in the arm. He went down with a cry as his colleagues all grappled for their weapons, and the sorcerer raised his hands.

Chinita's skin prickled, all over her body. She started to turn, and then the air crackled like the lightning of Catequil. Kai was picked up and thrown backwards, as Chinita's hair tried to stand up on its own. Then the shock wave struck her and she was flung aside with the flash of heat against her skin, to land among the split stones of *jatun k'anchay*. She skidded, her feet sliding around her before she came to a stop against another rock.

She had been an outlaw though, and now was a warrior, and it took more than one little fall to keep her down. She rolled to one knee, realised only then that she'd lost one of her knives, and shrugged to herself. The other was still in her fist. She'd bitten half through her lip, but she swallowed the blood and looked at once for Kai.

Terzian still stood in the middle of the clear space, staring at the forest where the *kamachi* had vanished. He wore an expression of faint puzzlement. Two of

200

the soldiers were down with arrows sticking out of them, one dead she thought, but no more flew. Some distance away Taruka and Evain were picking themselves up, looking dazed, but she couldn't see Kai. Chinita choked back a sob and stood.

One step, and she stopped.

Kai came out of the trees. He was limping. Smoke rose from his clothes in a dozen thin tendrils. His left hand was burned raw. The same side of his face was covered with a spreading yellow bruise, puffing the flesh around the eye so the mark of the snake seemed larger than ever. But he was alive, incredibly alive, and breath left Chinita with a whoosh. She was afraid her heart had died. Kai limped forward until he was back where he had stood before, and there he halted and looked at Terzian with his one good eye.

"How," Gavair began, and then stopped. The soldiers gaped in disbelief. Ahead of them all the sorcerer's face had gone bone-white with shock. Then he snarled, and his hands came up once more.

"No!" Chinita screamed. A moment later Kai crumpled like torn linen, and she ducked as a second wall of burning air crashed into her. Draivan and two of the soldiers fell over. Taruka, staggering back towards the *kamachi,* was picked up and hurled sprawling into Evain, sending them both back to the ground. Small stones danced and rattled. Chinita's skin felt tight and hot, but she gritted her teeth and forced herself upright, and turned back towards the sorcerer.

Kai was getting up again. He pulled at his right sleeve, from which smoke poured in a steady stream, and at the second attempt managed to tear it off. He flung it to the ground. The skin beneath was cracked and red. Beyond him Taruka was groaning on his hands and knees, and Evain was trying to help him up.

"Why won't you die?" Terzian screamed in sudden, uncontrolled fury. His hands came up yet again. "For my son! For Ramian! *Why won't you –"*

Chinita was standing to one side, where the blast of Terzian's power had thrown her, and so she saw clearly when Gavair drew his sword and, stepping forward, drove it so hard into Terzian's back that the point burst out of his chest.

*

Chinita stood rooted, too stunned to move. One of the soldiers cried out in shock and surprise. The sorcerer staggered as the blade was pulled clear, and then very slowly he turned to face the general. Blood poured over his fingers from the wound in his chest. He shouldn't be able to stand with that great gouge in him, but he did, and the Marshal looked back at him. Terzian's lips writhed as he tried to speak.

"Because the soldiers *do* matter," Gavair said quietly, in answer to the unspoken question. "Because you have forgotten that, and allowed your hate and need for revenge to send too many men to their deaths, when all they wanted was to serve you. As I have served you. All my life."

The sorcerer stumbled. Air rippled around Chinita, barely touched by warmth, and the stones danced again on the ground. Terzian was expending vast amounts of power, but this time nobody was being harmed. He was using it on himself, Chinita realised, clinging to life by sheer force of magic. And he was losing. He faltered but stayed on his feet, blood pouring over his hands.

"It was my pride to serve you," Gavair said. "But my first loyalty is to the men who give me theirs. Always." He turned to Kai. *"Kamachi."*

"Yes," Kai said. What remained of his right sleeve was still leaking tendrils of smoke.

"I give my men into your care. I ask that you treat them with honour, as it seems you have for others." He indicated Evain. "Enough have died already, of both our peoples."

Kai nodded. His left eye was almost entirely shut now. People began to emerge from the trees, staring at the stricken magician as they came. They walked wide of Kai, as though afraid. "Why did you do it? Kill him, I mean."

"For the reasons I gave," Gavair answered. "I have always been loyal, but my first duty is to the men in my care. He forgot that." He looked at the sorcerer. "I stabbed him through the heart. Even magic cannot heal the heart, and it's taking all his power simply to hold on. It won't last."

Terzian managed a step towards the Marshal. His whole chest was crimson now, and more blood gushed between his fingers. He stopped, swayed for a moment. And then he fell, toppling to the stony ground. His hands came away from the wound as he struck, and a last gout of black blood poured onto the grass and he was still.

"You - you killed him," Draivan stuttered. "I don't – I don't understand."

"You never do," Gavair said.

One of the soldiers laughed at that, high and wild, and Chinita found that she could move. Her legs felt like thin cloth, but she wobbled towards Kai, stumbling over stones as she went. Taruka was on his feet, she saw. Half his crest was gone, and the bracelets on his right arm had melted and left seared flesh behind them, but he was standing. He gave her a crooked smile.

Kai reached into his coat and took out the *cizin*. The black sheath was melted half away, and what remained wasn't enough to hide the fact that the sickle was broken. Pieces of bronze fell off as Kai drew it out. Some clung on for a moment, but then it too crumbled away, leaving nothing behind but the cracked bone handle. The assembled villagers let out a soft murmur.

Chinita's skin crawled. One more attack would have killed Kai, then. The *cizin* had absorbed the magic somehow, had kept Kai alive, but it had broken under the strain. He must have known that, and still he'd come back to face the sorcerer again. She bent to pick up a fragment of the bronze, but it broke into yellow dust the moment her fingers touched it.

"Taruka," Kai said, "take Evain and go down to the armies. Tell them the sorcerer is dead and the Marshal has surrendered. Gavair had better go too, in fact, and the soldiers here. Take twenty or so villagers as an escort."

Taruka was still staring at the remnants of the *cizin*. Chinita had to poke him in the shoulder before he started and gave a jerky nod. "What? Oh. Yes, of course. Uh… what did you do, *kamachi?*"

Kai looked down at Terzian's body. "This is *jatun k'anchay*, where Catequil is stronger than anywhere else in this world. As for Viraca, he is strongest wherever I am. Two gods, at the zenith of their power." He smiled a little. "What did I do? I put my trust in Viraca. As a *kamachi* should. Go on with you, now. Not you, cleric."

Caught in the act of turning away, Draivan stopped and threw Kai a glance that was filled with terror. The priest hadn't believed the Ashir gods were real, Chinita remembered. He wouldn't know how to start dealing with what had happened here, and in that, he would not be alone. Chinita didn't know what to make of it herself. Her whole body ached.

"You ordered the temples burned in Chakanay," Kai said through his battered lips. "Did you think I'd forgotten?"

The priest, white-faced, made no reply. It was Gavair who paused at the top of the trail and turned back. "What will you do with him?"

"If I still had the *cizin* I would cut out his eyes and tongue to leave him blind and voiceless for eternity," Kai said. Draivan mad a mewling sound. "But that's lost, now. So I don't know. We will keep him under guard until I decide what to do."

"He likes burning," Taruka said.

"He does," Kai said, promising nothing. "Go talk to the armies, Taruka. There will be time for this another day."

The warrior nodded and went down the trail. Gavair and the soldiers followed, and Chinita thought *that shows how much they care for this cleric.* Not one of them spoke up for him after Gavair, and none glanced his way. Draivan stood passive while two of the villagers bound his wrists.

"We won," Achachi said wonderingly. He couldn't seem to take his eyes from the bone handle Kai still held. "We won."

"The *kamachi* won," Paqu said from the trees. "And Viraca won. But life in Apusuyu, humph, will still change."

That was true. How it would change was another matter. Suchi, for one, would no doubt want things to be as close to how they were before as she could make them. Others would not. The Thorns were here to stay, a fact as immutable as a mountain and as real as the Thrain themselves. Between those two truths, she supposed everything else would be argued over for years.

"There's a lot to do," Kai said. The side of his face had begun to turn purple, camouflage for the birthmark around his eye. "We'll need the nobles to meet and elect a new Qapac. The warriors need a new Auk, too. Whoever's in command of our warriors down there might do for that. The gods know he's earned it. And we need to learn how to write, and make iron and breed horses, so in the future we'll be strong enough to defend ourselves."

203

"And you need to get your wounds cared for," Chinita said. "Especially that burn on your hand."

He nodded. "Paqu, you and Taruka can take care of things here. I'm going to see if one of these villagers has some salve and bandages." He sighed. "And then I'll go to the Retreat, and sit in contemplation for about a month."

He was only two paces away when he stopped and looked over his shoulder at Chinita. "Aren't you coming?"

"I thought contemplation was always solitary," she said.

"Things are changing," Kai said. "Didn't anybody tell you?" He held out his good, unburned hand. "And you go where I go."

Her smile was so wide it hurt her scorched skin, and she put her hand in his.

They were sitting on their horses by the side of a muddy road in the southern highlands, passing a flask of *aqha* from hand to hand.

"Are you ready?" Chinita asked.

"If I ever get a sip from that, I might be," Kai said.

Taruka wiped the lip of the flask with his sleeve and passed it over. The corn liquor slid down Kai's throat with fire in its wake, putting tears in his eyes and flames in his stomach. He gasped and handed the flask to Achachi, who took it in his three-fingered hand and swigged heartily. When he finally lowered it he smacked his lips and let out an enormous belch.

"That's disgusting," Taruka said.

The old man grinned at him. "You should see what I can do after a dozen mugs of *chicha* beer."

"I'd rather not, I think."

Chinita grinned at them, then at Kai. His attempt to smile back was a sickly thing, and slid off his face as though ashamed.

"By the poisoned balls of the Blind God, boy," Achachi chided, "it will only get harder the longer you wait. Dig out your courage and let's move."

Kai sighed. "Appalling personal habits, and now bad manners too. And I seem to remember you hit me once. Is there no end to your rudeness, old man?"

"Don't know. Never found one yet."

Taruka snorted laughter, and Chinita reached across to take Kai's hand. "Come on, love. I'll be with you, so let's get it done."

This time he almost managed a proper smile. Which was, in the gods' capriciousness, when Taruka said, "Rider coming."

They turned to follow his finger. Someone was riding up the trail, a small figure with white feathers in his hair. A Runner then, though most of that group rode horses now. It was only on the stepped roads of the mountains that messages still went on foot. As the man came closer Kai saw that he wasn't much more than a boy, maybe only fifteen.

"He rides like a sack of oats," Chinita said.

"Better than me," Kai said. It was true. He was learning, but still tended to shut his eyes and pray when the horse galloped. Changes came, and new things, but that didn't mean he had to be good at all of them.

The youth drew up. His colour was hectic, a flush that was almost sickness. Kai checked the boy's throat and saw no spots there, no blisters. Not the red plague, then. These days it was habit to look.

"I bring news," the rider said. "For the *kamachi.*"

Achachi cackled. "There's a surprise."

"Hush," Kai said. "Be easy, lad. News from where?"

205

"The west, on the coast. A fishing village called Wari, between the desert and the sea." The boy was smiling, and Kai saw now that what was in his face was wonder. "There is a new *kamachi*. Born with the mark of the snake. And... it's a girl."

"A girl?" Achachi asked, shocked out of his cynicism.

Kai threw back his head and laughed. All their talk of change, all the arguments about how far to go and what to preserve, and Viraca had had his own plans all along. The priests would be in turmoil, and oh, the arguments they would have, the disputations between seniors who said *but, but, but*. They'd accept her in the end, because they had to. She had the mark. Argument was nothing in the face of that.

"You know what this means?" Taruka said. "You were right, *kamachi*. This is a time of change."

That must be hard for him. Suchi had refused to accept change, and then vanished into the countryside. Perhaps she was still out there, gathering support, but Kai didn't believe it. Suchi was the type who would have made straight for Hatun to build support to oppose Kai, and they all knew it. Taruka certainly did. If she was missing, it was because something had happened to her, between Kuska and the city.

To Catori, too. Kai mourned for him most of all.

"This means," he said, rousing himself, "that I must go to see the baby as fast as I can. I won't let the priests shut her away, the way I was caged. It's bad for the soul."

"The *kura* won't like that," Achachi chuckled.

Kai shrugged. "There are a lot of things the *kura* don't like. What difference one more or less?"

"Do we go now?" Chinita asked.

There was no undertone to her voice, no pressure on him to do what she wanted him to do. Kai knew what that was, though. "Not now. We do this business first."

She beamed as he turned back to the Runner. "Go tell the priests I'm coming. They are *not* to move the girl to the Retreat before I reach her. Tell them so, in those words."

"Kamachi –"

"Son," Achachi said, "if you're going to be a Runner, you'll have to speak hard words, without fear, to hard men. It might as well start now. Take the message you were given."

The boy hesitated, then managed a nod. He turned the horse, his touch clumsy enough that Kai nearly swore the animal shook its head in dismay. They the youth was gone, and Kai only then realised he hadn't asked his name. That wasn't like him.

"You're worried," Chinita said, as usual reading his expression. "Don't blame yourself."

"I don't," he said. "Not anymore."

206

He clicked his heels against the mare's flanks and started down the road, the other three clopping along behind and around him. None of them was a very good rider, if truth be told. Chinita was the only one of them who could claim to be capable, while the rest of them barely knew enough to keep from falling off. Still, they could take care of the animals themselves. Evain would no doubt find a dozen bad habits they'd fallen into when they saw him next, but he always did, so that was no great surprise.

Kai's burned hand had troubled him for months. Every time it seemed the flesh had healed over it would split again, suppurating an evil-smelling liquid that bubbled up from somewhere deep inside. Whatever the sorcerer had done to him that day on *jatun k'anchay,* it was no normal injury. Finally an old woman in Hatun had given him a pot of yellow-green salve, and though it stank worse than the pus it had done the trick. The swelling was nearly gone, and he could actually use the hand to hold his reins now, and keep his horse moving in a more or less straight line.

Nothing could put Taruka's hair back the way it had been, though in truth Kai wasn't sure he would even if it was possible. The front quarter of his crest had been burned away by the backwash of the sorcerer's assault on Kai, and grew back the pure white of freshly fallen snow. Everyone knew him, and even grizzled warriors from other societies muttered that he was very nearly brave enough to be one of them. That might be a problem when he went into battle again, if an enemy chieftain decided to make him a target. Until then it just meant he walked a bit taller among warriors, making sure the sun caught his tattoos just right.

But for now he travelled with the *kamachi,* so it didn't matter. Certainly it didn't bother Taruka. He had discovered that if he told the tale to serving girls in taverns, or young women weaving baskets on their mothers' porches, they would just about fight each other to spend the night with him, either in a bed or sneaking away into a hayloft. Kai had remarked that he remembered another man who was much the same. Taruka hadn't said anything, but Kai thought he was proud as a puma about that.

Achachi had lost two fingers, and nothing else. His pallor and wheezing breath went away after a week's rest, at which point he declared himself ready to brave that high pass again and return to Kuska. They had talked him out of that – he hadn't been serious, anyway – but he came with them when they left for Hatun, though nobody could remember inviting him. Whenever he was asked Achachi would launch into one story or another about the travels of his youth. Tales of monkeys who dreamed of flying, and men who tethered the sun to a hitching post. The others soon learned not to ask.

He had seen the sea, and pronounced it a disappointment.

As for Chinita, everywhere she went there were women who wanted to know what the *kamachi* was like in the bedroom. Some asked bluntly, unable to contain their excitement, while others sidled up to the subject with coy glances and careful words. Chinita had been angry at first, he could see that, but she'd soon learned to meet the questions with a smile and a shake of the head, and no words. Let them wonder. There was only one woman who knew what Kai was like in the night, and she kept the secret.

There was still a great deal to do in Apusuyu, and probably would be for years to come. There was a new Qapac, a man named Huema, from one of the great families of the coast. He was from the Tihuac people, who had tried to rebel against Apusuyu forty years ago, and been defeated. Achachi had muttered to himself for days after news came of that. But Huema was new to the role and still establishing himself, so much of the burden of government still fell on the priesthood. Kai wanted to open Apusuyu to outside influences, so the Ashir could never be caught so much by surprise again, but many among the *kura* insisted that Viraca had taught them all they needed to know. The Blessed Land had fought off one assault, after all, led by the *kamachi* and strengthened by Viraca's love. It could fight off others. The world outside held nothing of interest.

The faction had taken a blow today, a mortal one, if the Runner's news was true. A girl *kamachi*. Kai thrilled inside whenever he thought of it. Girl or boy, what mattered was that the child bore the plum snake around one eye. The God still loved his people, even now.

Some battles had already been won. The Thorn society had been ratified by Huema Qapac, the day after he took the throne. That might have been because Kai said privately that he'd defend their cause every day of his life if Huema didn't. The king agreed, and went on to appoint a new Auk, a Puma named Chimalli.

About *that,* there had been no argument. This was the man, after all, who had led the famous Rising in Chakanay, and then pursued the Thrain to Hirka. A group of artisans had already begun carving a relief of the struggle in Hatun, on a specially built wall inside the royal compound at the Kancha. Chimalli always tried not to look at it when he walked by.

Another new thing was horses, not yet a common sight in Apusuyu but destined to become one, when the stud farm started by Evain and some of the soldiers began to bear fruit. They had a hundred Ashir working with them, and needed the extra hands, since all the army's animals had been left to the Ashir when the soldiers departed, by the terms of the surrender. With fifteen hundred horses as stock, it wouldn't be long before the land was teeming with them. But for now there were hardly any in all the southern highlands, and four of those were being ridden not very expertly along a muddy track in the autumn sunshine, with quinine trees on either side and *ikaku* birds singing in their branches, for the last time. Males sang as they fed their young, until exhaustion overwhelmed them and they died.

The four riders came around the base of a hill and saw a village laid out in front of them, a hundred or more stone houses scattered along both sides of a small stream. An ancient village then, one which had stood on the same spot for generations, while wooden homes were rebuilt with stone as time and money allowed. It took a long time. There must have been people here before Viraca walked the land.

On the far bank stood a temple, with a tall statue of Quilla of the Moon outside it, clad in flowing robes that hugged her round figure and yet hid it too. The sculptor had been careful, trying to show the goddess as demure and fecund at the same time. He hadn't really pulled it off. Nobody would be inviting him to Hatun any time soon.

"*Carajo*," Kai swore suddenly, reining in. "I don't think I can do this."

"Of course you can." Taruka leaned over to catch the *kamachi's* reins. "And now's as good a time as any."

"Wait a moment –"

"He's right, boy," Achachi said from his other side. He had turned his face up to catch the evening sunlight. "On a day like this, what could go wrong?"

"We're with you," Chinita said. She'd been saying the same thing ever since they began the journey that had brought them here, to the market village of Feria at the tail end of autumn. "Don't worry. We're with you."

Kai looked from one of them to another and gave a sigh. "I hate all of you. I hope you realise that."

"I'm sure we'll bear up under our misery," Achachi said.

Some of the villagers had seen them now. A group of children playing in a meadow shrieked and fled for the houses, too far away to see the snake around Kai's eye but easily able to make out the horses. Rumour would have spread this far by now, and perhaps even been believed, but hearing was one thing and seeing quite another. A few of the adults scurried away and came back with pitchforks or wood axes. They formed a knot on the near side of the buildings, huddling close and staring as the riders drew closer. The women gathered further back, with small children clinging to their skirts and bigger ones looking as though they wanted to.

"Look at them," Taruka said disparagingly. "Ten good cavalry would sweep them away. They haven't even built any ramparts."

Before the summer they wouldn't have needed ramparts. Change would come, but it would take a long time to reach into the deepest corners of the Blessed Land, where seasons always changed a month late and people liked the old ways best. It might have taken a thousand years to turn all the wooden buildings into stone. It might take a hundred, or more, to persuade a man here to ride a horse.

These are my people too, just as much as the princes of Hatun, or the merchants of the Pasqa. But I'm glad I was at the heart of things. It's better to ride the puma, even with the danger, than not know how to ride.

Some of the villagers burst into excited conversation. The knot of waiting men broke up, and those who'd fetched weapons tossed them aside. People began to stream along the track towards the riders.

"I think they might have recognised you," Taruka said laconically to Kai. Achachi chuckled in his throat.

209

Kai didn't say anything. His hands were steady on the reins and his face calm. He knew how to impose serenity on himself, always had, but now he saw it for the strength it was, not a sign of his unfitness as Servant. He'd come through the storm, most of all that day on top of *jatun k'anchay*, as he waited for the lightning to strike. Whatever turmoil he felt was locked away inside, to be ignored for the present and dealt with when there was time.

"Love you," Chinita said.

He had no time to answer before the crowd reached them. The villagers stopped a few yards away as the riders reined in, which was unusual. Normally people couldn't wait to stretch out their hands in pleading to be blessed by the *kamachi*, but Feria was always going to be different. Kai studied faces and found what he was looking for.

The way the hair lay, the shape of the jaw. An expression of astonishment.

Kai went forward, neat and precise, and stopped in front of the man he had picked out.

"Hello, Papa," Kai said.

Puma and moon
wind and ice
beautiful enchantment
Night in the highlands
Thus am I fed.

I'm Ben Blake, and I hope you enjoyed Fanged Fish. Even if you didn't, please leave a review on Amazon. Reviews are life blood for an indie author.

Feel free to contact me, if you like. My Facebook address, website and email are all at the front of the book.

By the same Author

The Risen King

Songs of Sorrow
Blood and Gold
The Gate of Angels

The Troy Books
A Brand of Fire
Heirs of Immortality
The Ancient Dead

The Blessed Land
Black Lord of Eagles